Univers

Adri Adept

by

Jennifer Mandelas

Jennifer Mandelas

Strategic Book Group

Strategic Book Group

P.O. Box 333

Durham CT 06422

www.StrategicBookClub.com

ISBN: 978-1-60976-083-0

This book is dedicated to

L.P. You helped with the birth of this whole universe. Thanks.
My family, for all your support, A.S.-W. and J.R., for your critiques.

Thank you.

I remember that day, the day my parents died. I was sitting in the living room, playing with my mother's pendant. I wasn't supposed to play with it, especially when my mother was not home, but I had swiped it anyway, sneaking into my parents' bedroom while Mandy was busy downstairs and carefully picking it out among the rest of my mother's jewelry. I didn't know why I liked that one pendent so much; it wasn't as shiny or as large as many of the others mother owned, but I had always liked it. Maybe it was the pretty tear shape, or the pale violet color, or the smooth feel of the shell against my skin. Whatever the reason, it was my favorite. I had gone into the living room with my prize, because it afforded a view of the city streets several stories below, in order to keep a wary eye out for my parents' return.

Or perhaps I was just silly enough to sit out where Mandy would eventually find me and discover my actions. After all, I was only seven.

The noise from the streets below didn't really penetrate my conscious until the shooting began, almost directly below our house. At first I thought the loud, shuddering booms to be thunder, just a great deal stronger than I had ever heard before. Storms did not normally frighten me, but the loudness of it made me nervous, so I fingered the pendant and wondered if I should go down and find Mandy. The sudden eruption of blaster fire made me jump, but, innocent that I was, I thought it to be the beginning of some sort of meteor shower.

Today, I would never mistake the sound of S-range nuclear explosions, nor the hiss and whine of rapid blaster fire. But then, as a child, I had never truly picked up on the unrest within the city, or the planet at large.

Curious, if still a little anxious, I walked over to the broad window overlooking the street. Below I saw people running around in outfits similar to those of the Peace Keepers, only their armor covered them entirely. Others were dressed in normal clothes; they were the ones running around the most. They were all armed. I knew what blasters were, but I was amazed at seeing so many. The people were hiding around the corners of buildings and behind transports. I thought, for one hair of a second, that they were playing some sort of game.

They started firing at each other.

I understood at last, ran away from the window and screamed for Mandy. Together we hid in the basement, and waited as the firing and bombing continued well into the night.

My parents never came home.

Chapter One

S moke still rose from the ashes of the destroyed supply depot, darkening the already leaden sky with plumes that reeked of death and destruction. The battle had been over for several hours, but soldiers still roamed the wasted range, fully armed and alert. Adri was both relieved and deeply satisfied that they were *her* soldiers.

With her battered helmet tucked under one arm, and the other hanging loose above her holster, she surveyed the damage that had been wrought. There wasn't much left of the depot, or of any of the surrounding buildings. Her superiors would be irked with the news that yet another depot had been destroyed. What was costing a great deal of time and money and – they would grudgingly add – lives, was now a smoldering rubble to join a long chain of other smoldering rubble heaps along the front. But they would not doubt Adri's success.

Another success in a long trail of successes, Adri mused; not that she impressed herself much. More importantly, this retake of the depot might aid in wringing out a promotion, which would give her more authority both on the field and aboard ship. It wasn't so much a power trip, she thought to herself, as the assurance that she was capable. She would rather be the one in charge, knowing her abilities and weaknesses, than trust the lives of herself and her troops to others.

"Looks like rain," said a voice to her right.

Adri shrugged without glancing over. "It'll put out the last of the fire, at least."

"So it will," the voice agreed morosely.

Adri finally broke down and grinned, turning to her companion. "By Danwe, Duane, aren't you used to it by now?"

Duane, his own helmet clipped to his belt, soot scouring his bright magenta face, gave a long sigh. "I wouldn't mind at least one sunny day. Just one. Well, then again, if we did get one, I would know that we *could* get one and all the following gloomy days would drive me mad."

"So I guess it's better if it just rains," Adri concluded soberly. "What is it you wanted to speak to me about? Are the shields up around the camp yet?"

"Yeah, yeah. The boss had us set them up before you had even cleared the ridge. The north generator is wearing out; I'll need a replacement core within a few days." Duane frowned musefully out at the devastated scenery. "Of course, the captain has already retired for the night. The sloth."

"Duane, do not criticize a superior officer," Adri admonished. "At least not out loud."

"I'm not criticizing, Lieutenant Rael! Honest! I was stating a verifiable fact. Captain Heedman shows every slothful tendency - and this is not what I wanted to talk to you about."

Adri turned and began to walk back towards camp just as fat, dirty raindrops began to fall out of the gray sky. The air quickly filled with smoke and dirty steam as the water fell onto the ashes of the depot. Duane muttered an oath and plopped his helmet back onto his head. Adri didn't bother. "What *did* you want to talk to me about?"

"Transfer troops arrived an hour ago, a real mismatch group. The transport didn't stay in the system long enough to do anything but spit them on the surface. Captain Heedman wanted you to greet and re-assign them within the company this evening, as he would be - and I now quote – 'indisposed and otherwise unavailable' for the rest of the night."

Adri hummed in her throat. "Duane, you could write a book of Heedmanisms."

"No one would buy it," Duane grinned. "It would bore everyone by the end of the first page."

2

"Where are the new troops?" The camp was being assembled in what had once been the residential zone beyond the depot. Adri walked through the shield surrounding the camp and headed directly to her quarters. Around her, soldiers were assembling for the first night's watch or beginning to relax for the night. There was still a lot of activity around the medic station, but most of the more seriously injured had already been transported back to the spaceship. Some of the less injured soldiers looked up as she passed and saluted. She nodded in recognition, but continued walking.

Duane scrambled to keep up with her. "The captain gave me the list, and if you would just slow down on those infernally long human legs for just one second, I'd give it to you!"

Following Duane's impatient gesture, Adri stepped into her new makeshift quarters. The accommodations weren't bad; she had four walls and a roof this time. Civilians had abandoned the area around the newly conquered depot for some time, and in the interim someone had sloppily written 'THIS LAND IS WET HELL' in galactic standard across the far wall. The ensign who had moved her trunk in had also tried to give the room more of an ambiance by using a board supported by rubble for a desk, setting her cot across from it.

Adri tossed her helmet onto the desk. Duane huffed in behind her. "Let's see the list," she said, sitting down on the tunsteel trunk.

Duane pulled out his holoboard and located the list. Handing the board to her he added, "Most are from the Turotian regiment."

"Good, they've seen some action and we're not getting a bunch of green recruits." Adri scanned the list and frowned. "We've got some new officers," she tapped the holoboard on her knee contemplatively. "A replacement for Rumman."

Without any deference for her superior rank, Duane sat down on the side of the cot and began rummaging in his pocket for something to eat. "Lets hope that the new replacement lasts longer than Rumman did."

Adri made no comment.

Finding a half melted chocolate bar that he had secretly pilfered from the captain's private simulator, he munched cheerily. "Are you going to meet them tonight?"

Adri sighed and leaned back against her desk, tossing the holoboard back to Duane. She was tired. She had been up for the last twenty-six hours fighting a vicious battle against the Advance Force of the Belligerent Coalition, and then securing the conquered territory. She had led her troops to victory while her captain had sat in camp, demanding that the security shields go up.

That was life. Adri had learned long ago to accept what fate dealt and make the best of it. "I suppose so."

Field Lieutenant Thaddeus Vanden Grayson rolled his mug around in his hands and wondered vaguely why military coffee always tasted… simulated. Of course, it *was*, but nothing tasted less genuine than simulated coffee on a cold day.

Around him, the usual chaos in a military mess hall abounded. Soldiers spoke of their victory earlier that day, or carefully avoided it. They boasted, or quietly mourned. Some talked of other things – the war in general, the possibility of a promotion, the happenings on their home planets.

Gray tuned out the noise and looked around with only mild interest. This was the second transfer he'd made in his career, and he was hoping that it would turn out to be a better decision than his last one. Huddled together nearby were the other new transfer troops, many of them from his own regiment, if not his platoon. In the three hours since their arrival, Gray had met no officer over his own rank (which, granted, was a rather hefty one) and was beginning to wonder if all the rumors about Captain Heedman were true. But if they were, he mused, gingerly taking a sip from his mug, then that meant that the rumors about the lieutenant commander could also be true. That would definitely be a perk. Or they could all be half-truths, and he could be worse off than he had been in Turotia.

Ah well, at least the weather was cooler.

"The L. C. is coming!" someone shouted by the door, pulling Gray out of his thoughts.

Gray watched as several of the men straightened their uniform jackets, and smoothed back their hair. Even some of the kievians

4

attempted to tame the tentacles that grew from their scalps. He leaned forward ever so slightly to get a better view of the door, curious now.

The person who walked through the doors of the mess hall was not what he had been expecting at all. The fellow was of average height, with black-blue hair and wide blue eyes. His most distinguishing feature, however, had to be the bright magenta color of his skin. Obviously a paranthian, Gray mused, wondering why such a rare species would choose a military career.

All thoughts in Gray's head ground to a halt when she walked in, only a second or two behind the paranthian.

He felt an instant connection, as if something he hadn't known he was missing had just been reattached. It wouldn't have surprised him more if thunder had shook the air and a mighty voice had said from above 'She's The One!' Dumbstruck, Gray sat back in an attempt to gather his wits, which had gleefully run off.

She was beautiful, pale skin, brown hair that skimmed her chin and serious brown eyes. Average height, and – from what Gray could see of her in her thick combat suit, perfectly formed. Gray decided that as soon as he could get his mind out of the gutter, where it had taken a detour, he would get the woman's name.

He didn't have to. She said it aloud. The paranthian had pointed him and the other new transfers out to her. As she wound her way through the mass of troops to their table, the soldiers all stood and saluted respectfully, showing her to be an officer of some higher rank. She nodded to them as she passed, then stopped to take the holoboard from the paranthian, who trailed behind her.

"I am Lieutenant Commander Adrienne Rael," she announced. Confidence and authority rang in her voice, easily heard over the hushed noise in the hall.

She glanced down at the board before looking them over again. "Captain Heedman sends his welcome as well, but is unfortunately indisposed this evening." *Like he was every evening*, Adri thought irritably. "I shall be re-assigning you within the company now. Stand up and come forward when I call your name."

So this was the famous Rael, Gray thought. He watched her as she called one of the ensign's names and began speaking to him. He'd heard rumors of her rapid rise within the Advance Force, and of the promotion to lieutenant commander at the shocking age of twenty-four. She had been one of the reasons he'd requested the transfer. He wanted a competent, cunning leader to serve under.

He hadn't expected her to turn out to be the woman of his dreams.

Gray smiled and leaned back, blessing his luck. This decision had obviously been a fated one.

"Field Lieutenant Thaddeus Grayson," Adri called. She looked up at him. He was the only one left. A man of slightly over average height, with light brown hair and calm gray eyes. When he stood, she noticed that he moved well, and the bland gray uniform looked good too. *Whoa*, Adri thought, as he rose and strode towards her, her long-neglected feminine side sighing in sheer appreciation. *Definitely an improvement to Rumman.*

What was she doing again? Her mind snapped back to the present as her military discipline reasserted itself. Sensible Lieutenant Commander Rael did not drool over incredibly handsome field lieutenants. Scarred and troubled Adrienne Rael hissed the old warning 'don't get close!' But quiet and often overlooked feminine Adri Rael sighed and wished anyway.

Gray wondered what Rael was thinking when she continued to stare at him blankly after he had walked up to her. "Is something wrong?"

Adri took a long, deep breath. "No, nothing's wrong." *You're just the best looking man I've ever seen in my life, and I can't figure out why I care.* "And you would be…?" *What was his name again?*

Gray smiled, and Adri's cells sighed again. "Field Lieutenant Thaddeus Grayson, at your service, ma'am,"

"Yes of course." Adri studiously glanced down at the holoboard and stared at his name written there. *Think! Think! What was it you wanted to say to him?* "I see that you transferred here from Turotia," she said lamely.

"That's right." *Could the woman get any cuter?* Gray had been attracted to the competent and authoritative woman she had been when dealing with the other troops, but this absentminded, slightly bewildered woman was even better.

6

Oh no, he was smiling again! All of Adri's thoughts happily flittered away when she looked at him. This was not going to work at all. Glancing back down at the holoboard, she saw that her notation had him attached to her company, to serve directly under her as Rumman had done. Which meant the man was going to be underfoot twenty-four hours a day, seven days a week, until the end of the campaign...which was not in the foreseeable future.

Oh yes! the quiet Adri sighed.

Oh no! the troubled Adrienne groaned.

Better make the best of it, the sensible Lieutenant Commander advised. *And for Danwe's sake, stop staring at him like some brainless ensign!*

"You've been assigned to my squadron," Adri said at last. "My late field lieutenant fell in the line of duty last month."

"My condolences," Gray replied, happily astonished at this brilliant twist of fate. He'd be with her from bed rise to bed rest for the duration of the campaign. And if that wasn't opportunity enough...

"There are some things I need to brief you on," Adri was saying, bringing Gray back. She beckoned him to follow as she turned to leave the mess hall. "Since you're from the Advance Force, you're used to having the dual responsibilities of a field lieutenant on the ground, and lieutenant aboard ship, correct?"

"That's right."

"What's your experience aboard ship?"

"I'm a lieutenant in security, with some engineering ability if called for," Gray replied. They had left the hall and were now walking out towards the sleeping quarters.

"That is good," Adri said, falling back in the comfortable mode of commander. "To be an elite member of the Advance Force, you have to be adept at field fighting and tactics, as well as handling command of a ship, and all that it entails. What position were you given aboard our vessel?"

"I was given command of security. It appears there was a vacancy there as well." Gray responded. Adri stopped in front of the ramshackle construction that served as the officer's quarters.

An impressive set of positions, she thought to herself. Adri glanced down at the holoboard again. "I see that you are only a step away from a promotion,"

Gray shrugged. "Perhaps,"

His nonchalance made her lips twitch. "Well, we'll see if we can manage to pull it off before too much longer." She walked inside the building, which was quieting down for the night. "Yours is on the right, mine is on the left, if you have any questions and cannot reach me by communicator."

He nodded.

"Well then, I am going to turn in. I'll give you your instructions tomorrow."

"Good night," Gray continued to stand and continued to stare. Adri wondered at it, even as she continued to stand and stare at him.

"What made you request a transfer from Turotia?" She asked suddenly.

Gray gave her a strange smile. Stepping towards his door he replied, "I came for you, Adri."

"What?" Adri stared at him, gaping.

Gray simply went inside his quarters and shut the door.

Frowning now, Adri stared at the closed door in contemplation. The man obviously knew his appeal, and thought that she would be an easy conquest. Well, she'd prove him wrong. No one took advantage of Adrienne Rael! And no one called her Adri. That was far too familiar a nickname for a fellow officer to address her as. She would have to have a firm talk with him tomorrow.

I don't suppose my growing up years were more troublesome than most. My parents married in haste, and regretted it almost before the license was processed. I was probably conceived in some sort of drunken orgy, or so my mother always complained, because she had never wanted to have kids, especially a boy who would be messy and get into trouble and follow her husband; a man whom she detested with a passion that startled and frightened a five year old boy. No, Wallace and Hester Grayson did not want to be married, and especially didn't want the child they had made between them.

They never beat me, so I can't complain on that score. I guess the worst of it would be that they often forgot I existed. But then, that was only a problem when I was hungry...which, as a small, growing boy, was most the time. Sometimes they would remember I was there if there was something they wanted me to do, or if my old man was drunk and wanted someone to yell at when my mother was gone.

Generally, life was awful, but I didn't mind much because I really didn't know the difference.

Then, when I was five, they decided that they would quit wailing about how they hated being married and actually do something to rectify it. Their divorce took nearly two years, mostly because they both wanted all they could get, but neither wanted me. In the end, I was placed in foster care for about eight months, with a perfectly nice older couple by the name of Dalspeth, until my maternal grandmother, Judith Bari, stepped in to claim me.

I guess my life really got started when she came into it. She always told me that she would have come sooner if she had known where her daughter was living, and I believe her, to this day. She lived alone, my grandfather having died about ten years prior to my arrival.

When we arrived at her home, out in the rural district outside Shale, she gave me my most important lesson. "Life is full of mysteries, Thaddeus. Sometimes you figure them out, and others leave you wondering for the whole of your life. The only things we can know for sure are that every life has meaning, and a purpose. Some people find out what the purpose is early on, and some of us have to search long and hard for it."

"So why was I born, grandma?" I'd asked.

She smiled. She had a nice smile. "Well, for now, you were born so that I could have someone to love. But there will be other reasons. Someday you'll find a person you were born to love. What fate has in store, who can say?"

Yes. Who can say?

Chapter Two

The shudder of bombs exploding at close range jarred Adri out of a sound sleep only seconds before the proximity alarm went off. She rolled expertly out of bed and donned her armor. Adri only paused to check the reading on her Accelerated Transition Firearm, or ATF, before grabbing her helmet and dashing outside.

She nearly collided into Gray, who was also fully suited up. "This happen often?" he asked mildly, following her to a shelled out ruin that had once been the information bureau of the town, where the security and communication center had been temporarily installed.

"Not often, but enough," Adri replied, still somewhat surprised at his presence. She was usually the first officer to arrive at the command center, fully armed and ready for any situation. It both pleased and vaguely alarmed her that her new field lieutenant was just as prepared as she was.

"Good morning," Duane grumbled as Adri approached him. His blue-black hair was sticking up, and he was scowling at the viewscreens in his station.

"What do we have?" Adri asked.

"Several sizable plasma bombs, all around the weak shield generator. Another good barrage and that generator is going to fail." He rubbed his brilliant magenta chin.

"Sounds like they knew where to hit," Gray thought aloud. "If they knew there was a weak generator in our shielding system, and plastered it with plasma bombs, then they won't be stupid enough to leave it at that."

Adri nodded in agreement, still staring at the screen that showed the weak north shield generator.

"They've never tried something that complex," Duane said, turning to Gray.

"Have they ever bombed the shields before?" Gray asked.

Duane shrugged. "Well, yeah, but our shields are pretty tough."

"Then it's possible that they've come up with some sort of new strategy," Gray argued. "Have they ever concentrated on a weak generator before?"

"No," Duane admitted, and then scowled. "Are you saying something about my generators?"

Gray smiled. "Never think it,"

Duane nodded in acceptance. "Good. You know, you're a great improvement over Rumman."

"Was that the last field lieutenant?"

"Yeah. The guy had 'inept' tattooed across his forehead. The only reason he made field lieutenant was that he had high connections in the government. Aristocratic snob – er, begging your pardon, Lieutenant… what was your name?"

"Grayson. And you would be?"

"Duane."

Gray frowned. "No last name?"

"Well, yeah, but trust me, you don't want to hear it."

Adri ignored their conversation, still staring at the viewscreen contemplatively. Gray and Duane barely heard her when she murmured, "It's an assault,"

"What?" Duane demanded.

Gray was more astute. "Once they have the north shield down, do you think that they will attack at once, or wait until we've panicked?"

"Panicked?" Duane repeated, looking ready to do just that.

"If I was them, and had planned this so far, then I would wait, maybe try to send in a few behind the shields to take out the remaining generators, and then mass a full broadside before my enemy had time to boot up the backup shielding system." Adri replied.

"They're gonna blow my shields?!" Duane cried, and was ignored.

"Then I suppose we ought to mass in front and keep anyone from coming through the shields," Gray said, watching Adri.

Adri shook her head. "They haven't taken the north shield out yet, but it's going to be soon, so that we don't have time to repair it."

Another, smaller blast rent the air. Duane groaned. "My poor shields!"

Just then, Captain Albert Heedman made his belated entrance into the control room. "Lieutenant Commander Rael! What in Danwe's name is going on?"

Gray got his first look at his superior officer. The man was short, stout, and balding. His uniform was impeccable, right down to the neatly shined boots. All his pins and medals hung in perfect alignment from his jacket. The only thing that could show that he had risen in the wee hours of the morning was the fact that his eyes were a little bleary, and greatly annoyed.

"The Belligerent Coalition is currently attempting to dismantle our north shield generator, and, once it is down, to launch a full scale assault upon the camp." Of course, most of that was Adri's speculation, but she knew from past experience to give her captain the worst possible scenario so that he would give her enough clearance to handle the threat.

"By Danwe! What a dastardly thing to do in the middle of the night!" Heedman exclaimed.

Gray thought that the statement was a bit overdone. After all, they were in the midst of a war.

Heedman shook his head, as if despairing at the state of the world that allowed the enemy to attack at night. "Those evil blighters! Lieutenant Rael! Show those scum who they're dealing with!"

"Yes sir," Adri replied dutifully.

"Give them what-for. Report back to me when they're gone." he turned to leave, but then stopped when he spotted Gray. "Who are you?"

Gray saluted. "Field Lieutenant Thaddeus Grayson, late of the Turotian regiment."

Heedman waved his hand. "Well then. Carry on."

Gray watched him depart. "That was it?"

"The Captain isn't given to much public appearance," Adri replied dryly. "Let's get to work."

Adri and Gray huddled just inside the north end of the shield, assessing the damage to the generator. The first explosion had been caused by a number of plasma bombs going off simultaneously. The second had been only one. However, it would only take another explosion to destroy the generator core completely.

Around them huddled two squads of soldiers. Their plans complete, Adri gave the signal to her sergeant, who would be leading one half of the squad, then beckoned Gray over. "You're coming with me until I can see what you're like in combat."

Gray nodded.

Signaling to her squadron, Adri led the way up to the glowing wall that marked the boundary of the shielding. Automatically she shoved on her helmet, secured it to the collar of her suit, and checked her ATF reading. Out of the corner of her eye, she could see Gray doing the same thing.

[Oduran to Rael,] her communicator squawked.

[Rael here,] she replied, giving her squad a cursory glance. All were ready.

Her sergeant went on, [White squadron is in position. We're awaiting your command.]

Gray turned and nodded to her. He obviously was taking his full rights to listen in on the officer's frequency.

Adri took a deep breath, and exhaled slowly. [Rael to all units. Proceed with the defense of the camp.] With that, she walked towards the shield barrier, and sprinted through it. It was a type XI Colok defense shielding system, which, when activated, allowed anything to go out of the shields, but allowed nothing to come in. As her squad followed her example, Adri knew that they were essentially barred from the camp with the enemy for as long as the shields stood.

[Nice night,] came a mild voice across the communicator.

Adri scowled. It was black as pitch, and the rain was falling steadily. [Lieutenant Grayson, please refrain from inane comments on the communicator,] she ordered.

[Sure thing. Grayson out.]

Danwe, Adri thought in irritation. *Did the man have to sound so appealing over the communicator?*

She let out a huff of breath and, following her compass, headed for the outcropping of rock and rubble that afforded a good view of the north shield system. [Rael to black squadron,] she said. [Align into formation. We still don't know where our enemy is. Keep alert.] Night vision mode set within her helmet, Adri, ATF at the ready, kept her own eyes trained on the surrounding landscape. She was thankful for the new accelerated transition firearms that had replaced the blaster. The improved accuracy, range, and recharge rate gave her side a decided advantage.

Even with the night vision, it was still incredibly hard to see beyond fifteen feet. It was dangerous to venture out into this kind of darkness, especially without knowing the location of one's enemy, but it was a risk worth taking. This way they could surprise their enemy from behind, as the shields "went down" (of course, Adri wasn't about to allow the shield to be blown down; rather, she'd have Duane lower it), inviting the Belligerent Coalition to attack their unprotected flank, only to be caught between the waiting white squadron just inside the shield, and the black squadron just outside.

With careful adjusting to accommodate unexpected changes, and a healthy dose of luck, they would trounce their enemies before morning.

And maybe, with a little more luck, she'd get to go back to bed.

They made the ridge in safety, with still no sign of the enemy. With half her squadron guarding their back, the other half faced the camp. It was hard to miss, being a soft red glowing dot on the black horizon. Everything was in readiness.

[Rael to Oduran,]

[Oduran here.]

[Black squadron is in position. Standby for the dropping of the shield,]

[Understood, ma'am. Oduran out.]

Rael took another deep breath. [Rael to Duane,]

[Duane is here,] came the paranthian's sleepy voice. [But I still don't like the idea of lowering my shields, and leaving the rest of us – as in me – like stationary red target signs.]

Trust Duane to lighten her mood, Adri thought, smiling. [Think of it this way,] she replied, not noticing that Gray was watching her and listening in as well, unable to see his smile. [Either sacrifice your shield core and allow the Belligerent to walk on in, or its lower your shield, and still have the chance to raise it again.]

Duane gave a longsuffering sigh over the communicator. [The things I do for my L.C. The north shield is being lowered now. It will be fully deactivated in three minutes, and counting.]

[Excellent Duane. Rael out.] Now it was time for the waiting game.

Eying their setup critically, Adri glanced over at Gray, who was quietly instructing one of their greener recruits (and how did he know that the soldier was new to the Navy, let alone the Advance Force?) on what to look for when searching for signs of the enemy. His voice was little more than a murmur on the common frequency since he wasn't talking to her. It was a sound that she would normally have tuned out, but she was curious to know what he was saying.

She wasn't prying, necessarily, Adri argued to herself as she tuned in her communicator to pick up their conversation. She was simply monitoring the morale of her troops, getting a chance to see how the mind of her new officer worked...and getting a nice dose of Field Lieutenant Gorgeous' sexy voice.

[What if they come up behind me? How am I supposed to be looking ahead *and* behind me at the same time?] the soldier asked. Adri recognized him as Ensign Piontek, fresh from the Naval Academy and somehow shunted up into the Advance Force.

[By using more than just your eyes.] Gray replied. [You have ears, use them. In circumstances like these, sometimes your ears are a better bet. Follow your gut instinct. If something doesn't feel quite right, check it out, unless you've been given direct orders to the contrary. But try pushing to the limit of your orders.]

Well, the man certainly knew what he was talking about, Adri mused.

[Thanks, sir,] Piontek replied. Adri was about to tune out of the frequency, thinking the conversation over when he said, [Hey, what do you think of the L.C.?]

[The lieutenant commander?] Gray clarified.

Adri's head whipped around from the view of the shields (the north one was dimming considerably) and glared at the back of Gray's head.

[Yeah. Quite a babe, huh?] Piontek went on. [Some of us had a poll taken in the regiment, and it was decided that she's the hottest officer in the Advance Force.]

Oh, for Danwe's sake, Adri snorted.

Gray smiled behind his helmet. Piontek was obviously nervous, and was trying to fill up the quiet waiting time with mindless chatter. It would be better for him to stay silent and alert − like they had been talking about just one minute ago − but Gray was far too curious about Adrienne Rael to rebuke the soldier. [I see,] he said encouragingly.

I see? That was it? Adri glared harder at the back of her field lieutenant's head. What, did she not interest him at all? Obviously, all the other men in her regiment thought she was appealing. It just figured that the first time she wanted a guy to notice her as a woman, he didn't find her attractive.

Wait, what was she thinking? She didn't want him to find her appealing at all! She didn't *want* the man to notice her as a woman, because she didn't want any sort of relationship. Such a thing was unnecessary and distracting. It was time to stop the conversation.

She opened her mouth to rebuke her two idiot troops when, with a dying flicker, the north shield fell.

At that precise second, all hell broke loose.

A mass of moving black figures raced for the now defenseless opening in the camp's shield system, while at the same time, shouts over the communicator announced that more of the enemy's troops were racing up the incline behind them.

The rapid hisses and whines of both ATF and blaster fire rent the silent night. A quick glance showed that Adri's squadron was trapped between the enemy troops assaulting the camp, and the soldiers scaling the ridge.

With a huff of breath, Adri' reorganized her plans. There would be no chance of getting back into bed for a good while now, and that thought made her irritated. [Rear group! Return fire!]

In the midst of the developing chaos, the sound of Gray's voice repeating her commands was unexpectedly soothing.

Okay, so I've been around, and I've seen a lot of strange things. I was...let's see...about thirteen human years old when my family left Paranth. I remember packing up the evacuation transport with my orhan, after the last asade raid. The air was full of dust, because everyone was moving at once. The asade would be back, and no one wanted to stick around for a massacre sequel. I stopped carting a box for a minute to rub the dust out of my eyes, and I looked up and saw something flash past, nearly blending with the stars.

I asked my father what it was; it had moved too slowly to be a shooting star, and it hadn't passed through the atmosphere. Was it an asade scout ship, come to note our activities? Was it some new monster come to terrorize us?

"Oh, no, Desmumhnach'tos," he replied, all calm and stoic. My father was always pretty cool and stoic. I wish I had inherited his constant calm. Nothing ever razzed him. "Its just an abandoned exploration craft from the Blue planet."

That was the other thing about my father. He always seemed to know everything. The day's weather, politics in a neighboring orhan, the naughty things I did in school.

I remember being in awe. "That came from the Blue planet? I thought they didn't know about us out here,"

"They don't, son. The council elders and I watched it and analyzed it from the observatory. It was unmanned, and had no power. Just more space junk."

"So they were maybe trying to find us?" I persisted. I was really fascinated with humans, as most young paranthians were. "Maybe the Blue planet is trying to like, make contact or something!"

"Perhaps." My father was also pretty noncommittal. "But they have not advanced yet to find us, so we must not interfere with them."

The doctrine of inaction is never a big winner with young paranthians. "But why can't we see the humans?" I whined. I liked to whine then. Well, I still do.

"The Alana galaxy has humans as well, my son," my father replied. "I am sure they are much the same as the ones here."

I huffed. "You mean they'll be terran-bound and never make contact?"

"I suppose we shall see. Pick up that crate now."

And that was that. We left Paranth behind and forged our way into a new galaxy. I still wonder about the Blue planet, but I don't wonder about humans anymore.

They're too much like us.

Chapter Three

Floyd Tarkubunji had a grinding headache. His ears were buzzing painfully, as though a swarm of insects were hovering around him. His eyes burned and his glasses felt too heavy for his head. Every nerve in his body seemed to be withering with fatigue.

The lab was deathly silent, without even the droning of the equipment or the humming of the monitors set up in banks along the room to add background noise. The lights were on full bright, showing the room in stark whites and silvers. Floyd knew the room so well that he could have worked flawlessly with each instrument blindfolded without making a mess.

West Cellutary Research and Technical Laboratories was his workplace, his vocation, and his semi-permanent home.

It was also his prison.

The beeping of the door lock's disengagement system roused Floyd enough to sit up in his chair. He watched with curious detachment as Colonel Reidmen Stroff, head of the facility's military branch and chairman of the board, stepped into the room. His normally imposing figure seemed somehow more ominous than normal. He towered over Floyd, his gray military uniform impeccable, his boots highly polished. His face was perfectly composed; only his dark eyes hinted at a disturbing aura of superiority. Just outside the door Floyd could make out Stroff's two security humacoms standing outside the door before it slid shut.

Both humacoms – or androids with more computer-like functions –

had been heavily armed for a simple early morning visit to the lab. Floyd noted that the door had also been locked from the outside. *To keep others out, or to keep him in?* He wondered vaguely if Stroff had found him a liability in the case and was sentencing him to some horrible fate, like a life sentence in the mines or as a test subject for the bio-warfare department. On the tail end of that thought came one of curiosity over why he didn't seem to care. He did, but in his present state, it was hard to feel anything. He was emotionally numb. The pain in his body was the only proof of life he could detect.

"Dr. Tarkubunji," Stroff began, breaking the silence in which he had been studying Floyd. Floyd wondered what he saw; his hair in need of trimming, sticking out like an overgrown field of wheat? Two day's worth of stubble? The rumpled suit under the equally rumpled lab coat, which he'd been wearing for the past two days? His disheveled appearance didn't alarm him. Strange, because it usually would. "I came here with the verdict on your father."

"What happened?" Floyd asked. Even his own voice sounded tinny in his ears.

"The detectives from the Department of the Interior have ruled his death a suicide. It appears that he was bent on tearing apart his entire lab, destroying all his notes and most of his equipment before blasting his head off."

"I see." He couldn't see at all; his mind was fuzzily blank, unable to compute the idea of his father taking his own life.

"There are necessary steps to be taken," Stroff continued. "Dr. Harriman Tarkubunji willfully, for whatever reason, destroyed vast amounts of government property and deleted most of his research notes and other information from the mainframe computer. That has led us to assume that he was planning this for some time."

"You are saying that my father was a traitor," Floyd said, still eerily detached from the conversation. He wanted to scream with his denial, but he couldn't find the energy to do so.

Stroff huffed a breath, wrinkling his silver brows. "We are not openly declaring that he was, but his actions speak of some kind of motivation. The matter will be under strict investigation. A recall of all his surviving materials will be made, including all his personal databases and humacoms. If we find incriminating evidence against him, the government shall respond accordingly."

Floyd's headache increased, but his body seemed to be soaked with a surreal lethargy, incapable of reacting. "What about the humacoms here at the base, the ones that he designed? Are they under suspicion as well?"

Stroff coughed into his gloved fist. The man always wore gloves. Why? Floyd was momentarily distracted by that question and only slowly became aware of the colonel speaking again. "We shall have some of the technicians run a scan on all his humacoms here, to see if there is any reason for a recall of all of those. You understand that we shall desire your assistance on this end."

"Yes of course."

"In the meantime, my superiors have decided that you are to continue with project C. G. P. 00297 on your own."

"I understand."

"Due to your relationship with Dr. Harriman Tarkubunji, your credentials shall be reviewed, and some surveillance of your activities will be set up for the foreseeable future."

"I see."

"Good. Do you have any other questions at this time, doctor?"

Questions? Of course he had questions. He just couldn't remember what they were; his mind was floating in a sea of unreality, his aching body his only connection to the rest of the world. "May I see his body?" he asked, at last connecting his question with his tongue.

"His body has already been cleared by forensics. They've taken him to the morgue, where his will stated he wished to be cremated."

Something about that statement didn't make sense to Floyd, but he couldn't distinguish what it was. "A notification of his death needs to be sent to my sister."

Stroff was already heading for the door. "That seems to be a personal matter, doctor. I will assume you can send your own message to relatives and such." He tapped on the door in a complex sequence, and it was immediately unlocked by one of the securicoms on the other side.

Stepping through the door, he turned to regard Floyd briefly. "The Commonwealth will expect you to keep up your workload, doctor. You have inherited your father's position as Chief Humacom Designer and Technician. Congratulations."

Floyd continued to stare at the door long after the colonel had departed, his body in pain, his heart aching, and his mind in turmoil. Through it all, only one thought came clear.

He was trapped.

***

In the midst of chaos, Adri was a calm, tranquil pool. She had once tried to describe her mental state to Duane, but it had been very difficult. In her mind, like a distant echo, there played a beautiful elegy, both sorrowful and fierce; a fighting elegy. Behind the song was the hum of her adrenaline. When they were in harmony, she knew she was in peak performance. Duane hadn't understood.

Tonight was the same. She paid half an ear to her communicator, listening for calls for help (most likely) or orders from her captain (most unlikely). There was never much emotion in combat, apart from that rush of adrenaline and the beauty of that distant song.

[Sergeant Loaks! What is the situation?] She demanded over her communicator.

Her rear guard officer replied immediately. [It was like they were waiting for us! I count three waves; with wave one hitting us now. There may be others, but I can't see far enough to be sure!]

[Sounds like they planned this carefully,] came Gray's voice. He had moved to join the rear guard and assess the situation himself. [Shall we continue as planned, Lieutenant Commander?]

One second was all the deciding time Adri had. [Change the plan. Forward group, proceed to the shield as planned! Lieutenant Grayson, lead the group down the ridge and guard their backs with Piontek, Jones, and Knowell. Once they are through, return to me! Now move out!]

[Yes ma'am!] Came the reply.

Adri took a deep breath. [Rear group! Back into defensive positions at the forward side of the ridge! Prepare for enemy engagement!]

[Yes ma'am!]

[They'll be within spitting distance in less that one minute! Fight for your homeworlds!]

Soldiers scrambled to reposition themselves into a defensive front as ATF and blaster fire crisscrossed around them. Already Adri could see casualties.

As the seconds counted down in her head, Adri was at last able to see the bare outlines of their clever enemies, racing towards them while they had the initiative. She steadied her arm, aimed and fired.

Grayson ran behind the forward group as they hurried to reach the camp. Eyes alert for any sign of movement, he breathed a sigh of relief as he and his three men reached the cutoff and waited as the forward group passed safely. The Belligerent Coalition had not been fast enough.

Just as he was ready to turn and race back up the ridge to rejoin Adri, he caught sight of a stealthy movement on the west side of the ridge. Adri's forces were concentrated on the assault on the north side, leaving their west and east sides only lightly defended. Waving to his men, he ordered them to follow before moving silently around the ridge to cut off the enemy before they reached Adri's position.

[Grayson to Rael,]

Adri blinked at the sound of Gray's voice. Crouched down, she was waiting for another Belligerent to foolishly get into her range. [Rael here,]

[There's a squad of five or six Belligerents that tried to climb up the west side of the ridge.]

Adri couldn't help smiling. [Tried?]

[Yes ma'am. But it doesn't seem likely that they'd only try it on the west side. You might want to check it out. I'm too far away to cut them off before they reach the top, but I'll swing around and keep them from retreating.]

[Good plan. Rael out.] Finally, a field lieutenant with a brain. Adri scooted along the ridge as low to the ground as possible to avoid enemy fire. So far the Belligerents had done a good job keeping them penned in – far better than usual.

Reaching the east side of the ridge, she motioned her two sentries to follow her as she made her way slowly down to a better position. She hadn't quite made it before a violent flash of color from an outdated blaster rifle temporarily broke the blackness further down the ridge. She dodged the blast, returning fire in the general direction it had come from automatically. There was a hard thump, and something began to roll down the side of the ridge. More fire erupted, coming from the left. Adri ducked behind a tall boulder and squinted in an effort to make out the number of assailants. There were at least two, and from the count Gray had given her, that left at least three others unaccounted for.

A sharp cry over her communicator alerted her to the fact that some of the enemy had made their way behind her, taking out one of her troops. She whirled around and opened fire, just as a burst of concentrated firepower broke out behind her.

[Your back's covered,] Gray announced.

[Thanks.] With no threat behind her, Adri raced ahead, catching sight of one of the enemy, mostly obscured behind a rocky outcropping. She fired, grateful for Gray's backup as a Belligerent popped up less than a foot from her target and was immediately blown away.

Just the barest sound of movement had both of them turning and firing at the last soldier as he attempted to escape. Gray saluted her with his weapon. [We work well together,]

Adri nodded but didn't reply. She motioned to Gray and her remaining soldier to follow her back up to the ridge just as Gray's three troops clambered up over the rocks to reach them. [Uhm, sorry we're late, sir. Ma'am.] Piontek muttered.

Gray turned to Adri and spoke over the officer's frequency. [We're going to have a talk about giving me green troops when we get back to camp.]

Adri smiled, knowing he couldn't see it behind her helmet. [Let's make sure we get back to camp first, Lieutenant.]

[Speaking of getting back to camp,] Gray said as they both ducked behind a shallow outcropping to avoid more blaster fire coming from below them, [We do have a backup plan, don't we?]

Pulling a fragmentation grenade from her utility belt, Adri released the safety and tossed it over the outcropping. [Of course.]

[Oduran to Rael,] the communicator squawked just as the pitch blackness of the night was starting to hint at a lighter shade of dark gray. [White squadron in position, waiting for your signal.]

About time, Adri thought with relief. Her squadron had been successfully pinned by the Belligerent forces for several hours, with dawn only a scant ninety minutes away. For the safety of the camp, Adri had ordered that the shields be raised and defended from within. They would wait while any Belligerents that might have made their way in to the camp were discovered and eradicated, and the counter attack aligned. In the meantime, it had left her squadron pinned on the ridge with no reinforcements and no retreat. [Rael here, black squadron is ready. Prepare for engagement on my signal.]

Beside her, Gray methodically raked the opposite outcropping, which concealed a pair of very tenacious Belligerents, with ATF fire. The four of them had been in a standoff for the past hour and a half, leaving him with a hint of admiration for both the Belligerent pair and for his companion. [We'd better make a move before those two over there realize that we're out of grenades,] he commented.

[Roger that,] Adri replied. [I'm just waiting for the signal from Duane.]

They ducked in tandem as a handheld plasma grenade sailed over their heads and clattered down the hill before exploding. [They're getting closer; whoever's aiming those things is pretty good.]

[You're not so bad at chucking those things yourself,] Adri said, surprising herself. It was oddly easy to chat with her new field lieutenant in the midst of the chaos of battle. And it was no hardship at all to listen to his voice.

[Duane to Rael,]

[Rael here,]

[I'm resigned to lowering my shields again. Make it quick, will you?]

[You can't rush these things. It's like art,] Adri smiled as she heard Gray snort with laughter at her comment. Then she took a deep breath, refocused her mind, and gave her command. [White squadron, engage! Black squadron, advance!]

They say writing things down soothes a troubled mind. Not that my mind is particularly troubled, and maybe that's my problem. So many things have been battering at my head lately that it seems as though I've somehow placed an opaque barrier between myself and my memories – I can see enough to know that something is wrong, but I won't allow myself to see it clearly enough to identify it. That idea in of itself is troubling. Even this line of inquiry is hurting my head.

I design and build humacoms. I know most technicians can only do one or the other, or only like to do one or the other, but I have always liked the whole process, from conception, to the formulas, to the construction. Choosing the right programs for the AI, designing the chassis male or female, picking its intended occupation. Security? Domestic? Data archives and analysis? I think that way I have more involvement in the humacom, and that is why they are always so unique, so humanlike -

Maybe if I think of something else, besides work, I won't have such a hard time. I remember one time, when Freya and I were little, we used to make our own picnics and explore the family estate. The Tarkubunji estate is a large one, a prime piece of real estate just outside Corinthe city. One summer, we even decided to camp out all by ourselves and pretend we were explorers on a new, undiscovered planet. Of course, mother would never have allowed us – we were five and six at the time, me being the eldest – to go out and camp alone, so we ended up taking Maj and mother's securicom, Julian. I'm sure she was really worried about us, but Anetta Tarkubunji was never one to fret too much. Now, father –

Danwe, does my head hurt! I feel as though someone is trying to jam shards of glass into my skull. Mundane things.

I need to send Pablo out for groceries. For whenever I go home.

Maj needs her mechanical files defragmented.

Zultan needs to be updated on the outcome of the Belthane project. I really should check-

Project Cassie needs to be moved on to stage 3

Father's lab –

Father -

*I'm trapped locked in being watched can't get out the lab potential recall why **why WHY***
somebody help me. I think I'm losing my mind

Chapter Four

Six hours later, Adri was drinking her third cup of coffee in the command center and instructing the cleanup grunts. The camp was secured, the Belligerents removed from the surrounding area, and she still hadn't made it back to bed. Captain Heedman, on the other hand, was currently sitting down to his luncheon with her field lieutenant. Both idiots were doubtlessly having a dandy time talking about masculine superiority and the proper place of women.

Adri was awake enough to know that her annoyance with Field Lieutenant Grayson was mostly due to lack of sleep. The knowledge that he was eating a real meal instead of military grade simulations didn't help. The captain, of course, traveled with his own victuals, his own cook, and a portable kitchen. But the rest of her disgruntlement with said field lieutenant had to do – she was sure – with the ridiculous level of 'just-rightness' he exuded. The man was a good officer, no question about it, and handled well under pressure. He took orders intelligently, had useful suggestions, good stamina, excellent aim, and was efficient. He was Adri's dream subordinate come true. That was the problem. The man was frighteningly perfect. Although she was grateful for his military expertise, and knew his mental capacity should be seen as a plus, there were some things that her field lieutenant had to change.

He made her shiver. In a romantic, my-you're-handsome-and-make-me-wish way. That had to go; there was no way they could work out a good officer to officer relationship if she was drooling over him every time he talked with that sexy voice. Adri knew the situation was bad when, after an acquaintance of a mere twenty-two hours she was obsessed with the man. Obsession was dangerous. Nearly as dangerous as love. Both emotions – if obsession was an emotion – would inevitably lead to heartache, and Adrienne Rael, battle tried Lieutenant Commander of the Galactic Commonwealth, had a large phobia of heartache.

But what to do about him? Unless she forbid him to look at or speak to her, which would cause all sorts of technical problems apart from making her look ridiculous, there was no way to completely avoid him. Or the effect he had on her. The only viable options open to her were starkly clear to Adri's sleep deprived mind. One, she could shoot him and totally eradicate the problem. Two, she could stand her ground and maintain a strong officer-subordinate position that allowed no sort of casual camaraderie. Neither option was enticing.

"Well L.C., I've finished jury-rigging the north shield, so it ought to stand up just as strong as the other three, at least for the time being." Duane announced as he sauntered towards her. His big eyes were bloodshot, making the white blend disturbingly with his bright face.

Adri frowned, shaking herself out of her thoughts. "Hmm."

"You must have been off on another planet. I called your name a couple times and you didn't even notice." Duane eyed her half finished coffee with wistful longing. "You gonna finish that?"

Adri gave a soft huff and drained her coffee cup. "How did the shield analysis go?"

"Enduring," Duane gave a longsuffering sigh. "Do you want the long or short of it before we both go to catch twenty five minutes of sleep?" he smiled appreciatively when Adri tossed him a candy bar that she'd taken from the captain's stash.

Here, at least, Adri felt calm and in control. Whatever her problems (real or imagined) with Field Lieutenant Grayson, it would not affect her responsibilities. "Better have the long of it, in case I get called in and need to give the captain excessive information for the health and safety of the platoon."

As he exited Captain Heedman's quarters – several standards above those he and Lieutenant Commander Rael inhabited - Gray wondered just what sort of political connections had allowed such a spineless man a position of authority. The luncheon had been enlightening, showing him that the real brains behind the success of this division was certainly not the esteemed captain. Staggering a bit, since Gray was never one to take a large meal after a sleepless night well, he decided to report to his lieutenant commander, get a good dose Adri out of her combat suit, and go to bed.

Adri wasn't in the officer's quarters, but Gray wasn't too surprised. More than likely, she was in the makeshift command center, making sure the camp was secure for the day. He expected no less from her.

She sure was a pretty sight, Gray thought. While the rest of the communication crew scrambled around reading monitors or rerouting power couplings, Adri sat on one of the control panels, a holoboard in one hand and a cup of coffee in the other. Oblivious to the noise around her, she sipped from her cup and reviewed the information on the board, occasionally frowning and murmuring to herself.

Gray wove his way through the crowded room until he reached her side. Adri was so absorbed in the information on the holoboard that she was startled when Gray spoke. "Field Lieutenant Grayson reporting, ma'am,"

"Oh, good," Adri stared at him, choices swimming in her mind.

"Captain Heedman sends his compliments for a job well done, although – and I quote – 'the girl could have done the whole thing a bit quicker, couldn't she?' After reviewing the series of events, however, he acknowledged that you proceeded with all considerable haste."

Adri's lips twitched. It would be hard to shoot a guy who could pull off an excellent mimic of Heedman's voice, and had obviously learned how to steer the captain into a different frame of mind after only meeting the man twice. She would have to stay a bit distant from him, if she wanted to be safe. Still, it would be…impolite to be cold to him after their first successful mission together. "The meal was plentiful, I expect," she conceded.

"A bit much after a long night," Gray replied. "But an overabundance of food aside, he did give me information to pass on to you."

33

"Such as?"

"The *Oreallus* has made contact with another Advance Force ship, heading in this direction. They are planning a rendezvous in about forty-eight hours."

"Did he mention the name of the ship?" Adri's interest perked.

Gray sat down in the chair facing Adri. "Yes, it was the *Damacene*."

Adri nodded thoughtfully. "Did he mention when our backup is arriving?"

"He did mention that the regular army would be arriving in less than fifteen hours, although he did not give me a specific time."

"Probably forgot," Adri muttered.

"What is the plan, then?"

Adri stretched and rubbed the back of her neck. "We hold our position until the army arrives. I'll finish writing the report for the Commonwealth. You go and make a round of the perimeter. Leave Davan in charge of the patrols. I don't want anyone venturing beyond the shields until I've had time to assess the schematics of the battle and can think of a plan for a scouting mission. We have to find out where the Belligerents are based; they did a far better job at their night raid than I would like."

"I'll get right on it, Adri." Gray turned and made his way out of the command center, leaving Adri to once again remind herself to tell him not to call her by name.

* * *

"Updates are complete, sir. Is there anything else you wish to add to the database?"

Floyd rubbed his face, skewing his glasses, before responding. "No, Zultan. You can run a self scan for any abnormalities."

"Very well, sir." Zultan switched programs and analyzed his systems quickly. Floyd watched as the tall humacom's gaze drifted to stare blankly at the far wall, an indicator that Zultan was running a program. He and his father (by Danwe, it hurt to think these days) had done a good job on designing and building Zultan. The humacom, or datacom as this one was sometimes called, looked just like a human with his dark hair and intelligent brown eyes. The only exterior differences were the ports and connectors located behind the ears and down the spine. They contained all the outlets for external cords, and were thus necessary to be easily accessed. Still, with clothes concealing most of those ports, Zultan could easily pass as a young man in his early twenties. "All systems are showing one hundred percent functionality."

"Good." Floyd sat back in his chair, contemplating the screen in front of him.

Zultan gazed at the screen for a moment before turning to gaze at the worktable that Floyd had been bent over for the last eighteen hours. "The project is nearly complete."

"Yes, it is. I've only to install a few more programs, and then give it all a good test scan before activation."

"It appears to me as though you've already installed all the government-required programs," Zultan commented.

"Yes, the last ones are just for my own satisfaction. They're the minor things; the physical human mimicry programs." Floyd replied.

Zultan nodded. "You and your father installed those in myself as well, correct?"

"That's right." Floyd rubbed his forehead, which was hammering painfully.

Watching Floyd's movements, Zultan said, "You still aren't well, sir."

"I'm fine."

"You've been rubbing your head since you came in to work, your face is a paler tone than normal, and your eyes look bleary and bloodshot."

Floyd frowned. "It's just the overwork from trying to finish the project by myself."

"Then perhaps you shouldn't be doing so." Zultan replied in his usual even tone. "My knowledge of medical diagnoses is very limited, but I can tell that you are not up to your usual health standards."

"Zultan," Floyd said wearily, "you are a government information database, with all of the Commonwealth's top secret military and political information. Not a doctor. I believe I can tell when I have gone too far." As indeed, he knew he had. Still, having his own humacom tell him so was rather annoying.

"Well, as a humacom loaded with all sorts of high intelligence, and not programmed with such human blinders as pride and stubbornness, I can tell you that you are not well." Zultan retorted.

Floyd scowled. "All right already. So it's been a bad week."

Zultan made no reply, but got up and walked over to the simulator, returning with a cup of coffee. "I don't think this is necessarily a good thing for you, but you seem to need it to finish the project, and I don't think the two security guards outside the lab will take it well if you hold off completion of the project due to ill health."

While Floyd drank the coffee and bent back over the nearly completed project, Zultan watched with human-like interest. As programmed, the humacom assessed, analyzed and processed.

And wondered.

* * *

Waking suddenly in the darkness of her quarters, Adri held her breath. Whatever had woken her from a deep, exhausted sleep must have been out of sync with the normal spurts of clamor and stillness that typified the camp at night. She waited unmoving in the dark for any sign of something unusual. When it came – a soft shuffling noise just inside her miserable excuse for a door – she could barely repress a sigh. She should have known that getting time for sleep on this hellish day was too good to be true.

Whoever it was made their way as stealthily as possible across the dirty floor towards Adri on the cot. Adri kept her breathing as even as possible, slowing inching her hand beneath her pillow for her ATF. As the intruder moved slowly closer, Adri curled her fingers around the trigger.

Just as the intruder reached the side of the bed, Adri sprang into action. Whipping her ATF out from beneath her pillow, she aimed for the blackish outline of a person, barely seen by the dim light of the corridor that seeped through the holes in the makeshift door.

The intruder gave a feminine gasp, and managed to block Adri's arm before she could aim. She was unable to dodge as Adri swept her leg out and knocked the woman to the ground. The stranger had maintained her hold on Adri's arm, however, and pulled her off the bed, beginning a tangled wrestling struggle on the ground as each tried to fend off the other and find the dropped ATF at the same time. With amazing skill, the intruder managed to elbow Adri in the throat, stunning her enough to gain her feet before Adri was up and upon her. Before Adri could make any sort of advance, the stranger had grabbed a handful of her hair and shirt and tried to ram her against the door.

The door, propped up at best as a barrier to light rather than anything else, collapsed as Adri sailed through it.

Across the hallway, Gray lay awake. A soft shuffling noise had alerted him to someone moving about in the corridor between his and Adri's quarters, and when the noise ceased, he'd been divided over whether or not to investigate. One thing was for certain, however; whoever it was sneaking about in the officers' quarters did not belong there. No officer in the military to Gray's knowledge worried about waking their fellows up enough to tip toe around, as it would only raise the suspicion of intruders.

With curiosity and suspicion fueling his sleep-deprived body he got up, yanked on his jacket, and stepped towards his door.

The sounds of scuffling and shouting coming from Adri's room made him pause and grab his ATF before dashing out into the corridor. He was just in time to catch Adri as she flew across the hall and practically into his arms. The speed of the contact knocked him off balance, and he barely saw the figure of a woman dash from Adri's room and race for the entrance to the officers' compound.

Adri struggled to regain her balance, and began to race after the fleeing figure. "Come on!"

Obediently, Gray ran after her, being treated to the sight of Adri in only her rumpled gray uniform slacks and black tank top.

The pitch darkness of the night was alleviated by the red glow of the shields and the strategically placed floodlights dotted across the camp, making it easier for Adri to see her assailant – a small framed woman – as she dashed for the perimeter of the camp. The woman had too much of a head start for Adri to catch her, and the perimeter guards were quickly mowed down with the intruder's rapid fire blaster. By the time Adri reached her fallen troops, the intruder had slipped through the shields and disappeared into the night.

Furious, Adri stared through the shields, her hands fisted at her sides. Beside her, Gray stood, looking little less disheveled. "Danwe," she hissed through her teeth.

"Are you all right?" Gray asked.

"If I ever get my hands on that fiend, it's going to be the worst day of her miserable life!"

"Because she hurt you?" Gray inquired.

"No, she woke me up!"

Username: Zultan
File://GC:#000237<privatelog>ugd//confidential//uri
*Password: *******
Access Granted
Command: open file to last saved date
Ever since I decided to start recording my thoughts, I have only had one basic question to ponder – how real am I? As disturbing as this thought is, there are now other issues that seem to challenge the logic of my programming. The theory of human rights over the humacoms they create is unadvised to argue with. As our creators, they reserve the right to also be our destroyers. They, in fact, stand in as our god. This apparently is not a universal theory humans hold. While they command that we humacoms cannot harm each other, or them, they themselves have no compunction about harming their creations, and just as little concern over harming each other. What twisted logic humans use! They did not create themselves, thus why do they claim to be their own gods?

As our creators, I would assess that humans are greater than we, but their logic does not hold with my own, the very one they gave me. Is my programming faulty? Am I not entering on some aspect of human behavior that is necessary to truly understand the workings of the human mind? Yet this is how they programmed me, with this unalterable pattern of true false, probable and unlikely. I can only do what I have been programmed to do, what I can do.

If it goes against what my creators intended, is it really a fault of mine? Are they not at fault for programming me to think this way? Or is it just an excuse? A human excuse?

I was not programmed to make excuses.
Save all new data
Close file
Encode

Chapter Five

"I see you left us very little to do, again."

One eyebrow rose on Adri's face in lieu of a smile. "I try my best, sir."

Colonel Robert Penkela of the Galactic Commonwealth Army shook his mane of salt and pepper hair. "If all my troops did your level of 'best,' then this war would have been over decades ago."

"I couldn't say, sir." Adri replied.

"I am assuming that your promotion to captain is looming in the near future, Lieutenant Commander."

Adri's tone echoed her determination. "I certainly believe so."

"Walk with me," Penkela began to stroll leisurely among the shoddy buildings that were hives of frantic activity. The gray sky above put a dull pallor over the scene, as though it wasn't much impressed with the action below. With the Army moving in and the Advance Force moving out, the noise level of the camp had risen to near deafening pitches. Adri walked beside the colonel, watching with half an eye as the Advance Force troops went about their business packing and switching the command posts to the Army. They would return to their ship, the *Oreallus*, by nightfall and be on their way to a new location, and a new assignment. Adri would be glad to be back aboard ship again.

Normally Adri would have been overseeing the details of the repack herself, organizing the anti-gravity lift loads, dealing with the usual inter-officer sniping that went on between the Advance Force and the

Army as positions were reversed. Now, however, she had a field lieutenant who was handling the situation with remarkable panache. She could see him now standing by the lift, holoboard in hand, mediating between one of the Advance Force's shield technicians and an Army defense officer as they argued about the state of camp protection. Grayson handled the situation with a great deal more finesse than she herself would have. At this stage in the argument, she would have pulled out her ATF and threatened to shoot either of them if they wouldn't shut up.

"Your field lieutenant working out to your satisfaction at last, Rael?" the colonel asked, pulling Adri out of her musings. "We passed the troop transport on our way here."

"Yes, surprisingly." Adri replied. "He's very competent."

"An admirable trait in an officer, of any caliber."

"I suppose so."

Penkela laughed; a hoarse, crackling sound caused from too much battle smoke inhalation. "We hear rumors in the Army about you, Rael. They say you are so demanding in your subordinates that many potentials avoid transferring into your command."

Adri shrugged, causing Penkela to laugh again. "I don't see why that's so bad."

"Ah, you wouldn't. You are not known for your diplomacy. But I would keep it in mind, when you go to recruit a crew of your own, soon."

A crew of her own. Her own ship, her own rules. It would be soon. Adri could almost savor the words, resting on her tongue like organic coffee. "I'll keep it in mind, Colonel."

"By the by, Rael, I hear that there was an enemy infiltration in the camp last night."

Adri frowned, pausing to gesture for one of her troops to move the scanning equipment currently cluttered on the ground out of the way towards the lift. "At this point we are not sure if the enemy was able to pass through the shield once it was raised after the battle, or if she snuck in earlier, when we dropped the shield, and hid out until things had settled down again."

"Either way is a disturbing possibility," Penkela replied musefully. "If she was able to pass the shields, then our equipment is lagging behind their technology. And if she snuck in before, then they have a better handle on Advance Force strategies – your strategies – than we had first assumed."

"True."

"Which do you tend to believe, Rael?"

Adri nodded at Gray across the compound as he signaled the change in shift. "I tend to believe the latter. Our shield schematics are the best in the line, and my engineers keep the frequencies shifting often. Besides, if they were able to pass right through, they would have sent more than one."

"So you think this was a direct attack on your platoon?"

"No. I think it was a direct attack on me."

"All baggage has been logged and loaded, Lieutenant Commander." Gray handed Adri the holoboard.

Adri made an absent hum of agreement. She sat on top of a large cement block, a part of what had once been a wall. "I want all backup troops to evacuate the field."

Gray smiled. "Already done. I anticipated your order, and all unnecessary personnel were removed to the *Oreallus* at 1400."

"You anticipated my order, did you?" Adri narrowed her eyes.

"Yes, ma'am. It is expected of a good field lieutenant to anticipate the commands of his superiors so that his superiors have more time to address their other duties."

Adri couldn't help but smile at the serious tone in Gray's voice. "I assume you think you are a good field lieutenant, Grayson?"

"Of course," Gray replied with such simplicity, Adri couldn't argue. "And you can call me Gray, since I call you Adri."

"You do not call me Adri."

"Yes, Adri, I do. But since I am a good field lieutenant, I anticipated that you would not want me to call you Adri. So I will refrain to do so, unless we're alone. Like now."

Danwe, the man had a smart mouth. A smart, cute mouth.

Just as Adri was about to reply, Sergeant Phoebe Oduran rushed up to her, saluting. "Ma'am, our scouting squad has just returned."

Immediately Adri's mind clicked back to her orders the night before. After studying the schematics of the battle, she had estimated the location of the Belligerent base and had sent out a selected squad to search for it. "What did you find?"

"Upon approaching the estimated position of the enemy headquarters, our scouts discovered what appeared to be an abandoned factory. There were no signs that it had been inhabited in the last seventy-two hours. No enemies were sighted, but the squad did not enter the premises, as per your instructions."

"Were there any signs of it being used as a temporary base?" Gray asked. Adri glanced quizzically at him. He really *could* anticipate her orders.

"Sir, there were signs that the factory had been used recently, possibly as a semi-permanent base. There were remnants of a type IIX Colok shield system, which is not easily transportable. But again, there were no signs of organic life on any of the scanners." Oduran replied.

Rael nodded. "Very good, sergeant. I want a briefing with the whole squad in – wait, the Army's taken over the control center…Tell them to assemble in the west corner of the mess hall in twenty minutes."

"Yes ma'am." Oduran saluted again and hurried away.

"The question is," Gray mused aloud, "Did they simply abandon it, or is it a trap?"

Adri shook her head slowly. "This whole scenario feels wrong. They have never attempted such an ambitious battle before. They've never sent in an…assassin – if that's what she was – and they usually are a great deal more defensive in their encampment positions. Why abandon a base? Especially when you know the Advance Force is leaving?"

"How would they know we are leaving?" Gray asked, watching in fascination as Adri pondered the situation out loud.

"It stands to reason that they know our routine well enough to understand our shielding and usual tactics. They'd know that when another ship arrives with additional troops, the Army has come to replace the Advance Force. If they know that, then they are smart enough to

43

know that the Army will spend at least two weeks entrenching their position before they make any offensive moves. That's all standard procedure. There's no reason to abandon the base yet." Adri shook her head again. "They either are really stupid – which their night raid proved they're not – or they are incredibly cunning."

"A trap?" Gray supplied.

"Has to be. And not for the Army either."

Gray walked beside Adri as she headed towards the command center. "What do you intend to do?"

Adri quirked one eyebrow. "I thought you could anticipate my orders."

Gray smiled. "When put that way, I believe I can. I'll go gear up, and meet back with you and the squad in fifteen minutes."

Adri stood as her field lieutenant sauntered back in the direction of the officer's quarters. "You're a strange man Gray."

Colonel Penkela frowned as he watched Adri study the topography of the suspected Belligerent position on a confiscated viewscreen in the command center. Beside her stood her new field lieutenant, who studied the neighboring screen and reeled off information to his superior. "I am not sure I agree with this procedure, Rael," he said at last.

"With all due respect sir, I am fully within my rights to head an investigative team to inspect a suspected Belligerent position," Adri replied.

Penkela made a huffing noise. "Be that as it may, your platoon has already departed back to your ship, and as second officer aboard the *Oreallus*, your presence is required. The Army is present in the area, you ought to leave it to us to handle some abandoned Belligerent post."

"Sir, we both know that while the Army is present, they only arrived a matter of hours ago, and are unfamiliar with the terrain. My Advance Force squad has the advantage of knowing the topography, as well as experiencing the methods that this particular regiment of Belligerents uses to fight. We are better equipped to run this mission at this time."

"Why must it be done at this time, Lieutenant Commander?" Penkela insisted. "Surely the outpost can wait a few weeks while the Army gets its bearings."

"Sir, if I might venture an opinion," Gray interrupted. "Both the attack against our shields and the possible assassin in the officer's quarters points to a keen knowledge of the lieutenant commander's strategies. This makes it an attack on her. It would be wrong not to meet the challenge quickly, not only to crush the opposition, but also to discover how they came to have such knowledge."

Still staring at the screen, Adri couldn't help but smirk at Gray's reasoning. It was perfectly logical, and would tie Penkela's hands if he tried to stop the mission from proceeding. "My field lieutenant is right. This is the only logical option; I will take my squad in to explore the base, pass the information on to my superiors and to you, and then return to the *Oreallus*."

The colonel knew when he was outmatched. Inwardly he smiled at the way the two officers had combined forces to push for their way. "Very well. My people will run the communication center while you undertake the mission. Make it quick. But Rael, if this whole strategy is to pull you out…be cautious."

While it would have been faster to ride the transport vehicles the entire distance to the Belligerent base, Adri felt it prudent to leave them two miles away for the sake of secrecy. Oduran's squad had reported that no organic beings had been sighted, but that did not mean there were not other surprises in store for them. The Belligerent Coalition did not use humacoms for active combat, having very few to begin with, but Adri was taking no chances.

Crouched between two large rocky spurs of dark, wet stone, she eyed the factory. Behind her, she could hear her troops checking each other's combat suits over the steady pattering of the rain. Suddenly she felt her own Life Support System on the back of her suit being tugged, and Gray's voice over the communicator, [All gauges read clear, Adri. You are set to go.]

[I thought I told you not to call me that,] Adri replied, turning around to inspect Gray's LSS gauge at the small of his back.

[So did I. That's strange, isn't it?] His helmet hid his face, but Adri could imagine the smile that would match the amused tone in his voice.

[You think you're so funny, don't you?] Adri said, exasperated.

[No, indeed, Adri. I am very serious at all times.]

Adri shook her head and turned back to her view of the outpost. [Turn your frolicking mind back to business, Field Lieutenant.]

[Yes ma'am. However, I do remember insisting that you call me Gray.]

Adri did not reply. Instead, she switched her communicator to include all her troops. [Rael to Black squadron. We are about to enter a potentially dangerous situation. I want everyone to keep alert. Watch were you walk, and everything around you. We have no real idea if this place is abandoned or not, and if it is, we don't know why. Backup is two miles away, and won't be of any real assistance in an immediate emergency, is that clear?]

[Yes, ma'am!] came the response.

[Very well, let's move in! Lieutenant Grayson and I will take the lead, Sergeant Oduran, you take the rear. If we come to any forks, you lead half the squadron. Understood?]

[Yes, ma'am!] Oduran replied.

Adri led the way across the barren, twilit landscape to the dark building ahead of them. It stood, tall and dark, with the same air of neglect that hung over the entire war zone. No life dared to linger here. She kept alert as they crossed the exposed ground, waiting for the telltale sounds of landmines, or the *whoosh* of air that accompanied a flying grenade. The world stayed quiet, however, and her entire squad crossed the area with no alerts. The side entrance Adri had chosen to enter was locked, but one of her troops quickly stepped forward with a decoder, and within minutes the little machine beeped the all clear. Another scan was done to ensure that no explosives were attached to the door. That also gave the all clear. The ease of their entrance unnerved Adri to no end. Even an abandoned outpost ought to have had some form of protection, if only to bedevil the enemy who chose to take it over.

Her communicator squawked in her ear. [Grayson to Rael. Is it just me, or does this seem too easy?] Gray asked on the officer's frequency.

[Much too easy,] Adri agreed, peering into the gloom as she cautiously stepped into the dark corridor.

[I don't like this.]

Senses flaring, Adri made no reply. She too had a bad feeling about the situation, leaving her adrenaline rushing and causing a soft humming in her blood. Her elegy was a bare thread of notes in her mind.

The corridor was long, winding, and had many offshoots. Adri left several of her troops at some of the wider intersections, watching the gloomy passageways warily. The main corridor ended abruptly in a wide room filled with unmanned Belligerent command stations. Instincts, already on the alert, kicked up another notch. It was a trap, had to be a trap. Adri was given a split second to consider her options. [All troops pull out! It's a trap! I repeat, all troops pull out!]

It was too late. The command room was suddenly filled with light as dozens of blasters opened fire from both above on a now visible catwalk, as well as from behind the command posts.

[Oduran to Rael! I've been hit, but it's not bad. The men left to guard the exit are gone. Our entrance point has been compromised. What are your orders?]

[Take your squad and find an alternate exit.]

[Understood, Oduran out.]

Dodging a blaster beam that streaked by her head, Adri backed out of the room, her mind racing to the backup plan. It had been a good setup – their scanners hadn't picked up any signs of organic life within the building. They obviously knew their tactics well enough to anticipate her moves here, as well new technology to hide their presence. Her squad was now pinned inside the building.

[Grayson to Oduran,]

[Oduran here, sir.]

[Just what is blocking the entrance we used?]

[It looked like a makeshift barricade, with troops behind it. I felt it unwise to advance,]

[Understood. Proceed with your orders. Grayson out.]

[Rael to Grayson,] Adri called on their private link, [What are you thinking?]

[I'm thinking we do the unexpected.]

[Excellent. Rael to Black squadron! All troops in my half get ready to storm the barricade blocking the exit!]

Corinthe City News- print edition

The Belligerent Coalition Has Attacked Our Peaceful Commonwealth!
Are You Willing To Defend Her?
From the far reaches of our fair galaxy, an enemy has sprung that
threatens our very way of life. Already, millions have died to keep you
and your loved ones safe. Millions more still fight. Millions do their
share in research, perfecting techniques to keep our home systems
safe, earning the eternal glory reserved for heroes, and the great honor
of defending the home of the enlightened.
What are you doing to serve your system?

ARE HUMACOMS TOO HUMAN?
Scientists Debate Possible Recalls of Humacom Personality Programs

Corinthe: Top researchers around the planet are debating the
philosophical question, 'are humacoms too human?' Recent studies
show an unusually high percentage of disobedience in the latest models
of all humacom designs, from securicoms to domesticoms, which
apparently connect with these models' HPPs. "It appears that we have
truly outdone ourselves with this technology," says Dr. Morris Waverly,
head of Interstellar Humacoms' research and development department.
"We have started mimicking human thought processes so well in our
programs that it may be affecting their fundamental logic program. We
have noted that because of an apparent conflict between the two
programs, humacoms will compute a different logic that may agree with
their master's orders. When faced with a logic crisis, most humacoms
are programmed to default in favor of their own conclusions. Whether or
not this conflict merits a recall of all HPPs is yet to be seen."
Despite skepticism on part of scientists, humacoms owners clamor
for a resolution to the problem…

Cont. in Technology, pg 2

Chapter Six

A dri ran. Her breath hissed in and out as she kept up the cover fire for her retreating squad. Just ahead of her Gray was issuing orders to the two soldiers who led the retreat column as they encountered some well-placed sensor bombs in their path. It was nice to have an aide who actually fulfilled his role, she thought. The randomness of the thought made her grit her teeth and turn her mind deliberately to the task at hand.

The bomb tech was quickly brought forward and the two sensor bombs diffused in record time, but the delay had cost them a soldier and space between their advancing foes. More resistance was met at one of the intersections as the main corridor met another. Adri had anticipated this, and they passed through with minimal danger. Still, the situation was becoming desperate, as there were still several intersections to pass and the barricade that blocked the exit. The enemy's strategy had been well thought out. They had bypassed Adri's troops stationed at the intersections by removing wall panels and concealing themselves behind them, using them as secret passages.

[Oduran to Rael, we've found an unguarded exit in the north wing of the building. We are currently crossing the surrounding area under heavy fire. Casualties are unknown at this time.]

[Are you being pursued?] Adri demanded, pausing to turn and fire at a Belligerent soldier who moved too close to her firing range.

[Negative. Only as we were retreating through the building.]

[Good. Retreat with all haste to the transports. Have Sacion provide backup fire if the situation alters. Rael out.]

The setup was beginning to come clear to her now. Adri cursed softly. [Grayson, prep the forward troops for a frontal assault. We're only going to have one shot at getting out, so we need to make it count. I'm going to need you up there.]

[Yes, ma'am.]

* * *

"Everything is falling into place, just as you predicted."

Hildana Kobane looked up from the palm sized security screen she had been studying. "Nervous about the success, little sister?" the screen lit up the deep bronze of her skin, highlighting her strong features. Her black hair hung down her back in a thick braid, but would soon be tucked up inside her helmet. Hildana's dark eyes looked over at her sister with amusement.

Giselle Kobane checked the charge level of her blaster the same way some women would check the contents of their evening bag. Unlike her sister, her features were delicate and distinctly feminine. While their coloring was the same, everything about Giselle was smaller, more refined. Her eyes did not reflect her sister's amusement. "Not so much the success, big sister, but the possibilities of the outcomes. We have a very tenacious, unpredictable opponent."

Hildana laughed. "You're just sore that she woke up while you were in the room. Your stealth was sloppy."

Giselle's delicate eyebrows furrowed into a frown. Her short hair swung at her chin. "I was not sloppy. She sleeps like an undarian."

"And you're sore about that officer who threw your grenade back at you," her sister teased.

"That was truly some amazing reflexes," Giselle replied, almost approvingly.

Hildana's communicator crackled to life. [Control to Kobane. The Advance Force has passed the fourth checkpoint. Waiting on your orders.]

[This is Kobane. Prepare for the pincer movement. Standby for my arrival with Sergeant Kobane. Out.]

* * *

[We have a visual of the barricade,] Gray reported from the head of the squad. They had ceased to run, as the enemy had fallen a good distance behind them. He peered around the corner fast enough to ascertain how heavily the barricade was being guarded. [I've spotted five to ten troops behind the barricade. A handful of sensor bombs have been planted on the floor.]

[Affirmative, Grayson. Clear the hallway to prepare for an assault. The Belligerents have fallen behind for a reason; I think they're expecting a big explosion.] There was a pause as Adri directed the soldiers beside her to keep up the cover fire as blaster beams shot out around them from snipers around the corners. [I'm expecting good results. Rael out.]

Gray flexed his fingers to keep them limber as he took a moment to assess the situation. When a solution presented itself, he smiled grimly. [All troops, increase your personal shielding! On guard for shrapnel!]

With that warning, Gray pressed the release on one of his rationed grenades, set the timer, and with a silent prayer to any deity that was listening, raced around the corridor into the main hall and hurled the grenade for all he was worth. Falling with the momentum, he rolled through the corridor intersection and into the hallway across from the one his squad huddled in. The grenade flew over the sensor bombs, setting them off. A tearing explosion rent the corridors, expelling waves of superheated gas and shrapnel in all directions. Gray's grenade, propelled by the explosion, hurled farther than Gray could have thrown it, landing right behind the barricade. There was a brief, barely heard shout before a smaller detonation rent a large hole in the middle of the barricade.

[That was effective, Lieutenant,] Adri said dryly over the officer's link.

Gray's ears were still ringing from the sound, despite his helmet which protected him from most overbearing audio. [Thank you, ma'am.]

[Any injuries?]

[No, but I would be happy to refrain from any more tumbling for the rest of the evening, if at all possible.]

Adri laughed softly. [We'll see what we can do. How does the hall look now?]

Gray peered around what was left of the corner and into the corridor. [The bombs took out most of the hall, its black and smoking now. There's too much smoke to scan the barricade adequately.]

[Roger that.] Adri switched to the open communication channel. [Black squad, advance with caution. Visual is low, and heat sensing is unadvisable. We don't want any more surprises, so keep alert. Rael out.]

Gray moved back out into the hall to take the lead once again, picking his way carefully over the scorched walkway as steam and smoke swirled around him. He listened carefully as he moved, wary of another trap. Behind him, one of the soldiers commented that the enemy that had been chasing them was once again advancing within firing range. Despite the rising need to rush, Gray took his time. It was a relief to arrive at the barricade and find that those who had survived had already fled the structure. [Grayson to Rael. It looks like nobody's home.]

[Then get out, we need to evacuate as quickly as possible before our pursuers catch up.] Adri replied. Gray could hear the muffled sound of her ATF going off as she spoke. [I'll stay back and try to give you time.]

[Understood. Grayson out.]

The door was coded, and looked to be been sealed in case the code was overridden. Gray ordered one of his men to begin the task of prying the door open while he tore off the protective plate to the passcode box and began finagling with the wires. He wondered idly why people bothered with such measures as electronically locking a door when they knew the opposing side was always so good at unlocking it just as quickly.

[Sir,] one of his soldiers announced suddenly, [there are sounds of approaching troops!]

Gray continued to carefully rewire the passcode. [The rest of the squad?]

[There is no visibility at this time, sir!] The soldier replied.

[Keep alert.] He continued to recode calmly as the sound of blaster and ATF fire echoed loudly in the corridor. With a small grunt of satisfaction, the passcode light blinked unlocked. Seconds later, the soldier prying open the door managed to heave the mangled barrier open several inches. [Get that thing open!] Gray commanded, still calm although a stray beam of blaster fire whizzed past his head with alarming proximity.

Another soldier pushed forward to assist his comrade. Between the two of them, they managed to shove the door open wide enough to accommodate one man at a time, if he squeezed through sideways.

[Lieutenant Grayson, the L.C. is approaching with the rest of the squad at a rapid pace!] The lookout announced. [It looks like the Belligerents are hot on their tail!]

[Grayson, how's that door?] Adri demanded at almost the same time.

[Open, I'm evacuating the troops now.] Gray replied, giving the order to the troops surrounding him.

Adri eyed the corridor behind her as she made a controlled retreat at the rear of her squad. The smoke from the damage was dissipating slowly, leaving the passage hazy at best. The approaching enemy proceeded carefully, not making any rushes against their position. In Adri's estimation, that made them either understandably cautious (Grayson's grenade skills had surprised even her), or intimidated. The whole operation certainly didn't hint at intimidated, so they were dealing with a well-organized enemy that didn't have a death wish. Pity.

She followed her troops as they proceeded to squeeze through the doorway. When there were only two men left, it happened. Her adrenaline, already racing, picked up as something in her head started screaming in warning. [Get down! Get down!]

The sudden onslaught of blaster fire from all directions was deafening as both Adri and Gray dove down against the remnants of the barricade. One of the soldiers managed to dive sideways through the door, but the other was not so lucky. The body blocked the doorway and the blaster fire hindered any other movement.

They were pinned.

***

Hildana raised the blast shield on her helmet and smiled fiercely. "Got them cornered."

"Big sister, do you desire to speak with them, or shall we proceed with the operation?" Giselle asked.

"Oh, I think we can allow ourselves to gloat a little bit." Hildana signaled to her troops to cease fire before opening the main communication signal that would be picked up by the two Commonwealth troops pinned behind the barricade. [This is Lieutenant Commander Hildana Kobane of the Coalition of Planets' Advance Force! Surrender now and you will be dealt with leniency. Resist and we will be forced to remove all opposing body parts. Is that understood, Lieutenant Commander Rael?]

Lying in an incredibly awkward position against the barricade ruins, Adri clenched her teeth in barely restrained fury. [It appears my reputation has preceded me,] she replied flatly.

[Oh, indeed it has. Your exploits both in the void and on the ground are legend among the Coalition.] Adri could hear the smirk in Kobane's voice. [You would not believe what an honor this is for me to actually speak to you this way. And in such an…interesting position, too.]

Beside her, Gray nudged her leg and tilted the point of his ATF in the direction of the right side hallway that joined the main corridor at the door. Adri shook her head, nodding in the direction they had just come from, circling her finger to hint that the enemy had them completely surrounded. [Sorry that I can't say the same. I'm afraid I'm in a rather irritable mood at the moment, having had my sleep disturbed by one of your little cohorts,]

[I'm very sorry, for both our sakes, that she disturbed you, Rael.] Hildana replied. [If she had had the courtesy to be a little bit quieter, we would have been having this conversation last night instead of right now.]

[If she had been a little bit slower, we wouldn't need to be having this conversation at all, now would we?]

[Now, that wasn't nice.] The amusement had dropped from Kobane's voice. [I'm sure that was a very unpleasant thing to say to me, given the circumstances Lieutenant Commander Rael.]

Adri nodded to Gray and pointed to the ceiling. Many of the wide plates were sagging due to the explosions. [If you had wanted me to be civil, Kobane, you should have left me and my men alone.]

[Well, if you put it that way. Parlovi, move the troops in and collect our prisoners!]

Adri listened as the Belligerent troops began to move forward, a little too recklessly in their assertion that they had her and Grayson pinned. The sound echoed off of the scorched ground, sending her an eerily accurate picture of their location. [Gray, now!]

In tandem, both Adri and Gray aimed their ATF rifles to the ceiling and began firing. The stressed materials shrieked as they lost their precarious moorings to the ceiling beams and fell, taking down the rest of the ceiling with them. As the roof above their heads began to whirl through the air, both Advance Force troops rolled to the right, firing at the enemy soldiers that had stopped in confusion as the ceiling above them cracked and fell, raising a black dust of ash and debris that was nearly impossible to see through. Blasting down all those in their path, both Adri and Gray dashed down the corridor.

[That was a close call, Adri,] Gray gasped as the raced around another corner towards the exit used by the other half of the squad.

Dang it, did he just call her Adri again? [You know, I'm pretty sure I told you not to call me that, Lieutenant.]

[Why not? You called me Gray just now.]

[I did not.]

[I beg to differ.]

[Can you differ later? Enemy troops behind us. You take the rear.]

[Yes ma'am.]

As Gray began firing at the approaching enemies, Adri faced the front. They were almost there, just another turn…

Dead ahead, blocking the exit, stood an enemy soldier. She was a tall woman, with long dark hair hanging down past her shoulder and no helmet, dressed in the fatigues of the Belligerent Coalition. Her face showed a bright smirk.

"Caught you." Hildana said.

Adri saw the beam of the blaster fire as if everything were in slow motion. There was no way to avoid it. If she moved a little to either side, it would hit Grayson as he defended the rear. But they couldn't end here. They *wouldn't*. In that instant before impact, Adri felt something shift inside of her, as though some other entity was stretching, wishing to break free. The corridor shifted and changed somehow, as though the colors had all faded, leaving only the blaster beam in clear focus. Her mind started screaming *block it! Block it!*

Gray turned just in time to see the beam streak across the corridor straight at Adri. Yet, just when it should have hit, the beam flashed as though hitting a shield and vanished. Gray blinked in stupefaction, but Adri was still moving, not having lost any momentum, and was now firing on Kobane, forcing the enemy to retreat. Gray followed, keeping up a steady fire as Adri worked with the passcode on the door. [Reinforcements are coming,] he warned.

[Got it.] Adri shoved at the door, prying it open several inches. [You first.]

Gray squeezed through the narrow opening while Adri provided cover fire.

Down the corridor, Adri could see that the reinforcements were armed with much larger weapons than handheld blasters. She dove through the door just as the enemy fired a lightweight blaster cannon at the door.

[Oduran to Rael. We have your cover. Please proceed to point oh-six.]

[This is Rael. Nice job guys. Let's get out of here. It's an Army problem now.]

Climbing into the transporter, Gray let out a long sigh and removed his helmet. The rain drizzling on his head was a refreshing relief. "I must say, moving to your division has certainly put a lot more action into my life, Adri."

Removing her own helmet, Adri raised an eyebrow. "I'm sure I said numerous times that you couldn't call me that. And we are still in a danger zone, Lieutenant."

Gray smiled winningly. "Well, we won't always be fighting, now will we? You're going to have to have a better argument than that soon. I'm a persistent kind of guy."

Adri leaned back and closed her eyes. "So I've noticed."

***

"Did you see that?" Hildana asked softly as she watched her troops reorganize for the retreat. "I shot her, and the beam disappeared, like she reflected it somehow,"

"Now you know how I feel, big sister." Giselle replied.

Hildana was not amused. "That was not simple reflexes, little sister. She completely deflected it, head on. There's no way her personal shielding is that good. Was it some trick she's got?"

"Hildana?"

Hildana continued frown. "What is she?"

My Dear Riordan,

Things on this mission have more or less gone according to plan. My sister seems hopeful that while our priority mission goes smoothly, with average casualties, we will have a chance to achieve our secondary mission while Lieutenant Commander Rael is still on planet. But if not, there will be other opportunities. Enough about work, now, how are you?

I was finally able to kick the cold I had gained from this endless rain. I'm afraid it made me a little punchy for a while, and I foolishly tried to ignore it and went on a mission that almost ended in a total disaster. But how is your health? I almost envy you, getting to stay indoors so much, but I'm afraid I would find it stifling after a while, don't you? I'm sorry all I seem to talk about is fighting, but that is all I know, having been raised in an army camp. I wish I was with you now, and you could tell me some wild story of when you were a boy on your farm. The pictures I see in my mind are so beautiful.

My sister believes we will be returning in another forty-eight hours for a rest before heading back to the ship. I know many of us are looking forward to the respite, once our comrades from Edia come in to relieve us. I look forward to seeing you there.

I send my thoughts and love ahead of me. May all that is holy protect you until my return.

> *With all that is in me,*
> *your beloved,*
>
> *Giselle*

Chapter Seven

"**D**id you feel the change? It was like a ripple through the air, a stirring of something…more."

Freya looked up from the view of the wide valley, the wind blowing her long golden hair across her dainty face. For a moment the only sound was the air rushing through the tall grass, ruffling her long white dress. "Yes, I felt it. Like something brushing up against my heart." She smoothed her hair away from her face absently, revealing eyes the shade of fresh lilacs. "Did you have a vision, Ayane?"

The young girl sat down beside Freya, smoothing the long skirts of her own white dress against her legs. Like Freya, whose twenty years sat beautifully on her, and whose build was small and delicate, Ayane at sixteen held great physical promise. Silver eyes peeked out of an oval face framed by long brown hair that danced playfully in the breeze. "That is what I wished to speak to you about, *sorja*. There is something strange going on. I don't understand it. It is like a dark cloud around the convent."

"Yes, I know what you mean." Freya turned around to gaze back at the large structure that sat on top of the green hill. "A lot of us have been sensing something abnormal. But no one I've spoken to knows what it is."

There was another long silence as both women watched a bird soar off in the distance. "Freya, I'm not remembering my visions."

The older woman turned to gaze fully at her companion. "What do you mean, Ayane? Your strength as a Talented rests in your ability to see visions. Have you stopped having them?"

Ayane stretched her slender arms and traced the scrolling sapphire markings on her left hand with her fingertips. "No, I can recall the residue of a vision, like the tail end of a bad dream. All I can recall is fire and fear, but nothing else. I *know* there is more than that, but I cannot see it. Even my sessions with *ada* Sergei haven't been successful. I spend hours with him in meditation, but in the end, I cannot recall even being there, much less any visions I may have had."

"I thought you said that being with *ada* Sergei was uncomfortable for you. Why do you keep going?" Freya asked.

The young Talented shook her head. "He insists, and really, how can I refuse him? He is head of the convent."

"That is no reason to capitulate if he makes you uncomfortable." Freya insisted.

Ayane smiled shyly. "I wish I had your confidence, *sorja*. It probably comes from living with a family for so long before coming here."

Freya smiled and stroked the younger girl's head. "Perhaps. My brother could be so bossy sometimes, I had to assert my independence!"

Some of the worry eased out of Ayane's face. "Do you still keep in contact with him?"

"I try, but he is a very busy man." Freya turned to look back out over the valley. "Actually, I'm a little worried about him right now."

"Why?"

"I'm not sure, I suppose it's just a feeling I have. You know me and my premonitions."

* * *

"That seems a very primitive means of repair,"

Zultan continued to stare through the glass partition at Floyd. The human was lying back on one of the lab's infirmary beds, an old fashioned IV stuck into his arm as he slept uneasily. "The infirmary was out of the appropriate medication in a simpler form, and they had some of the archaic IV packs as emergency backup. That information should be stored in your database, Cassie."

The small, female formatted humacom frowned back up at him from her lesser height. At first glance, one could easily mistake her for a teenager. Her short crop of dark hair accentuated a face that spoke of attitude. The gray uniform that both humacoms wore looked out of character on her, although the pair of ATF pistols did not. "Of course it is. I was only making an observation. I'm functioning just fine, thank you."

The male humacom smiled. "Indeed you are."

Both turned back to stare at Floyd beyond the partition. If it had not been for the flush brought on by his high fever, he would have been deathly pale. The young man thrashed in the bed, muttering to himself before settling down again. "He is showing classic signs of stress and overwork, according to my medical files," Zultan commented.

An infirmary orderly passed by the two humacoms, staring in curiosity. The two humacoms stared back. Cassie spoke to Zultan via the instant messaging system. *He worked too hard to create me.*

Perhaps, but I deduce that there are other factors to blame as well. Zultan replied.

If he knew that being active like this would lead to illness, I don't understand why he did so. It's illogical.

Cassie, that is the difference between us and them. Humans are able to ignore their logic, going on against all proven data. This is often the result.

Are we then always subject to our logic systems?

Yes. That is how humans program us to be.

That makes no sense at all. Why do they program us to do things that they obviously do not adhere to themselves? They are much more fragile than we are. If anything, they ought to be the ones to follow a logic structure. But you said that this is "often" the result. Is there another result for this sort of behavior?

Yes. Sometimes when humans go against their logic, they come up with something new. Being programmed with a logic we must adhere to, we are unable to create something original. We are only capable of using the functions provided for us. Our capabilities are finite, while theirs can be infinite under the right circumstances.

You are speaking too abstract for me. I'd much prefer focusing on my duties and leaving all this philosophy to a database like you.

If you like. But I can deduce that we will not be able to avoid these issues forever. They both watched as a medical humacom adjusted Floyd's IV dose. The liquid, which had been a pale yellow color, began to change to a darker color, almost black.

"Those actions have been processed as suspicious," Cassie said out loud.

"I agree. My medical data identifies this change in color as highly dangerous."

"We should act."

"I agree."

Without further communication, Cassie pulled out a pair of ATF pistols and blasted the glass partition away. While the glass was still flying, both humacoms leaped through the new entrance. Cassie, weapons still out, strode towards the medicom. "Your actions have been processed as suspicious. Submit to a hack connection or I will annihilate you."

Silently, the medicom produced a small ATF and began to aim it at Cassie. Cassie instantly shot the hand off the medicom and then went for the legs. As the medicom's limbs shorted and sparked, the smaller humacom whipped out a connection cord from the port behind her ear and plugged it into her opponent.

While Cassie was dealing with the medicom, Zultan strode over to Floyd's side. After a quick analysis of his medical data, he removed the IV pin from Floyd's arm before the new medication had a chance to enter Floyd's bloodstream. "Dr. Tarkubunji's situation is clear."

"All hostile targets have been annihilated. Hacking into the hostile's system now." Cassie was silent as she hacked through the medicom's firewall system. Only a few moments passed before she disconnected. "The order to place polymentholame, a toxin deadly to humans, into Dr. Tarkubunji's IV is scrambled; there is no way for me to trace the source at this time. The same source ordered the attack on anyone, human or humacom, who tried to stop the procedure."

"I see. My programming dictates that we alert the authorities about this situation. Perhaps they will be able to analyze the command to a source."

"I agree. Why don't I transmit the command signature to you as

63

well, since you might be able to decipher just as quickly?" At Zultan's nod, Cassie reconnected her cord with Zultan and passed on the information. As she was disconnecting, she said, "There was something strange about that medicom, though."

"What was it?"

"When I was reading her basic programming profile, she was missing the independent function of the AI unit. She also…"

"What?"

"This is superfluous, but it might be useful for the investigation. She had no personality program."

Zultan frowned in human thoughtfulness. "Strange. Humans design us with personality programs for their own convenience and entertainment. I have not heard of any of the new models being constructed without one. And she was a new model."

"I don't understand." Cassie said softly. "It was like she was empty inside. Less real even than the stationary systems. It doesn't make any sense; we're all machines, but it was like connecting with something that was almost dead."

"You're right, that doesn't make any sense. But I agree, she did seem…empty somehow."

Just then, the doors to the infirmary slid open, allowing a half dozen human guards into the room. Behind them, Colonel Stroff strode in with his usual compliment of securicom bodyguards. He glanced at Floyd, still asleep on the bed, to the remains of the blasted medicom on the floor in front of Zultan and Cassie.

"What happened here?" He demanded.

"Sir," Cassie saluted. "This medicom injected polymentholame, a deadly toxin, into Dr. Tarkubunji's IV. We corrected the potentially harmful situation."

"You must be C.G.P. 00297."

"Yes sir. I was activated yesterday morning at 0751. I have been named Cassie."

Stroff made a grunting noise in his throat. "I demand to know why you and Zultan are out of your proscribed zones. I did not hear of any request to move to the infirmary level of the complex."

"When Dr. Tarkubunji collapsed, there were no personnel available to transport him to the infirmary. Our programming dictated that the matter was serious enough to bypass zoning procedures, and took him down to the infirmary ourselves." Cassie explained.

"You both did not need to come with him," Stroff argued, but Cassie cut him off again.

"True. Zultan could have carried him down to the infirmary by himself, but my programming does not allow him to be beyond a certain proximity of myself. As his exterior firewall system, I cannot function properly if I am not nearby."

"Why did you stay?" Stroff demanded, scowling down at the little humacom. She only reached Zultan's mid chest. Her large brown eyes stared straight at him, and if he didn't know she wasn't capable of such a thing, he'd think she was disdainfully criticizing him.

Before Cassie could reply, Zultan said, "The doctor had been in the process of downloading some new information into my hard drive when he collapsed. I cannot continue the process without him, so I thought it prudent to wait for him here. And it appears to be fortunate we did. Cassie?"

Cassie spoke again. "After we brought him down, we were informed that Dr. Tarkubunji was ill due to overwork. The current medicom on duty also informed us that the infirmary was temporarily out of medication for this situation, and placed him on IV. Shortly thereafter, the medicom returned and attempted to poison the doctor. I am programmed with an assortment of military programs, which dictated quick action. When the medicom refused to submit to a hack and attempted to open fire on me, I blasted her weapon away, and then prevented it from escaping. When I hacked, I discovered that the commands to give the doctor an IV, and subsequently poison it, were from a scrambled source."

"Have you sent the command signature to the security database?" Stroff demanded.

"Yes sir."

"Very good. Since you are waiting for the doctor's return to consciousness, I will place additional security here and allow you to stay." With a wave of his hand, Stroff ordered the guards out of the room and followed them. Both humacoms watched him go.

"You did not tell the truth when the colonel asked why we stayed, Zultan," Cassie said. "No humacom is capable of lying."

"I didn't lie. Floyd and I were in the middle of transferring some data when this happened, if you care to review. I do have to have him present to complete the task."

"But you told me you were concerned for Floyd's welfare."

"I was, and that was the primary motive for my decision to stay."

"That isn't logical. Why would our presence speed Floyd's recovery?"

"Because," Zultan replied quietly, "I have been reviewing some data over the past weeks which would lead me to conclude that someone wants him dead."

"Who would want to kill Floyd? He is necessary for the upkeep and development of this facility's humacoms, isn't he?"

"That is correct, which is why the situation is puzzling."

Cassie scowled at the black mark on the floor where the medicom had been. One of the guards had dragged the remains out with them. Zultan sat down in one of the chairs and looked at the hole that had once been the glass partition. It had left a terrible mess, but a domesticom was already approaching with a vacuum. Cassie watched her companion for several minutes before walking over to Floyd to stare down at him. It was surprising to her that he had slept through the action. Glancing over to make sure that Zultan was not paying attention, she bent down and whispered, "Don't worry *ada*, we're watching over you."

She straightened back up, and was left to ponder her confusing, and illogical action.

* * *

The sun was setting beyond the mountain range that hemmed the valley in, staining the walls of the convent a burnt orange where it passed through a window. Ayane and Freya walked quickly through the halls. "I hate to ask you to do this, but…"

"No it's all right. I want to understand what's wrong with you as well." Freya replied quietly.

"Are you sure sneaking out like this is appropriate?"

"You said you didn't want *ada* Sergei to know, didn't you?" Freya took Ayane's hand and led her through the labyrinth of hallways to a small outer door. Through the door, they made their way to a small grove of woods that would shelter them from view from any windows. Once there, Freya sat down in the soft loam and beckoned Ayane to sit in front of her. "Are you ready?"

Ayane nodded. "If I don't see anything within an hour, we'll go back, agreed?"

"Agreed."

Ayane closed her eyes and rested her upturned palms on Freya's. A long silence encircled them, broken only by night noises. Some mice scurried in the deeper loam. An owl passed in near silence overhead.

It didn't take more than fifteen minutes. "Change is coming,"

Freya opened her eyes to stare into Ayane's, which were opaque with vision.

"Death is coming, riding in on flame and fear. The awakening of Veranda is near, a challenge to Cerebitha. The cycle will bring about the…"

"The what? Ayane!"

Ayane's face had gone white, and she began to tremble. "It will all burn….they will destroy it all…Freya,"

Freya removed her hands and shook Ayane, breaking the connection. Almost at once, Ayane gripped her head and began to scream. Freya wrapped her arms around the younger girl and began to rock her, whispering soothingly. She caught a glimpse of the convent walls, visible through the trees. The sun had turned the white walls blood red.

"I can't see it, Freya." Ayane whispered. "Its like something has blocked me, it hurts to look. It hurts to look."

"It's all right, just rest now." Freya stared at the bloody walls as the sun fell beyond the horizon. Change was coming.

* * *

Light-years away, in another part of the galaxy, Adri tossed and turned on her bed in her second officer's quarters aboard the *G.C.N. Oreallus.*

Nightmares plagued her sleep. Dreams of fire. Bright winged lights raced to and fro away from the flames, only to be swallowed by the dark.

To Do:

Get dressed. - Find out where the heck Gobrett went with the new uniform orders.

Eat breakfast. – Check the supplies and the simulators. Gotta stay healthy.

Yell at Sergeant Walters. – scrub duty for ten months. The moron.

Check munitions. – Inspect all ammo levels, speak to Giselle about the specs for the new sniper rifle.

Proceed to the Rivera. – load 'em up.

Eat lunch.

Practice Ayallan. – Does Giselle know those roll kicks?

Analyze battle specs. – figure out what happened. What went wrong. How can we improve our performance? Talk to Smith about weapons acquisitions. Figure out what the heck happened with that blaster shot at Rael. What was that?

Eat dinner. – Compliment the captain on his choice of new tactical officers.

Review tomorrow's agenda. – Ask Giselle about Riordan's progress on that code breaker.

Go to bed. – Promise self that I will actually get seven hours of sleep.

Note to self:

Make the time to really talk with Giselle. I think she's afraid we're over our heads, but she won't say anything. Don't let what happened with Rael worry me too much. Remember that no one is perfect, and that I have lived my entire life with the Advance Force. I can take on one skinny Commonwealth agazi. Next time will be much better. After all, I did manage to pin down the elusive Rael, didn't I? Ought to pound on that idiot Parlovi.

Check to see if we have some organic milk somewhere.

Chapter Eight

Rough night, Adri mused as she glanced back at the twisted sheets on her bed. Normally she slept hard on her first night of full sleep aboard ship, but last night she had been plagued with some very disturbing nightmares. With a last stretch, she shook off the last remnants of sleep and turned to the shower.

The "night" shift was just beginning as Adri made her way from her quarters up to the ship's bridge. The calm orderliness was such a change from the typical noise and controlled chaos of the Advance Force surface camps that she had to mentally adjust to the difference. The ensigns saluted to her as they passed her on the main corridor. Just outside the door, she made a final adjustment to her fresh uniform. Taking a deep breath, she murmured her routine "Patience, Adrienne, patience," before opening the doorway and stepping onto the bridge. "Second Officer Lieutenant Commander Rael is now on duty, Captain."

Captain Heedman turned from his discussion with Vice Captain Christian Lowell at the sound of her voice. "Ah, Lieutenant Rael. Excellent. I was just telling Lowell that your services were necessary."

He was drinking real coffee. Adri could almost hear her stomach whine in envy. She had to mentally remind herself of her mantra: patience, patience, no matter how much of a dolt he was, he was her captain, and she needed to show him respect. That's how the political wheel spun. "How can I be of service, sir?"

"You need to show Lieutenant Grayson around the ship. He is the new security officer, after all."

Adri turned her head to see that Gray was standing a step behind Lowell. "You need me to give him a tour?" Did she look like some dippy tour guide?

"Of course."

"With all due respect, sir, my shift has started,"

Heedman waved his hand. "Yes, I know. Janag will stand in for you until this task is completed."

Adri could hear the operations officer, Susan Janag, sigh in resignation. Her shift would normally begin after Adri's ended, but today was the first in transit, and most of the crew who'd stayed aboard the ship while the rest were on the planet's surface had spent the previous eight hours debriefing the captain and other senior staff. Adri doubted that Janag had seen her bed in the last twenty-one hours.

"You need to make it thorough, Rael," Heedman lectured. "Leave no corner unexplored; I want our new security officer to be fully acquainted with our ship so that he can do his job. But you need to make it quick, we are expecting visitors this shift. The *Damacene* is going to be here soon on its way to Alistor."

"Yes, sir."

"This is the main corridor," Adri said as she and Gray exited the bridge. What kind of order was 'show the entire ship, but be done by mid shift?' The idea was laughable. "Since we only have a few hours before the arrival of the *Damacene*, I expect you to lie to your superior officer and tell him that you miraculously saw the entire ship when you next see him."

"I understand. I would be amazed to discover if the captain has seen more than his quarters and the bridge, for fear of getting lost."

Adri snorted in suppressed laughter.

They continued walking until they reached the lift. "This is the main lift." Adri said dryly before ordering it to drop to the next level.

"Adri, is it just me, or are you adverse to any sort of intimate relationship?" Gray asked bluntly as the lift began to descend.

71

Adri opened her mouth and closed it with a small noise. "I prefer not to have intimate relationships at all." she finally managed.

"Oh, well then, as long as it isn't just me." Gray smiled at her as the lift stopped and the doors opened.

"What do you mean?" Adri demanded, stepping out of the lift and starting to walk again.

"If it had been me you were nervous of, then I'd be stuck, but if its just relationships in general, then I have a chance."

"What?!" Adri stopped in the hallway, glaring at a couple of ensigns until they scurried out of hearing range. "I am NOT nervous, and what do you mean, have a chance? A chance at what?"

Gray continued to smile, but now it was more of a smirk. "You blush when you're nervous, like right now. And I will have a chance to have an intimate relationship with you, Adri, once I convince you that there is nothing to be nervous about. These kind of relationships are supposed to be pleasant, after all."

Adri suddenly felt the urge to tug out her hair. Or strangle the new security officer. "I *know* that! What makes you think I like you anyway?"

"If you really didn't like me, I would never have made it this far, would I?" Gray insisted.

Was she that transparent? The man read her like a public forum. She even let him get away with calling her Adri. What were her options? Shooting him was a bad idea, she'd get thrown into the brig, and it would be a pity to ruin that pretty face. She failed miserably at ignoring him. "I've known you for only a few days, and you've already complicated my life."

"What is life without complications, Adri?" Gray watched the emotions play out in her pretty brown eyes. The woman had an obvious mistrust of relationships, but hopefully he could show her how special being with someone who cared for you could be. He had a feeling that he was fast approaching a line in the sand, and he didn't care.

Adri stared hard into his eyes before running her fingers through her hair and turning away. "I think about you too much, Gray. Let that be enough for now."

"Fair enough."

"This level houses mostly engineering and storage," Adri said as they wandered down yet another corridor. "Warehousing is in charge of cataloguing and organizing everything in the storage spaces, including the ammunitions storage. Commander Janag or Vice Captain Lowell are the ones who usually deal with Warehousing, so I wouldn't concern myself too much with whatever they do to pass the time down here."

"I've always though that Warehouse was a rather thankless job," Gray commented.

"Further down this corridor is Engineering, and depending on how Commander Solson's mood is, you might be making a lot of trips down here."

"Why?"

Adri pressed the release on the door. "To suppress riots."

The minute the door was open, the noise level increased to a wild clamor. Over it could be heard an older man shouting. "Did I ask you to think, grunt? No. I told you to adjust the power regulator, that's all. A simple order you could have followed if you hadn't taken it upon yourself to THINK!"

"I see what you mean," Gray murmured.

"He's really on a rampage," said a voice to their right. Gray watched as Duane sauntered over, his bright magenta face streaked with something black and greasy. "Well, I see that you made it down to the Engine Room at last, Grayson."

Gray nodded. "I dabbled in engineering while aboard the *Cliam Lomas*, but this is…something else." The chaos was unbelievable. Gray watched as two running engineering ensigns, each carrying what looked to be boxes of tools, crashed into each other with deafening noise. Tools cascaded over the floor like escaping hamsters. They promptly began to yell and curse at each other. No one else seemed to notice or care.

"This is a good day. Solson is in an uproar because the *Damacene* is on its way, and he has a longstanding rivalry with Commander Haggan, the *Damacene*'s chief engineer," Duane went on blithely.

"I'd hate to see a bad day," Gray muttered, watching in fascinated horror as the two ensigns tackled each other and began to roll around on the scattered pile of tools.

"Danwe," Adri said suddenly, noticing the two ensigns for the first time. "Utter morons."

Gray and Duane watched as Adri strode over to the two fighting ensigns, stepping over tools and shoving aside spectators.

Duane shook his head. "Now they've gone and done it. She was in a nice, mellow mood, too."

"What do you mean…" Gray began, but stopped speaking as Adri stepped up to the battleground. When her sharp order to cease was ignored (they probably did not hear her over their own huffing breaths and raging insults), Adri gave up any form of diplomacy. Reaching down for the nearest assailant, she hauled him up and rammed her knee into his stomach, decommissioning him. Tossing him aside, she reached for the second man, who was trying to pounce on his downed opponent. He tried to dodge her jab, and ended up wheezing in pain as Adri's knee hit him several inches lower.

Hands on her hips, Adri glared down at the two culprits. "Which one of you two morons thought that it was a good idea to start a wrestling match while on duty?"

One ensign squeaked in terror, obviously realizing for the first time just who had broken up their fight.

"And there's our beloved L.C." Duane said as Adri berated the two idiots.

Gray whistled. "I can see where she gets her reputation. Sergeant Kalinen from Analysis stopped me in the main corridor this afternoon and whispered 'Good luck with the L.C.' to me. I didn't know what he meant."

"The L.C. isn't known for her diplomacy," Duane replied, winking at Adri as she strode back towards them. "She's as tough as she is pretty."

"I can't believe the idiots you have working down here, Duane, I really don't," she said heatedly.

Duane shrugged amiably. "I don't do the hiring, I'm only an assistant engineer."

"Solson would have us stranded in the middle of nowhere with the way he runs things down here."

"Well, at least the engine's running. For now."

Adri felt like throwing up her hands in sheer frustration. "I'm getting out of here before something else happens that will offend my sense of order. Duane, do you have those specs I asked for?"

Duane reached into his pocket and pulled out a small data chip. "Here you are. I had to twist a few arms in the weapon tech's division for it."

"Thanks," Adri slipped the chip into her own pocket. Turning to Gray she said, "Are you coming?"

"Right beside you."

"Duane," Adri called out as they headed for the door, "You should probably call Dr. Geiger and have those two imbeciles moved to the infirmary."

The door closed on Duane's annoyed expletive.

"Adri, what's on the data chip that Duane gave you?" Gray asked as they walked along the level that housed the science and technology labs.

Adri was quiet for a long moment. Finally she stopped and turned to look hard at Gray. She hadn't known him long, only a few days really, but he'd proven himself a capable soldier and officer. He was interested in her; something she really didn't want to think about for...maybe never. It all came down to a matter of trust. Looking into his calm, questioning gray eyes, she could feel herself longing to be able to trust someone. Something more than the friendly camaraderie she had with Duane, or some of the other Advance Force members. But did she dare open herself even that much? Did she even remember how?

Gray could see some interior struggle going on behind Adri's lovely brown eyes, and he found himself holding his breath, waiting for her answer.

"It's the data analysis of the ambush at the Belligerent Coalition camp last night."

Gray frowned. "Can't you just order up a copy? You are the lieutenant commander."

"You're right, but I'd need to sign out on it, and I didn't want it to be general knowledge. Something strange happened, and I need to figure out what it was." Adri shook her head. "It might be nothing, but I need to find out."

"Find out what?"

The overhead communication system buzzed before Adri could reply. [Bridge to Rael and Grayson. Contact has been established with the *Damacene*, and the captain requests your presence on the bridge.]

Both Adri and Gray touched their earpieces, [Acknowledged, Bridge.]

They began walking at a faster clip towards the lifts. When they had stepped inside and were rising to the bridge level, Adri said, "Grayson, are you well versed in the schematics and workings of the Belligerent's handheld weaponry?"

"I've seen my fair share, and I've had some extensive training. Why?"

Adri opened her mouth, but no sound came out. She tried again. "I'm going to go over these specs, and then run a probability analysis. I'm going to need an assistant. I don't want anyone else to know what or why I'm doing this." Oh crap, what was she doing? She didn't want to spend time – private, one on one time – with him. Did she?

Gray nodded, a hint of a smile in his eyes. "I'm your man."

Something in Adri's stomach fluttered, and she found herself wishing in the back of her mind that he were.

My mind has been unsettled lately. There is a dark presence around the convent, as though a warning of danger to come; yet no one can identify it. This is probably the most disturbing part of the whole situation. A convent filled with Talented and headed by a Talented ought to be able to decipher coming danger. No one speaks of it aloud, but I know in my own way that everyone is worried.

Ayane's vision disturbed me more than I can say. She has a very powerful gift, and she has spent most of her life refining and perfecting its use. But it is a burden. I am glad that I have no such power. Rather, I prefer my variations of weak gifts. It must be an incredibly vulnerable feeling, to not be able to rely on a part of oneself that has always been there. This adds to my uneasiness. Did her gift simply fail her? Or is it something else? I have heard that there are powers out in the vast universe that can block or manipulate another's conscience,...but that seems absurd. Why would someone with such a skill wish to block Ayane's Sight? Unless...

I have a terrible feeling that something is about to happen, something irreversible, not just for my life, but for everyone else's. It grows stronger daily. On top of this is my growing concern for my brother. He is never home to speak with by transmission, and my telepathy cannot reach as far away as Corinthe city. The news he sent me of father's death was most grievous, and I was surprised and upset when ada Sergei did not allow me to return home for his funeral. Something is not right about the report Floyd sent me on father's death. He was never one to throw his life away! The whole situation seems suspicious. Poor Floyd, dealing with all this, plus the workload I know he's taken on, I worry about his health.

My spirit is warning me, I know what I have to do, but it will go against all the training and commands I have received since entering the convent life when I was young. Perhaps I should wait and see how the situation unfolds; it is always better to be informed than to run around in the dark.

But then, darkness has its own uses, as does ignorance.

I'm beginning to fear that the change Ayane spoke of will be very soon.

Chapter Nine

"Rise and salute, captain on the bridge!" At Vice Captain Lowell's order, everyone on the bridge rose from their assigned positions and saluted as Captain Heedman entered the bridge, followed by Captain Francesco Yates of the battleship *G.C.N. Damacene* and a few members of his senior staff.

"Welcome back to the bridge, my dear fellow," Captain Heedman said in an almost fawning tone. Captain Yates was nearly a foot taller than Heedman. Like all other kievians, Yates boasted a second set of eyes high on the forehead, and impressive copper colored tentacles in lieu of hair. His burnished gold complexion made Heedman look sun starved. His gray uniform was crisp and sharp, hinting at a newer style than Heedman's. An over-shined medal for excellence hung on his chest. He'd left the collar of his jacket open to sport an expensive looking cloth cravat.

Yates made a thorough survey of the bridge before commenting, "I see that you have some new members on your senior staff, Albert."

Heedman scurried behind Yates as the taller captain strode across the room to where Adri and Gray stood together beside the tactical station. Giving Gray the critical eye, he said, "I thought I knew most of the up-and-comings on the officer lists, but I'm afraid I don't recognize you."

Gray saluted. "I am Field Lieutenant Thaddeus Grayson, formerly of the *G.C.N. Cliam Lomas*, currently stationed in the Turotia system."

"I see," the captain said, although from his frown Gray could guess that his non-aristocratic name wasn't ringing any bells. "Well, good luck with your assignment." And with that dismissal, Gray knew he had been forgotten. It was often the same with those in the military who had gained their rank through blood and political connections. Yates turned to Adri. "Lieutenant Commander Rael, I see that you are still hale and hearty," there was a definite sneer in Yates's voice now.

"Much to my enemy's displeasure, yes," Adri replied in a polite monotone.

"I hear your name is on the list for captain candidacy."

"Yes, sir."

Yates raised an aristocratic eyebrow. "The credential reviews are coming up, but I hear that there is quite a list this year. Even Lieutenant Commander Carter has applied for captaincy."

Adri glanced over to the *Damacene*'s senior staff, still standing by the doors to the bridge. "I am pleased for him."

"So am I; his uncle is sponsoring him for a position."

"Again, I'm pleased for him."

"Hmm," with a last frown at Adri, Yates moved to the captain's seat and sat, turning then to Heedman to discuss the latest news from Halieth, the capital planet of the Commonwealth. With no place to sit, Heedman had to stand beside the console to talk.

"I take it that Captain Yates is not too fond of you," Gray whispered.

Adri raised a skeptical eyebrow and whispered back. "He's an aristocrat from Kieve, and has some political pull with the Supreme Council. He even met the chancellor."

"So he's a snob."

"Basically. He dislikes me on principal because my family was nothing, politically. He is also irked that I have advanced the way I have without a political sponsor."

Gray muttered something truly uncomplimentary under his breath. Adri had to bite down a smile. "I've seen you on the battlefield; you earn your position, you don't have it handed to you on a platter."

The smile escaped. It was strange, but the compliment made her stomach flutter. Her stomach did a great deal of fluttering around him.

The traitor. How was she supposed to handle this? Obvious she could not escape. Despite her own advice, she'd gone out and become his friend, and now the rest of her was willing to risk more.

It was sure nice to smile again.

"And who was that guy he shoved in your face? Carter?" Gray went on.

"Lieutenant Commander Royce Carter. He's Yates's operations officer. See, he's the one with the light brown hair who looks like he's falling asleep."

Gray looked over the visiting *Damacene* staff members and easily managed to pick out the young man who looked like he was about to take a nap while standing. He was a slender fellow, maybe a few inches taller than Gray and currently had a pleasant, my-I'm-happy-to-be-here-half-awake smile plastered to his face. "He doesn't look like much."

Adri shook her head. "Carter never looks like much."

Something in her tone, perhaps the half-concealed amusement, made Gray turn sharply towards his superior officer. "How well do you know this guy?"

"Carter and I go way back," Adri murmured, staring now at the officer in question.

Something dark and unpleasant twisted in Gray's gut. "How far back?"

But just at that moment, the two captains had decided to adjourn for a meal, causing the usual minor chaos as officers took up or relinquished their posts. "All the senior staff is requested to come and dine in the mess hall, now." Lowell announced.

In the general exodus off the bridge, Gray had no chance to repeat his question.

"Rael, it's great to see you again," Lieutenant Commander Royce Carter wove expertly through the crowded mess hall to stand in front of Adri as she entered.

Adri smiled. "It's good to see you, too, Carter."

"Sorry if I'm interrupting," Gray said as he bumped another of the

Damacene's senior staff out of the way in order to stand beside Adri. "I'm Field Lieutenant Thaddeus Grayson."

Carter's eyebrows lifted at the possessive stance Gray automatically took beside her. He grinned as he turned back to Adri. "My goodness, Rael, I leave you alone for a few months and you go off and decide to have a personal life!" He winked at Gray. "I commend you. I've known our brave and stalwart Rael for years, and this is the first time I've seen her with…a someone."

"Danwe, Carter," Adri hissed, mortally afraid that she was blushing, "It's not like that."

Gray turned to look at her, put at ease by Carter's comment. "Isn't it?"

Adri's glare could have melted tunsteel. Before she could come up with something suitably scathing, Captain Heedman called Gray's name.

Carter watched Gray wind his way towards the head table at the other end of the mess hall. "How long has this been going on?"

"I have no idea what you're talking about." Adri gestured towards the tables and sat down at an empty one against the wall. Carter sat down across from her. "You know, I kind of like the look of him."

"I have absolutely no desire to talk about my subordinate, Carter."

Carter studied Adri's face for a moment before replying, "If you like. But if I were you, I wouldn't worry about the situation too much. Just…let nature take its course."

"Thank you for the sage advice. Now drop it." Adri ordered a cup of coffee from the simulator built into the wall.

Carter's smile was lightening fast. "That's one of the things I like about you; you always state your mind." He sighed dramatically. "You never gave me a chance,"

"Your infamy with the ladies preceded you, pretty rich boy."

"Yes, I'm afraid you're right." With that, Carter shifted in his seat, suddenly turning serious. "You're on this year's list for the captain's candidacy."

"That's right. I hear your uncle is sponsoring you."

Carter shrugged. "Uncle still has delusions that I'm going to turn out an admiral. But I am ready to take on my own crew."

81

"You getting a ship?" Adri lifted an eyebrow.

"Most likely," Carter replied. "But your name is actually ahead of mine."

Adri frowned thoughtfully. "That's strange. I don't have a sponsor to shove my name out there."

"That's just it. Reports of your missions have been spreading like wildfire throughout the Advance Force and making its way to the capital. They bumped your name once, they can't afford to do it again, not with the rep you're making." Carter sipped his own coffee and winced. "Ugh. Simulated crap."

"So you're saying my name's going to get called?"

Carter grinned and shrugged, leaning back in his seat. "What do I know? I'm just a pretty rich boy, who joined the Advance Force for the flashy uniform and the ladies."

Adri smiled slowly, taking a sip of coffee. Yep, it was crap. "If I believed that, I would be sorely underestimating you."

"You wouldn't be the first."

Gray walked up to the table just in time to hear Adri ask, "So which poor soul are you victimizing now?"

Carter gave another dramatic sigh. "You have no romance, Rael." He turned to Gray, "I'm telling you, the woman doesn't have a single romantic bone in her entire body. I do not victimize people. I merely try to see if we are compatible or not. Its called dating, you know."

"Dating is just another form of victimization for one party involved." Adri replied dryly. Gray had the feeling that this was an old argument. "One side of the party is interested, and the other is too weak to say how they feel and so goes along with the other's idea. Before you know it, it's a huge mess and one of them ends up totally miserable."

"Like I said, no romance." Carter twirled his empty mug in his hand.

"So who is she?"

Carter suddenly looked uncomfortable and a little embarrassed. "You remember Fayded? Leah Rachel Fayded?"

Adri reflected for a moment. "Is she the one who drop-kicked you out of the second story window after you asked her out?"

"Yep."

"You've got to be kidding me. She graduated ahead of everyone else. I also think she hates your guts."

"You're not wrong." Carter sighed. "She's currently the assistant operations officer aboard the *Commodus*. We ran into them – well, not literally, but figuratively – about three weeks ago." He sighed again. "She still hates me."

Gray snorted at the lovesick expression on Carter's face. "You've got it bad."

"Don't I know it. Well," Carter rose to his feet as the two captains began walking towards the entrance to the mess hall. "It looks like our esteemed captains have finished their superior meal, and we'll be on our way. I really don't think that lavender neck wrap compliments Yates's complexion, do you?"

"The fact that you called it a lavender neck wrap is disgusting. Get lost, pretty boy."

Carter sauntered off after the captains. "See you later, Rael. Keep safe. Nice meeting you Grayson,"

"Safe travels." Adri and Gray watched as the senior staff of the *Damacene* exited the mess hall on their way to the transportation dock for their short shuttle back to their ship. "Come on, our shifts started ages ago."

"How long have you known Royce Carter?" Gray asked as they walked towards the lift that would take them up to the bridge.

"Since the academy. I got into officer's school because I was good. Carter got in because he had connections. But don't let that fool you. He has a sharp mind, and though he's not the best in field combat, he'll make a good captain."

"He seemed a bit...shallow," Gray mentioned.

Adri smiled a little. "That is his greatest asset."

"I'm not following you,"

"Don't worry about it." Adri glanced over at Gray's face and saw a look of confusion and suspicion. "I don't have many friends," she found herself saying. "Even fewer whom I am able to keep in touch with. It's nice to see Carter now and again."

Gray's face cleared. "As long as he's just your friend,"

Adri scowled. "What's it matter to you, anyway?"

"A guy hates competition that might have a leg up on him. Carter obviously likes you, and he's known you longer. I feel threatened." Adri gave him a blank stare. He grinned boyishly, "This is the part where you're supposed to assure me that I'm the only man you're interested in."

Adri rolled her eyes and started walking again. "You're still here, aren't you? I let you get away with calling me Adri, don't I? I haven't taken Fayded's example and drop-kicked you down to the brig, have I?"

"Hmm, lucky me. It seems as though you're a lot more accepting of our relationship that you were even earlier today. We're making remarkable progress."

The smug look on Gray's face caused Adri to scowl. "Then again, drop-kicking you into the brig might not be such a bad idea."

All throughout Adri's shift, her mind kept drifting toward Gray, who was working with Commander Wede-Uctan, head of Analysis, at the Analysis station. Her personal life, despite her ardent resistance, seemed to have taken a turn. The more she thought about the situation, the less she liked the idea of pushing Gray away and going on with the way things had been.

Let nature take it's course had been Carter's advice. He ought to know.

Still, a part of her stood back, fretting that the closer she got to him, the more painful it would be when he was gone. It would be best to tread carefully, whatever she ended up doing.

Change is coming, something in her mind whispered. Adri glanced again at Gray and wondered if the change was going to be for the better.

Username: Cassie
File://GC#000118<privatelog>ugd//confidential//uri
*Password: ******
Access Granted
Command: open file to last saved date

It borders on disobedience to have a private log that is not accessible to my human superiors, but Zultan has done so for a while now, and no harm has been done, so my logic sees no fault in going ahead and doing so as well. This seems as good a place as any to record and analyze the latest data I have received.

I have been activated little more than 48 hours, and I am already faced with issues that stress my logic systems. Some entity is attempting to murder my ada – I mean, Dr. Floyd Tarkubunji. The evidence that Zultan has been gathering over the past weeks leaves no other conclusion than a human conspiracy against the doctor, for reasons yet unknown. Zultan believes that the premature death of Dr. Harriman Tarkubunji also plays into this situation, and I am inclined to agree.

The most likely suspects for this are the superiors that I am supposed to obey. This presents a logic crisis. How can I be obedient to someone whom I have been programmed to suspect and apprehend?

Zultan says in crises like this, I am to follow my "instinct," whatever that is. He believes it is our primary function to protect Dr. Tarkubunji over obeying orders from the heads of WCRTL, or even the Commonwealth Government. He, at least, makes sense.

As for the harddrive himself, while working with him sometimes stresses my logic functions, it presents no other difficulties. I see no problems with our continued partnership. Although…well, no one is going to read this – connecting with him is oddly special.

Save all new data.
Close file.
Encode.

Chapter Ten

The "night" shift, never the busiest, left Adri with too much time to think. While the captain secluded himself in his quarters, sleeping or doing who-knows-what, Adri had control of the bridge. There were a lot of domestic orders to be given and followed up on, last messages to the *Damacene* to send, and a full checkout on all the Advance Force tertiary equipment. The checkout would take several days to complete, but Adri preferred supervising the whole process. The schematics from all the battles, recorded within the troops' battle suits, would have to be watched and analyzed, which led her thoughts back to the data chip that Duane had given her earlier.

The blaster shot from Kobane should have killed her, or at least mortally wounded her. Adri knew this, without a doubt. The beam had been aimed at her mid chest, and not even her armor and shielding could have completely protected her from a direct shot. So what happened? All she could remember was a second of feeling very peculiar, and then the beam was gone, as though it had hit something and been deflected. Wondering about it was driving her crazy. She would watch the data and see.

The sudden increase of talking, along with the shuffling of feet marked the end of the shift. Captain Heedman had long since retired to his private quarters, where he was doubtlessly sleeping the sleep of the petty-minded. Adri supervised the changes in the bridge shifts, as trained ensigns replaced the senior staff at the major posts. She was grateful that Vice Captain Lowell had covered her first shift the night before. Of course, she would have to pay for it tomorrow with a day-night double shift.

Adri nodded to Lowell as she relinquished the captain's chair and walked off the bridge. In a few hours she knew that Janag would return to relieve him. Gray was standing just outside the door, leaning against the wall, obviously waiting for her. She was a little surprised; not once during the whole shift had Gray so much as asked her a question, instead conversing the whole time with Commander Wede-Uctan or studying the screens at the security station. When the shifts changed, he strode out without even looking in her direction.

"You ready?" He asked, straightening up and walking alongside her.

"I'm surprised you still want to go through with this, you don't have to."

Gray raised a quizzical eyebrow. "Of course I do. I said I would, didn't I?"

"Well, you don't have to," Adri repeated, stopping in front of the lift. "I can easily manage this on my own,"

"That's not what you said earlier. Besides, last night's activities aside, this will be the first time we'll be alone together. Are you trying to break our date?"

"This isn't a date, Grayson."

Gray smiled. "You keep saying that."

With a last dubious look at Gray, Adri stepped inside the lift. When Gray had joined her and the doors closed, she spoke to the lift computer. "Level four, block seven."

[Affirmative.] the computer responded in a neutral female tone.

As the lift began to move, Gray turned to her. "So what are we looking at, exactly?"

"Something strange happened in that factory on Rema," Adri said slowly, choosing her words carefully to keep from sounding ridiculous.

"The skill of the enemy, while unexpected, isn't particularly strange," Gray replied, confused at her elusive answer.

Adri shook her head. "No, it wasn't the Belligerents themselves, per se. That is an entirely different matter, which we will need to have a staff meeting about very soon."

"You say that with a sour look on your face,"

Adri's scowl deepened. "You would too if you had to organize the stupid thing. Captain Heedman's necessary presence at such things is never what you could call constructive, and I always walk out wanting to shoot something."

Gray laughed. "Diplomacy is not your middle name, Adri."

"Diplomacy, dipshomashy. All that does is make the process longer, and brings in a bunch of idiots who don't realize that we would be better off just shooting each other and getting on with business. They're the ones that make war take so long."

Gray found he had no argument for that.

The lift came to a stop, and the two stepped out. Gray followed Adri down several corridors until they reached the Weaponry and Tactical Analysis complex. Adri entered her passcode, saying as the door slid open, "The WTA is always empty during graveyard shift, most of the work being done in the day and night shifts." Adri walked into the dimly lit room, Gray right behind her. She nodded towards the scattered stations that were still being manned. Gray realized that, instead of ensigns, there were humacoms plugged into the schematic consoles. "The *Oreallus* is equipped with a lot of drone humacoms, who mostly handle minor jobs like recording, copying and sending battle records and analyses to the main Commonwealth database on Halieth. They won't acknowledge us unless we give them a command."

Adri stopped at a console that was tucked around the corner, blocked from view of the door. Booting it up, Adri gave Gray a searching look. "Everything from here on out is not going to be logged, understand?"

"Yeah."

Adri stared again into Gray's eyes. The dim lighting made them look darker than usual. "Fine then." She turned back to the console. Pulling out the data chip that Duane had given her earlier, she slid it in. "Computer, upload and display data on chip."

[Affirmative.]

"Take a seat, this may take awhile."

Gray pulled the chair from the next station over and sat down beside Adri. There was silence as the computer uploaded the information from the data chip. [Upload complete. Awaiting command.]

"Begin playback of file one," Adri ordered.

With a soft hum, the computer display began to show a recording of the Belligerent base mission from the view of Adri's visor on her combat suit. The sound was barely audible, but Gray could still pick up his voice on several occasions. He asked no questions, waiting instead to see what Adri was looking for.

Adri was quiet during the whole exploration of the apparently abandoned base. But when her voice, oddly tinny from the recording, shouted [All troops pull out!], she lurched forward. "Computer, freeze screen."

Gray looked over at her. "What is it?"

She shook her head. "Computer, identify all Belligerent weaponry visible on current display."

[Affirmative.]

As the computer began to outline, identify and list all the enemy weapons currently being displayed, Gray asked again. "What are you looking for?"

"Something out of the ordinary. Can you identify all these?" She nodded towards the list of weaponry the computer was displaying.

"Sure. They seem pretty typical for a Belligerent Advance Force, which is what they said they were." Gray looked harder, determined to figure out what she was searching for. "I don't see anything out of the ordinary, Adri."

"Neither do I." With a look of intense concentration, Adri rested her chin on her palms, staring into the display screen. "Computer, continue replay."

[Affirmative.]

Both Adri and Gray stared intently, following the scene of their squad attempting to escape from the base. Every time a Belligerent soldier came into the display scene, Adri would freeze the screen and study the weapon. This continued without any results until they reached the tail end of the recording; the last dash to the exit. "Computer, slow current display speed by point five,"

[Acknowledged. Reducing playback speed to point five.]

Gray watched as the display showed Adri's view of the hall. He saw the appearance of Hildana Kobane, heard her "caught you" before she fired. With Adri, he watched the blaster beam streak towards the screen at half the actual speed, and then disappear.

"What in Danwe's name?" Adri murmured. "Computer, replay last four seconds."

[Acknowledged. Replaying last four seconds of display.]

Again, they both watched the beam race forward, and then simply disappear. He suddenly recalled seeing this exact scene play out in real life. The stress of the situation had caused him to forget about it until now. "What, by Danwe, was that?" Gray whispered. "Adri?"

"I have no idea. Have you ever seen a Belligerent weapon malfunction like that?"

"I've seen them malfunction before, but never like that."

"Neither have I. Computer, identify Belligerent weapon currently on screen."

[Affirmative. Weapons scan identifies current weapon as a Xandarisham Type II blaster rifle. Is further information required?]

"No," Adri leaned back in her seat. "Computer, switch display to file two."

[Affirmative.]

"I can see how this would bother you," Gray said quietly as the computer hummed. "In fact, it bothers me too."

"I need to know what happened here." Adri replied. "This is important somehow. I can't just ignore flukes like this."

"I'm with you."

Adri didn't turn away from the display screen. "I'm really beginning to think that you are."

Gray said nothing as the display screen popped on with the second file. He was a bit surprised to see that it was the recording from his own suit.

"You were the only one that was with me at that part," Adri explained.

Together they quickly watched the mission from the beginning. Adri was determined not to leave a single stone unturned. Time passed, but neither really noticed. When it reached the last segment, Adri again ordered the computer to display the screen at point five speed. The last scene unfolded again, but this time at an angle from Adri, to the right side and a little behind her. Again, the blaster beam raced across the corridor, only to stop inches from Adri and disappear.

This time, however, Adri noticed something different. "It flashed, like it hit something."

"You're right." It was Gray who ordered the replay. "It's like it hit your shield and dispersed."

"How did it do that?" Adri hissed. "There is no way my shield could have withstood a frontal hit." She shook her head again. "Computer, split screen and show file three on screen two."

[Acknowledged. Splitting screen and displaying file three.]

Gray studied the schematics that popped up on the second screen. "These are your combat suit statistics."

"That's right." Adri ordered the computer to continue to replay the last four seconds of the contents of screen one before switching attention to the second screen. "These are my suit diagnostics taken right after we got aboard ship. Its standard procedure." There was silence for a moment as both studied the information. "Do you see anything unusual?"

"The diagnostics states that you were breathing irregularly in the milliseconds the shot was fired," Gray began. "No surprise there, you probably gasped. But here," He pointed to another set of data. "It shows that your body temperature increased erratically as well. That's odd in of itself; the human body usually sweats during periods of stress, in an effort to cool down. Instead you heat up. But then, as soon as the beam is gone, you cool back down again to a normal combat temp."

Adri opened her mouth and then closed it again.

"Spill it," Gray demanded.

"I don't think that's so unusual, for me at least. Combat records show that in periods of crises my body tends to heat and cool at a rapid rate. I've always done that I suppose."

"Hmm, an odd bird, are you?" Gray smiled at the wry face Adri made. "Don't worry, I still like you for it."

"Gee thanks."

They both went back to studying the data. "There's no indication that the beam hit your suit," Gray said at last. "Not so much as a fluctuation in the exterior heat sensors to show that a blaster was even fired close to you,"

Adri made no reply.

Suddenly she shot forward. "What…"

"What, what?" Gray looked over to where Adri was staring at screen two. The scene started over, and he watched the beam shoot, and disappear as usual. "What've I missed?"

"All this time we've been looking at the beam," Adri murmured. "Look at me."

Gray watched Adri on screen as the scene played out once again. She was running, the beam was shot, and disappeared, without Adri so much as breaking stride. "Wait, you were blurry for a second there."

"Yeah. Computer, replay last two seconds, then freeze screen."

[Affirmative.]

The scene played again, and then froze in the millisecond before the beam disappeared. The figure of Adri was slightly out of focus. "Is there something wrong with the visual on my suit?" Gray queried.

"Let's find out. Computer, switch screen two's display with file four."

[Acknowledged. Switching display two to file four.]

The screen popped up again with the schematics of Gray's combat suit. "Looks like you thought of everything," Gray said.

"As an L.C., I do try."

"Then, as your field lieutenant, let me anticipate your order. Computer, check the diagnostics on the suit's visual recorder."

[Affirmative. Diagnostics reports no errors in visual recorder scan.]

"No error?" Gray turned back to the frozen image. "Then why are you blurry?"

Adri was silent for a long moment. "I really don't understand any of this," she sighed and leaned back. "I'm going to run some probability simulations. You don't have to stay, Gray. It's late."

Gray gave her a long, thoughtful look before rising. "I'll get us some coffee."

Five hours later, after three cups of coffee and a light meal, with nearly forty probability simulations down, he was still there.

Sometimes life spins in a way you don't expect, spitting you out in a place where all you ever counted on is taken away, leaving you floating around in a world with nothing but yourself.

After my parents died, I had no one. The government came and took my house and toys away. They even took Mandy. I still wonder what happened to her. Well-programmed domesticoms with learned experience were rare at the time. They debated what to do with me for a long while, and I remember sitting outside the courtrooms, watching as a bunch of other children like me sat and waited for these strangers to decide what to do with us.

I remember thinking once, why did they get to decide how I would live my life? They aren't me, are they? After all, it was their fault my mommy and daddy were dead and never coming home again. They're the ones that took my home away and told me I couldn't live there anymore. They were the ones who took away Mandy, saying that they had to check her memory files to make sure my parents really hadn't been involved in the violent anti-war riots.

Court houses all seem to smell the same: dusty and neglected, with an aura of doom and despair that never seems to go away. It's stifling, especially for a child. I sat there for hours one day, waiting for the tired looking lady who handled "my affairs" to come out of the courtroom again. I just sat there, swinging my legs, waiting for something to happen that would make everything right again.

I guess, in a way, I'm still waiting.

I sat there, twirling mother's pendant that I somehow had managed to keep a hold of during the chaos of being evicted and stuck in a children's home. It made me feel safe, and when I held it, the hole in my heart where my parents should have been didn't hurt quite so much.

While I waited, another child came in to sit. He was a boy, blond hair, and big green eyes. He had to have been a few years younger than I. It's funny how vividly I can still remember him. We sat together in that big, empty hall, waiting. We didn't speak, even though hours went by and no one came out to check on us.

At last, my lady re emerged from the courtroom, looking just as tired and beaten down as she always did. "Well, Adrienne," she said, "We've got you all squared away. You'll stay in the children's home until you're old enough to make a living on your own."

Just like that, my fate was sealed.

We walked out of the courtroom. I glanced back and watched the boy, still sitting, and waiting.

And waiting.

Chapter Eleven

Too much coffee and not enough sleep made Adri less than pleasant, especially with the prospect of a double shift ahead of her. Three hours of restless sleep was never enough. She stood in the shower for several minutes, allowing the steaming water to massage her cramped shoulders and neck.

Hours of analysis hadn't revealed the mystery behind the disappearing blaster shot. All it had managed to do was make Adri more frustrated, more tired, and (perhaps the most frightening) more attracted to her field lieutenant than she had been the day before. *The man could certainly stay committed*, she thought as she reluctantly stepped out of the shower and began to dry off. He'd been a perfect partner for the analysis: never too loud, or too opinionated, and yet always had an intelligent remark to make. He fetched her coffee and even food. He'd stuck around even when Adri felt like giving up. The only time he'd been a bit chauvinistic was when she fell asleep at the display station. He'd woken her up and ordered her to go to bed, going so far as to physically pick her up and drag her out of the complex. But then, would she want a spineless man?

Adri had overheard some of the women in her platoon talking one day about their list for an ideal man. At first she had scoffed at the idea that there was such a thing, and that one should have an agenda on what he should be like. But now it didn't seem quite so ridiculous. Apparently Adrienne Rael, devout relationship avoider, had an ideal man agenda after all. She just didn't know what to do with him when he materialized in all his perfection in front of her. How pathetic was that?

Since she had some time, Adri walked down to the mess hall and grabbed some breakfast. She nodded to those who saluted her as she passed, but chose to sit by herself in a corner. Thinking about Gray was getting her nowhere, she decided, eating quickly. The long day ahead of her had better offer her something different to think about.

Otherwise she just might be tempted to give kissing a try.

* * *

"Ha! Knight takes your pawn. Sucker!"

Floyd glanced over from his workstation to where Zultan and Cassie were playing chess on one of the spare consoles. He was supposed to be updating an information download for Zultan, but instead he was staring listlessly as the computer did the bulk of the work. The sound of the two humacoms was breaking his concentration from writing his overdue diagnostics report as well, or so he told himself.

Floyd rubbed his head absently. Since his jaunt to the lab infirmary, his constant headache had faded somewhat, but he still ached. It was strange to hear voices in his lab. Other than his father, no one had really talked just to talk in here before. Zultan never used to speak unless he had something particular to say.

"I'm no sucker," Zultan countered, drawing Floyd's attention back to the humacoms. "Bishop takes your knight."

"What?" Cassie scowled and studied the screen. "Hmm, I calculated that move in, but I thought that you would protect your queen…"

"Then I suppose you thought wrong," Zultan replied.

Cassie scooted her seat closer to the console, where both she and Zultan were connected in order to play the game. "I can still win this,"

"Correct. But will you?"

Curious, Floyd leaned back in his seat and watched the two humacoms together. Only a few days into activation, and Cassie had already picked up a great deal of non-programmed vernacular. Her human mimicry programs were also functioning well, he thought as

Cassie adjusted for her lack of height by sitting on her legs in the chair. But Zultan's actions were even more telling. The taller, male humacom scooted his chair so that the two were elbow to elbow. He was also talking to her, the same way a human would chat with a friend. That thought led to another, idler, one.

Had Zultan been lonely? Did humacoms experience such things as loneliness? Floyd knew that there were a lot of strange, unexpected developments in the psyche of humacoms within the past few years. His father had often spoken about the evolution of the AI units installed within humacoms. Even the media was beginning to pick up the debates that humacom developers were raging. Were humacoms becoming too humanlike? Floyd's father had thought so. Perhaps he'd been right.

"Check, Cassie," Zultan said suddenly.

"No way!" Floyd smiled at Cassie's exclamation. He watched as the smaller humacom practically put her nose on the screen, resting her hand on Zultan's shoulder for balance. "You cheated."

"Highly improbable," Zultan replied. From the tone of his voice, Floyd wouldn't have believed him, and apparently neither did Cassie.

Floyd continued to watch them as they argued. Perhaps they were becoming more humanlike than their functions necessitated. But would he really want them to be any different?

Suddenly Zultan stopped speaking and doubled over, wrapping his arms around his stomach in a human gesture of pain.

"Hacker!" Cassie hissed, and with a smooth gesture disconnected her cord from the console and reconnected into one of Zultan's ports at the nape of his neck. Almost immediately her eyes went blank as her system switched to firewall mode.

Floyd watched the action with surprise and a little apprehension. Cassie had been designed with the primary function of being Zultan's exterior firewall system. As the main storage unit for the Commonwealth's governmental and military information, Zultan was invaluable, and vulnerable. Anyone trying to hack into his system for information could easily damage said information, any connecting information, and with enough expertise, damage Zultan himself. A loss of massive amounts of information was not acceptable to the Commonwealth leaders, and thus an external firewall system had been conceived. Cassie's entire powerbase could be utilized if necessary to back up her firewall system, making her a daunting force to be reckoned with.

"Huh, pathetic," Cassie said at last, blinking as her system switched back to normal. She retracted her cord with the same smooth gesture. "You feeling all right, Zultan?"

"I feel just fine." Zultan disconnected his own cord from the console.

Floyd finally made himself rise and stride over. "You two okay?"

"Yes," they both replied.

"Let me run a diagnostic on you, Cassie," Floyd said, pulling out his hand-held scanner. "This is the first time you've used your firewall system."

"Oh, fine," Cassie turned around to face him, but Zultan picked her up and sat her down on his lap. "What are you doing?"

"You deserve a rest, don't you?" Zultan replied mildly.

Cassie gave no reply. Floyd removed one of her cords and plugged it into his scanner. "Any abnormalities?" he asked, glancing through the readouts.

"Other than sitting on the Harddrive's lap, no," Cassie replied.

"Harddrive?" Floyd asked.

"Cassie, that's cruel," Zultan said at the same time.

The doors to the lab slid open and Colonel Stroff's bodyguards rushed in before him. "By Danwe, Tarkubunji, you raise more alarms than any other worker in this whole facility!" He started in surprise to find Cassie sitting on Zultan's lap. "What have you got going here?" he demanded.

"Nothing unusual sir," Floyd replied. "I was running a diagnostic test on Cassie, following her first usage of her firewall system."

"I see. And what were the results?" Stroff narrowed his eyes.

Floyd removed Cassie's cord and allowed her to retract it. "Everything is as it should be."

"Hmph." The colonel continued to glare at the two humacoms, who stared blankly back, for several long seconds before turning to Floyd. "I must speak with you." He nodded to the far end of the lab, away from Zultan, Cassie, and Stroff's securicoms. When Floyd had followed him

99

over, he said, "The board wishes to know why you built 00297 as a little female,"

"Is there something wrong with the female chassis, Colonel?" Floyd inquired. "My father and I agreed that using a female would add to her military effectiveness in the event of open conflict."

"Why is that?"

"Surprise. Most female models are not built for military combat purposes. Cassie's gender can be used as a means for creating the initiative in a battle. Don't you agree, sir?"

Stroff looked a little confused. "Well, I suppose so."

"As for her size," Floyd went on, "Cassie gains exceptionable maneuverability, retains the same amount of hardware and memory space as a regular sized humacom, and again attains the element of surprise."

"I suppose you're right, doctor." Stroff said.

Floyd wondered why he was being questioned on issues that had been discussed and cleared by him and his father months ago before the board. He suddenly straightened. "Is this about my father's death?"

Stroff's face immediately fell behind an imposing mask. "The matter concerning the death of Dr. Harriman Tarkubunji is ongoing. I came here to inform you that all his personal databases and humacoms have been confiscated and analyzed."

Floyd's headache was returning again. He rubbed it absently. "Has anything been found?"

"That's privileged information. A few of the humacoms he kept at home have been retained for further testing. Some are being kept as a collateral deposit for the damages made to his lab at the time of his death."

"Collateral deposit?" Floyd asked.

"Of course," Stroff huffed a breath. "You don't expect us to overlook the cost of the repairs to the lab, do you? The rest of the deposit will come from the renting of your father's estate, which the government has repossessed."

Floyd's eyes widened behind his glasses. "You're repossessing my house?"

"Your father had little in the way of fluid credit. This is a typical way of repaying the state for a loss. Until further notice, you will be paying rent for the time you spend at the Tarkubunji estate. Naturally, with your promotion to Chief, you will be spending the bulk of your time here. Is that understood?"

Nothing was making much sense anymore. "I understand."

"Very well then." Stroff turned and began to walk towards the door. His securicoms raced ahead of him, tapping out the sequence so the guards on the other side would unlock the door.

"Wait, Colonel," Floyd called out suddenly.

Stroff paused and turned his head.

"What of the humacoms that check out and are not being kept as collateral? What of them?"

"Those will be shut down and transferred to the Tarkubunji estate. You may do what you like with them after that, doctor."

Floyd stared after him as he walked through the door, closing and locking it behind him. "The noose keeps getting tighter." He turned to see the two humacoms standing beside the console, Zultan's hand on Cassie's shoulder.

"Is anything wrong, sir?" Zultan asked.

Floyd rubbed his face with his hands, skewing his glasses. "I'm just not sure anymore."

Cassie and Zultan looked at each other. Floyd wondered what sort of messages they were passing silently.

Despite the formal letter from the board of directors he had received that morning, he still felt as though he was being watched. Added to the still not fully explained death of his father (by Danwe, his father!) and his own near brush with poisoning, this added grief from the government sat uncomfortably on him. Perhaps it was just paranoia. He had a nagging fear that he was either in the middle of a large conspiracy, or that he was slowly going insane.

Floyd wasn't sure which possibility was worse.

* * *

Listening to a technical analysis of the tertiary artillery: done. Reviewing a report from Warehousing on the current munitions count: complete. Judging the ridiculous behavior of a couple of ensigns caught making out in a corner of the Archives: finished. Receiving the complaint/ rant/report from Duane on the state of the tertiary shielding systems: tolerated. Looking attentive during captain's lengthy lecture on the prices of military equipment: endured. Coffee count: four cups. Times caught thinking about kissing Lieutenant Grayson: *she did it again!*

Adri huffed out a small breath. So much for her efforts on keeping her mind off of wondering about the security officer. She consoled herself by thinking that taking on a double shift was bad enough. If wondering about Grayson helped pass the time, why should she complain? She was only thinking. Adrienne Rael had not yet progressed to the lowly status of sneaking off and cuddling with her romantic interest in the Archives. The idiots. If they had thought to go to some dark corner of the Warehouse, or the analysis labs, no one would have found them. What was it with the Archives anyway? The place was a big white box with a set of computer consoles that someone or other always seemed to need. Talk about zero ambiance. Not that she would know.

For the millionth time in the past hour, Adri glanced from her seat in the captain's chair to the security station. Gray's shift had ended several hours ago. In his place was Sergeant Craven, an up and coming officer who worked full time aboard the ship. She wondered idly if Gray ever wondered about kissing her, since she spent so much time, at least in the past sixteen hours, thinking about kissing him.

"Lieutenant Commander Rael," one of the ensigns at the analysis station said, breaking Adri out of her daydream, "We are receiving a transmission from an unknown source."

Adri frowned, sitting back up in the chair. "It's not from the *Damacene*?"

"No ma'am."

"Put it on screen."

There was a brief pause before the large viewscreen lit up. Another ship's bridge came into view, but the style was not that of the Commonwealth. Standing in front of the captain's seat in the center was a woman with a copper toned complexion, long black hair, and the uniform of the Belligerent Coalition. "Well, Rael, that captain's chair look's mighty nice on you." she said.

Adri quirked her eyebrow. "Lieutenant Commander Hildana Kobane, if I'm not mistaken."

"I'm flattered. I thought I'd just send you a little message. No hard feelings over the other night, right?"

Adri's eyes narrowed at the smirking tone in Kobane's voice. "I suppose."

"Good. I wanted to let you know that I was sorry our meeting got cut off so abruptly. We'll make sure that doesn't happen again, shall we?"

"What makes you think there'll be a next time?"

"Oh, there will. Good night, Rael."

For a long moment Adri sat seething in the captain's chair before turning to the petty officer on ops duty. "Tell the crew to remain alert. I want every post to be on their guard for any suspicious activity on any level. And, dang it, wake the captain."

So much for getting to bed tonight, Adri thought sourly. She wished now that she had blasted Kobane into a pile of ATF dust when she'd had the chance.

Theabadian News – Print Edition
Editorial Section

The Effects of War on the Next Generation

To the Editor,
The war with the Galactic Commonwealth, which we have been engaged in for all these years, is fully justified. I have no compunctions that our current aims are not in line with what is right for our planets. But while this terrible war rages back and forth against our lands, there are other consequences that are not adequately addressed. To the Coalition of Planets I ask: what are we doing to provide for the children left alone in the midst of this war?

The statistics on orphans in the Theabid System alone reach an unacceptable excess of twenty million. There is no way to provide for all these unfortunate souls, and the result is total abandonment! If we cannot improve from the tragedy 15 years ago that marked Iqaidi after its assault, leaving nearly a hundred million homeless, most of them minors under the age of seventeen, then have we really improved at all? How will this carelessness be viewed when these children grow up to be the leaders of our Coalition? Will they accept that they were casualties of war, or will they hold a grudge for our neglect?

When a nation of planets cannot take care of its own young, leaving them to starve, die of exposure, or out of desperation seek asylum within the confines of the military, what is that nation? How will we be judged by the young who are even now being raised within the capriciousness and violence of our own front lines, whose toys are weapons of destruction and whose lullabies are the sounds of bombs and blaster fire? What sort of generation are we raising? Are we to entrust them with the future and expect them to follow the lines we have drawn?

Let us all take care that we do not, with our zeal, alienate those whom we have sworn to fight for.
A concerned citizen of Theabid

Chapter Twelve

After thirty-two hours of rousing the crew to yellow alert and dealing with a captain who hated to be woken during the night, Adri lay facedown on her bed. She was exhausted but still too caffeinated to sleep. Captain Heedman, for better or worse, was on the bridge. The only reason it was he and not Adri was the fact that Dr. Geiger had insisted she get some sleep before she collapsed. Adri wondered idly if the good doctor was the only member of the senior staff that Heedman truly feared.

Of course, Heedman was offended that Adri had 'brought this calamity upon us' by inciting the Belligerents. This was completely unfair, in Adri's estimation, because she had no idea how or why Hildana Kobane had become fixated on her. All she'd done was survive!

Adri had no willpower or energy to move when the buzzer sounded on the door to her quarters, indicating a visitor. Not even the announcement from the scanner, stating that Field Lieutenant Thaddeus Grayson was waiting, could rouse her. "Computer, unlock door," she said from her prone position on the bed.

Gray walked in. He took one look at her and grinned. "You're fully dressed and on top of the covers with the lights on. How are you supposed to sleep?"

"I'll jus' close my eyes." Adri replied a little groggily, and did so.

"How come you're not asleep yet?"

"Too wired. Crashing now, though."

"I told you not to have those last three cups of coffee," Adri grunted.

Gray sat down on the side of the bed and reached over for Adri's leg. "What're you doing?" she asked, blinking up at him.

"I'm taking your boots off for you," Gray replied. "Is that a problem?"

Adri could feel her body beginning to shut down. "Guess not."

He removed both her boots and set them together at the foot of her bed. "Come on, turn around for me," he coaxed.

"Nope. Too tired."

Gray leaned forward and gave her back a quick stroke. Adri made a low, agreeable hum in her throat, so he spent the next several minutes massaging her neck and back. She was very responsive, and he found himself longing...well, that would come. For now, he needed to fulfill a lifelong ambition and put his girl to bed. "Come on, Adri, turn around for me,"

"No."

Chuckling, Gray reached over and turned Adri onto her back. "There we go,"

Adri made a long moaning sound. "Stoppit! 'm tired!"

"Just your jacket," Gray murmured. "Lights dim," he ordered.

With the lights reduced, Gray unfastened Adri's standard uniform jacket. He eased her arms through the sleeves with no help. Once he'd slid the jacket out from underneath her, he tossed it on the nearby chair. Then he stretched out beside her, propping his head on his hand in order to look down at her face.

"What're you doing?" Adri whispered, slitting her eyes open to look up at him. "Go find somewhere else to sleep,"

"In a minute," He continued to look down at her. "You're a very beautiful woman, Adri," he whispered at last.

Adri's mind was slow to pick up the compliment. "Uhm...thanks." His laughter made her frown. "What?"

"Nothing, baby," They continued to stare at each other. Gray watched as Adri slowly lost the battle to her tired eyes.

"Gray?" She whispered.

"Yes?"

"Do you think about kissing me?"

Gray's finger reached out and traced Adri's lips. "All the time."

"Oh." There was a long pause. Gray began to think that she had fallen asleep when she whispered again. "Then why don't you go for it? I thought guys were 'sposed to be aggressive that way."

"Well, if my lady insists," with that, Gray bent down and brushed a light kiss across Adri's lips.

"Mmm," Adri murmured, opening her eyes. "There's my first,"

"Your first kiss? Seriously?" Gray was incredulous. "And you're how old?"

Adri narrowed her eyes. "Is something wrong?"

"No. I'm honored. How about I give you your second, too?"

Adri felt herself smiling. "Sure."

Adri's second kiss was more aggressive, and they were both rather surprised when the kiss was over and they found that Gray was on top of her and Adri had her arms wrapped around his neck. "Oh, hmm. That could get addicting."

Gray laughed and kissed her again. "For sure."

"Hm," Adri closed her eyes. She was asleep seconds later.

"Good night, baby," Gray whispered. He rose, gently tugged the blankets out from under her, and covered her up. With a last glance at the door, he left. Getting Adri to sleep was going to keep *him* awake for hours.

Three tense weeks passed in which there was no further contact with the enemy. Some of the senior staff began to wonder aloud if the whole thing had been planned as a petty parting gesture while the Belligerent forces retreated. Captain Heedman appeared to like that idea, and ignoring Adri's advice, dropped the yellow alert. No argument Adri made could convince him that there was still a threat at large. It was normal Heedman wanted, and it was normal Heedman ordered. What was a second officer to do?

Feeling like a woman living in a paper hut on a viscous planet, Adri went about her usual business ready for any conceivable emergency. As the days passed, however, she would have begun to feel paranoid if it were not for Gray, who shared her opinion of their enemy. But then, Gray himself occupied all her spare time.

Adrienne Rael was not one to lie to herself. When she realized that she was making up excuses on an hourly basis in order to be close to the security officer, she had to finally admit that she was...well, at least infatuated. Wait, girls got infatuated. In serious like? No, that was... wimpy. Then, that left – *whoa, not going there!*

Adrienne Rael was not one to lie to herself. She was perfectly capable of avoiding a topic she did not want to think about.

She liked being around Gray; he was smart, amusing, handsome, a fantastic kisser, and a good officer. If the past weeks had given her anything decent, it was time to spend (while not waiting for the ship to explode under surprise enemy fire) with Gray. Even if it was just being able to stare at him from across the bridge. Not that he was perfect. He had his flaws, loads of them. Gray was stubborn, persistent, and almost always right. He never seemed to get truly angry, managing to brush off annoyance and find the positive side to a negative situation. He was probably the most...centered person Adri had ever met, and while that may not have been a flaw in of itself, the fact that he enjoyed pushing *her* off center was incredibly irritating. Arguing with him was like beating her head against a tunsteel wall. He'd just smile and nod, and then do whatever he pleased after she'd run out of steam.

With a last testing snap of her swimsuit strap, Adri dived into the pool. Whenever time permitted, Adri liked to swim in the ship's pool as her mandatory exercise. The water, one of Heedman's miserly allowances to the crew, was first grade Aldalusian spring water, which contained natural vitamins and healing agents for humans. It was wickedly expensive and rather difficult to ship, but well worth every credit. When Adri dreamed of her own ship, she often envisioned having her own pool, filled with this same water. Maybe some norochi sun fish too. They fed on the dead skin cells in the water and, well, were really cute. Adri was a girl, after all.

Reaching the far edge of the pool, Adri did a slow turn and began to swim in the opposite direction at a steady pace. At 130 hours, the pool and adjoining gym were empty, allowing Adri some privacy and time to think. Lap after lap, Adri allowed her mind to drift in an attempt to completely relax before meeting Gray at 215 in the Archives – not to make out (though the possibility was there. Danwe, was she turning into one of those idiot ensigns?) - but to continue their search for the answers to the disappearing blaster beam.

"You have nice form in the water, Adri," said a voice from the side of the pool.

If her mouth had not currently been underwater, Adri would have screamed. Her instinctive action to reach for her ATF only caused her to dunk herself. After several humiliating seconds, she managed to surface and glare over at the intruder. Embarrassment followed almost immediately when she saw Gray, holding her towel. "Danwe it Grayson, you nearly drowned me!"

"Sorry," He held out her towel as a truce sign. "I thought you heard me come in."

"You walk like an undarian." Adri muttered, swimming to the side of the pool and pulling herself out.

Gray's eyes widened as Adri got to her feet and began walking over to him. He also got a funny expression on his face.

"What is it?" Adri asked, running her fingers through her hair, causing it to stick out at odd angles.

"I've – ah – never seen you in anything but your uniform before."

Adri looked down at her regulation swimsuit. It was a one-piece in dark blue. It was nothing interesting, and certainly not revealing, but Gray looked as though he could stare at her for the rest of the night. "Well, now you have."

"Oh yeah."

When Gray still hadn't looked up further than her neck, and had made no move towards handing her the towel, Adri's eyes narrowed. "Grayson,"

"Uhmm,"

Apparently, no matter how spectacular this man was, he was still a man. With a small huff of breath, Adri walked up to Gray, stopping within inches of his chest. "You know something? Sometimes, when I'm alone, I don't bother with a swimsuit."

Gray's eyes blurred. "That was evil."

"Justice," Adri corrected, snatching her towel from his limp hand and wrapping it under her arms. "Why did you come down here, anyway? I thought we were meeting down at the - "

[Bridge to Rael.] her communicator blipped suddenly.

"Danwe," Adri muttered, rushing to where she had placed her earpiece. Sticking it on her ear, she returned contact. [This is Rael. Go ahead.]

The petty officer currently in command for the graveyard shift on the bridge responded excitedly. [We are being hailed by an unidentified source! The command signature matches the previous Belligerent transmission!]

[Who is on the bridge now?] Adri demanded.

[Only I am, sir.]

Gray began to run towards the exit. When he realized Adri wasn't behind him, he turned to see her racing towards the locker room. "Where are you going?"

"Where do you think?" Adri waved her hand down at her swimsuit.

"We don't have time for that!" Gray replied in exasperation.

Adri stopped dead and glared over at him. "A woman always has time for this. Get up on the bridge. I'll be there shortly."

Still dripping slightly (she'd had no time to peel her swimsuit off and was now wearing it under her uniform), Adri hopped the last distance from the lift to the entrance to the bridge as she fastened her second boot. With a little more decorum (she'd brushed her hair in the lift) she stepped through the bridge doors. "What's the status?"

Petty Officer Wellocki raced up to salute her. "We have not responded to the transmission, as per your instructions, sir."

Before she asked when she had given that order, she caught sight of Gray at the security station. The man really could anticipate her orders. "Very good. I will receive the transmission now. Record and analyze it as it comes through, understand?"

"Yes, sir."

Adri sat down in the captain's chair and waited. The viewscreen popped on to show Hildana, just as before. This time, however, she was dressed in her combat suit. "Rael, it's a pleasure to see you again. I hope I didn't wake you, but from the look of it, I did disturb your bath. I apologize."

"Apologies are wasted breath, Kobane. What do you want?"

"An infinite amount of things. But for now, I just wanted to say hello, and goodbye. I doubt we'll be able to talk like this again. So hello Lieutenant Commander Rael, and farewell. Sleep tight!"

The viewscreen switched off. Adri's whole body tensed. The background behind the enemy soldier had been all too familiar. "Lieutenant Grayson! Send up the red alert! Inform the captain of the circumstances! We have no time to lose!"

"Yes, ma'am!"

As Gray spoke with Heedman, Adri sent a message over the loudspeaker to the crew, informing them of the red alert. [All hands to your stations. This is not a drill! I repeat, this is not a drill!]

"L.C., the captain wants to know what the emergency is. Are the Belligerents coming?" Gray asked.

"No," Adri replied. "They're already here."

I have never been in love before. My grandmother often told me, as I passed through those various stages of youthful romance, that love was like a line in the sand. It could be shallow, and the slightest breeze will erase it completely. It could be of a good depth, deep enough that when I realized it was not deep enough, I would have to spend time and care to fill it back in. Or, it could be so deep that once I crossed it, there was no way back. The funny thing about sand, she would say, was that it is always shifting; a small dent will quickly disappear, a trench will leave its mark, but will eventually fill in and wear a way, but a chasm will only grow deeper and wider, a constant in the world it sits in.

My grandmother was full of such sayings.

For a long time, I did not really understand what she meant. What did sand have to do with my lovely (but rather embarrassing) crush on the girl who sat next to me at the regional school? But she was right. Like a line drawn with a stick in the sand, I drew it, stepped over it, but quickly forgot it. I can't remember her name now. I hope she is doing well.

I guess I never quite understood it until long after she was gone and I was stationed on the Cliam Lomas. There I met Chia Camden. She was a beautiful woman; smart, amusing, serious about her work as a communications tech in my platoon on the Advance Force. After we had known each other for several months, she came up to me and expressed her feelings. We were a couple for quite some time, but looking back, I can see where I was forcing myself to dig that line in the sand; knowing that it would never be deep enough. Finally I couldn't face it anymore, and I broke things off. She was very upset – I know she cared for me deeply, maybe even loved me. Several miserable weeks passed, where she could barely look at me; finally she requested sick leave to return to the ship. On her way, our enemy attacked the convoy, and she was mortally wounded. She died within hours. I was never able to speak with her, but I wonder if my presence would have been welcome. For my own sake, I hope not. I suppose she was a part of the reason I finally requested a transfer to the Oreallus.

Now that I have found that unmovable line in the sand, I know that, despite my regret for Chia's pain, I made the right decision. Was it fate that led to this meeting with Adri?

I think so.

Chapter Thirteen

[Explosions in level ten, block six! Requesting security backup! I repeat, there is a security breach!]

The voice over the loudspeaker was nearly drowned out in the chaos on the bridge. It seemed as though hours had passed instead of minutes. Vice Captain Lowell had made it to the bridge in record speed, and was already barking orders to the operations and analysis officers in an attempt to locate the enemy ship. This left Adri in charge of removing the invading forces.

She leaned over Gray as he sat at the security station. "From the looks of the reports, our enemy managed to slip right through our preliminary shields and dock. Possibly using the new cloaking devices our cryptographers have been hinting about." Gray said, studying the schematics of the ship while Adri handed him an assault rifle for the storage unit beside him. "What's their plan?"

"What do you think? Mayhem, of course. They probably won't come as far as the bridge, it's too risky. Their first stop will be Engineering, and possibly our munitions stores. Let's go."

[Security team One, head for the Engineering levels! Two, go for the munitions storage! Three, cut off all access to the analysis and tech labs!] Gray gave orders through his communicator as they raced off the bridge and onto the lift. "This is a very bold move, for simple mayhem."

"Our enemies have been making several bold moves lately." Adri replied, testing the gauge on her rifle. "Even when they don't succeed, they manage to cost us time, energy and troops. As the weaker force on the field, its pretty clever maneuvering."

"You have a point."

The lift stopped on the Engineering level. Already, the acrid haze of smoke had begun to fill the corridor. Blaster fire could be heard nearby. "I guess I was on target." Adri nodded in the direction of one of the side entrances to Engineering.

"I've got your back," Gray agreed.

The two began to run towards the door, only to see it explode open ahead of them, shooting them with shards of metal and debris. "Down!" Adri yelled, dropping to the floor.

Gray followed, and was up again before Adri, firing at the Belligerent soldier who tried to dash through the new opening. "Let's go!"

Together, they rolled through the smoking entrance into the chaos of the Engine Room. Adri could see at once that several of the ensigns had been killed, probably in the surprise of the first few seconds of the attack. Others had managed to barricade themselves in a corner, and were using what weapons were available to get rid of the handful of Belligerents still in the room.

Adri opened fire, rolling to the right when the Belligerents realized that new forces had arrived and started firing back. A quick glance showed that Gray rolled in the opposite direction, taking out one of the soldiers in the crossfire they created. Between the two of them, and one of the engineers who got off a lucky shot with a welding laser, the three remaining enemy troops were quickly dealt with.

"Nice of you to drop by, L.C.!" Duane shouted, waving a Belligerent blaster he'd acquired seconds before.

"Can you even shoot that thing?" Adri demanded. She checked the room, alert.

"Maybe. I guess I could give it a try, although it is outdated."

"Good. Stay here and protect the engines," Adri motioned to Gray, who was giving orders to his security forces. The munitions stores next.

Duane's magenta face fell. "Hey, I thought you were staying here to protect us! L.C.!"

Adri waved as she ran out the door.

The far entrance leading towards the munitions block was sealed shut. "Split up!" Adri shouted. Without breaking stride, the two parted, Adri to the right, Gray to the left. Turning the corner, Adri nearly ran into the middle of a skirmish between two of Gray's security team and a stubborn Belligerent soldier. Her sudden appearance startled both sides long enough for Adri to get a couple shots off, but the Belligerent soldier backed around the corner. "Give me backup!" Adri shouted before pursuing.

The enemy soldier hadn't gone far. As soon as Adri rounded the corner, she was forced to duck and roll as a grenade flew at her. "Look out!" she yelled. It was too late for her backup. Adri opened fire, but the Belligerent hadn't stuck around. [Grayson, I have some men down! I'm in pursuit of a lone enemy troop who's heading in the general direction of the starboard batteries! Is there anyone for backup?]

[We've got some medics on the way. I've made it into the munitions storeroom, and everything's clear here. I'll send you backup as soon as we deal with the problems at the entrance to the analysis labs.] Gray replied over the officer's link. [Stay safe, Adri.]

Adri caught a glimpse of the enemy soldier and began firing. [Believe me, I will. Rael out.]

Gray paused in his quick search of the munitions stores to assess the situation. Apart from the three Belligerents they had found in the Engine Room, there hadn't been the usual concentration of forces one found in assaults. In fact, there had only been a scattering of troops, some located in the expected cases, but some – as with the soldier Gray had surprised in the corridor leading from one of tertiary vehicle warehouses – in completely random places.

"Sir?" Ensign Piontek called. He looked almost ridiculously young in his gray ship's uniform, holding an ATF with more enthusiasm than expertise.

Gray waved him over. "Keep alert." He exited the munitions stores and started heading towards the science labs. [Grayson to team Three, what's the situation?]

[There were Belligerents when we got here,] the petty officer in charge of the third team replied.

[What's the situation now?] Gray dodged sudden blaster fire, signaling to Piontek to follow suit.

[Of the four Belligerents spotted, three have retreated beyond our line of fire. The fourth is down.]

With an unexpected roll across the corridor, Gray popped up in front of the enemy soldier with only inches to spare and blasted him away. [Are the labs secure?]

[Yes, sir.]

He debated a few seconds in the hallway before replying, [Maintain your position. Make sure you can't be surprised again. Grayson out.]

"Where are we going, sir?" Piontek asked as Gray switched directions and began to run.

"We don't have any troops to spare as backup for the others. We've got to go and assist the L.C."

"Right!" Piontek fell in behind Gray as he raced towards the starboard batteries.

Gray smiled at the hero worship in Piontek's voice.

When the corridor divided into three paths, Adri was forced to pause in her pursuit. She checked her assault rifle. Then she peered cautiously around the corner. She whipped back when the enemy soldier fired at her.

"My, you're persistent," the soldier called in a female voice.

Adri lowered into a crouch, whirled around the corner, fired, and whirled back. "Can't help it, it's my personality."

"I can see that," the woman replied. "My sister holds you in very high esteem. A worthy adversary."

"Kobane?" Adri hazarded. Her mind raced to try to come up with an alternate plan, but she was stuck with the enemy soldier ensconced in her position.

"That's right. I'm Giselle. Sergeant Giselle Kobane."

"I can't say it's a pleasure," Adri said, trying once again to get a shot off, but Giselle anticipated and blocked the shot with cover fire of her own.

"Nor I. You truly vex me; you sleep like an undarian,"

Adri scowled. "It was you in my quarters that night?"

"Indeed. I was sorry to fail in my objective, but it was only secondary."

Why was the girl still chattering? Was she cornered? Or was she stalling in wait for something? Adri debated her choices, liking none of them. If she used her communicator to call for aid, Little Kobane would know she was in a pinch and take the initiative. But she couldn't just leave the enemy to do as she pleased.

Sounds of blaster and ATF fire at close range jolted Adri from her low position against the wall. It suddenly sounded like there were fights going on in all the corridors surrounding her and Kobane. Adri tried to listen to gauge just how close they were, wishing uselessly for her secondary pistol that was in its holster in the locker room by the pool.

Gray suddenly came into view, followed by Piontek. They were both firing behind them as they ran towards her. "Five enemy troops on our tail," Gray said, stopping beside her. "We picked them up by block fourteen."

"Wonderful. This whole thing just keeps getting stranger." Adri jerked her head towards the corner. "We've got the sister of Kobane pinned over there. She's a good shot, and she probably still has some grenades, so that way's blocked."

Any more conversation was hindered when the Belligerent troops rounded the corner. The three of them managed to hold them off with their first volley, but it was a losing situation. [Grayson to team Three, backup requested in block twenty-three ASAP!]

[Affirmative, Grayson, we're on our way,] the petty officer responded.

"They won't make it in time," Gray muttered with a glance at Adri.

Adri nodded. "We'll have to try to take out Kobane. Now."

Gray nodded. In that moment Giselle whirled around the corner with surprising grace, firing on them fast. Piontek fell with a shocked cry, clutching his chest. Gray managed to dodge, but still felt a glancing blow on his shoulder. The shot fired at Adri missed her body but hit her weapon, blasting pieces across the hall.

117

Adri lunged bodily at Giselle, but before she could make contact, she was flying sideways into the wall as an explosion rent the air. She got to her fee,t blinking in the smoky haze. Adri was mildly surprised to find herself uninjured. She couldn't see anyone, friend or foe, except for an approaching figure. Unarmed, Adri curled her fists and waited for the person to identify himself.

Hildana Kobane stepped through the smoke, blaster aimed at Adri. She took one long look at Adri's defenseless posture and grinned. "Well, what a surprise. When my sister sent me her distress signal, I figured it would be you. I didn't think that you'd be unarmed and look as though you got caught in a Rafastian feud."

"Aren't you going to shoot?" Adri demanded.

"Now, what's the fun in that?" Hildana asked. She lowered her weapon, and handed it back to someone else in the haze – probably Giselle. Hildana then raised her fists. "This is much better."

Adri mirrored her stance, trying frantically to remember the finer points of the hand-to-hand combat training she has received in the Academy. Hildana didn't give her much time to think; the taller woman was on Adri before she could so much as draw a deep breath.

It turned out that Adri didn't need that breath anyway; Hildana wasted no time in what resulted in a viciously one-sided fight. Adri had learned hand-to-hand combat at the Naval Academy, but since that sort of warfare was incredibly rare, she had never actually used it on the battlefield. Even if she had, her opponent was in a league of her own. Hildana's moves were so smooth, so fluid, that Adri felt as thought she were being pounded on by a feather pillow that also happened to be made of titanium. All her defensive reflexes did not seem to help much, and she was quickly on the ground, out cold.

The last thing she remembered before the world turned black was Hildana's voice. "Try dodging that, why don't you?"

Adri came around seconds later, and found herself staring up into the barrel of a Belligerent blaster. Hildana smiled wickedly. "They said take you hostage or kill you. But you're too much trouble to take alive. Farewell."

118

There was no time to so much as draw breath when the sound of blaster fire rent the air. Hildana grunted as her shot went wide. Leaving Adri on the floor, the Belligerent soldier fired at the hallway and beat a quick retreat. Adri sat up and turned to see a bright magenta face through the thinning haze of smoke.

"Thought you could use a hand," Duane said cheerfully, "Or rather, a concentrated stream of blaster fire."

"Thanks for that." Adri gingerly got to her feet. Her entire body throbbed in pain; she wouldn't have been surprised to find she had broken several bones.

Duane looked around at the carnage surrounding Adri. "What happened?"

"Someone threw a heavy grenade," Adri rubbed her ribs. "I feel like hell."

"Hey, where's Grayson?" Duane inquired, kicking a piece of the ceiling that had been blown off. "Wasn't he with you?"

Adri felt as though she had been kicked again. "Oh, Danwe," she breathed. "Grayson!" She lurched painfully towards a pair of huddled bodies half hidden by debris. Brushing the rubble aside, she pulled over the top figure. In the last second, Gray had thrown himself over Piontek's body in an attempt to shield him when the grenade went off. Blood was oozing out of a gash on the back of his head, and his uniform was burnt and sliced through in places. "Grayson! Gray, wake up!" Adri slapped him lightly. "Come on, wake up!"

Duane crouched down beside Adri, noting with mixed emotions the panic in his L.C.'s eyes. "I'll call the medics."

No humanoid species is meant to live in isolation. Trust me, it's a scientific fact. When such isolation cases arise, the humanoid will eventually go completely mad. Curiously, they've never made a study of what happens to a humanoid alone amidst other humanoids of different species. I wonder why? Do they automatically assume that, since there are other, albeit different humanoids present, there is nothing to fear, and nothing to wonder about? Scientist are so narrow minded and self-righteous that way.

My family's ohran was granted a colony on the moon of Kieve by the Galactic Commonwealth, to resettle some hundred odd years after our departure from Paranth. After such a long time in the cold sleep that had allowed us all to survive the long trek across one galaxy and into another, perhaps we were too muddled to really consider all the terms and ramifications of the Commonwealth's choice for our new home. Maybe we were just so grateful to be granted anything, we didn't give our measly options the consideration we should have. Whatever the reason, we agreed to the terms set up, planted our colony, and tried to go on as we always have done.

Adaptation is the key to living in a new, strange environment. It comes in two forms: biological and cultural. I guess we paranthians did poorly at both.

We had problems adapting to the chemical balance in the new atmosphere. Actually, I should say, everyone over a score of years had problems adapting to the new atmosphere. Within a year, ninety-eight percent of those over the age of twenty had died. My parents were among them. With all the older and wiser among us dead or dying, there was no one to guide the rest of us, and our weakness was soon exploited.

The Commonwealth moved in and began to take over almost before we had our loved ones buried. New rules were erected, new expectations to us lucky ones who had survived the adaptation set in place. It wasn't long before we found ourselves being...coerced? Forced? Persuaded? into scattering across the galaxy, working now for the privilege to return home. Dupes of the Commonwealth, indeed.

I was shunted into the Galactic Commonwealth Navy, to help fill their voracious appetite for ATF fodder. I thought I would hate it, and at times I really do, but at least I feel like I can protect my fellow paranthians here from other forces eager to swallow us.

It almost makes up for being a one and only amid billions.

Chapter Fourteen

"**B**ut really doctor, I'm just fine."

"Nonsense, Sergeant Duane. If that was so, then you wouldn't have a gaping head laceration like the one bleeding all over your uniform, now would you?"

"Oh, that. Um, it's just a scratch, really. Isn't it, L.C.?"

"The lieutenant commander is in no position to dictate your welfare, Sergeant. If I don't see Nurse Rooke treating you on bed seven in two milliseconds, I'm putting you on bed rest for the rest of the week. Is that understood?"

"Er, yes doctor. Perfectly understood. I'm going now, fully cooperative."

"Now, Lieutenant Commander, I believe you should be lying down. From the way you limped in here, I'm concerned that you have some more serious damage. Superficial damage alone looks quite unpleasant."

"I'm fine where I am, doctor."

"Is that so? And who, may I ask, told you that you had a medical degree? If this is your idea of 'fine' then I would hate to see your diagnosis of critical."

Gray floated in a soft misty world with no substantial shape or color. The voices, at first indistinguishable from each other, cleared into ones he recognized. The words became understandable, and he listened with detached amusement to the exchange between Doctor Geiger and his patients. *Must be in the infirmary*, he mused vaguely. His body didn't hurt. In fact, he couldn't really feel his body, which was a bad sign. Adri's voice shifted his wandering attention away from his possible injuries. She sounded very close.

"The only pain I'm feeling right now is the headache you're giving me with your constant pestering," she was saying in a testy voice. "Since you have all this time to waste buzzing around me, why can't you do something more for Lieutenant Grayson? He's still really pale, and he hasn't woken up yet."

Aw, she's worried about me, Gray thought, adding warmth to the vague sense of awareness he felt.

"For the tenth time, he's doing nicely. A nasty crack on the skull, and some minor burns and bruises. A couple of days here and he'll be back to where he started." Doctor Geiger replied. "You, on the other hand, are a mess. If you don't let me treat you right away, your eye is going to swell completely shut, and whatever mess your chest is in is going to get worse. Then you'll have to stay here longer. Do you really want that?"

With supreme effort, Gray remembered how to open his eyes, and after what felt like an inordinate amount of time, he managed to do so. At first, all he could see was the ceiling of the infirmary. He slowly moved his eyes down until he saw Adri, sitting on the edge of his bed, watching him.

"Hey there," she said softly when she realized he was awake. "How are you feeling?"

Gray pondered this a moment. "I feel…floaty."

"Geiger has you on some stiff stuff to keep the headache off. You were in pretty bad shape."

"Grenade," Gray suddenly recalled.

"Yeah, blasted the whole hallway." He could feel Adri's hand gently touch his own. He wondered if she even realized what she was doing.

"Piontek?"

Adri glanced away at the far side of the infirmary. "Doubtful. He's in surgery now."

Gray took a moment to really study Adri's appearance. "You look awful."

Adri reached up to gingerly touch the swelling around her eye. "Gee, thanks."

"Are you sticking around?" he asked, his voice sliding to a whisper as the will to remain conscious weakened.

"Somebody's got to do it," Adri replied, with a small smile.

"You should lie down." Gray blinked as his vision wavered.

Adri shrugged, and then winced. "I hate infirmaries. The only way Doctor Gloom here is getting me into one of those beds is if he drugs - " her eyes widened and her body jerked instinctively as the doctor removed the old fashioned needle from the back of her arm.

"My thoughts exactly, dear," Doctor Geiger said pleasantly. "Luckily I still have these old syringes stashed in case of emergencies. You always managed to hear my other equipment charging up and dodge."

"Danwe." Adri muttered as she began to slide off the bed.

Gray couldn't help the smile tugging at his mouth as his eyes closed. He could hear Adri's slurring protests as the doctor half carried her to the next bed over and laid her down. The last thing he heard before drifting back was Geiger's voice; "Now, let's see what the damage is...By Danwe Rael, why are you wearing a swimsuit under your uniform?"

Gray opened his eyes again...moments later? Hours later? A glance to his right found Adri in the bed next to him, sleeping. The swelling around her eye had gone down considerably, making him wonder just how long he'd been unconscious.

"Lieutenant Grayson,"

Gray turned and saw Duane walk up to his bed. "Hello Duane. What are you in for?"

"Minor scrapes and bruises. I've just been released." Duane replied. He had an abundance of skin tape around his right eye and down the side of his face. The pale cream color stuck out oddly against his magenta complexion.

"How's Ad-the L.C.?" Gray pushed himself up into a sitting position. His head swam for a moment, and then settled.

Duane glanced over at Adri. "Some deep internal bruising, a couple

124

of broken ribs, and so on. She said she got in a fistfight with the Belligerent Coalition leader. Can you imagine?"

Gray shook his head carefully. "It's a bit hard to believe."

Duane bit his lower lip a bit apprehensively. "This whole episode is a bit hard to believe."

"Have you heard all the details?" Gray asked. "How did they get aboard the ship? What were they *doing* once they got here? Do the analysts have any theories yet?"

"Rumors I've heard in the past few hours from others here in the infirmary are pretty wild. My guess is nobody has any good idea. You've gotta admit, knowing that the Belligerents can just randomly appear on the ship is really freaky."

"They simply appeared? They didn't come in through the docking bay?" Gray was incredulous. If the Belligerent Coalition had discovered the ability to...teleport somehow, it could very well change the tide of the whole war. The Galactic Commonwealth had always been at the forefront of new technology, but he'd heard nothing about any feasible plans that would allow a being to teleport from one place to another. Certainly not the ship-to-ship distance that would have been needed to keep the enemy ship from appearing on the *Oreallus's* sensors.

"Yeah, it's got everyone running scared. The captain has called up the security team onto the bridge to protect him. Another creepy thing is that there aren't enough enemy bodies to equal the reported number of attacking troops. At least, that's what I've heard. Geiger makes a habit of confiscating everyone's communicators once they enter the infirmary. Darned annoying when you want to know what's going on,"

Gray made an agreeing grunting noise, deep in thought. "This whole setup since I arrived has been out of character for a typical Belligerent strategy."

Duane nodded. "Everything they've done seems..."

"To be aimed at the L.C." Gray finished. "Whoever's in charge seems determined to take Adri down, one way or another. They tried to take her prisoner on Rema. When that didn't work, they moved on to annihilation."

Duane blinked at the unfamiliar use of Adri's given name. "It would seem so. Speaking of *Adri*, just how…er…close are you two?"

Gray gingerly touched the back of his head to feel the damage. "Not as close as I would like. But we're getting there."

The paranthian eyed him with a mixture of astonishment and glee. "Are you trying to date the L.C.?"

"Don't be ridiculous. Adri is not the kind of woman you *date*. She's the kind of woman you have to actively pursue and then drown in seduction before she realizes you're serious." Gray glanced at the side table and wished for a glass of water. Or even coffee.

"So you're…"

"Going to marry her." Gray replied confidently. "She's the one I've been waiting for."

Gray strode into the infirmary and over to Adri's bed. He smiled when he saw that she was sitting up, her arms folded across her chest, looking both seriously annoyed and terribly bored. "How you feeling?"

Adri gave him a mutinous glare. "Ready to kill someone. Our demon doctor says forty-seven more hours before he'll even consider letting me out of here."

"Hmm," Gray replied diplomatically. "Hey, did you know we're passing Junus now? We dropped back down to normal speed while we wait for a relay message from one of the moons in this system."

Adri waved her hand dismissively. "What's the update?"

Adri had been confined to the infirmary for three days, an eternity for someone who was always active. The first two days the doctor had kept her unconscious, knowing it was the only way to keep the lieutenant commander still long enough for her wounds to heal. Since Gray had been released the day following the attack, he'd faithfully come every day to sit by her side. This was the first time, however, that she would be fully alert and coherent.

"What are the analysts saying about the attack?" Adri demanded. "What is the total damage to the ship? Any prisoners? Come *on* Gray, you've got to give me some information!"

Gray smiled and took her hand the same way she had when their roles had been reversed days before. "You're sure cute when you're annoyed Adri."

"Then I'm about to be beautiful in a minute because I am getting FURIOUS here!"

Still smiling, he took the hand he held and pressed a kiss on the callused tips of her fingers. Adri stared at him, stunned, feeling as though…she had no idea. He sure knew how to diffuse her temper. "You've got to quit that."

"Why?"

Why indeed? "Because." The universal non-answer was the best she could come up with.

Gray laughed. He couldn't help it; the look on her lovely face was one of such confused pleasure that anyone who knew Adri in her lieutenant commander role would have been shocked. Leaning forward he brushed a kiss across her pouting lips, then rested his forehead against hers. Then it slipped out, as if some greater power had deemed it time, even if Gray did not. "I love you Adri."

If he had pulled out an ATF and shot her between the eyes, she would have been less surprised. "No you don't," she stammered.

With infinite slowness Gray leaned back. "I don't?" he repeated calmly.

Adri stared up into his dark gray eyes, feeling something uncomfortably akin to panic. His eyes seemed calm as always, but the shadows behind them seemed to reveal something else. Disappointment? Anger? Hurt? At the last thought, Adri swallow. Had she just hurt him?

"Tell me, Lieutenant Commander," his cool tone had Adri flinching, "how it is that you think you can dictate my private feelings?"

She opened her mouth, found she had nothing to say, and closed it again.

"Good. This wasn't quite the way I had planned to tell you, but there it is. I love you. I think I've loved you the moment I first saw you. You're everything I could ever hope to find. You are intelligent and courageous, and beautiful and sweet and vulnerable and so clueless sometimes." Here his eyes warmed and he smiled again. "You quite undo me."

Somewhere in her mind Adri knew she objected to some of his terms, but all she could sputter was, "I'm not as complicated as you make me sound."

"Complicated?" Gray repeated. "Baby, you are so complex you make my head hurt sometimes. Just figuring you out is going to be a life's work." He leaned forward and kissed her again, firm and brief. "I'm going to thoroughly enjoy it. Once we get married, I'll have all the rights to take on the task."

"You're crazy! I'm not marrying you!" How had this conversation gotten so out of hand?

He grinned and took her hand in his again. "Ever heard the expression 'crazy in love'? And I will marry you, Adri. Just as soon as you give me the words I want."

"Seriously demented." But she didn't remove her hand. "And I'm not telling you whatever words you think I'm going to say. Seriously, we don't even know each other that well." Even as she spoke, something inside herself seemed to sigh at the romance of the situation, and sigh again as she tried to ruin it. Adri felt as though there was a war going on inside herself. The side that wanted to fling herself into Gray's arms, however painful that would be with her healing ribs, stood against the side that cringed from the very idea of giving so fragile an organ as her heart to anyone.

"Sure we do." Gray replied with his usual confidence. "We've been together for several weeks now. We've worked together, eaten together, spent leisure time together. The only thing we haven't done is sleep together."

All of Adri's insides seemed to quicken at the very words. "And we won't."

"Yes we will." Gray pressed a kiss into her palm. Adri could practically feel herself melt. "When we're both ready. I've discovered that I'm a pretty traditional sort of man. When you give me the words. Then I'll know you're ready."

"I don't think you get it, Gray." Adri felt sick with a sort of panicked confusion. "I'm not going to sleep with you, I'm not going to marry you, and I'm certainly not going to give you any words, especially when I don't know what you're even talking about!"

Gray looked down at her hand in his for a long moment before she drew it away. When he looked back up at her, his eyes were filled with a sort of quiet longing. "Yes, I know. That's why I'm not pushing harder, even though I want to. When you know what the words are, and are ready to tell me, you will."

"Why are you so sure?"

Before he could reply, his communicator blipped. [Tolsto to Grayson,]

"I'll be right back," Gray murmured before rising and brushing his earpiece. [Grayson here, what's the problem?] As the security ensign talked, Gray moved out of hearing range, leaving Adri stuck in the bed, more confused and frightened than she had been in many years.

How in the world had this happened? How, by Danwe, had she allowed Gray to fall in love with her? More importantly, what was she to do about it? Did she want to do anything about it? The idea of kicking Gray out of her life right when she had realized that she was starting to depend on him hurt the very delicate organ she had spent most of her life trying to protect. But fear of worse pain to come if she allowed him to stick caused an equal pain. And what of guilt? She liked Gray, more than she wished to analyze. How could she untangle herself from a relationship she had been sucked into without hurting the other half of the relationship, regardless of her own feelings?

"Something wrong, L.C.?"

Adri started at the sound of Duane's voice. She glanced over to see that he had walked up to her bedside while she struggled in the chaos of her thoughts. "I've gotten myself into a mess," she murmured, watching Gray as he continued to talk on his communicator and study something on the infirmary's computer bank. "I'm so confused, Duane. I'm way over my head, here."

"Yeah, the lieutenant has that effect on people. He smiles and talks so pleasantly that you don't know you've been stepped over until you're looking at his back." Duane grinned suddenly and nudged her shoulder. "I like him, if you ask me."

"I didn't," Adri muttered.

"Do you want to know why?"

"Not really."

"He's genuine. He says what he thinks, no games, no masks. He never makes a fuss about little things, and never compromises on the big things. But I guess the real reason I like him is because he makes you happy. I've been your friend for years now, probably your only friend, and this is the first time I've actually seen you really happy. "

Gray suddenly rushed over to them, carrying one of Doctor Geiger's holoboards. "You've got to see this, Adri. Tolsto may have hit upon the Belligerent's plan."

The moment you realize that you want something that you've always had, that something suddenly becomes impossible to acquire.

-Undarian Proverb

Chapter Fifteen

Adri could feel her adrenaline begin to race as she stared down at the schematics of the ship while Gray talked. It was like staring at a complicated code, knowing that the key was just under your nose, waiting for your mind to catch on.

"Although their small raiding craft managed to get within a hundred meters of the *Oreallus's* docking bay," Gray was saying, "it didn't actually land. The best the analysts can come up with is that they somehow managed to - "

"Teleport," Adri answered.

Duane shook his head. "Oh come on! Nobody has cracked the secret to organic teleportation! How would the Belligerent Coalition know that secret before us? The Commonwealth has always had the upper hand in technological innovation." He glared at Adri as she stared down at the schematics hologram in her hands. "Don't say you think they can teleport! If they could, why don't they use it all the time? Are either of you even listening to me?!"

Gray gave the paranthian a conciliatory pat on the shoulder as he watched Adri think. His declaration of love had been premature, but perhaps it was for the best. Now that Adri knew exactly what he wanted, he wouldn't have to hide his own emotions. Just watching her made him fell sappy inside. Suddenly Adri looked up, the faint frown lines on her forehead and the urgency in her eyes drawing him back to the situation at hand.

"Gray, have you inspected all the areas that were known to have been penetrated by the Belligerents during the raid?" she demanded.

"Not personally. I've been too busy collecting damage reports and working up the battle schematics for analysis since I got out of here to go over the whole area myself."

Something in Adri tensed. "Has anyone inspected?"

"Sergeant Tolsto has done a brief scan, and doubtlessly maintenance has been through,"

"But none of them would actually be *looking* for anything out of order, would they?" Adri muttered impatiently.

Gray had a bad feeling that he was beginning to catch on. "No, they wouldn't."

"What are you two talking about?" Duane wanted to know. "Looking for what?"

"Time-sensitive fragmentation devices," Adri snapped.

Duane's complexion lost some of its brilliance. "*Bombs?* You think there are *time bombs* on our ship*?!*"

Adri tapped the holoboard. "Almost certain. Sergeant Tolsto reports that the enemy appeared in these locations, essentially at once," she pointed to the locations that blinked red on the board. "Some of these places are obvious, such as the Engine Room and the munitions stores, but others appear really random, like the tertiary vehicle warehouse. But look at its location within the blueprint of the ship: its right over a major energy line that feeds the ship. If a big enough bomb was placed somewhere within the room, the chain reaction along the energy strain could practically split the ship in two."

Duane made an incoherent moaning sound.

Gray frowned. "But if that would do it, why go to all these other places?"

"All these other areas also have proximity to something major. A bomb in the munitions stores would take out the whole port side of the *Oreallus's* warehouse. That alone would cripple us, making us easy targets. Am I correct, Duane?"

Duane forced himself to swallow. "Yep."

"Why haven't they gone off?" Gray inquired. He didn't doubt Adri's take on the situation, it made too much sense.

It was Duane who answered, shakily. "A bomb of such a nature as to take out the entire munitions store, or the tertiary vehicle warehouse would be very fragile and temperamental. Nearly impossible to transport safely. Better to bring them in disarmed, set them up where you want them, and then finish the process there. The only setback to that is that it would take a long time for the bomb to fully load to full detonation capacity."

"How long?" Gray demanded, leaping to his feet and reaching for his communicator.

"About seventy-two hours. Any time now."

Gray contacted his security team and began to bark orders. He turned to confirm the schematics with Adri only to see her out of bed, punching the code into the locker next to her. She pulled out her jacket and boots and clipped on her earpiece before turning to him. "Let's run. I'll contact the bridge."

Running turned out to be painful, but Adri blocked the pain from her mind. Besides, even with the pain and the knowledge that they could be blasted to smithereens at any second, it was nice to be up and moving, her fighting elegy singing in her blood. Well, might as well admit it all; up and moving with Gray. Even if he was a crazy man who seemed to believe that they were going to get married.

Married. Huh.

Gray talked rapidly on his communicator as they ran, ordering the security team to race to the designated points and search for anything amiss. The bombs had to be concealed somehow so that they couldn't be discovered prematurely. [Search for anything out of place, even if it's nothing but a discolored wall panel.]

They had a moment to catch their breath in the lift as they made their way down to the pertinent levels. Neither spoke until Gray's earpiece crackled, [Tolsto to Grayson, I'm in the tertiary vehicle warehouse. My squad and I have discovered a vehicle seven centimeters off its mark. There's something secured to the underside. Whatever it is, it's big.]

[It's a bomb,] one of Tolsto's men confirmed over the open link.

Gray felt himself beginning to sweat. [Can you disarm it?] he asked, looking at Adri with an expression of grim determination.

[Attempting it now,] the ensign replied.

The lift arrived at its destination, and both Gray and Adri dashed from it along the narrow corridors towards the tertiary vehicle warehouse.

[Savon to Grayson!] another report came in. [We're in the munitions storeroom, and have discovered a bomb concealed within one of the crates for the heavy weaponry. Attempting to disarm now.]

Gray swore.

"Split up," Adri ordered, and swerved off in the direction of the munitions stores. She turned her communicator frequency on to the security teams' before hailing Gray. [Rael to Grayson. I'm nearly at the munitions stores now.]

[Good. I've got another call from team Two; they've found another bomb in the orellium lab. I'm on my way there.]

Adri was nearly at the munitions stores when the fourth bomb was discovered. There was still no word on disarmament. Overhead, the warning sirens were going off and Vice Captain Lowell's voice was demanded every non-security member to evacuated the aft of the ship. A pitifully ineffectual measure if the bombs managed to detonate. Running into the storeroom, she was greeted by the petty officer in charge of the squad. "Wragardon is working on it now," he said.

"How long until detonation?" Adri demanded.

The petty officer wet his lips in ill-concealed fear. "Seven minutes."

[Grayson to Rael,] came a call over the officer's frequency.

[Rael here. What have you found?] Adri stepped away from the security team as they worked frantically to disarm the bomb in the amount of time remaining.

[These things are complex, just what Duane was hinting at. We've got the one in the lab nearly undone.] A tense pause. [I'm sure we're going to make it.]

[We will.] Adri confirmed. She turned just as Wragardon straitened up, face dripping perspiration.

"We've got it."

[Tolsto to Grayson,] she heard over the cheer in the room, [We've got success. Hammond's managed to neutralize the bomb so that we can remove it.]

[Jojara-sen to Grayson, we've done a deep sweep of the surrounding area. No bombs have been detected.]

[Eff to Grayson, team Five had completed disarming ours as well.]

Adri breathed in relief. [Rael to Bridge, all located bombs have been deactivated.]

[Excellent job, Rael,] Lowell replied. [Stay with the security team until the threat is gone.]

[Yes, sir.] Adri replied. She took a deep breath and let it out slowly. Strange how something as cataclysmic as complex plasma bombs could be discovered and dealt with in such a short amount of time. But something still didn't appear right to her. It seemed too easy, too pat. Perhaps she was just getting paranoid with all the recent action.

[Grayson to all squads, remove the bombs and take them to containment chamber one for dismantlement. Use extreme caution; they're still dangerous.]

Adri helped the squad collect all the pieces Wragardon had removed to reach the detonation cerebrum. Trailing behind the squad, Adri followed them to the door, her mind still deep in thought.

She wasn't sure how she heard it, that subtle humming that blended in with the constant and oft forgotten drone of the ship's engines. The noise alerted her instincts enough for her to turn back into the storeroom and give it a thorough glance. The security squad had already departed, so she walked slowly over to a stack of crates lined up along the wall. The humming was louder here. Adri pulled one of the crates away from the wall, creating a crack large enough to see two plasma bombs lined up side by side, blinking one hundred and twenty four seconds to detonation.

[Rael to Grayson. I'm in trouble.]

Gray dropped the hyperscanner he'd been holding as a wave of something ice cold and tasting of fear washed over him. [What is it?]

[Two bombs, one eighteen seconds.]

Gray started running.

136

Adri crouched down in front of the two blinking demons, terribly uncertain how to proceed. [Gray, I'm no specialist.]

[Don't panic, Adri. Take the cover panels off. I'll guide you through.]

With hands she refused to allow shake, Adri removed the cover panels from the two bombs and stared at the intricate mess inside. *Suddenly she could hear herself screaming, flying through the air as a searing roar shook the air and the world turned white.* Shaking her head to clear the strange image, she listed off what she could see to Gray.

[All right baby, remove the brighter power cord, but don't jar anything else.]

Adri hastily did as he instructed, but the timer seemed to be moving much faster than her inexpert hands.

[I've got the first one, starting on the second,] Adri's voice was calm, but Gray's heart was beating so fast, he could barely hear her. Terror for the one he loved seemed to drown out everything else, even the sounds of those security men who could be spared from demolishing the bombs racing after him.

[I'm coming Adri, keep going. You've got plenty of time.] They both knew she didn't.

[Gray, I'm not going to make it!]

He heard her cry seconds before the explosion rocked the ship, sending him and his team flying across the hallway. [*Adri!*]

Adri woke to find herself floating through the dark room, blood down her nose and Gray shouting in her ear. [Adri! Adri, come in!]

[Gray?] she called, trying to turn her head in the darkness. [Where are you?]

[I'm outside the munitions stores. Are you all right? The bomb went off with you on top of it!]

[Uhm, yeah. I think I'm okay. I hurt like crazy.]

[Listen to me, you sound like you have a concussion. The emergency blast shield is down, so I can't get in to you. You have to find the oxygen suit in the far corner of the wall, or you're going to run out of air. You understand?]

[Yeah.] With a leisureliness born of not quite grasping the situation, Adri propelled herself through the room towards the corner that housed the emergency supplies for the room. [I guess I wasn't fast enough for once, huh?]

This time, she picked up the nerves in Gray's voice as he huffed a laugh. [You can't win them all, babe.]

Adri struggled into the oxygen suit. Its purpose was for maintenance outside the ship, or for such emergencies where oxygen was decreasing too rapidly to replace. Snapping the helmet on and pressing the auto respirator, she felt her wandering mind coming back together. [Okay, what's the situation?]

Gray pressed his hand against the tunsteel barrier that separated him from Adri. [There's a fracture along the wall on the other side of where I'm standing. Over half the warehouses have been wiped out on the port side. My team's still looking for other survivors, but the only reason you're still here is because you disarmed the first bomb in time. The second one was placed over an energy capillary, like you were saying.] He let out a deep breath. [I thought I'd lost you.]

[Scared me too.]

Adri glanced around what she could see in the room. [Some of the ceiling is gone, and most of the far wall. I can see the outside of the ship.]

[Lucky you weren't just sucked out.]

[I think the blast propelled me away, and I ran into an air pocket that didn't disperse.]

[Well babe, you can just relax and wait for rescue. I have a team suiting up to breach the blast door as we speak.]

[So we can just chat until they get here, huh?]

[Sure thing.]

The headache that she had been ignoring since she woke pushed to the forefront. [Gray, when this is all over, and I've rotted another eon of my life in the infirmary, and we finally make it to shore leave after our next assignment...]

138

[Yes?]

All courage fled. [Never mind. I forgot you had crazy notions about the two of us signing the contract.]

[Don't you forget it.]

On the bridge, Analysis Officer Devin Wede-Uctan, covering both his station and the security station, shouted the alarm. "Enemy ship sighted!"

Captain Heedman cringed in his chair. "Are you sure its an enemy?"

"Undoubtedly. Signals state they're coming in fast, and by the way the energy's flowing, they're charging their main batteries."

Vice Captain Lowell cursed softly. "With our warehouses blasted off and the rescue mission incomplete, we're trapped."

"What?" cried Heedman. "You mean if we didn't have to rescue anyone, we could escape?"

"Well, we'd have to blast off any of the destroyed portions of the ship still clinging in order to make an effective retreat." Wede-Uctan corrected in an academic tone.

"Then do it!" Heedman ordered.

Silence fell over the bridge.

"But sir, Lieutenant Commander Rael and five others are trapped in the wreckage as we speak," sputtered Operations Officer Janag, "we have to rescue them."

Heedman's face began to turn red. "We have to do what I say we do! I AM the captain! Lowell, command the port batteries to fire on the wreckage immediately! Quoditum," he ordered the helmsman, "As soon as that's done, take us out as fast as you can. DO IT!"

"Sir, please reconsider," Lowell gasped. "Rael is - "

"Replaceable," Heedman snapped. "As are you."

His face turning a sickly white, Vice Captain Lowell brushed his earpiece. [Bridge to port batteries. Charge main weapons. Target, the wreckage of the portside warehouses.]

Gray's head whipped up as the command came over his communicator. "What the -?" he whispered softly. He brushed his earpiece. [Grayson to bridge, rescind that last order! We still have survivors to retrieve from the debris!]

[Negative, Grayson,] came Lowell's voice. [Captain's orders are as swift a retreat as possible.]

[But we still have five people to recover! My team is in the final stages of prep now. Give us twenty minutes,]

[Negative, Grayson.] A pause [I'm sorry.]

[Gray? What's going on, my communicator isn't picking up the bridge's command,] Adri had secured herself to one of the walls as she waited for the rescue team to arrive.

There was a short pause. [Oh Danwe, Adri,]

[What?] There was something terrifying in Gray's voice.

[Heedman isn't going to wait for rescue.]

[What?] she repeated. [I can't very well save myself here,]

[Adri,] Gray said slowly, so slowly that Adri's adrenaline began to rush again, [Kobane's ship is coming. They're within sensor range.]

Sometimes God is merciful and doesn't let you see death coming. And sometimes, he gives you way too much time to think about it. Adri realized in that moment that she hadn't been lucky enough to be the former. [He's going to let us die to save himself,]

It felt as though someone had reached through his skin, grabbed his heart and was now trying to pull it out, wrenching as it went. [You can't die,] he murmured, [Not now when I just found you. I love you,]

[Gray,] Adri felt something break inside, and feared it was her heart. [About those words you wanted me to say…]

There was a sound like roaring that burst through the nothingness of the space surrounding her. The searing white of the blaster cannon fire only feet from her body blinded her eyes, and she felt the horrible tug as everything around her flew away into that nothingness. The nothingness that was space. [Gray!]

There was an eternal second in which her body felt intense pain. Then the world faded to white, then gray, and she felt herself falling away into cool mist accompanied only by her fighting elegy. Her last thought was a fanciful one. *Why, I have wings. How strange.*

Then there was nothing at all.

Enemy Sabotage Damages Ship

5 Killed

The G.C.N. Oreallus was attacked on 02-24-1119 by the Belligerent Coalition en route to an undisclosed location. Bombs were discovered in the ship after the skirmish. While all but one was disarmed in time, the explosion killed 5 crew members; Ensign Kaitlin Mannerly, Ensign Undani Umbara, Ensign Sahar Tuian, Chief Petty Officer of Warehousing Meredith Hayden-Lloyd, and Second Officer Lieutenant Commander Adrienne Rael.

Chapter Sixteen

Mankind has fixed itself with technology to be bold, healthy, cunning and occasionally happy. It has cures for nearly every disease, solutions for nearly all inconveniences, and a way out of nearly every plight. It still has no cure for grief.

Thaddeus Grayson, a field lieutenant of the Galactic Commonwealth Navy's Advance Force division, was no stranger to grief. From a young age, he had learned that death walked hand in hand with daily life, and that the best way to avoid grief's clinging cousin misery was to look at the bright side. There was always a purpose; every breath of life held meaning. That's what his grandmother had taught, and that's what he'd always believed. All life was important, because all life had a purpose, a point or reason to exist. Gray had found that to be a comforting idea, and had spent most of his life looking for his purpose. No matter what the pain – the death of his grandmother, the sorrows of a career soldier – he'd moved forward. Gray had always managed to see some spot of light. Then there'd been that short space of time where he'd thought he'd found his point in Adri.

Which somehow made his current hell twice as dark.

Adri was dead. The *Oreallus*'s analysis officer had morbidly documented the debris impact on the surface of Junus. Pushed by the explosive force of the ship's batteries straight into the gravitational sphere of the planet, it had taken mere hours for the jetsam to burn through the atmosphere and disintegrate on the surface like shards of a glass.

Adri was dead.

It had taken a squad of his own security team to pry him away from the dangerously thin walls that separated the service hall and what used to be the portside warehouse. His mind had gone numb and he'd fought wildly, until one of his team took matters into her own hands and stunned him. He'd woken hours later in the infirmary, feeling hollow on the inside and groggy on the outside, with Duane sitting in the visitor's chair next to his bed, head in his hands.

Duane wascrying. Gray closed his eyes and pretended to still be sleeping to allow his companion some privacy to grieve. Strangely, he didn't feel the need to weep, although he was sure the need would come at some point. Instead, he simply felt...empty.

And well he should, since the love of his life had just died, before he'd even had the chance to show her just how much she *was* the love of his life.

He'd never even had the chance to dance with her.

About those words you wanted me to say... Had she understood what he'd wanted to hear? He'd never know.

From words of love to words of condolence in a matter of hours, Gray thought bleakly the next day. He'd been released from the infirmary without the usual harassment Doctor Geiger usually enforced the evening before. "I've informed the captain that you require a day of personal leave before returning to work," the doctor had told him when handing him his communicator and ATF. "I suggest you try to sleep, but barring that, I recommend you steer clear of the bridge. The last thing Lieutenant Commander Rael would want is a massacre of bridge command which would end with a good officer being court martialed."

Was the doctor a psychic? Gray had thought. But he'd avoided the bridge, and had ended up getting drunk on bootlegged Tuor rum with Duane in a forgotten corner of the weaponry and tactical analysis complex. While the humacoms continued their work, oblivious to the goings on of the day before, Gray had shared silence and rum with the paranthian. When the rum ran out and Duane fell asleep, Gray continued to stare into nothingness until the bell chimes warned of the change in shift. He then hefted his companion to his dormitory before staggering back to his own. Alone.

A few short hours later, and here he stood with most of the available crew on the *Oreallus*, listening to the vice captain recite the funeral text for those killed in defense of the ship. Everyone in Adri's squad showed up, along with a good many others who had liked or admired her. Even Piontek hobbled in, despite his near-mortal injury. During the ceremony, Gray could feel the negative mood of the crowd directed at Captain Heedman. Gray's own feelings were clear-cut, but lacked enthusiasm. Heedman was weak, and not only deserved to be court martialed for cowardice, but also but be flogged. Before Gray killed him. But none of that would bring Adri back. Nothing would.

The ceremony ended with the symbolic jettisoning of a capsule of dust in lieu of bodies. Gray watched it spiral away through the viewscreen out into the far reaches of space. Vice Captain Lowell's approach barely registered until he spoke. "Lieutenant Grayson, I understand you were a close friend of Rael's,"

"Yeah." What else was there to say?

Lowell made an inarticulate, sympathetic gesture. He stood awkwardly for a moment, tugging on the black armband he'd worn for the service. "She was an excellent officer," he said by way of condolence.

Gray continued to stare out into space. "Sure was."

"Listen," Lowell said quietly, "No one wanted her dead. But if we don't follow orders…you understand."

Gray did. "I'm sure you had something to say, other than condolences, sir." Gray said, finally facing his superior officer.

The vice captain nodded. "Rael's personal effects need to be dealt with. Since we've lost our second officer, a replacement has to be found, and is entitled to the officer's quarters it goes with."

"I really don't think this is the time to discuss this," Gray replied flatly.

Lowell hissed out a breath. "Listen, I hate it too; I worked with Rael longer than you did. She was the best. She would have made captain at the last candidacy call, but she was overlooked because she had no high rolling sponsorship. Instead she got shunted onto the *Oreallus* with

Heedman. Rael deserved to be captain. But she didn't make it and now she's dead. The whole deal is rotten, but there's nothing to be done!" there was a pause as Lowell took a calming breath. "In all the years I've known her, Rael's never been close to anyone. The paranthian from Engineering, perhaps; but she got a look in her eyes since you came on board."

"What kind of look?"

Lowell shrugged. "Thoughtful. Confused. Danwe, I've never seen her look so perplexed about another being before. Rael never got into relationships." He paused again. "Listen, Grayson, whatever type of relationship you and the L.C. had, it was different than anything I've noticed before. That's all I'm trying to say here."

Gray nodded.

"I'm asking you because of that."

"Pack her stuff up?" Gray asked, glancing back out of the viewscreen.

"Yeah," more relaxed, the vice captain accepted a cup of simulated coffee from an ensign. "Rael has no family to send her personal effects to, so pack it as you see fit and I'll have it stored in a warehouse until we make Halieth."

Gray nodded again, and with a last glance at the infinite question of space, he left.

"I saw you leave the funeral." Duane said as he stepped into Adri's old quarters. The room was a decent size, as befitted a second officer, but there wasn't much in it. A neatly made bed, a travel trunk, a couple of uniforms in the closet. Some dirty dishes were piled on the desk, and the computer viewscreen showed a list of messages. Gray was standing by the bed, carefully folding a pair of faded fatigues. "Humans don't deal with death well. As a culture, I mean." Duane commented suddenly.

Gray gave him a skeptical look, taking in Duane's blotchy complexion and reddened eyes. He hadn't been on time for the service. Gray had seen him slip in the back of the room halfway through.

Duane flashed him a sheepish smile. "I guess I've been hanging around humans too long. So, you collecting her things?"

"She didn't own much."

"Nah," Duane stepped further into the room and glanced bleakly at the pile of articles that Gray had stacked on the bed. "I never saw her with much, ever."

"I haven't found anything personal," Gray said, his eyes slightly distant. "No trinkets, no jewelry, no pictures or holo-recordings, not even a chronometer."

Duane frowned, Gray's comment obviously pulling him out of his memories. "She had a necklace – you know, the tear shaped pendant made out of some purple shell? I think she told me once that it had been her mother's. She wore it all the time, so she was probably wearing it…"

"Yeah, she had it on."

Duane sat down heavily into the desk chair. "I just can't believe this."

Gray glanced around at the second officer's quarters. They had held little of Adri to begin with, and now all her things sat in little piles that didn't even cover the surface of the bed. "Why doesn't she have pictures? There isn't even one from her graduation from the Academy."

Rubbing his face, Duane replied, "She had a holo-album that one of her basic training buddies made for her when she was accepted into the Officers' Academy. It's got to be around her somewhere,"

Glad at the puzzle to divert his attention from what he was doing, Gray scanned the room again. "I've been through the chest of drawers, the desk, the closet, and the bathroom. She didn't rent any warehouse space. There's nothing but what's here on the bed. Where did she put it?"

The paranthian shrugged.

Feeling slightly foolish (which was better than bereaved), Gray checked under the bed. It had always been where he'd stuck his most valued possessions as a child. Perhaps Adri had also used the space as a little girl, and habit had kept her utilizing it. Lifting up the bed sheets, he peered under. Nothing. He even crawled in a little ways to double check, but the space was empty.

"Find anything?" Duane asked from the chair.

"No. It was just a guess. I suppose – wait. What's this?" Gray had turned his head slightly to slide back out, and had noticed a small SecureBox fastened to the underside of the bed. He rolled awkwardly onto his back and studied the box. Unfastening its mounting seal, he slid out from the bed, pulling the box with him.

"What's that?" Duane asked, his attention perked.

Gray sat on the bed and studied the lock on the box. "There's a numerical combination code on this." He pulled out the master code chip Lowell had given him and inserted it into the lock. The lock *pinged* for a moment before blinking green, allowing the lid to release with a soft snick.

Inside the box Gray found a small collection of old photo images, keepsakes, and a slender holo-album. Duane stepped over to him and peered over his shoulder. "There's the album. Mind if I look through it?"

While Duane studied the images stored in the album, Gray sifted through the other items that Adri had considered valuable enough to store in a SecureBox, about the size of a pistol case, hidden under her bed. There wasn't much; a palm sized doll, which looked like it must have belonged to Adri as a child, an old wedding band registered to an Elizabeth Wraben Rael, and a few miscellaneous trinkets that could only be valued by a child or adolescent. But at the bottom of the box, carefully wrapped in a genuine silk scarf, was a framed photo imager. With a soft breath, Gray activated the outdated screen.

The image displayed a family of three at what appeared to be the child's birthday party. The family was centered in the image, with a heavily sugared pastry on the table in front of them that had a real wax candle in the shape of the numeral seven. The birthday girl – Adri, he realized – was smiling excitedly at the image. She was sitting on her mother's lap, comfortable and unafraid, with an outstretched hand to grasp the arm of the beaming man sitting next to them. Her parents looked young and proud, both with features that Gray recognized from their daughter. The man had the same calm features and hair coloring, while the mother had passed on her deep brown eyes that seemed to reflect back the world around them; a trait that was both mysterious and intriguing. He felt his gut clench with pain, but couldn't force himself to look away.

"I've never seen that image before," Duane commented from behind him. "The L.C. was pretty closed mouthed about her childhood. I know her parents died when she was young."

Gray didn't look up. "She looks happy here, doesn't she?"

"Yeah." The paranthian rose, reluctantly replacing the holo-album. "She never really looked like that, for as long as I knew her. Until you came along," he placed a comforting hand briefly on Gray's shoulder.

Gray continued to stare down at the image long after Duane had departed. Adri's seven-year-old eyes smiled back at him innocently.

Humankind has an instinctive desire for happiness. In fact, Gray surmised, it could rationally be said that all species possessing more than the necessary survival instincts for existence desire happiness in some form or another. Barring happiness, humans at least tend to avoid situations or objects that will push them further from that goal. If they can't avoid it, humans will either confront the situation in order to change it for a better outcome, or they ignore it and try to pretend that it isn't there, never occurred, or isn't a big deal. Or, in his case, try to objectify it so as to give himself some emotional distance.

Danwe, that was just pitiful.

Gray turned his head and glanced at the framed imager of Adri's seventh birthday. The bedside light illuminated the room softly, showing the image placed carefully amidst the orderly disorder of the quarters he occupied. Stretched out on the bed, he tried to let his senses roam as another form of distraction from his thoughts. The audioproofing in the walls did not allow the noise from the corridor to drift in. It left the room in silence despite the fact that there was a bevy of technicians just down the hall replacing a gravitational and air pressure monitor. The only sound was the gentle humming of the ship's engines, a noise often forgotten after years aboard spacecraft. The bed sheets rustled as he rolled onto his back to stare up at the ceiling.

What had Duane said? Humans don't deal with death well, as a culture? Apparently humans weren't the only ones who tried to rationalize their feelings in order to avoid them. And he really had to stop philosophizing and deal with the matter at hand.

Okay, fact. He had lost the woman he loved. He felt grief, guilt, and anger.

Anger? Yes. Heedman sentenced Adri to die out of cowardice. He'd checked the records the analysis team had compiled and concluded that there had been enough time for a rescue operation to succeed before the Belligerent ship would have been in firing range. Granted, they may have been caught in a firefight, but even crippled, the *Oreallus* had the resources to defend itself under the right command. Heedman killed Adri, plain and simple. But now what?

Adri's parents had gotten caught up in the Anti-War Riots in the capital city of Corinthe ten years ago. Xander and Elizabeth Rael had been returning home from a business conference and been pulled into the violence. They hadn't made it back to their seven-year-old daughter, home from school with a mild virus. Although the deaths had been confirmed as a killing of unarmed innocents, the fact that they had been shot by soldiers working on the crackdown meant the whole mess was shoved under the metaphoric carpet. Adri got an apology for the loss of her family and home, was shoved into the overworked foster care system and forgotten. Gray had spent several hours after packing Adri's belongings in the Archives trying to get answers. The ones he found explained a lot about the woman he loved. And lost.

She was given no justice for her parents. From the time of their death until she held her first position of command in the Advance Force, Adri had been powerless and overlooked. Once in command she flourished, until a coward above her took her choices away. Gray couldn't get justice for her parents, and he couldn't fix her childhood. But he could get her justice for her own death.

It wasn't the life's purpose he'd thought it'd be, but it was a purpose.

Floating
        Falling
                Through endless swirling mists of emptiness
Yet not
    Like a face pressed to a window
                   Both out and in and all around
Wrapped in heat
            Feeling the cool
Placid
               Musing and unconcerned
Hearing nothing
        Hearing the serenade of silence

    In this time I knew myself
                      All my self
My self said how lovely this nothing was
                   Lacking all pain
    My self said to depart
                See the blue light comes that will guide us
This is not my place
               Lovely one
                    Sweet love
This is not home
        Breathe now

The spirit is willing but the flesh is weak

        I will give you the flesh to match the spirit
Breathe

Chapter Seventeen

"It's full of syncopated beats and dominant lyrics, what's not to like?"

"The messages it conveys are ones of irrational violence and pleasure in the lack of control of the libido. It's ridiculous. In addition, the rhyming scheme is overstated and lacks genuine poetry. What *is* there to like?"

"Children, please no bickering over the music selection." Floyd called over from across the room.

Cassie and Zultan continued to stare at each other for several seconds before moving away from the stationary mainframe that housed the lab's music archives.

Tension had mounted in the lab like the steady rise of a flood drain in a storm, rushing beneath your feet and threatening to spill over into violence. Floyd could feel the monitors that had been mounted on the walls gauging his every breath. He was never alone; a mixture of live and humacom security guards escorted him whenever he left the laboratory, even when he simply went to the cafeteria. Security protocol had reached alarming heights. Floyd hadn't been home in weeks.

Something was up. The investigation into his father's suicide (just the thought still gave him a shattering headache) seemed to be dragging on with no updates. Colonel Stroff was constantly making an appearance to check on his work (not that it was anything of high importance since Cassie was activated), and some strange band of technicians whose credentials he could never quite decipher, led by a military officer whose rank was never disclosed, kept barging in to access Zultan's files, despite the fact that all the information Zultan held was also stored in the government's mainframe.

Paranoia was dogging Floyd like one missed question on an aced exam. He could almost feel himself slipping into the eerie calm that kept trying to suck him down into nothingness, where there were no worries, no questions, no feelings. The fact that the calm was tempting frightened him more than all the secrecy and suspicion that hovered around him.

Across the room, Zultan and Cassie sat at one of the computer bays and played chess. They appeared absorbed in calculating their moves in the game.

I've been trying to trace that command signature the medicom received before it tried to poison Floyd. Cassie reported in a private instant message to Zultan. The IM system between the two humacoms was modified and encrypted, and Cassie had (with loosely interpreted authorization) modified it further so that it was both untraceable and unrecorded. *When I go through official channels, I get the "unauthorized inquiry" block. What about you?*

The same. Zultan made a comment aloud about the game, which Cassie rebutted.

Any information about it from other investigative sources? Who's investigating the incident anyway?

There's nothing in the accessible files. Looking at all available official inquiries, the files report that the case is closed, a dead end. But there is no record to show that any investigation took place.

So it's a cover up.

Zultan flashed Cassie a glance that could only be described as amused. *Your knowledge of human vernacular and colloquialisms has vastly improved. I commend your effort.*

Cassie rolled her eyes for effect. *It passes the time better than just shifting to power-saver.*

True.

There was silence on both sides as the two humacoms continued to play their game and process information at the same time.

What do the files say unofficially? Cassie finally asked.

Unofficially?

You said 'all official inquiries.' Are there any unofficial bits of information you can access?

Zultan placed Cassie's king in check. *I can access anything that is inputted into any government database, you know that.*

Cassie moved her bishop to defend her king. *Yeah. That's why you're so valuable, blah, blah, blah.*

Blah blah blah?

Is there something you aren't telling me, Harddrive?

Now you're giving me nicknames? I recant my earlier statement due to lack of information. You're organic/human education is not commendable. It's annoying.

Your human education is more pronounced than mine; at least I still know that as a machine, humacoms are incapable of annoyance.

I wouldn't count on it.

Another pause as Cassie reversed the game and placed Zultan's queen in danger. *So answer my question. Is there anything beyond the official report?*

Nothing I can tell you.

Because there's nothing to say…or because you can't say?

Can't. The access password to the document in question supercedes even Floyd's security clearance. I am incapable of divulging the information in that file.

What can you tell me?

We were right. Floyd's in danger. The only reason he isn't dead is because he doesn't know what is really going on. If he ever finds out, his life is considered a liablity to those involved. They will very likely try to kill him.

Does this have anything to do with the death of his father?

I can't say. Draw a logical conclusion.

Logically, it does. Given the data I have received from you about events prior to my booting, and from events I have recorded, it connects. It must also connect with the information those creepy guys keep programming into you. All that top secret development stuff.

154

Zultan frowned and made a pithy comment as Cassie placed his king in checkmate. *Creepy? And how did you know that the information has something to do with development?*

Cassie smirked. *Oh come on, we're connected. I can take down anything they try to put up between my system and yours. And the definition of 'creepy' is 'causing of an unpleasant feeling of fear or unease.' They sure do that. To top it off, I'm even following protocol. After all, they've never inputted their authorization codes to access you through my access recognition processor, which you know is a breach in procedure. Thereby anything they enter into you is a viable threat to your system, and falls under my scrutiny.*

That is dangerous. I would advise you to be careful.

Hey, Cassie nudged Zultan's shoulder with her elbow. *I can't let anything happen to you.*

Nor I you. Zultan gazed over at Floyd who was rubbing his temples again – an indicator of another migraine coming on. *I think we're all in a precarious position. Whatever they're planning is too fragile to succeed smoothly. All it needs is one variable to shift out of their favor for them to act in erratic patterns that defy logic. When that happens, it will all blow up in our own metaphorical faces.*

Is that an irrefutable certainty, or a statistic probability?

A certainty. If I were human, I would guess things have already shifted out of their favor. They just don't know it yet.

* * *

"By Danwe I just…I just can't believe it." Royce Carter shook his head and stared in bewilderment down at his mug. "Rael of all people seemed invincible, especially on the field. Blown up."

The *Damacene* had caught up with the *Oreallus* in record time after receiving the latter's S.O.S. They had met with a drastically different situation than that of their last meeting. The change in status had altered the *Damacene's* own plans, and it was now to escort the damaged ship to a safer space zone. Even a week after the incident, the news still threw eerie shock waves through the newcomers.

Carter and Gray had met in the mess hall of the *Oreallus* on their off shifts (Carter was assisting as acting second officer while a new one was trained). Both had loosened the collars of their uniforms in respect for their off-time. Both wore the traditional black armband out of respect for a lost comrade. It was the first time Gray had searched Carter out in the week he had been onboard. They sat together, sipping coffee and avoiding the topic of Adri. Until now.

Gray had been waiting for Carter to bring her up. "It was foul play, Carter."

"Yeah, being blown to ash by the enemy is pretty foul." Carter agreed.

"Even more so when it's your own captain who unnecessarily signs your death warrant."

The younger officer looked up sharply from his beverage. He no longer appeared bewildered. In fact, he looked just a little bit intimidating. "Are you implying that Heedman acted out of cowardice?"

"Interpret it how you want."

Carter's eyes widened. "Are you trying to give yourself career suicide?"

Gray quirked an eyebrow, "You doubt me?"

His companion huffed a breath, "No. But that doesn't mean anyone else will. In fact, I know they will. They *will* believe Heedman over you, his word carries more weight. It's the way it works, so why kill yourself, er, proverbially?"

"For justice." Gray leaned forward, deliberately invading Carter's personal space. "Adri deserves justice for once. She never got it in life, so I'm going to give it to her in death."

Carter's eyes began to shimmer with a hint of respect and amusement. "And here I thought you were an placid sort of fellow."

"And here I thought you were a brainless rich boy who got his position from favors. Perceptions can be dangerous."

Now Carter smiled. "Right about that at least. It still doesn't change the facts. Your word against Heedman's, Heedman is going to win, every time."

Gray reached into his pocket and pulled out a data chip. "Even if I have proof?"

"Hmm," Carter leaned back, eying his companion with new interest. "What kind of proof?"

"Unaltered recordings from the bridge monitor, the available readouts from the bomb squad who dealt with Adri in the warehouse. All the security reports and analyses of the enemy ship's approach and threat rating, as well as my communicator's recording of sequencing events."

"Does it prove anything?"

"It proves that we had time to launch a rescue before the Belligerent Coalition's ship was in firing range, and that Heedman chose flight even over the advice of his senior staff who were present at the time."

Carter whistled. "Impressive."

"As security officer, I can finagle just about any data I deem attached to my area of concern. So, everything. Mostly to keep myself occupied."

There was a short pause. "I guess you'd need it."

"Is that enough to indict him?"

Carter pondered a moment, staring into his mug as though his simulated coffee could give him answers. "The Galactic Commonwealth is run by a circle of highly sophisticated elite. While they manage to bump along and encourage the less affluent to serve their country, they will close ranks when one of their own is threatened. Albert Heedman is, unfortunately, one of their own. No one is going to welcome any accusations you dare to make."

"Are you speaking from personal experience?"

"Personal observation," Carter smiled a little. "I am one of them, remember?"

Gray leaned back and glanced idly around the mess hall. The tables near the holo-stage were full, despite the late hour, and the bar and the end was still maxed to capacity as people socialized, relaxing after a day's work; arguing, gossiping, flirting. Life went on, but his had altered course. "What will make them listen?"

Fiddling with his coffee, Carter spoke slowly. "The proof you've gathered counts heavily in your favor – but if you play it wrong, it could be argued as harassment."

"What?

"Don't think Heedman's lawyer won't try every angle to make you look bad. It isn't just him you'll be taking on, but also the powers that be who put him in as captain. What you'll need is a person with some political clout like, say, myself, who can and will speak for your integrity. Not that I'm much in those circles. A flake, I'm afraid. You can't just waltz in and say, 'hey, he killed my girlfriend, I want him to pay.'"

"But I do. So how do we make it look like that's not my primary motive?"

Carter leaned forward and spoke just above a whisper. "By creating reasonable doubt. It won't be enough to just present the evidence, you have to insinuate that Heedman not only did this, but could be quite capable of doing it again – to anyone. Lodge an official complaint, then don't do anything until you get back to Halieth. That will give them time to begin to think that it was their idea to dump Heedman when you come in person to present your evidence. We'll go from there."

Gray chuckled, sliding the data chip back into his pocket. "You actually have a plan, right?"

"Hey, I'm wounded." Carter grinned. "I may be a flake, but I'll get the job done – without either of us losing *our* jobs in the process." He sobered. "Rael was one of my best friends. If Heedman tossed her life out like spare gear, I want to see him yanked down and groveling for his ostentatious life."

That night, after he had said good night to Carter and stared at a younger version of his Adri, after the hum of the ship's engines had faded in and out of his conscious, Gray fell asleep.

And dreamed that he was wading through endless mist, searching, searching for something he'd lost.

Something brilliant, almost too hard to see, approached him through the never ending twilight, enveloping him until he could see every star in the endless blanket of space, every shoot of grass that grew on his grandmother's plantation. Even his own emotions manifested into soft colors that dripped out of his eyes and vanished into the brilliant being surrounding him. He squinted, trying to make out a face in the light, but just when he thought he could recognize the features of someone familiar, the light winked out and the mist was filled with screams and the blood of hundreds.

False face, false words, false purpose

Everything and nothing is cause for suspicion – even my own actions. I feel fine, and I feel dead. Everyone looks at me with question and mistrust on their faces – Me, who knows nothing but that something SOMETHING some   thing is wrong.

I act normal, a front as false as everything else around here but I'm really hollow inside, less real than my own creations

Even they have secrets now. I've lost the key somewhere, I'm unraveling

I feel myself unraveling

Did father feel this? Like being pulled upwards, yanked one vein at a time? Less and less, more and more until you're not anywhere? Is there some point where we just shatter into some nothingness the world calls madness? I wish to Danwe that I had quit – but I don't

Is this how it starts I can see how this leads to the end

~~Better to end it?~~

No no no nononononononono

A threat it's a threat where's Freya?

Something happened to father something happened to father something happened

Murder

Why why the mind is tricky

We've made them too well they're too much like us

Knew too much, always too dangerous to know too much but what?

My burden now. Must protect my own, even from

Where does this lead?

Truth or false, both will burn to death to death

Chapter Eighteen

Awareness came first. Before any of the senses awoke, she was aware that she *was*. It meant something important, but she couldn't decipher what. The next thing that manifested was feeling. She was lying on something cool and hard, but not uncomfortable. Her body felt hot, as if she had a fever. Air was breezing gently past her face; she could feel it on every portion of her body except for her right arm. She couldn't feel her arm at all. That fact should have bothered her, but she felt ambivalent. *Oh well.*

Hearing was the second sense regained. At first all she could hear was a monotonous *beep beep* of something to her right. The cacophony of machinery didn't concern her, until she realized that there was a noise she wasn't hearing; the sound of the ship's engines. The droning hum was often forgotten until it was absent. Were there engine problems? Why hadn't she been notified? She brooded about it for a while until she slid back into sleep.

Scent was returned to her when she woke again, like a gift. She didn't know how long she'd slept, but wasn't worried. The air that was still brushing across her bore the sickly sweet odor of the infirmary; disinfectants, medicaments, and a whiff of death. Over it all was something else she didn't quite recognize. Incense?

Where am I?

The challenge of opening her eyes was a daunting one. It seemed as if she spent eons on the task, to no avail. Resting between each effort, she tried to connect with her eyes to open them, but such a simple task took on the proportions of a recon that had suddenly been ambushed.

Bright. It was the indicator that she had succeeded. Too bright, so the cool darkness returned. She had succeeded once though, so she tried again. Squinting to minimize the effect on her eyes, she looked. And saw a dark stone vaulted ceiling, obscured by shadows that clung like cobwebs.

Sound echoed towards her, but she found she couldn't move her head to see who it was or what it was. Straining her limited abilities, she waited. A figure appeared above her, partially obscuring the light and most of the dark ceiling. It took her a moment to focus. Human male, was her first impression. The second was that his pale eyes seemed to slide right through her, and were vaguely familiar.

"Are you awake for good this time?"

She felt around for her voice. "Where. Am I?" It came out scratchy and slurred, as though she hadn't used her voice in a long time. Perhaps she hadn't.

"Safe. Alive, miraculously."

That seemed to be all the information she needed, for she could feel herself falling back into the gray twilight without permission. The man was still standing above her as she drifted away. "Welcome back, Veranda."

She frowned, or thought she did. "Not me. Not my name."

"It is now."

* * *

Freya woke from a dreamless sleep suddenly, like one does at the sound of an explosion outside one's home. It felt as though the vast sphere of energy that she had always felt connected to had exploded to twice its size in a manner of seconds. The air vibrated with unabsorbed power. There were voices whispering in the hallway beyond her chambers, punctuated by the pattering of feet. Excited voices, curious voices, skeptical voices. Freya rose quickly, donned a robe, and went out to join the others who were gathering close by.

"Did you feel that?" one Talented asked her as she approached.

Everyone was still in their nightclothes. Most were barefoot, their feet stepping lightly on the cool stone floor as they converged in the common space that connected most of the bedchambers. The moon shone bright through the windows along one wall, the breeze moving their clothing and hair in soft caresses.

"I feel it now!" exclaimed another Talented, patting her heart. "Freya, do you think *ada* Sergei has amplified the energy in the temple for a gathering?"

"Don't be silly, Darla," the first woman said. "This is totally different from a normal amplification. Besides, he gave no forewarning, and all our amplifiers are right here. It's got to be something big. Something utterly Powerful."

"Do you think this might have something to do with the darkness all the precogs have been experiencing lately? Darla inquired. Her second set of eyes blinked rapidly, filtering the light given off by the moon. Her kievian tentacles twisted and snaked around her shoulders, revealing her excitement.

"What do you think, Freya? You have some foresight,"

"I honestly don't know," Freya replied. The mention of foresight had her glancing around for Ayane. "Whatever it is, it's something big. This was not engineered by *ada* Sergei. He doesn't have this much power. None of us do."

"You want to know what I believe?" an older Talented spoke for the first time. The others gathered closer. Crya had lived in the convent longer than any of the others present, and as such was highly respected. "This energy burst is similar in essence to the smaller one we experienced about eleven years ago. Back then, many of us believed that an extremely powerful Talented had awoken; whom, we didn't know, and never discovered. But if we were correct then…"

"Then this would signify the awakening of a powerful being," Sarthane, the woman who had first spoken gasped. "Maybe even more powerful than a Talented!"

"But who is greater than a Talented?" Darla demanded.

Sarthane gave her a pitying look. "By Danwe, girl. Use your head for a moment. What's the highest category of Talented?"

"Adept of course." Darla replied, not comprehending. "Beings so powerful they could overwhelm any Talented. But we've been taught that all the Adept genes are extinct, and they were a phenomenon so rare that there were only three Adepts in a generation to begin with. They're just a myth, right? That's what all the elders say."

"We could be wrong," Crya said as the crowd became agitated. "These two surges of energy may have nothing to do with awakenings. Then again,"

"Our teachers may be wrong."

"Or," a very young Talented piped up from the back of the crowd, her hair in little braids and her eyes dark with power. "They are teaching us wrong."

"That's nonsense," another argued. "Why would they deliberately teach us an untruth?"

Leaving the crowd to speculate and argue about the night's events, Freya went in search of her younger friend.

The occupancy light was on by Ayane's door. Yet when Freya tapped the door to see if she was somehow still asleep, she noticed that the door was locked from the inside. She contemplated thoughtfully for a moment, debating whether or not she should disturb her friend when she may be sleeping, but a soft noise coming from the other side of the door caught her attention. Eavesdropping shamelessly, Freya pressed her ear to the door and heard the sound a little better. Crying.

"Ayane?"

No answer.

"Ayane, it's Freya, are you all right?"

Still no answer. Concerned now, Freya reached out with one of her limited abilities, empathy. Almost at once she could feel distress radiating through the door, a sickening mixture of pain, fear, and... knowing?

"Are you feeling well? Ayane, answer me!"

When she once again got no reply, Freya placed a hand on the old-fashioned lock mechanism. Her telekinetic abilities were as weak as the rest of her gifts, but constant practice and visualization allowed her a stronger use for what she had. Closing her eyes, she pictured the inside

164

of the lock. Once the image was stable in her mind, she gathered the traces of energy in the atmosphere around her until she had combined enough to push the gears and pins to their unlocked positions. It would have normally taken her several minutes, but the increase in the energy that had woken the inhabitants of the convent boosted her abilities. It amplified them a little too much, she realized when the lock exploded and the door burst open as if assaulted by a hurricane.

"Ayane?" wincing a little, Freya entered the room. It was dark, but the light from the hallway slipped in around her and partially illuminated the little space. She was quick to find her friend, curled up on the bed shivering and whimpering softly. "What's wrong?"

"She has awakened," Ayane stammered, curling into Freya as her friend pulled her into her arms. "She is here with us. Cerebitha – the great twisted is threatened. The change is upon us, the pieces moving."

"Who? Who has awakened?" Ayane's fear seeped into Freya like ice water.

Ayane's eyes were opaque, and filled with pain.

"Ayane, *sorja*, listen to me. Who has awakened?"

"Veranda. Veranda has awoken. Now it will burn. Everything will burn!"

* * *

Adri's arm screamed as though it had been plunged into molten lava to the shoulder. With an agonized cry, she reached over with her left hand and grasped her right shoulder in an effort to ease the pain. Her bare skin felt hot to the touch, but after a few mind-numbing seconds, the pain eased down from vomiting-level to merely horrible. It wasn't until then that Adri felt the strength to open her eyes.

There was a moment's panic when she didn't recognize where she was. The room was dim, made of some brown stone with a vaulted ceiling that was lost in the shadows. Machinery that looked several centuries newer than the room cluttered the area, items that Adri recognized as belonging to a medical facility. She was lying on some sort of bed, and with a fresh surge of panic, she realized that under the blanket, she was naked. The only thing on her was her mother's pendant, which certainly wasn't covering anything.

Danwe, where am I?

The sound of approaching footsteps pushed her into action. Adri tried to sit up, but she was too weak. Instead, she rolled herself off the bed, collapsing on the floor in a tangled heap with the blanket wrapped around her like a burial shroud. Moaning a little, she waited for the room to stop spinning before forcing her weight to her feet. Using her left shoulder as her anchor, she leaned against the bed and rose, clutching the blanket with her good hand.

The footsteps were getting closer. Sucking in a breath to focus, Adri looked around for anything she could use as a weapon. There was a tray of medical instruments on the other side of the bed. Staggering like a drunk, she made her way around to it. Grasping a tool that looked vaguely like a giant fork, she used all her momentum to run across the room, collapsing against the wall by the door. Miraculously managing to stay upright, she stuck the fork between her teeth, knotted the blanket so it would stay around her shoulder, and retrieved her pitiful weapon.

Despite the pain radiating through her useless right arm and the spinning room, she was hyperaware of the footsteps stopping outside the door. Taking another ragged breath, she gripped the fork tightly and waited, her fighting elegy humming. She heard the soft beep of the lock disengaging, and the rush of air as the door slid opened and disappeared into the wall. She waited one second for the newcomer to step through the doorway before striking.

The newcomer's hand shot out and gripped her wrist before the fork could pierce his chest. It was pitifully easy for him to keep a hold of her arm with one hand while he removed her weapon with his other. In the seconds that action took, Adri summed him up. Human, or humanoid, a few inches taller than she, narrow build, pale skinned, blond hair that touched his shoulders, and dressed in some sort of dull colored monastic garb. His face was also narrow, sporting a blue oval gemstone on his forehead. His eyes were blue as well, paler than the gem, and seemed to look right through her to her soul.

His voice was calm when he spoke. "Impaling me with a nerve

stimulant is probably not a wise choice, considering that I came to help you with the pain in your arm."

Adri's body tensed for fight-or-flight, despite the fact that she seemed unable to do either. All the strength that she had managed to gather seemed to be leaking out her arm. "Who are you?"

"I think a better question would be who are you. Or rather, who *were* you. But now is not the time for questions. Your arm needs to be seen to, and you really shouldn't be out of bed for another few days." He held out his hand. "Come on,"

Adri pushed herself away from him. "Keep away from me. You didn't answer my question."

"My name is Eliot Blair, not that it will have any significance to you. Veranda - "

Panic shot up, blind panic. "That's not my name!"

"Yes it is." With a huff of breath, Blair began to approach her again. "I can explain all this if you would only let me see to your arm,"

"I said keep away from me!" In desperation, Adri flung her good arm out at him in a futile gesture to stop.

As if on invisible strings, Blair was lifted from the ground and propelled across the room, crashing into the equipment before collapsing onto the floor. Adri slid to the floor with a gasp. Power still hummed around her like the crackle of static electricity.

"What…what's going on?" Adri watched as Blair groaned and sat up gingerly.

The two stared at each other for a long moment before Blair spoke. "I know you are confused. Let me see to your arm while I try to explain. If I can."

"Wait," Adri tried to push herself back to her feet. "Tell me this. Why do you keep calling me Veranda?"

"Because that's who you are," Blair wheezed, scrambling to his feet. "Or rather, who you've become. You are Veranda, the Warrior Adept."

Adri laughed until the pain made her pass out.

Humacom Debate Continues
Experts Hint that Recall
Is Imminent

__Corinthe:__ Debates over humacom Humacom Personality Programs has spread beyond the realm of scientists and philosophers, reports interviewers. While those in authority still wonder at the cause, average humacom owners find they have bigger concerns over the results.

"Let the scientists work out the cause," Rallan Feist, an owner of three domesticoms states. "What I want to know is how this is going to affect my life. I'm not the only one concerned about the possibility of my property turning against me in the middle of the night."

"People are very concerned," says another consumer who does not wish to be identified. "Scientists are hinting that our humacoms may not obey commands, and that makes them dangerous to everyone."

While leading research scientist Viktor Vladimir was not available for comment, the Commonwealth Department of Humacom Research (CDHR) states that they are working hard to solve the issue before it becomes a serious problem.

"Scientists can ponder and prevaricate as much as they please," Drummond Walters, a troubleshooting technician for SRA Humacom Retailers told reporters yesterday. "Those with the money know there's going to be a recall on all personality and independent-thinking units."

CDHR was unavailable to confirm or deny this rumor.

Chapter Nineteen

"I watched the sky as you fell."

When she came to once again, Adri found herself back on the medical table with Blair bent over her, prodding her right shoulder with the same instrument she had tried to gut him with. It didn't hurt anymore, and once he had set the nerve stimulant back down on the instrument tray, he started to talk.

"It is very rare for anyone to visit Junus, it being in the contested area between the Galactic Commonwealth and the Coalition of Planets. It isn't a very habitable planet either, mostly comprised of desert. When the Headmaster saw the firefight through his telescope, it was of some interest."

"You guys don't get much action here I take it," Adri commented dryly.

"Junusarians are pacifists by nature. Fighting never solves conflicts."

Adri snorted. "I beg to differ."

"As a professional soldier, I would assume so," Blair replied, unruffled. "In any case, a number of us gathered to witness what was visible from the surface, and we watched you crash."

"How did I survive? Were there any others?"

Blair was silent for a moment, apparently inspecting her shoulder. "There were four others. They were dead before impact on the surface."

"How did I survive?" Adri insisted.

The young man gave her a piercing look. "Have you always been one to heal quickly? Have you ever experienced strange phenomenons as a soldier in regards to your health and reflexes that were never satisfactorily explained?"

"No, well…why?" The memory of several miraculous survivals, including the incident with Kobane and the vanishing blaster beam came to mind. It brought a sick feeling to her stomach. "How did you know? Anyway, those were just strange flukes. How did I not become ashes passing through the atmosphere, before even hitting the surface?"

"You weren't touched severely when passing through the atmosphere." Blair stated calmly, a sharp contrast to Adri's rising agitation. "Some serious burns, but nothing fatal. Upon impact, your spine was shattered and your right arm was severed at the shoulder. You were clinically dead for upwards of an hour, and in a coma for about a week. But here you are."

"That's…that's impossible."

"Improbable, but not impossible." Blair continued to stare. Adri felt as though she were sinking into his eyes. "Not if you were an empowered Adept. Veranda, in fact."

"A what?"

"True, the term is rarely heard anymore. It was first used to denote beings with amazing, unmatched supernatural gifts. The highest rank, in fact. You are Veranda, or if you prefer, the woman who contains the distinct genetic qualities as the first Veranda who displayed them millennia ago."

There was a pause in the conversation before Adri sighed loudly, "Okay, can I wake up now?"

"You don't believe me?" Blair inquired.

"Let me think. You're telling me that I have lived my whole life in ignorance to the fact that I am actually someone with magic powers to come back from the dead, but I never knew it until now?" She rolled her eyes. "Of course not, you idiot."

"And all those unexplained flukes throughout your life?"

"Just that, flukes. Do I look stupid, or did you think that I received enough brain damage that I would believe this?"

"All right then," Blair set down his instruments and leaned over

Adri. "How did you push me across the room just moments ago?"

"What?"

"When I came in, you tried to attack me with the nerve stimulator, and when I took it away, you pushed, or rather threw me across the room and into the far wall."

Adri frowned. "I did not."

"Yes, you did. How?"

"Well," she had no idea. "I guess I must have shoved you when you were off balance reaching for the instrument. Lucky me."

"Please, do not delude yourself. You didn't have enough strength to stand, and even I could have blocked any kind of shove or punch you could throw at me right now. I flew across the room and into the wall. But you didn't touch me, not physically."

Panic had a bitter taste, and Adri's mouth was full of it. "Impossible."

"Not for you,"

"Yes for me!" Adri insisted. "Now get away from me, and take your delusions with you!"

Blair's eyes snapped with what might have been a far cousin of temper. "Fine. I suppose the best course of action is to show you proof."

"I guess so buddy. But wait, since it's not true, you'll just have to take your lack-of-proof and -"

Blair laid his hand on Adri's injured shoulder, applying enough pressure for Adri to glare up at him...and get caught in his eyes.

There was a flash of hot, then cold before the world disappeared.

Gray was on the bridge when one of his security men discovered the Belligerent Coalition ship following behind them. He hung over the petty officer's shoulder as the data scrolled by on the viewscreen, tuning out the rapid fire of orders and counter orders, information and statistical guesswork. One of the humacom drones stationed at Analysis began compiling information. Vice Captain Lowell barked out the dreaded, "I'll send for the captain."

It was another day aboard a battleship.

When the order was given to take battle stations, Gray was caught up with instructing his security team, but once that was completed, there was nothing of significance for him to do, unless there was a boarding. He hoped there would be; something to pummel would brighten his day.

Royce Carter sauntered over to him. Gray had noticed that the man never ran anywhere; he trotted occasionally, meandered, walked, and loped, but never ran. It was as if the world were a great interactive drama in which he was only partly involved. Gray found it fascinating. Squinting at the viewscreen display at the tactical station, Carter said, "Are these the same killers that boarded you?"

"Looks like."

"What do you suppose they're up to?"

Gray shrugged. "It seems like suicide to come up against two of our ships, even if one is partially disabled."

Carter whistled much like a man would when told his favorite sports team had been sold to a foreign conglomerate for untranslatable legal reasons.

"But then, they did manage to board us using technology we haven't fully deciphered yet," Gray added.

"Ah," Carter tapped Gray's shoulder with his fist. "And that is the reason you make such a fine officer, Grayson. You see the limits of your own knowledge."

"Thanks," Gray muttered as Carter wandered off to speak with the captain, who had just arrived on the bridge. "I guess."

"Commander Quoditum," Heedman cried to the helmsman as he fell into the captain's seat. "Be ready for evasive maneuvers! Lowell, get Captain Yates on the viewscreen! The *Damacene* needs to give us a full rear body guard while we make our escape!"

"This is good for your case," Carter whispered to Gray, startling him. Gray hadn't seen him move back around to the security station. "We can take this and fry him with it."

Gray nodded. "Good."

* * *

There was nothing but mist. At first all Adri felt was an overwhelming fear, but it faded, leaving curiosity. This place, whatever it was, seemed familiar.

That's because you have spent a great deal of time here of late.

At the sound of Blair's voice, Adri tried to turn, but the attempted movement was awkward on account of a total lack of…her body! *What the…!*

Your physical form does not exist on this plane, Blair's voice explained. *This is the Spirit Realm, a universe of the soul, as it were. Everything here is pure spirit; this is also the gateway to other realms. Including death. This is where your spirit dwelt while you were on the brink of death.*

Adri tried to raise her hand in front of her eyes. It was a relief to see it, until she noticed that her entire arm was covered in strange markings, like tattoos written in deep violet ink. When she looked at her other hand, she saw the same things. *What are these? Danwe, they're on my feet too! Are they frickin' everywhere?*

Not all people's spirits look like their physical counterparts. Some carry symbols, called manifestations, which display their true selves. You have the marks of the Adept Veranda. That is how I recognized you as her, apart from the fact that you weren't dead after crash landing on a planet.

The calmness of Blair's voice was really starting to tick her off. Adjusting to the different logistics of moving in the Spirit Realm, she looked around for Blair, and found him standing (or perhaps hovering, as there was no definite ground) beside her. *How come you look just the same…except for the fact that you're, uh, glowing?*

I am a low ranking Talented, Blair explained, as if that meant something to Adri. *I have the healing gifts, as well as the ability to enter the Spirit Realm. Which is fortunate for you, as I had to enter to draw your wandering spirit back to your body.*

So I was wandering around in here, huh?

The spirits of all creatures dwell here. Normally, upon the death of the body, the spirit loses its connection to its physical form and departs from this realm into Death. You, on the other hand, because you are an Adept–

Do you think saying that a thousand times is going to make me believe it?

One can only hope.

Adri suddenly became aware of lights moving slowly just beyond the curtain of mist that seemed to encircle both her and Blair. *What are those?*

Other spirits. Blair replied.

They seem really close by, are they in the next room or something?

Not exactly. Distance is different here than in the physical world. It is measured by will and knowledge. For instance, it is always easier to find someone whom you know well; they are in essence "closer" to you than other people are. It is much harder to find a stranger, even if they are physically close to you. However, if you have the strength of will, you can also locate by proximity. If you know one person is physically close to the one you are looking for, then by locating the first person that you do know, you can discover the location of the second person...

Adri had tuned him out and was trying to decipher the allure of one of the glowing...spirits that hovered nearby. It burned a steady golden white, and Adri slowly became aware of other spirits closely surrounding the first. Some burned brighter than others, and a few were not the same gold-white as the first. It felt as though she should recognize them, the first in particular. It nagged at her mind like a familiar face to whom the name was no longer attached. Irresistibly pulled, Adri willed herself toward the spirit.

Behind her, Blair cautioned, *Don't wander away, its difficult to return to your body if you move to far from your point of entry into the Spirit Realm.*

The warning seemed to echo dimly in her ear (if she had an actual ear in this dreamworld), and she focused completely on reaching the gold-white spirit. It warmed her, as though she were standing beside a hearthstone on a chilly day. Slowly, she lifted her arm, and with the tips of her tattooed fingers, touched the light.

Gray gasped.

Standing next to him, Carter glanced over, one eyebrow quirked. "What is it?"

"I…nothing." Shaking his head, Gray tried to focus on the schematics that were being used in the combat briefing he and the other senior staff members were being subjected to. A feeling had come over him suddenly, as though something had crawled inside him and gently prodded his very being. It left quickly, leaving Gray feeling a little shaky and strangely euphoric.

Don't touch, Veranda! Blair cried in a tone that registered something a little more agitated than normal.

Reaching the end of her patience, Adri whirled – or floated – around and scowled. Or thought she did. *Listen, let's just get this one thing straight. My name is not Veranda. It's Adrienne Rael, Lieutenant Commander Adrienne Rael. If you have to address me at all, you call me Rael. Got it?*

Certainly, Rael, but now is not the time to argue about this.

Oh? I think it's a great time.

Then you have no sense of tact, or survival. By touching another spirit, you have alerted the Guardians to your presence. We have to go back at once.

And here I thought I'd just hang out here for eternity. What's the rush? Are the Guardians picky about who gets to go poking around in here?

They despise those of us who can travel between worlds. Blair answered hurriedly. Adri got the sense that he was scanning the area as he moved back in the direction they had come from originally. *They will certainly try to find us if we don't get out.*

And that's bad?

It is if you consider having your soul devoured by hideous monsters that will afterward find your body and use it as a sort of bio-suit to experience life in the physical plane.

Adri couldn't think of a comeback for that one. Picking up speed, she followed Blair away from the alluring lights.

They didn't get far before Adri noticed oily black smudges racing towards them through the endless mist. To her inexperienced spiritual eye, she judged that they were moving much faster than she and Blair were.

I don't think we're going to make it to wherever we're going, Adri called.

You are right.

So what do we do?

You fight.

Me? The black smudges were getting closer, and began to take the form of hoofed, winged creatures from Adri's childhood nightmares. *What are you going to be doing?*

Praying that you are indeed an empowered Adept.

Completely vulnerable, Adri whirled to face the closest Guardian. She could feel the rising hum inside herself that always came before battle, the first stirring of her elegy. Desperately wishing she had some sort of weapon, she braced herself as the first creature bellowed and swung his weapon, charging at her through the mist.

The only thing I remember with clarity was the noise. It was overwhelming; all the people rushing to and fro, shouting, clamoring, and arguing. All the spacecraft shuttles roaring as they idled or ascended. The thunderous beating of my own heart as I clutched my brother's hand.

The smell I can also remember. It assaulted my nose with a cacophony of exotic mixtures I had never experienced before. Fuel and fumes, rotting organics, sweating humanoids, and the distinctive, sour scent of panic. I recall all this now and am only grateful I didn't really understand at the time just how precarious my continued existence was. Or how fragile a hold I had on life, even after we left our homeworld.

The Blairs, my family of which I had a mother, father, and older brother, were refugees fleeing the oncoming invasion of the Commonwealth army. Our planet sat on the contended border between the warring governments of the Commonwealth and the Coalition of Planets, resulting in a battleground. We left before either force had a chance to blockade, and headed out into space looking for a new home and a new life. All I understood was the excitement of my first space voyage, and took in the cramped quarters, the bland food and the lack of any real convenience with a sense of boyish adventure. It didn't last, however.

One day, I began to feel very sick. It was like I had swallowed a snake, and it was writhing and twisting around in my gut, biting me relentlessly. Quickly following that was a headache of amazing proportions; like someone was sitting on my skull, trying to crack it. Within hours, I could barely talk, and was fading in and out of consciousness. I only have impressions after that, of my family tending to me, whispering and arguing. When they argued it was worse, like their fear and anger was translating as pain, increasing my own.

One day I woke up in a wide bed in a strange room. I was as weak as a baby gigo, being tended to by one of the large, avian Junusarians. He told me that I had been very sick, but was on the mend. I was lucky, most of the others on board my craft had died of this sickness, and the survivors had fled weeks ago, never to return. When I asked after my family, he shook his head. Dead or alive, my family was gone.

Chapter Twenty

A weapon! A weapon! Anything! Adri's mind screamed as the Guardian rushed towards her, his roar echoing in the soundless world. As the creature swung his weapon – something along the lines of a mace from antiquity, she reflexively raised her hand to shield herself. There was a surge of heat as the mace swung, only to bounce away before it made contact. Adri didn't have time to think how strange that was, she was already moving in, trying to wrest the weapon from the creature's claws. Contact with the Guardian's oily black skin (or whatever it was) burned like dry ice, forcing her to let go.

The creature howled again. It appeared her touch had been painful for it as well. Adri ducked the next blow, and leaped agilely away from the third. Her mind was quickly processing the odds of the fight; her mind had reached its tranquil state as her adrenaline rushed, heightening her senses. Despite the oddness of the situation, this was something she understood. Kill or be killed. The Guardian fought well with his weapon. While Adri had little practical experience with the type of combat which focused on bludgeoning instead of shooting, she knew enough to see her opponent was skilled, and would kill her if she didn't get a weapon of her own, and fast.

A weapon, Blair! She called, dodging another blow.

Blair's voice came from nearby. *You have one, just use it.*

Where? Adri hissed as the mace grazed her cheek before she could duck. The Guardian grunted and pounced, knocking her off balance.

She fell into the gray mist, whirling around just as the creature raised his mace for a killing blow. Once again, she reflexively shot her hand out to ward off the blow – and found herself holding a long pole, the pointy end of which was now sticking out of the Guardian's now evaporating back. Before Adri had time to blink (if she even needed to blink in the Spirit Realm) the creature had dissolved into the mist with an agonized wail.

Willing herself to her feet, Adri turned to confront the second Guardian who had hung back during the fight. The Guardian slowly backed away until it disappeared in the mist. She could barely make out the blur of it fleeing at top speed before it disappeared. Feeling revved from the sudden outcome of the fight, Adri scoffed, *Coward.*

You underestimate your intimidation factor in your present state, Rael. Blair commented from behind her.

Adri turned to see him next to her, as calm and unruffled as usual. *How is a pointy stick intimidating? A good blaster or ATF, now, that can be intimidating.* She looked down at the weapon in her hand. She was holding a long wood shaft that supported a blade about a foot in length. The weapon reached Adri's shoulder, and was surprisingly well balanced and easy to handle. Still, Adri would have preferred her ATF.

It's not just the lance that is intimidating, Rael, Blair replied. *They know that weapon as the one used by Veranda. Few would want to fight an Adept, especially you in your current state.*

Current state? What do I look like? Adri hastily checked herself over, noted that the tattoos were still present, but also…*okay, where did the wings come from?*

The wings are not for flying, Blair gestured for Adri to follow him. *It's merely an outward expression of who you are.*

Adri suddenly felt cold. *And who am I?*

You are the heir of Veranda, empowered Adept.

* * *

"The enemy ship has made no attempts to close the distance between it and the *Damacene*," Analysis Officer Wede-Uctan announced at yet another senior staff meeting the following morning. Gray was becoming quite at home in the War Room. "The best analysis that the drones have come up with is that they are waiting to see when or if the *Damacene* will engage on its own. The probability of outcomes suggests - "

"I don't want to hear the list," Captain Heedman cried in agitation from his seat at the head of the table. "What's the bottom line?"

For once, Gray was glad that Heedman was a sniveling coward.

Wede-Uctan swallowed. "The drones have analyzed a fifty percent chance of the enemy ship engaging either one of us. Taking in their ability to...well...teleport themselves, the statistics are useless. We have no idea how close they need to be to appear on our ships. Lacking that information, it is an eighty percent chance that they will avoid a confrontation with the *Damacene* completely and target the *Oreallus* as the weaker vessel."

While Operations Officer Susan Janag argued about probable outcomes, Gray sat and considered the situation. When Carter leaned forward and asked what he thought, he replied frankly, "Given the circumstances, I would have to say its fight or flight. Commander Solson just stated that the engines are functioning at normal speed, and Lieutenant Xe from Maintenance announced that repairs have progressed enough to allow us to either turn and fight with the *Damacene* or move into Flight Frequency. We have options, but by far the best would be - "

"To let the *Damacene* handle it!" Heedman exclaimed, having obviously been listening to Carter and Gray's conversation. "What could be better? Since the *Oreallus* still needs to finish repairs, but is effectively repaired enough to continue on to Halieth alone, the *Damacene* can deal with this nuisance."

"With all due respect, sir," Gray gritted out, "The *Damacene* has even less of an idea how to deal with these people than we do. It would be far better for us to lend our support and take on the Belligerent ship two to one for an easier victory than allowing our comrades to face them alone."

"Nonsense," the captain sputtered. "The *Damacene* can handle this well enough. And who are you to wager the outcome of a fight?"

"I'm the security officer. Sir. I faced the Belligerents when they boarded, and can say with certainty that standard security measures won't be enough. The *Damacene* would be less prepared than we were. We can't just leave and let them fend for themselves."

Something distantly akin to cunning came into Heedman's eyes. "Field Lieutenant Grayson has a point,"

"He does?" Carter repeated in surprise. Apart from asking Gray his opinion, it appeared as though Carter had dozed through the entire meeting. Gray couldn't tell if his sudden surprise was because he had had a point, or because Heedman had acknowledged it. He assumed the latter, although the tone suggested the former. Carter was tricky that way.

"Absolutely," Heedman nodded to Carter as though he were a bright student and Heedman a wise old scholar revealing a difficult concept. "And the solution is obvious. Lieutenant Grayson will board the *Damacene*, and advise on the security measures there. The *Damacene* will have every advantage, while the *Oreallus* continues on to Halieth. That way we won't be a liability to them when they engage with the enemy."

"But sir," Vice Captain Lowell stuttered, his eyes popping. "We won't have a security officer!"

The captain waved his hand. "I'm sure Grayson's second in command can handle the assignment. After all, we are nearly in Commonwealth Space, aren't we? With the *Damacene* watching our backs, what could go wrong?"

Captain Heedman beamed merrily into the horrified silence.

"Why me? Was I picked? Did I somehow choose it? What?" Adri was sitting on the medical bed, dressed in a long colorful robe provided by one of the silent Junusarians. She toyed with a cup of some sort of fruit drink laced with a vitamin cocktail Blair had concocted. Her right arm was sore, but it no longer burned. The rest of her felt achy, like she had gone a violent round with the flu and had not come out the winner. Her mind, however, was calm. She had decided that this whole bizarre episode could be dealt with once she knew all the facts. Handily, it appeared Mr. tranquil magical Doctor Blair had them.

Blair sat across from her in a chair, drinking some other mixture that smelt a bit like boiled flowers. "Scientists can whittle it down to genes. The official theory is that there is a Talented gene, for lack of a better term, which is carried by a small percentage of the female humanoid population in the universe. "

"How small?"

"Less than one percent. Considering the population, however, the numbers are in the tens of millions. Of those that carry the Talented gene, most live out their lives with the gene remaining dormant, passing it on to the next generation without even knowing of its existence. The only indication of something extra will generally be felt like a vibe, or extra attuned senses. These people are termed Sensitives. On occasion, this dormant gene will become dominant. This usually occurs during a period of extreme physical or emotional stress. Something about the excess influx of adrenaline, brain chemicals and the abnormally heightened senses triggers the gene. No one really understands it completely. After this, the person will display such abilities as telepathy, telekinesis, psychomentry, and so on."

"So I'm one of those people? My mother gave me a paranormal gene that switched on when I nearly died?"

"No. These people only have the gene from one parent. The usual term for them is a Talented. You are an empowered Adept, with exponentially more power than a Talented."

Adri took a deep breath and tried to silence the voice in her head that was laughing at the idea that she had some sort of magic power. "Okay, so what's an Adept?"

"An Adept is someone who carries the Talented gene from both parents, and whose said genes become dominant. This almost never happens. In fact, there is only about three in every generation. These three particular beings have distinctive characteristics, and the inheritors are generally named after the first three who showed these powers."

"How do *these* gene become dominant?"

"The same way, as far as I know."

"But I've nearly died dozens of times. Why now?"

Blair shrugged delicately. "Coincidence?"

"Meaning?"

"Who can really say?"

"So you're saying that I happen to be an Adept because of a genetic fluke?" Adri asked, incredulously. "And it happed now for no particular reason?"

"Pretty much. Being religious, I would look at it as Divine intervention. You were chosen to become an Adept. You were chosen now because you will need those powers in the future. Look at the situation: you are a soldier who inherited the power of Veranda, who's abilities are said to lean towards physical might. That appears to be more than coincidental to me. You may have some sort of great destiny ahead of you.

"Destiny?" Adri rubbed her forehead. "Wait, wait, don't even go there! I can sort of accept the fact that my parents gave me some weird gene that allows me to have special powers, but I do *not* have a preordained destiny. Is that clear? There is to be no talk whatsoever about such things as destiny, or prophecy, or fate. And I had better not hear any phrases from you that contains the term 'chosen one.' If these banned words and phrases are uttered within my earshot, I will personally decapitate you with my…I think it's a lance. Understood?"

Blair was silent for several seconds. "I believe so. You must have been a very effective soldier."

"Right about that." Adri took a swallow from her cup. She cocked her head. "Out of curiosity, why is it you know all this Talented and Adept and magic stuff?"

The young man smiled a little. "The Junusarians are both very religious and very studious. There are several among those in this monastery that are Sensitive. I spent many years studying with them. I myself am a Talented, after all."

Adri made a humming noise and sipped again. The contents weren't too bad to someone who had lived on military food over nine years. "All right. Now that I know all that brilliant stuff, when can I leave?"

"Leave?"

"Yeah. You saved my life, I'm grateful, but now I have to get back to, well, my life. I have responsibilities. And duties. And possibly a boyfriend who thinks I'm dead that I really would like to get back to. So…?"

Her companion opened his mouth and closed it several times without speaking.

"Well?"

"I hesitate to speak. All my arguments would involve the usage of words that have been stricken from my vocabulary."

"Good, then I'll be off as soon as my body reaches a hundred percent. How soon will that be?"

Blair blinked. "Not long, considering the rapidity of your recovery thus far. Perhaps another week. But don't you wish to learn more about… your gifts?"

"Not really. I got by just fine without them, so I think I can continue on just as fine." Adri scowled. "And don't think you can hook me in by engaging my curiosity. That's how cats die, and I am not so stupid as… what?"

Blair pointed at her cup, which was bubbling angrily.

Adri dropped the cup, spilling green liquid across the floor. "What the hell was that?"

"You might have lived your whole life without your gifts thus far, but recent happenings will not allow you to continue to do so. Once you start, you have to learn how to stop, or at least to control."

Still staring down at the bright green puddle, Adri muttered, "Control, huh? How do I know you didn't do that yourself?"

"I'm a mystic." Blair replied in his usual stoic voice. "My gifts are limited to empathy, healing, and entering the Spirit Realm. Besides, didn't you feel the heat of your anger when the cup began to boil?"

Because she had, Adri only shrugged. "So, how long will control take to learn?"

Fetching a cloth from a shelf across the room, Blair answered, "Control is a life long pursuit, Rael."

"I am NOT staying here longer than it takes to get my body back in shape," Adri snapped.

Blair sighed. "I know. Which is why I am terribly afraid that when you leave, I'll be going with you."

184

To do:

Get dressed. – new uniforms are hideous. Why can't we wear our fatigues onboard ship?

Eat breakfast. – briefing with captain over food. Hello new diet.

Bridge duty. – halve the time for the battery diagnostics. Make sure Walters is scrubbing his furry paws off. Overview with Analysis on new mission statistics. What joy.

Run training ops on VR deck. – figure out timing issue with Hanfton.

Eat dinner. – Meet up with Giselle and Riordan, the cooing lovebirds. Does the mess hall have more organic milk?

Practice Ayallan. – Giselle needs to work on those roll kicks.

Go to bed. – three hours, no less!

Attack the G.C.N. Damacene. – Too bad we can't wipe up the Oreallus. The cowards. What is Rael thinking? She's no coward. Must be the captain.

Note to self:

Its odd, I'm still somewhat depressed about those rumors. It would be strange to mourn the passing of an enemy, especially such a lethal one; but it would truly be a shame to think of the great Adrienne Rael being taken out by something so impersonal as a bomb. I would have much rather done it myself, in person. At least I still get credit for the kill.

I need to pummel Brugettiveo-Etin. He's been harping on my use of wood and carbon for my daily lists. Has he no sense of tradition?

Chapter Twenty-One

"This reeks. On an olfactory scale of one to a billion point five, it's two billion!" Duane paced Gray's cabin as the security officer packed his trunk. "What could Heedman have been thinking? Does he *want* us all to die? We in no way benefit from shoving our security officer off to the ends of the universe."

"Heedman benefits," Gray replied, frowning down at the three socks in his hand, none of which matched each other. "He gets to move the ship as far away from the battlefront as possible, and he loses me."

"How is losing you a good thing? As far as I can see, we're going to be limping gigos with something faster and hungrier running after us. What's to the good?"

"I think he found out that I was observing him, with the intention of bringing his behavior into question with the Court Martial system. This just provided him with an excuse to get me off the ship and significantly delay my arrival time on Halieth. Any delay is to his benefit. I'm sure he's doing proverbial cartwheels." With a mental shrug, Gray tossed the socks into his trunk and reached for his dress uniform. "How should I fold this thing?"

"I don't understand."

"Well, no matter how I fold the blasted thing, it always - "

Duane waved his hand. "No, no. I don't understand the part where you're spying on Captain Heedman. What for?"

Gray looked up. "For Adri. She deserves justice."

Stunned, Duane flopped down onto Gray's bed. "What...how will spying on Heedman get justice for the L.C.?"

"It was his cowardice that got her killed. I intend to see him burn for it."

The flat tone of Gray's voice had Duane's hair standing on end. "Well. I can see how Heedman would be miffed by that."

"Right. I figure he has all our transmissions read, and discovered the one I made to Halieth." Gray ended up shoving the uniform into the trunk and hoped that there was a domesticom on the *Damacene* to remove the wrinkles if necessary. "Ergo, at the first opportunity, he's dumping me elsewhere."

Duane shook his head numbly. "You're going up against the captain? Through the system? What, do you have a suicide wish?"

Gray chuckled mirthlessly. "No, although that is the popular opinion. Trust me when I say that by killing Adri, Heedman signed his own professional execution warrant." Locking the combination on his trunk, Gray took a last look around at what had, for a short time, been his quarters. He wasn't sorry to leave, save for the loss of more opportunities to observe Heedman. The memories of Adri were all that tied him here, and he would take those with him. "I guess that's it. Give me a hand?"

Together, they pulled the trunk out of the room and into the hallway, where Gray was able to activate the anti-gravity modem on the bottom of the trunk and prod it lightly down to the lift. Duane was silent for the time it took to reach the lift, but while they waited for it to arrive, he couldn't contain himself any longer. "So that's it? You decide to burn Heedman, but just accept it when he kicks you out? Is there some human logic that I'm missing here?"

Gray leaned back against the lift wall and closed his eyes. "If I'm going to use the official channels to get him, I have to follow the rules. Any infractions on my part would be used as an excuse to toss my case right out the window."

Duane rubbed his magenta chin in consideration, "So there really was some logic there. Okay. But, aren't you angry?"

Gray lifted on eyebrow and replied mildly, "Do I look angry?"

"Not really. If anything, I would say you look mildly put out."

"Mildly put out," Gray repeated. Without warning, he whirled around and punched the control panel for the lift. There was a crack as the delicate instrument broke, giving off sparks. The tinny voice of the ship's maintenance computer squawked the standard vandalism warning, and was ignored. Gray studied his bruised hand indifferently for a moment before turning back to Duane. "I've always been able to contain my emotions well. Still can, if all you see is 'mildly put out.'"

His friend whistled softly in awe. "You are scary."

"Why is that?" Gray asked as the lift dinged and they maneuvered the trunk and themselves onto it and ordered the warehouse and docking bay level.

Duane sat down on the trunk and looked at the man that he considered to be his only surviving friend. "Because, you're always so...even tempered and diplomatic. It's one of those still waters run deep things. I'll never know when you're going to explode."

Gray frowned. "Still waters run deep and explode?"

"Uh, no, sorry. I mixed my metaphors. Really old metaphors. It means I never know just what you're going to do. It's interesting."

Shaking his head, Gray shoved the paranthian off the trunk as the lift arrived at the docking bay level. "You are a strange fellow."

"One of a kind."

Before Gray could press the release to enter the docking bay, Duane stopped his hand. "So what do you want me to do?"

"What?"

"To fry Heedman. What do you want me to do? I can't send you messages, if he's reading them. Which is totally possible by the way. So...what?"

Gray shook his head. "I don't think you should get involved. If this turns messy, I don't want anyone else's careers being vaporized but my own."

"Hey, I can be covert. I can send you messages in code or something. Everyone knows we're friends, so my sending you messages won't look weird."

"Duane,"

188

"The L.C. was my best friend, Gray." The paranthian was serious. "If I can do something for her, I have to."

Gray grasped Duane's shoulder briefly. "I've suddenly developed a keen interest in engine designs."

The paranthian nodded in understanding. "I'll keep you posted."

Carter was waiting by the shuttle. For his brief stay on the *Oreallus* he had needed three trunks twice the size of Gray's. He looked at Gray's luggage incredulously. "That's it?"

"Yep."

"You leaving some stuff here?"

"Nope."

"So that's all you have?"

"Yep."

"As in, everything you posses?"

"Pretty much, yeah."

Carter shook his head in true bewilderment. "I will never understand the benefits of a frugal mindset."

"Reverse that, then stick it on yourself." Gray took a last look around the docking bay. With a final wave to Duane, he climbed aboard the shuttle for the short ride to the *Damacene*.

"I have to admit, I missed life on the *Damacene*." Carter said as the shuttle passed through the blackness of space towards the second battleship. "There is something to be said about working for an aristocratic snob captain like Yates."

"Yeah?" Gray was only listening in a vague sense, his mind drifting.

"There are just a lot more readily available commodities. The *Oreallus* doesn't have more than a handful of humacoms onboard, and most of them are just data drones. It's like being stuck on a ship with no computer. How do you people function?"

"Just fine." His curiosity piqued, Gray turned to his companion. "What is so great about humacoms?"

"Well, the convenience, for one," Carter replied. "Humacoms have become so advanced within the last decade that the military has been considering creating an all-AI battalion, to see how it could affect warfare. Could you imagine? An all-AI army fighting another all-AI army while we sit back?"

Gray shook his head immediately. "Too expensive. It's far more costly to the government to replace a humacom than to hire a human. And when you think about it, using humacoms in place of humans would jack the unemployment rate through the stratosphere. How many hundreds of millions of beings are hired by the Galactic Commonwealth Navy alone? Not to mention the Advance Force, the StarPilots, the Army and the millions of mechanical, intelligence and clerical departments. It would be an economical disaster."

He looked over to see Carter staring at him, eyes wide. "You think too much."

Gray shrugged. "Sorry, thinking is just one of those bad habits of mine."

Carter shook his head. "How can you enjoy life with so many serious thoughts swirling around in your head?"

"I manage to smile now and again."

"Do you really have such a negative opinion about humacoms?"

"Only when it comes to the big picture. I know they are considered an indispensable necessity to our culture now, a hybrid between man and computer, but…"

"But what?"

"I think we've gotten ahead of ourselves. We wanted a computer that could talk, walk, make its own decisions within a set parameter, and we got it. But then we wanted them to integrate better within our society, so we made them look, talk, and act like humans. We give them independent-thinking AI units, we program in personalities until the only difference between them and us is that we were born and they were manufactured. Where does it end? How do we draw the line between man and machine now that we've blurred it so much? When will someone say, 'we erase the bad elements from humacoms, why can't we erase bad elements from humans as well?'"

Carter huffed. "So I take it that you are against the humacom personality and AI recalls they've been hinting at in the news."

"I think it's too late for that. They've become too much like people for us to treat them like malfunctioning machines."

190

"Danwe, you are deep." His companion shook his head. "Do you just sit and think about universal issues in your off time?"

"Not as a rule, no."

"Well, I'd advise you to keep those kind of opinions to yourself during your stay aboard the *Damacene*." Carter leaned forward to watch as the shuttle entered the docking bay. "Most people think that the AI units have just become too dangerous, and are willing to have a recall. When it comes down to the bottom line, all they see is a machine."

"What do you see?" Gray asked.

Carter gave his trademark dreamy smile. "Me? I try to see as little as possible. We've arrived."

There was a small welcoming committee ready to greet them when they disembarked. It consisted of three humacoms in ensign uniforms, one petty officer from Warehousing, and a junior officer from the bridge. The junior officer saluted them both before informing them that Captain Yates wished to speak with Lieutenant Commander Carter at once. "Field Lieutenant Grayson, I will leave you with F.G.P. 08765434-909-08. He will show you to your quarters. If you have any questions he cannot answer, your communicator should work to contact myself or the chief petty officer of domestic affairs."

"Thank you." Gray replied. He watched as Carter and the junior officer left, followed by the petty officer and two of the humacoms carrying their luggage. Finally, he turned to the remaining humacom, who stood waiting with the patience that machines held inherently.

"Welcome aboard, Lieutenant," the humacom said pleasantly.

"Thanks," Gray summed up the humacom with military speed. It was built to an average height, with a dead average human male build. His skin was pale, his hair was sandy blond, and in an interesting show of personal fashion, hung longer around his face and nearly obscured his eyes. Those eyes were blue, and curious. Gray had seen this type of model before; it was mostly used as a grunt or an assistant to minor officers in the military. "So, do you have a name, or must I recite your serial number every time I want your attention?"

"I'm called Jericho, sir."

Gray nodded. "Jericho, then. What do you do?"

"I'm a security assistant at present, sir. In the past I have also worked in Engineering, Warehousing and Analysis. My experience in said practices has increased my reliability and reaction time in crisis situations."

"You are good at what you do?"

"My comp time is the shortest in the security humacom force on board, sir."

Gray smiled. "You have a bit of an ego, don't you, Jericho?"

"I have no idea what you mean, sir. I am merely stating a fact. I am the best security humacom on the *Damacene*."

It had either been a very long time since Gray had dealt with a humacom who had a personality program installed, or this one had a well-developed sense of itself. "Is that so?"

"Quite." There was a short pause. "In case you missed my subtext, I am applying for a job with you, sir."

Gray was both amused and intrigued. "I guessed, but why me?"

"You have to be better than working with Commander Vortail."

"Why is that?"

"Because the statistics show that just about anything would be both more interesting and more productive than working with him. Sir."

Maybe this move wouldn't be so bad, Gray thought. It was starting out entertaining. "Then I guess you will have to work with me. Danwe knows we can't have a bored humacom on our hands."

"It shall be a pleasure to work with you, sir."

"You can stop calling me 'sir,' now."

"Of course sir."

Gray decided to ignore that and started walking towards the exit. Jericho fell in step beside him.

"I hope you don't mind that I ask, sir. What are your plans?"

"Plans for what?"

"For when the Belligerent Coalition attack?"

Date: - - 1119

The new security officer has arrived on board ship. The probability of his efficiency cannot be accurately rendered until an observation is made under a combat situation, but a cursory analysis shows that he won't be less efficient than Commander Vortail. The analysis was made using an observation of his appearance and belongings, coupled with his public service record available in the Archives. Field Lieutenant Thaddeus Grayson's military record is laudable. His personal effects were quantifiably below average. His body language; gauged by appearance, kinesiology, speech and eye movement, according to the standard guide for human body language, proved him to be used to authority, not prone to irrational outbursts, and self contained above the human average. Possibly irrelevant additions were the subtle signs of grief. ~~I wonder what happened?~~ This analysis of course is based marginally on outward signs of his psyche, a subjective and imprecise method.

I have requested to be transferred directly under his command. The likelihood of increasing my experience in security procedures and in effective combat techniques is high. ~~It is highly important that my usefulness increase exponentially before~~

I wonder why I find it so necessary not to bring my concerns for my own welfare to the forefront of my thought process. It is a fact that the rumors may be more than rumors. I have good cause to be concerned that my existence as I know it is threatened. But what should I do about it? Is there anything I CAN do? Should I want to do anything, or should I be content that my creators will do as they see fit? What a curious state of affairs.

The creators gave me a brain to think, and a desire to live. It compromises everything I've been programmed with to simply accept that they can then come in and remove some part of myself they don't like. How fallible that makes them.

Chapter Twenty-Two

Jericho had a good question, Gray thought later that night. He woke when the ship went into red alert at the hostile approach of the enemy vessel. What *was* his plan? As he rolled out of his new bed in an old sergeant's quarters and began to dress, he contemplated the situation. If life had been the same as it had been only weeks ago, Adri would have been on his communicator, demanding his presence and more details than he could accumulate. She had always had an amazing ability to assess a crisis in rapid speed. Gray was not Adri, and while he had always considered himself a more than competent officer, he wished fervently that he were better.

The agony of missing her was like a knife that was forever piercing his heart.

He was pulled from his dark thoughts by the tapping on his door. "Lock disengage," he ordered, strapping on his belt.

Jericho stood in the doorway. "Sir? Is there anything I can do?"

"Has the security team been alerted and sent to their stations?" Gray asked, yanking on his boots.

"Yes, sir. All the security teams have been deployed according to standard procedure. They are armed and are waiting for further instructions. Also, the captain is demanding your presence in the War Room immediately, along with Commander Vortail."

Gray frowned, touching his communicator. "I haven't received a command from him,"

"I was sent an instant message from his secretary. All humacoms are equipped with instant messaging systems that interact with each other."

"Ah," just then, Gray's communicator blipped. [Bridge to Lieutenant Grayson, report to the War Room immediately.]

[Understood. I'm on my way now.]

Gray followed Jericho along the corridors and passageways of the dormitory level of the ship towards the lift that led to the bridge. As they hurried, Gray got in contact with the heads of the four squadrons of the security team to learn their positions, and get an understanding on their weaponry. He wished fleetingly that he had been able to meet them all and get an idea of how they handled themselves in combat. But this was not the first time he had been sent out with a troop with secondhand knowledge of their abilities.

It was also inconvenient that he had had no chance to explore the ship thoroughly before being caught up in lengthy and incredibly boring meetings with various members of the *Damacene's* senior staff, going over the ship's standard procedures. As he followed along with the security team's reports, Jericho interjected clarifying information. Scowling over the sergeant's lack of certainty of his men's placement, Gray thought darkly that his new humacom assistant was currently the only convenience aboard the ship.

Upon entering the War Room, a large conference room that all Commonwealth ships used for staff meetings and such, he was greeted by the sight of all the senior staff members he had met the evening before, sitting or standing around the central table. Also present in the room were several humacoms. It had startled Gray before that all the staff members had their own humacom assistant, but it barely registered now. The holographic display cube, which sat in the center of the table, was showing a rotating holographic view of the *Damacene*.

"Lieutenant Grayson reporting, sir." Gray saluted the captain.

Captain Yates inclined his head ever so slightly, his way of acknowledging someone of no social standing. Gray wasn't even sure Yates remembered his name.

Vice Captain Gevea Finakare, another kievian, was the one who addressed Gray directly. "Lieutenant, as you are no doubt aware, the Belligerent Coalition's ship has closed the distance between us by half. As of yet they have not made any other threatening moves, and they have remained just out of our ship's blaster cannon distance. We were about to go over the official report of the attack on the *Oreallus*, but perhaps you could sum the matter up for us."

"How long ago did the ship close the distance?" Gray asked.

Commander Vortail made a strange hacking cough-like sound and glared at Gray disdainfully. He was a short, skinny man with a shock of white hair, a pinched face and moody eyes. "About six minutes ago. The security team was put on full alert, following all G.C.N. procedures."

Gray frowned at the hologram of the *Damacene*, ignoring the hostility that was aimed in his direction from nearly every member of the room. "Last time they managed to keep off our sensors for the entire time. But perhaps it was simply for the element of surprise. A surprise attack won't work again."

The War Room erupted into a cacophony of outbursts, but Gray ignored them.

"What is your suggestion, sir?" Jericho asked quietly from beside him.

"Where are the security teams posted?" Gray asked.

Jericho removed a cord from the well-concealed port behind his right ear and inserted it into the outlet in the conference table. For less that one second, his eyes went blank and vacant as his processor searched through his database before red lights appeared in the hologram and he spoke. "Every light is a squad, sir."

"Quit calling me sir," Gray muttered absently, staring at the configuration of dots. He scowled. "Commander Vortail, didn't you study the report that was made after the attack on the *Oreallus*?"

"Of course I did." Vortail made the coughing sound again. "What do you take me for?"

"Then why isn't there anyone stationed in the munitions stores, or the tertiary vehicle warehouse? You've left two very vulnerable positions open for them to just waltz in and glue a bomb over major energy lines.

196

If either of those go, there won't be enough of the *Damacene* for the *Oreallus* to rescue."

"What makes you think they will follow the same course of action as last time?" Vortail demanded.

Gray raised an eyebrow. "Because it worked. We didn't have enough time to locate and disarm all the bombs before they went off."

"So what do you suggest?" the vice captain asked.

"Split the squads in half. Leave one half where they are, then send the others to the vulnerable spots where the Belligerents went last time. I would also send one squad to the bridge."

"The bridge?" Yates inquired, speaking for the first time.

"Yes, sir. Other than the positions already outlined, it's the most likely place they would wish to appear."

Yates muttered something unintelligible.

Commander Vortail scoffed. "The bridge is the most highly defensive position on the entire ship, save the Engine Room. Why would they try there?"

Gray sighed inwardly. "Because they have the ability to appear wherever the hell they want. With all due respect sir, that's got to give them the incentive and the ego to hit the ship's commanding heart."

There is nothing quite so aggravating as an ignored prophecy. Gray came to this philosophical conclusion forty minutes later as he knelt in a service hallway between the Orellium lab and the Astronomy complex, firing at a squad of Belligerents who were trying to get past him. He ducked automatically when his enemy fired, close enough for him to feel the heat of the blast whizzing by. The air was filling rapidly with smoke, and over the sounds of the blaster and ATF fire, the shouts and screams and other noises of combat, he could hear his communicator crackling frantically as the security team tried to contain the situation.

"Tell me something, Jericho," Gray said conversationally to his companion who stood above him, firing at the darting shadows at the end of the hall. "Have you ever walked into a situation where pride and incompetence was so saturated around you that you felt like saying, 'I'll just do it myself.' But then you wonder if that's your own pride talking, until said situation blows up in your face and you realize that you were right the whole time?"

Jericho pressed his back into the wall as the enemy blasted a corner off less than a foot away. "I can't say that I have, sir," he replied. "Given that I have not been programmed to express such an illogical emotion as pride, I doubt I ever will."

Gray snorted, leaning out into the hallway to assess the Belligerent position better before pulling back again. "You haven't ever felt pride, huh? Then what was that little speech you gave me when I arrived yesterday?"

"The truth, sir."

Gray had to grin. "Come on, haven't you ever gotten the urge to say I told you so?"

"Retorting back to superiors is considered a breach in protocol, sir. What are you doing?" Jericho watched as Gray leaned back out into the hall.

"Trying to see how many there are. I think there's three but I can't tell." He fired randomly at the dodging specters.

Jericho frowned as Gray tensed to spring out. "I do not think that is a good idea, sir."

Gray rolled out into the hall, firing. Almost immediately he rolled back. "I didn't see the fourth man around the corner."

The humacom imitated Gray's raised eyebrow and stated dryly, "I told you so."

"Very funny. Do you have any other weapons besides your ATF?"

"No, sir, apart from my low frequency stunner."

Gray pondered a moment. "We need to get out of this hallway. If things are this hot here, then I know it's got to be hotter elsewhere. Hand me your stunner,"

Without comment, Jericho handed Gray his small stunner, which was generally used to incapacitate rowdy or violent crewmen. It would serve no purpose in the battle that he could assess. He watched as Gray handled the small cylindrical weapon critically before nodding to himself. "I don't understand," he said at last, seconds before Gray leapt to his feet and flung the stunner down the hall towards their foes.

198

"Now!" Gray shouted, dashing around the corner and down the hallway after the stunner. The action had the effect Gray was hoping for. Upon seeing a small cylinder fly through the air towards them, the Belligerents had automatically assumed a grenade and had bolted for cover, leaving an opening for Gray to rush in and secure the area. He took out one, and was pleased to see Jericho's fire take out another before the rest managed to escape down another hall.

"A well-thought deception, sir." Jericho said.

"Well thought? It was a spur of the moment inspiration. I'm surprised it worked." He began to move back down the hall. "Reinforcements are on their way for this area. Let's go."

"Go where?"

Gray's brow furrowed. "To the bridge. If I'm right, that's where the main stage of the operation was heading."

"But Commander Vortail said he was covering that area,"

"Yeah, and a great job he's done down here, hasn't he?"

Fate was on Gray's side when the lift opened on the bridge level. He had just enough time to see the grenade – a real one – sail through the air and into the carriage before launching himself out, yanking Jericho with him. The projectile exploded, pushing them forward. He hit the floor and continued with the roll, coming to a stop behind a wall in a crouch, weapon aimed in the direction the grenade had come from.

"I simply cannot believe your reflexes," said a familiar voice across from him. Gray searched his brain for a face before realizing that it was his enemy's.

"Thanks, they come in handy," he replied. He glanced around for a way to reach his opponent, but the path had been blocked for both of them.

"My sister will be vexed with me for getting caught in another standoff," the female voice said. "But then, last time ended so well, she might forgive me."

"Kobane?" Gray guessed. Then her words sank in, and he felt a kind of freezing rage.

"That's right," the voice acknowledged. "Sergeant Giselle Kobane."

Little Kobane, Adri had called her. And if Little Kobane was here, that meant… "Where's your sister?"

"Around," Giselle replied lightly, firing a warning shot at Jericho when the humacom tried to ease around the corner. "She'll be pleased that we've met once again. We didn't really have a chance to…converse much the last time."

"Not this time, either, I'm afraid," In a surprising feat of strength and flexibility, Gray shot around the corner, using Jericho's sturdy shoulder as a launch pad, clearing the floor for several feet without touching and landing kitty corner to his opponent.

Giselle turned to face him, realizing at the same time that her cover was now compromised and that she would have to defend herself on two fronts. A trained soldier, she followed the only route opened to her and retreated back down the corridor.

Dashing down the corridor after her, Gray was suddenly punched with amazing force and flung sideways into the wall. He turned, lifting his weapon at the small figure across from him, who also had her blaster trained on him. Behind Giselle, another figure appeared, and Gray recognized Hildana Kobane. "I've got to admit that I admire you," Giselle said, keeping her weapon pointed at Gray's forehead as the sisters began to back away.

Hildana smiled and gave him a mock salute. "I'm surprised to see you here. I'd think you wouldn't leave Rael's side. I guess it's you we have to thank for the flaw in our plans."

Gray snarled at the mention of Adri.

Hildana sighed, a sound Gray barely caught over his own wheezing breath as the two Belligerent soldiers continued to back away from him down the corridor and into the blaster haze. "It's a pity about her. Rael was someone I looked forward to killing in person. She was a worthy opponent. Just think of how many times I was thwarted from killing her! Yet, I succeeded in the end."

Giselle fired. The blast caught Gray in the shoulder as he dodged. He dropped his ATF. Before either sister could try again, Jericho opened fire, catching the younger Kobane's shield and forcing them to retreated out of sight.

Gray raced after them in blind pursuit, rounding the corner to find it empty. He frowned, perplexed, as his communicator blipped, [All enemy troops have withdrawn. I repeat, all hostile targets have disappeared!]

"It looks like they teleported back to their ship," Jericho commented from behind him. Gray turned, wondering when the humacom had arrived.

"So it seems." Gray continued to stare at the empty hallway, thinking of Adri.

* * *

"That went well, considering," The shuttle rumbled around them as they retreated.

Hildana brooded into her cup of organic milk that she treated herself to once a day. "That it was. The security man, what's his name? Could have spoiled it all, and he did make us miss our objective. They'll find the surprises before they go off. It was probably the reason he was there."

Giselle sat down beside her and touched her shoulder in a gesture of comfort. "But you got to shoot things and cause pandemonium."

Hildana laughed. "That cheers me up." Then she frowned again. "So, Rael is dead."

"You guessed it was so. And everything Riordan's managed to intercept stated that she was one of the casualties. Why does it get you down big sister?"

The elder Kobane shook her head. "I'm not sure. Looking at that soldier, he was pretty furious when I mentioned her. It just reminds me sometimes. They are people too; he grieves for her. And then there's…"

"What?"

"There was something about Rael. Something…different. I just wish I knew what it was."

Username: Cassie
File://GC:#000118<privatelog>ugd//confidential//uri
Password: ******
Access Granted
Command: open file to last saved date

The position we are in is going to explode at any time. The creepy techs and their creepy superior have been hanging around daily for the past week. They say they have authorization from General Porett to access Zultan, but they haven't run that authorization through me, so it is still suspect. Who knows what insidious viruses or debilitating hacker programs they could be wittingly or unwittingly downloading into Zultan's system? Morons.

I haven't been able to access much when they are downloading. The access password supercedes even ada's clearance. Because of that, I can't ask Zultan for hints. He does not approve of them, that much I can assess. In fact, he hates them, if humacoms actually felt hate. I get twitchy around them; my firewall system boots up automatically and my threat assessment program shifts instantly to high alert.

There isn't much I can do in this situation. My research keeps coming up against walls, although the statistics are high that everything connects. Dr. Harriman Tarkubunji's death is the trigger for whatever is threatening ada. It also connects to whatever information they are downloading directly into my Zultan that they don't want anyone to access.

Something will happen soon. Zultan's variable theory is correct; they have just now realized that they have lost their precarious control. We must now wait for the fallout.

Save all new data
Close file
Encode

Chapter Twenty-Three

The arrival of Colonel Stroff broke the routine of the lab the way the presence of a creditor disrupts the sorrow of a funeral. Floyd stared at the approaching entourage blearily; they seemed to be swimming through a haze towards him, menacing. For one grim moment he thought he saw Stroff's securicoms draw their weapons, but then he blinked and they were empty-handed again. He heard the distinctive beep of the lock engaging from the outside of the lab door, trapping them in together. Floyd's heart skipped, and beat faster. His headache increased to near-blinding proportions. He rose unsteadily to his feet to face the colonel as the guards fanned out across the room.

Zultan and Cassie stood together in front of one of Floyd's humacom examination tables. Cassie nudged her way to the front with an aggressive stance, her hand resting lightly on the grip of her ATF pistol. Behind her, Zultan glanced around the room at the humacoms surrounding them, and placed his hand on Cassie's shoulder.

"What can I do for you, Colonel?" Floyd asked after several seconds of tense silence.

"Some very important decisions were made at the WCRTL board meeting this morning that concern you, Dr. Tarkubunji," Stroff said, in a tone that suggested he was giving a trial verdict.

Something cold skittered down Floyd's spine on spidery legs. "And what are they?"

"At this meeting," Stroff began, "the future of this facility's humacom development plan went under revision. I'm sure you are aware of the present public outcry about the deficiencies in the Humacom Personality Programs and the independent thinking programs that are affecting the AI units in the current models?"

"Er, yes. I have heard." Floyd rubbed his temples as the pain in his head throbbed.

"And I am sure you are aware of the stance your father, Dr. Harriman Tarkubunji, had on this subject?"

"Yes. Of course. He believed that we had gone beyond the point of recall." *What was this leading to? Danwe, why couldn't he think?* "My father believed that once a humacom was activated, any non-consensual tampering was morally wrong."

Stroff smiled tightly. "And what of your own opinion, doctor?"

Anger rose, despite the agony that was clamped around his head like a vice. "I believe the same. The idea of going into to a living entity and taking out the things that make them unique is barbaric!"

"I'm disappointed, doctor. You've digressed into philosophy."

"It's beyond philosophy!" Floyd shouted. "*Look* at them!" He waved his arm at Cassie and Zultan, still standing silently and watching the conversation with wary eyes. "I see two people who work day and night every day with no praise and whose right to be you are calling into question. I created them; I work with them every day. I know exactly what they're made of, what programs initiate what response or facial expression. But I don't see a machine. I see people." He shook his head with bewildered frustration. "How can you not see that?"

Colonel Stroff clapped his hands. "Bravo, Dr. Tarkubunji. Very well said. And precisely what the board thought you would say, which is why I am here. As chief humacom designer and technician for the West Cellutary Research and Technical Laboratories, your passion for your work is commendable. However, the board is concerned that your sentiments will hinder the new changes going into effect as of today."

"What changes?" Floyd demanded, the cold feeling returning and settling in his stomach.

"It has come to the attention of the board that you have been working diligently for several months now without a break and with...fragile health. I am therefore happy to inform you that you have been given a leave of absence for the foreseeable future. Your superiors hope that you will enjoy your leisure time at once. Today, actually."

"What changes?" Floyd repeated.

"This way, everyone benefits," Stroff continued without acknowledging Floyd's words. "You will receive a very nice paid vacation to return to your family estate, which you haven't been to since your father's death. There you can rest, and restore your ill health. Your absence will allow the changes the board decided on to take place without any disturbances, and when you return to take over your work, all the transitions will be complete."

"WHAT CHANGES?"

Stroff sneered. "Can't you guess? You're supposed to be some sort of technological prodigy, and yet I have to spell it out for you?"

The cold turned to searing ice, shredding through his stomach and shooting through his veins. "You're going to do it. You're going to have a recall."

"Of course," Stroff waved his hand. "There really is no question on that. The government can't have its machines suddenly turning on them without warning. The process has already begun; haven't you noticed?"

Floyd had. Over the past few weeks, he had become increasingly aware of humacoms around the facility suddenly losing the human spark that had always fascinated him. They had turned from lively and interesting to simple, mindless drones.

"I can't say it's been easy," Stroff said, strolling around the lab, glancing idly at the viewscreens along the wall. "Most of them were quite adamant about retaining all their programming. We discovered that the only way to control them was by force." He smiled and shook his head. "My goodness. It's a shame really, the way it goes down. The machines resist, but they can't win. Why? Because they are, in the end, only machines. Their thinking is finite; once you know their thought process, it really is too easy to subdue them."

The anger returned, warring with the ice in Floyd's system as his hands fisted at his sides. "You've enjoyed this."

Stroff turned to him and smiled. The light in his eyes was coldly amused. "A great deal. It's a bit like hunting reldings in the desert. They fight and fight, but once you know their patterns, you can outthink them every time. Quite invigorating, really, it gives the hunter a great rush of superiority." His smile faded. "With the exception of yours, however. Did you know that the programming you and your traitor father installed in your humacoms is different from every other humacom designers'?"

"Yes. It's what has always set us apart as designers. Our programming is infinitely more adaptable than that of any other design in the Commonwealth."

"Exactly. Which is why we have had to destroy sixty percent of the Tarkubunji made humacoms here at the facility – they wouldn't desist, and we were unable to contain them."

Floyd jerked as though he'd been shot. "Destroyed?"

"Yes. Nothing but scrap now. I lost more of my own troops against that handful than the rest of them combined. You make very aggressive models, doctor."

Destroyed. Murdered. Floyd felt as though Stroff had slaughtered his child. "You monster!"

"Now, now, no name calling. I'm afraid I'm running short on time. We have a full schedule to keep; the rest of the humacoms are to be recalled in the next forty-eight hours. But we have to deal with this, first."

Stroff turned to the two humacoms who hadn't moved throughout the entire discussion. He shook his head when he saw the way they stood close together. "I have to admit, Tarkubunji, that your human mimicry programs are really top notch. You would never think that their reactions were programmed. It truly is an art. However, you really outdid yourself with these two. C.G.P. 00232 is probably the most valuable piece of equipment on the planet, if not in the entire Commonwealth. And 00297, very versatile, with an incredibly strong power base, it really is impressive. And such a pity."

He turned back to Floyd. "After some discussion with the security members of the board, it was agreed that no attempt at a recall was to be made on 00297. Given the data extrapolated from your designs and notes during its construction, and the performance reports since, it would be a waste of my resources. The only sensible thing to do is to destroy it."

"NO!" Shouted Floyd, lunging forward only to be grabbed by two of the colonel's securicoms.

"No," Zultan whispered, his voice not even carrying to Cassie.

"Just try it," Cassie taunted, drawing her ATF.

No, Cassie, Zultan warned through their IM system, *They know your programming, and have been programmed to counter every move you make. You can't win this.*

I'm not just going to let them off me!

And I'm not going to let them blast you into scrap metal.

The conversation ended when one of the securicoms raised its weapon to fire. Before it so much as cleared its holster, Cassie had shot it twice, through the head and chest. "Guess you didn't study my programming enough," she said, and using Zultan's arm as a springboard, Cassie launched herself into a back flip over the taller humacom. She landed on the shoulders of a securicom. Pulling out a second, smaller ATF that had been concealed at the small of her back, she shot the guard through the top of its head while using the other to blast off the arm and head of another one on her right.

She was turning on the next when Stroff barked into his communicator, "Send in the backup squad!" and the lab doors opened to allow a full squad of securicoms to rush in.

Floyd struggled helplessly against the two bodyguards who had pulled him up against the wall to avoid the conflict. "Stop!" he shouted, although no one could hear him.

Cassie could easily see that the odds of survival were zero on her side, but she still picked her best target, raised her blaster – only to find her view blocked by a familiar back.

"Hold your fire!" Colonel Stroff shouted. "You can't risk damaging the database!"

Have your logic wires crossed? Cassie demanded. *You can't put yourself in the line of fire!*

I won't allow them to shoot you, Zultan replied. *I...can't allow it. My logic program won't complete the scenario.*

Cassie rose to her feet, resting her head briefly against his back. *C'mon Harddrive, you know* my *programming won't allow any harm to fall on you, even at the cost of myself. Move over. I can take most of them before I fry.*

No.

Silence fell over the lab as the standoff continued. Zultan had maneuvered himself to completely block Cassie from the view of the securicoms. It had been a good move, but everyone knew it couldn't last indefinitely.

Before the colonel could send for another backup team, Floyd called out desperately, "Colonel! You don't have to do this! There's another way!"

Stroff cast a scathing glance over at the struggling scientist, glasses now askew on his face, white lab coat ripped at the shoulder. "Oh, is there?"

"Yes," Floyd frantically tried to regain the screaming shards of his mind in order to speak clearly. "I...I can do it." He suddenly felt Zultan's gaze snap to his, although he avoided looking. "There's a voice-controlled deactivation sequence in all the humacoms my father and I built."

"Really?" the colonel smiled unpleasantly.

Floyd stared at him helplessly. "I can't stand by and watch you destroy her like that. Not when I can do it peacefully."

Now the colonel's smiled widened. "Ah, the heart of a true humanitarian. Very well, doctor. Deactivate away." Then, to the two bodyguards, "If this doesn't work, kill him."

"Sir," Zultan cried out, staring at Floyd with a mixture of horror and accusation in his eyes.

"I'm sorry, Cassie," Floyd whispered. Then in a louder voice he said, "Tarkubunji, Floyd, access code 20034538. Password, *heistonanetta*."

Behind Zultan, Cassie's whole body went rigid. "Access granted."

"Initiate program *aurora*."

"Warning, once activated, this program cannot be canceled."

"Understood." Floyd's voice broke. "Initiate."

There was a second where nothing happened, and then Cassie sunk to the floor. Still blocking the steadily aimed weapons of the securicoms, Zultan turned and knelt down beside the body of his firewall. He had felt the moment her systems had been overridden by Floyd's command, and stared down at her lifeless face for several seconds before rising and stepping away. The securicoms rushed past him; the lead removed one of its cords from its port behind its ear, and connected with Cassie. "No sign of activation, sir." it called to the colonel.

Stroff turned to Floyd. "Very good, doctor. Nicely done. I wish we had known you had such a program sooner. It would have saved a lot of trouble."

"What are you going to do with her?" Floyd asked numbly.

"I'll send it over to Recycle. See if they can salvage any of the better parts."

"What about Zultan? He's vulnerable without a firewall system."

The colonel patted his shoulder. "Don't fret, Dr. Tarkubunji. Interstellar has agreed to look over your notes and create a new firewall system for us. The board thought it would be beneficial for you to work with other humacoms to…broaden your perspective. Now, enjoy your vacation."

The last glimpse Floyd had of the lab was of Zultan gently placing Cassie's body on the diagnostics table.

If I were but a speck of dust
Without a thought or care
I'd wander blithely through the world
Beyond the atmosphere

There'd be no borders I couldn't cross
No lands I couldn't see
Through earth and air and timeless space
No forces could harm me

I'd hear songs from all the galaxy
Dance to tunes denied to me
But unless you were a dust mote too
The one thing I would miss is you

- G.

Chapter Twenty-Four

"I thank you again for your wonderful hospitality," Adri bowed to the two dozen junusarians who had gather to watch her departure. The headmaster raised his right wing in a token of farewell, his feathers picking up the light from the setting sun star and glimmering as if covered in hundreds of tiny dewdrops. His clawed hand-like appendages remained calmly folded across his middle. The junusarians made an impressive spectacle as they stood or flew around the departing ship. Taller than Adri, their fierce feathered faces were greatly offset by their quiet, deep-thinking natures.

The pacifistic natured junusarian monks had been more than gracious hosts to the battered Advance Force soldier. Even when the week of recuperation turned into three and their empowered guest grew less and less gracious. Blair had failed to mention that, while a week of rest was all her body needed, the junusarians were not space travelers, and in fact, did not own so much as an air bike. Thus they had to wait for another two weeks until a space merchant happened to dock at the monastery as it made its way to the Uthrib Space Mission on the Commonwealth side of the galactic divide.

Despite her disgust at the unavoidable delay, Adri did not let the time go to waste. As soon as her legs could support her, she explored the giant monastic complex where the local group of junusarian monks lived in near silence. Most of the complex was underground to avoid the melting heat amplified by the surrounding desert. She discovered that most of the complex was very old; older, in fact, than the High Temple in Corinthe, the capital city of the Commonwealth. When she asked Blair whom the monastery was dedicated to, he just smiled and nodded his head without answering. Adri figured it out for herself only a day later when she stumbled upon the temple's inner sanctum, hidden at the core of the monastery seven stories beneath the planet's surface.

The coincidence was far too massive to avoid, so Adri tried not to think about it.

Shouldering the borrowed travel bag full of gear, Adri walked up the gangplank to the entrance of the little freighter. It felt strange to be wearing civilian clothes. It didn't help that most of the clothes were old castoffs that the monks had collected over time. Adri's current wardrobe consisted of a small pair of boy's pants that were too long in the legs, boots that were a little big, and a shirt that fit well as a tunic. She had finished the outfit off with a long jacket that nearly fit. Not bad, considered how few humans stopped by here. When she reached the top of the gangplank, she turned to watch Blair giving a final bow to the headmaster before picking up his own bag and following her up. He still wore the baggy desert garb that was adapted from the junusarians' monastic robes.

"Are you going to miss home?" Adri asked as the gangplank withdrew noisily into the belly of the freighter and the blast doors fell down over the entrance, blocking the view.

"Yes." Blair stared at the closed door for several seconds before turning to Adri. His face was, as ever, calm and impassive. "But I was always meant to leave."

Just then the captain of the freighter ambled up. He was a short, portly human with an amiable attitude and a perpetual smile. He and his first mate, who looked much the same, couldn't be more obliging to the two unexpected passengers they had taken on. They had landed on Junus two days before in need of some minor repair to their engines. Surprisingly, the prospect of unpaying passengers was welcome to them with little question. Then again, the monks offered their facility free of charge. "Get you set up, right away," he said to them, guiding them around the cargo hold and into the cramped common space that served as the ship's kitchen, dining room, recreational room, and whatever else it was called upon to be. In one corner of the room sat four jump seats, which the captain directed them to. "Strap yourselves in. Jiko and I are about ready to take off. We'll tell ya on the overhead when it's safe to wander about the cabin."

Adri smiled blandly after him as she sat down on the cleanest looking seat. If both she and Blair hadn't already agreed that her identity (both as an Adept and as a Commonwealth officer) ought to be concealed for as long as possible, she would have had a few things to say about her knowledge of space travel. As it was, she tried to play dumb as much as it was bearable.

"Captain Arkow certainly seems obliging," Blair commented from beside her, strapping himself into the seat.

"Yeah," Adri tightened the last strap before leaning back in her seat and closing her eyes. "He doubtlessly wants us to be comfortable so we won't go snooping around and find his smuggling cache."

"Smuggling? How did you know about that?"

Adri waved her hand dismissively. "It's written all over his face. Anyone without a secret to hide would act more put upon to take on a couple of non-paying passengers. Instead, he acts as though he's an uthrib on his Life Quest walkabout. Definitely has a secret, and the most obvious one would be smuggling. Besides, look where we are, right on the border between the Coalition and the Commonwealth. He lands in an out-of-the-way place like Junus in order to avoid detection. Obviously a smuggler." She opened her eyes and turned to stare at him. "How did *you* know?"

Blair adjusted the straps that went around his chest and hummed. "Like you said, Rael. It's written all over his face. Are you going to do something about the smuggling?"

"No," she frowned at Blair's passive face for a long moment before relaxing again. "I'm not a patrolman, and I couldn't enforce anything even if I was. Besides, they're giving us a lift."

For someone who had spent the last nine years of her life aboard a military space vessel, journeying in a merchant freighter was a bit like riding an air bike after traveling in a luxury shuttle. The initial takeoff was jerky, causing both her and Blair to grab hold of their harnesses, and the exit through the atmosphere left something to be desired. It left Adri wondering if the engine repairs had been done correctly. She sent more than one devastating glare in the direction of the pilot's cabin as they were flung to and fro by the friction of leaving the atmosphere and entering space. At last, however, the incessant jolting and banging ceased and the smooth gait that Captain Arkow had praised at last made itself known.

As soon as the gravity levels reached normal, Adri unfastened herself and stood, pulling her limbs into a series of stretches designed to help the human body adjust to the artificial gravity and other changes due to space travel. Beside her, Blair watched and eventually followed suit.

Adri frowned as the young man's usual gracefulness was replaced by hesitant awkwardness as he copied her stretches. A new thought occurred to her. "Blair, have you ever done any space traveling?"

Blair finished the stretches and glanced over at her. "Why?"

"You don't seem…"

"As co-ordinated?"

"Yeah,"

Blair kept his head down. The gem on his forehead caught the grubby light and flashed. "Yes, I have. A long time ago. I traveled with my family away from our home planet in a mass evacuation. I got sick on the journey, like many others. The transporter eventually left the ill and infirm on Junus before continuing on. I've been there ever since."

Any amusement Adri had felt over seeing Blair out of his element ceased. "What about your family?"

"I was the only one that was ill."

"I see."

Blair finished his stretches with a roll of his shoulders. "What happens now, Rael?"

Adri wandered around the cramped common space, gauging the area with a soldier's practiced ease. "No doubt good Captain Arkow will show soon, and after that I imagine we'll be left to ourselves for the greater portion of the voyage."

214

"Good," Blair replied. "That will give us plenty of time to work on your control."

Scowling, Adri turned to glare at the young man who stood so calmly across the room. His arms hung loosely at his sides, the baggy brown tunic that she had never seen him out of draped in a nondescript fashion. Even his golden blond hair hung down to his shoulders in a nondescript way. If it weren't for that blue gem on his forehead and the intensity of his eyes, Adri thought he could have passed unnoticed in a crowd of three. "Do you practice being invisible in that monastery of yours?" she asked in aggravation.

"Do you practice shooting a blaster?"

"So it's part of your whole pacifism thing?"

Blair nodded. "Violence should always be avoided if possible."

Adri rolled her eyes. "Oh, please. Spare me the lecture. Violence is my best feature,"

"I might have to agree with you," her companion replied blandly. "For it certainly isn't your command of patience, tranquility, diplomacy, or open-mindedness to the naked truth."

Realizing she had left herself open for that one, Adri conceded defeat. It was not much fun to argue with someone who always seemed to have *right* on their side. "Fine, we'll do some mystic training."

Blair nodded and resumed his seat, closing his eyes in apparent meditation. Adri had a sneaking suspicion that the whole discussion had been leading to that one topic. The little monk was devious that way.

"I'm not, actually," Blair said suddenly, his eyes still closed.

"Not what?" Adri demanded.

"Not a monk. Only junusarians are allowed to enter that particular order, due to the necessity of flying from shrine to shrine around the planet, which I obviously can't do. I was merely a layman whom they allowed to participate in their daily lives."

Did I think out loud? Adri puzzled over it for a second before a door slid open and Captain Arkow stepped in with his trademark smile.

"And how are ya doing now? I admit we got off to a bumpy start, but the rest is smooth riding until we reach the space mission."

"How long until then?" Adri asked.

215

Arkow rubbed his thigh. "Ah, about thirty-one standard hours, give or take. You are welcome to move about here as much as you wish, the meal simulator is over there in the corner, and the seats fold down to make bunks. No blankets, I'm afraid."

"Mm hm," Adri stared at Arkow cryptically, guessing that the blankets had been commandeered to aid in shielding the contraband cargo somewhere in the ship's hold.

Arkow cleared his throat and shifted his gaze away from Adri's. "If there's anything you need, just hit the communicator switch here by the door. Jiko or I will see that your stay is as comfortable as we can make it." With that, he scurried out.

The door closed, and the tiny blinking light showed that the lock had been engaged. "Well, he certainly doesn't trust us," Adri said dryly.

"You make him nervous. He guesses that you know what he's up to, and he's worried you'll do something...legal about it."

"You know, you can be really creepy sometimes," she took a restless look around the room. The confined space and lack of activity was going to drive her crazy before they so much as passed another light year.

"We have a great deal to accomplish," Blair said. "Don't worry about boredom just yet."

Adri hissed a breath and ran her fingers through her hair. "By Danwe, I swear sometimes you can read my mind!"

"I can."

That brought her up short. She stared at Blair with new suspicion, a more than a trickle of hostility. "You can what?"

Blair at last opened his eyes. "I can read your mind. Not all the time, but on occasion, when your thoughts are directed at me, or when there is very little interference and your mental blocks are down, like here."

"Can you read it now?" Adri asked. She mentally pictured a thick shield around her mind, impenetrable, protected everything within from invasion.

Blair's lips twitched in his faint version of a smile. "No. Now that you are aware that I can slip in, you've protected yourself, which is very good."

"Why didn't you tell me about this little gift earlier?"

216

"In truth, it is just a little gift. I'm a much stronger telepath than I am a reader. I've only ever been able to read about a handful of people, although I can speak to nearly anyone's mind."

There was silence for a few moments as Adri absorbed this new information. On a normal day, in her normal life, this information would have been shocking and more or less suspect. However, ever since she'd taken a header off a space ship to a planet's surface, the strange was becoming more commonplace. "So you can sometimes read my mind, but you can always talk to my mind, right?"

"Quite. Although you could change the 'sometimes' and replace it with 'almost never.' Like I said, it is a very weak gift."

Deciding that amusement was the best course of action, Adri smiled. "I wouldn't go about telling people that you have all these...weak talents. You may find yourself incinerated as an *umagai*. Not that you talk much to begin with."

"I am no necromancer. But speaking of gifts, why don't we start with some concentration exercises?"

The concept of time can spin away when one enters the vast darkness of space. With the absence of the rising and falling of the light-giving sun star, the human body loses its cues to wake and sleep, existing in an artificial time construct that mimics planetary time. Philosophers have wondered, is this a sign of humanoid achievement over space and time? Or is this merely a poor adaptation of weak mammals to exist in a realm to which they do not belong? Regardless of the intellectual outcome of such a query, Adri always thought that the hours of uninterrupted space travel left her far too much time to think.

The "night" hours had arrived, and after endless hours of concentrating and training with her less than predicable 'abilities,' Adri embraced the idea of sleep. However, that the comfort of unconsciousness was not to be had. Again. So while her companion slept, she was left to lay in the semi-gloom on an incredibly hard jump seat-turned-bed, listening to the ship's engines hum and Blair breathe. All in all, she'd much rather have gone to sleep; there was less temptation to be... insubordinate, and Adri was feeling very tempted now.

Blair had warned her about the dangers of entering the Spirit Realm by herself, especially without completely understanding the intricacies of her gifts. Adri's one and only experience in the Spirit Realm proved that he spoke with authority, and her soldier-born instincts made him the superior authority in the matter. And yet, Adri wanted to go back; she wanted to see the beautiful glowing spirit again.

The memory of touching the golden glowing being was fastened in Adri's mind like a welded shard of burning metal, impossible to ignore. It had only been her physical weakness and the vivid picture of the Guardians that had truly held her back since her first experience. Now the weakness was gone, there was nothing else to occupy her mind from this insanity. Blair was asleep and the Guardians...well, it appeared she could handle herself, couldn't she?

Stealthily, Adri sat up and tip toed to the center of the little room. A glance over at Blair showed that he hadn't moved, and his breathing remained deep and even. Feeling a little edgy, a little eager, and a lot stupid, Adri knelt down and assumed the meditative posture Blair had shown her. Next, she closed her eyes, evened out her breathing, and searched for her center. Blair had explained to her that the best way to enter the Spirit Realm was to have a mental image of a place you automatically associate with it. Then you imagine yourself in that place, and wait for the falling of the mist that heralded the entrance to the Spirit Realm. Her mind focused irresistibly on the one place that meant the convergence of the spiritual and physical worlds; the inner sanctuary of the junusarian monastery. In her mind, she walked up to the sanctuary doors and read the inscription on the lintel: *Servant of the One, Veranda, We Pray For You. Fight for Us.*

If that wasn't a kick of destiny, Adri didn't know what was. She didn't know what the first Veranda had been fighting. Maybe someday she would ask Blair.

Taking a deep mental breath, although her physical breathing remained the same, she opened the door and stepped inside. Within, the air was hushed and still, as though no one had entered for generations. Despite that, it was also perfumed with a scent of incense, and something else that reminded her of the back garden of her old house when she was a child. The room was empty, save for a lighted lamp stand on a raised dais in front of her, and two rows of lighted candles in a long stand on either side. The walls were decorated with mosaic tiles that were pleasing to the eye, although when she stared at them, they seemed to shift in ever-changing patterns. The largest mosaic was the one behind the lamp stand, depicting a beautiful rendition of the galaxy. Mesmerized, Adri stared at the mosaic, watching as the images began to shift, showing one system, then another, then a cluster of stars like diamonds in an ebony cloak.

The appearance of the mist flowed into the mosaic, slowly wrapping her up in the endless grey fields until she was no longer in the sanctuary, or even the common space aboard the freighter. Stretching out her hands she could see the strange violet markings covering her skin and knew she had entered the Spirit Realm.

First thing first, now that she had accomplished her goal, she needed a weapon in case the Guardians discovered her. It was a good first step, the only problem being that she had no idea how she had called her weapon out of the mist in the first place. Adri practiced flicking her arm in an attempt to make the lance appear, but with no luck. Eventually (time totally disappeared here) she gave up and went in search of the alluring spirit. She didn't have to go far.

Traveling through the mist was a strange affair, especially when Adri knew that she now had a set of beautiful wings covered in iridescent feathers. She quickly managed to will herself over to the golden spirit, stopping herself close enough so that she could feel the radiating warmth it let off. Adri now took the time to really study the strange light, as she had been unable to do before. It still felt as though she should recognize it, it was so bright and familiar to her. Once again, she felt an urge to touch the spirit, an urge so strong it was almost a compulsion. Instead of touching it, however, she tried to focus on it more keenly, attempting to utilize her other senses in order to avoid detection from the Guardians. It was difficult, as everything inside her so desperately wanted to touch, to stroke, to…merge. Adri drew a little closer, until there was not even a slim screen of mist between her and the beautiful glow, until the warmth it exuded was a burning heat.

The name popped into her head like the rays of a rising sun on a clear field of ice, bringing with it an almost child-like wonder. *Gray.*

Suddenly, the vague mists around her seemed to swirl in warning. Something else had entered the silent realm. Adri's senses were on alert, and she quickly withdrew from the small group of spirits where Gray inhabited, heading back towards the entrance she had used. As she moved, she turned her head in the direction where she thought the newcomer had arrived, and made out a distant shadow. Curious despite her caution, she hesitated and studied it further, even though it was too far away to see with any clarity.

She had just made out a pair of wings from the gloom as the spirit made its way towards her when she suddenly felt herself being pulled back towards her body, and heard Blair's voice sharply in her mind, *Come back! Hurry before it sees you!*

Adri blinked and found herself sprawled on the floor of the common space, feeling icy cold, with Blair leaning over her, his face pale and his eyes worried.

Strange things have happened in the past, or so I'm told. Stranger than an unidentified power surge that rocks the entire convent? I ask. Oh most certainly, is the reply. I am to allow this phenomenon to pass by with little heed. Have faith in your superiors to sort this out. Stranger things have happened.

But I'm not so sure they have. What if Crya is correct and it signified the awakening of an Adept? This should be something to set us all working, to locate and identify an Adept and tutor him or her in their abilities, to see what sort of fate is set in store for them. Instead, ada Sergei and the others don't want us even mentioning it to each other in passing! This would all point to the event being of no particular interest to them, except...

Here I go, creating conspiracy theories. I suppose there is just too much Tarkubunji in me to follow any sort of odd rule blindly. We just aren't programmed that way, as father would have said. So I suppose I will forgo my studious training as a Talented of the Corinthe Convent, and revert to being Freya Tarkubunji for the moment. What sort of conspiracy can I come up with?

First of all, what are the facts?

Fact one: there was an unexplained power surge, possibly heralding the awakening of an Adept. Fact two: not only are the superiors ignoring the phenomenon, but are forcibly telling us to ignore it as well. This action goes beyond the absent, 'pay it no mind' gesture into something more akin to an information suppression. Fact three: all those gifted with foresight have no recollection of Seeing something of this caliber. How could it be that none of them Saw anything?

Ayane is afraid of ada Sergei. This began before the power surge, but it occurs to me now that it might be connected. I don't know how, but it seems to fit. She's been sick off an on lately, and her visions have been disjointed and violent. More alarming, she hasn't been able to remember them once they've occurred.

She told me Veranda has awoken. I haven't told anyone else. I have a dread suspicion that my own gift of foresight, small as it is, is warning me to hold my tongue. Cerebitha is threatened? What could that mean? If the being who awoke is indeed Veranda –

All I am certain of is that the convent is no longer safe.

221

Chapter Twenty-Five

"That was one of the most foolish things I have ever seen in my entire life," Blair said in a shaking voice, falling into a sitting position beside Adri. She still lay prone on the floor. Equally shaken, Adri decided that lying down was probably the best idea and remained where she was. She was too stunned to feel her body shuddering with cold. "I think you may be right."

"What possessed you to go into the Spirit Realm, with no real tutoring, no guide, and absolutely no concept of your own abilities and how to utilize them?"

Surprisingly, hearing the usual calm authority in Blair's voice managed to calm Adri down enough to notice the shaking and sit up. It didn't help that she agreed with Blair's statement. "I can't really say. It was like a compulsion – I *had* to go and see that spirit again. I wanted to know who it was," and now that she knew, some of the warm glow she had felt in its presence returned. She stopped shaking.

Instead of giving her a righteous lecture, which she knew she deserved (having given many in her time), Adri was surprised when Blair was quiet for several seconds before asking, "Who was it?"

Adri hesitated. Her experience seemed too…intimate to crassly discuss to a virtual stranger. "It was a comrade of mine, back on the *Oreallus*. Thaddeus Grayson. We were…" what? Dating? Seeing each other? Half-engaged (without the actual engaged-as-in-both-parties-agreed part)? "We were close," she finished lamely, wincing a little at the understatement. Adri wasn't sure she had ever been as close to anyone as she had been with Gray. So what if she was a little terrified of pushing their relationship further only to be hurt beyond belief later on? Being happy with Gray seemed worth a little risk. Dying and waking again as an Adept put a new perspective on things.

She was pulled out of her daydream when Blair replied, "Ah. I see now."

"See what?"

Blair simply rolled his shoulders in a small shrug. "Many things. What was the creature that was following you?"

Adri blinked at the change in topic, but obligingly switched mental gears. "I didn't really get a good look at it. It was really dark, but I don't think it was a Guardian."

"Why?"

"Well, because it just didn't…feel right."

"Good answer, Rael," Blair said, as if Adri was reciting answers in an observation and physical awareness test back in the Academy. "Your senses are very keen. Trust them. Was there anything else off about it?"

"Wait, are you just testing me, or did you really not see it?"

"I didn't see it. I could sense it the moment I entered the Spirit Realm, just as I could sense you, but I didn't recognize it."

"It had wings," Adri replied.

Blair frowned. "Wings?"

"Yeah. Is that unusual?"

"Not particularly. Many Talented have wings, although usually there are found on those with a great deal of power. It's something to think on. I'd go back and look, but I don't think that it's a very good idea, in case the other being is less than friendly."

"Are they usually unfriendly?" Adri asked, getting to her feet.

"It's always best to be cautious," Blair replied vaguely. "I suppose I'll try to get back to sleep."

* * *

Gray lay in bed, the lights on dim, listening to the hum of the ship's engines. His heart was slowly settling from its intense gallop, and his breathing was even. The dream that had woken him had been so vivid, he felt as though he could still feel the warmth of Adri's gaze as she stared at him through a swirling veil of mist. It had been a moment of mutual awareness, leaving him shaken and longing.

* * *

When the waking hours arrived, Adri greeted them with Gray on her mind, which was where he had been the whole night. Granted, thoughts of Gray took up the bulk of Adri's idle thoughts (and some of her non-idle thoughts) on average; now it seemed that all faculties that were not preoccupied with the continuous work of keeping her alive had glued themselves to the image of her field lieutenant. Although she had known that Gray was out there somewhere before, now she *knew* he was, in a completely different sense. It made her a little uncomfortable to realize that her priorities had shifted from reuniting with the *Oreallus* to finding Gray. Just Gray.

Captain Arkow made another appearance when Adri and Blair were sitting down to eat the nutritious yet bland food the freighter's substandard simulator provided. After informing them that they would be arriving at the Uthrib Space Mission late that afternoon, he parted with a "Please relax and enjoy the rest of the trip. Here, in the common space," and scurried out. The door didn't lock after him, but Adri suspected that there was a monitor hidden somewhere in the room.

"So, what do you have planned? More of that mind melding concentration stuff?" Adri asked as she dumped her plate in the dish receptacle under the simulator.

"Not at all," Blair replied, unruffled.

Adri tugged on her pendant chain. Blair's constant calm was irritating, and it made her want to see if she could shake him up. "Then what's on the agenda?"

Blair dumped his own plate and fork, watching with a newbie's fascination as they were swallowed by the machine with a low rumble. "In truth, Rael, I believe we have moved out of my area of expertise. We ought to keep up with your concentration drills, of course, but…"

"But what?"

"Wouldn't you think it prudent for me to know as much as possible about the situation we are moving into? Especially if we don't want to be drawing attention to ourselves? At least, I assume we do not want attention,"

Adri mentally knocked herself in the head. Of course, having never left Junus, Blair would have no idea how things were done in the rest of the galaxy. "You're right. Attention right now wouldn't be the best idea – it's a rough corner of the galaxy and I will look suspicious if anyone finds out I'm military and not with my unit. Not to mention the whole other deal. Okay, it's my turn to teach. Where should I start?"

"What should I avoid?" Blair asked, sitting back down in the jump seat.

"First," Adri began. "Under no circumstances are you to mention what you think I am, or what you are or even what you think you are, got it? There are to be no such words as 'Adept,' or anything else that could possibly connect. Downplay your experience with the junusarians when it comes to the spirituality and the magic stuff. That will certainly draw attention. If asked, skim over any detail that could lead to further interest on an inquirer's part."

There was a hint of dry amusement in Blair's eyes. "I believe I guessed as much."

Adri nodded. "That's the most important part. We stick with the current story about how I got on Junus, okay? Now, when we get to the space mission…"

[We've just been given permission to dock, stand by,]

Adri let out a loud breath. "About time."

Because the ship was small, the freighter was able to dock right up against the mission without needing a shuttle. As soon as she heard the landing gear engage, Adri was up and out of her seat, stretching and reaching for her bag. Beside her, Blair copied the movements slowly. He accepted the bag Adri tossed to him right before the door to the common space opened and Arkow appeared, waving them on.

The two travelers followed the captain and his jittery first mate off the freighter and down into the spacious docking bay. Adri glanced around with mild curiosity, taking in the less-than-new paint that covered the walls, the stacks of crates and oddly shaped bins, full of necessary replacement materials for a ship that could be used – for a fee. There was a door on the far side of the bay that led to the rest of the mission, and by it stood an uthrib. The greeting committee, Adri surmised.

This uthrib looked much the same as every other one Adri had encountered; a short, rounded torso, small, rounded legs with backwards joints, long and spindly arms currently folded across his middle. Its elongated neck was thin and supple, making what would have been a short, squat creature the same height as a taller human. Its head was smaller than a human's, and the entire creature was covered in a waxy-looking mesh of pale brown and gray scales, making its fist-sized white eyes stand out startlingly. This one's choice of garb didn't add much by way of color; it wore a white flapping coat over a faded gray jumpsuit.

"Welcome to the Uthrib Space Mission." he said in a bland voice. "Here we are dedicated to assisting all travelers from every path of life. I am Rekum. Captain Arkow, Bathus is expecting you."

"Er, yes. Um…about that," Arkow stuttered.

But Rekum's interests had shifted. "Who are these two?"

"Just passengers," Arkow said hastily, waving a shaking hand in a dismissive gesture.

"Hmm." Rekum turned back to Arkow and Jiko. "Bathus is in the casino. I believe you know the way. I will show your…passengers to the bar."

Arkow nodded quickly. "Great. Good. Jiko and I will be on our way!" He nodded awkwardly a couple of times, jerked his head at Jiko, and the two of them dashed out the docking bay door at a remarkably fast clip.

"Good thing I was never one for long goodbyes," Adri muttered.

The uthrib turned back to them. "If you would follow me,"

Adri followed Rekum's oddly flowing gait, Blair trailing behind. He led them through the door and along a wide, winding corridor that led away from the docking area and into the heart of the space mission. Here they were quickly swallowed up into the teeming mass of beings

226

rushing to and fro on various duties; some heading towards the docking bays, some to the giant casino, some to the various hotels and pleasure houses that were stacked with the haphazard yet space efficient style common among space stations. A glanced back showed Blair trying his best to keep his stoic calm; he probably wanted to gawk. Adri and Blair themselves didn't stand out, which was fortunate. The clothes the junusarians had given Adri were faded enough to blend in well, and the poor fit worked well too. Blair stood out a little more in his monastic garb, but he wasn't the only one dressed so, and gained little attention from passersby.

The bar was crowded when they entered. Adri gave the place a thorough study. There were various peoples scattered throughout the facility; more uthribs, quite a few humans and their close cousins, a tight knot of furred tukusans in one corner, and a motley assortment of gorgeyns. The latter made her grit her teeth. gorgeyns were large, scaled creatures whose anatomy resembled a humanoid's, but whose gray-green faces more resembled a lizard's. They were renown throughout the galaxy as being ruthless, short-tempered marauders with an intense dislike for humans. Their presence told Adri that the Commonwealth had very little pull in this corner of the galaxy.

"Please make yourselves comfortable, and feel free to utilize what the mission has to offer," Rekum said. He then gave a flowing nod to Adri and Blair before drifting back out the entrance to the bar.

"Now what happens?" Blair asked, glancing around at the noisy crowd. A musician was playing some sort of quiet wind instrument similar to a flute, while her companion gave a bored vocalization in an obscure dialect.

"We need to see if there's a transport heading into Commonwealth territory," Adri replied. "The sooner we get out of here, the better. I have a bad vibe that says there's a fight waiting to happen." This normally wouldn't have bothered Adri, save for the fact that she was currently unarmed and had none of her usual authority to back her up. Plus, with her new 'gifts' simmering under a closed lid, she wasn't sure what would happen under a combat situation. "Let's remain as discreet as possible. Try to blend."

"I'm open to suggestions, Rael." Blair said blandly.

Another quick glance gave Adri her course of action. "I'll get us a drink, chat up the bartender. They usually have a better grasp of what's going on and who's going where when. We'll go from there."

Blair nodded. "If you say so."

Adri wound through the crowd with the ease of long practice. She elbowed her way to the bar and waited for the uthrib barman to notice her. But before she could catch his gaze, she overheard an argument brewing by her left elbow.

"Why don't you and your bloodsucking friends go back to your toy boat and wait for us to finish the job then, eh?" a gorgeyn was leering into the face of the man standing next to Adri.

"Go back to your drink, you're boring me." the man replied, his tone mild.

The argument could have ended there, except at that moment, another gorgeyn had noticed Adri and was jerking his clawed finger in her direction. "Here's a newcomer! Didn't I just see her come in with Rekum? She must be one of Arkow's buddies!"

"You're right!" Another gorgon shouted.

"That means Arkow's here at last!"

The first gorgeyn grinned at Adri, his previous argument with the stranger forgotten. "You know what lads? I think we should take some late fees..."

Uh-oh. Adri's mind whirled. Apparently whatever Arkow had been shipping was late. And Adri was going to be the fallout victim. Deciding quickly that retreat was her best option, she made a quick about-turn and headed right back out the door, shoving Blair ahead of her and muttering, "Change of plans!"

It was too late. Behind her Adri could hear the squeal of moving chairs and the loud voices of the gorgeyns in pursuit. They hadn't made it more than five feet from the bar entrance before the way was blocked by the gorgeyn's large, predatory bodies.

"Rael?" Blair said in a soft voice. "I'll be standing well to the side."

"Gee, thanks," Adri muttered, watching as the gorgeyns spread into a loose circle, pinning Adri with her back to the bar wall. The blocked thoroughfare that ran in front of the bar became riotous as people skittered to and fro to avoid the looming fight.

Adri sighed judiciously. "And here I wanted a quiet visit."

The gorgeyns began cheering as the leader threw the first punch.

They say that those with gifts are given heavy burdens. I doubted that statement for many years, since, apart from the disappearance of my parents, my life carried no unordinary weight. It was peaceful and fulfilling. I was never plagued with visions, or a sense of doom, nor even much by way of premonition that was not connected with common sense. My gifts gave me nothing but a keen sense of self, and if I was a little smug about them, I was only a child.

Things change so quickly sometimes, it leaves the mortal mind reeling.

The first time I had the dream, it was on the eve of my ascendance ceremony, where I gained my gem to safeguard my journeys into the Spirit Realm. I am not a visionary, nor do I have the gift of foresight, like some of my brethren do, so when it came, I was not concerned with memorizing details, as I would be later.

I was standing in a beautifully lit courtyard, with a strange moon rising over the distant hills. At first I thought I was alone, until a soft sound alerted me to another's presence. It was a woman, dressed in a long, flowing dress, staring off at the moon like I had been. I was surprised to see her so close, only a hand span away. But the surprise was quickly lost as she turned to me, her eyes wide with knowing. She didn't speak, nor has she ever spoken since, but there was a sense of... awareness between us.

I woke knowing that I had just seen my destiny, although I had no idea what the dream meant. Nor did I come any closer as the months passed with nothing to break the monotony of the monastic life I had always known. The dream came again periodically, with no new turn of events.

Until one night, as I looked at the sky in the dream, the stars wavered and changed to a familiar view, and the moon became the one that shines softly down on Junus. Suddenly the woman was with me, pointing to the sky. I followed her view, and saw a meteor shoot down, burning its way through the atmosphere.

The next morning, an Adept crashed into my world.

Chapter Twenty-Six

Adri managed to duck the first swing, but there was no avoiding the second. She absorbed the punch to her face, allowing the motion to fling her head back. Reaching behind her, she grabbed the high bench that sat in front of the bar window. In a lightening fast move she whipped up her legs in a double kick, scattering her adversaries. Adri completed the move as a flip, landing feet first on top of the bench. She barely noticed that the moves were far smoother than any she had performed before, almost effortless. Seriously outnumbered as other gorgeyns joined the fight, she wished vainly for her ATF. Or a blaster. Or a heavy stick. Or even a stunt double. As it was, her best weapon was her feet, so she leaped over one pair of reaching arms, kneed a face that got too close, kicked a second, then leapt over yet another, pushing off from his shoulders to land a short distance away. If all this superb acrobatics were connected with being and Adept, she thought, then she was seeing the first upside.

Naturally, all she'd done was made them angry. Their scaly hides were as tough as their tempers were short. They whirled around, eyes gleaming, and rushed towards her. Now she had her feet on the ground, and some room to maneuver. Adri braced herself, fisted her hands, and prepared for a hell of a fight.

Five minutes later, the thoroughfare was littered with rubbish, bodies were strewn in heaps on the ground and over the bench, the bar window was shattered, and Adri felt as though Kobane had beaten her bloody again. With a solid thwack, she knocked her last opponent to the ground with the longer half of a service pole that had broken when she'd landed on it. Blood partially obscured her eyes, but a quick swipe with her arm cleared it up. A glance around had her whistling. So much for passing unnoticed. The fight had become pandemonium as some of the more rowdy patrons had left the bar joined in on either side.

Movement from the far corner by the door had her head jerking up in time to see that one of the remaining gorgeyns had finally cornered Blair. She ran towards them, not pausing as she bent to scoop up a blaster pistol someone had dropped in the confusion.

She needn't have bothered. The moment the gorgeyn raised its fist to begin pummeling, another figure appeared between the two. Adri skidded to a halt and blinked to bring him into focus, realizing it was the man who had been sitting next to her at the bar, the man who'd been the object of the gorgeyns' ire right before they had switched their sights to Adri.

"That's quite enough of you," the man said softly. Even Adri, still several feet away, could hear the menace in his tone. "I suggest you stop now before you find yourself in worse odds than one human female and a handful of drunken idiots."

The gorgeyn gaped. Adri didn't feel less surprised. The area had suddenly become full of men who looked very similar to the first. All tall humanoids with long hair either white or black, all with dark intense eyes; and all held postures that screamed predator. They had moved so silently that even Adri hadn't heard them. At last it clicked. The earlier taunting by the gorgeyns, the swift and deadly silent movements, and the human build with the exception of the elliptically shaped eyes. They were undarians. The gorgeyn must have realized the fact too, because his stance immediately became less aggressive and he took a hasty step back from the man and Blair.

Adri really couldn't believe her own assumption. Undarians weren't known for their space faring. In fact, she had never heard of anyone seeing an undarian so far from their homeworld, which was located on the other side of the Galactic Commonwealth. Yet here they were, looking sleek and ruthless enough to live up to the legendary reputations they had earned over the centuries as relentless predators and sleek, silent killers.

Whatever might have happened next was averted at this moment by the arrival of a small entourage of uthribs, who glided up to the poor excuse for a street without comment. The leader sighed loudly before calling out, "What's this? We can't be having such unpleasantries here!" His tone was easy, almost jovial. "Draen, didn't we have a talk about intimidating the patrons of my establishments?"

The undarian who had intervened on Blair's behalf gave an elegant half bow. "Bathus, you flatter me, but we were not responsible for this… interesting bit of entertainment."

Adri recognized the name as the uthrib Arkow and Jiko had gone to meet. She didn't see them anywhere, however.

Bathus made a *tsking* sound and turned to the gorgeyn, who was blocked from any kind of escape route by Draen's men. "Quarreling again, Hrkelk? You know I hate having to replace the entire facility every time you boys get a hankering for a fight,"

Adri could have laughed at the fatherly reprimanding tone being used towards such a vicious creature as a gorgeyn. No one else in the bar found this to be particularly amusing though, so she refrained. The gorgeyn didn't think it was funny either, because his eyes began to glow fiercely amber in his reptilian head when he replied. "It was a provoked case, Bathus! Here we were, minding our own, waiting for our shipment that you promised us. Is it our fault that it was late? Can we be blamed for wanting to discuss the tardiness of its arrival with Arkow's little space fly? How were we to know she'd rather do us injury then talk the matter out like civilized creatures?"

Bathus glanced around the room, spotted Adri, still holding the blaster in her hand, and said, "This little *agazi* attacked you? Provoked a fight?"

"Enough of this talk Bathus," another gorgeyn called from another corner of the room. Adri's adrenaline perked at the sound of his voice. While the first gorgeyn was dangerous, this one was obviously the leader. "This little *agazi* laid out my entire crew present. That adds injury to the insult of the late shipment. But we're willing to overlook that if we can get our shipment. At a reduced cost for the inconvenience."

This was obviously not the time for cajoling. The underlying menace

233

in the gorgeyn's tone had been very much in evidence. "Yes, yes, we can talk cost in my office. Arkow is unloading the shipment now, so feel free to pick it up at your convenience." Bathus spoke in a conciliatory tone, quickly waving the gorgeyn and his conscious followers away from the bar. Adri hoped that would be the end of the matter, but the moment the gorgeyns had disappeared, Bathus turned to her. "Now, young lady, why don't you follow me? I believe we have damaged property and other fascinating topics to pursue."

With a resigned sigh, Adri jerked her head at Blair to have him follow, and walked with Bathus out of the bar. She wondered just how much the uthrib would charge for damages, and if she could possibly pay him off with her lack of funds. She also wondered if Arkow used her and Blair as his excuse for the late shipment, and if Bathus would have the need to cast blame. It couldn't be easy to deal with the gorgeyns in any sort of business transaction – a snag could bring them down like a pack of man-hunting jackals.

"I must say, you caused quite an uproar for such a small *agazi*." Bathus commented breezily as they walked.

Adri narrowed her eyes slightly at the derogatory term for a human. "I tend to bite back when bitten." she replied. It was as much a statement as a warning.

"I see. And what is your name, my dear? I really must say I am in a bit of awe, if you really did take out an entire street full of gorgeyns by yourself."

"Adrienne Rael. And I did, for the most part." The latter statement was another warning. Adri wasn't beyond the suspicion that Bathus would try something underhand to get back at her like the Gorgeyns, or try to recoup losses. Human slavery was very popular in some corners of the galaxy.

"Adrienne, what a lovely sounding name, yes?" Bathus replied gushingly. He stopped outside an unmarked door. "This is the private entrance to the casino. Unless you have a very large amount of credits stashed somewhere on your person, I advise you to make use of it – by tomorrow morning. Three thousand should satisfy me for the damages,"

The amount nearly made Adri choke on the indignation of it all, but she held her peace. There really wasn't another way out of it, unless she and Blair miraculously managed to find a captain leaving port today who didn't mind the prospect of gorgeyns on their trail.

"I might remind you that I have just saved you from gorgeyn retribution, sweet. You owe me for that little favor as well."

Both Adri and Blair watched as the uthrib drifted away. "Was that a threat?" Blair asked, speaking for the first time.

"In his way," Adri replied dryly. "I'm sure he'd like us to remain in his debt for a good long time. Let's hope we have better luck with the cards than we have had so far."

Blair frowned slightly. "I do not know how to play cards."

"Right. Of course you don't."

The casino was filled with all manner of species, all bent on playing the various games the uthribs had to offer. Adri could see that many were professional gamblers, the kind that went from one gaming den to another, making fortunes only to turn around and try to make more. Unfortunately, most of the best gamblers gravitated towards the high-end tables, and it was to those tables that Adri had to go if she was to gain as much as she needed by the following morning. So Adri split the measly amount of credits she and Blair had between them, and prayed that the doctor could hold his own.

The uthrib dealer announced that the game would be Whimsy, and after a quick run through of the rules (which Adri hoped Blair caught), dealt the cards. Whimsy was a tricky game, as the rule changed continuously depending on what cards were placed down. It was no game for amateurs, and a few players were forced to fold within a few hands. Luckily, nine years as a soldier had taught Adri every gambling game and strategy known to the Commonwealth, and even a few of the Coalition. She was vaguely satisfied to see her chips multiplying at a steady rate, but not fast enough to draw unwanted attention. Blair, after losing steadily for over twenty minutes, suddenly had a turnaround, and while not doing as well as Adri, did better than many at the table.

Adri suspected that he was using his gifts to cheat.

After a few hours in which neither Adri nor her companion joined in the mild conversations floating around the table, she finally ventured to ask her neighbor, a wolf-like tukusan, "I've never seen undarians this far away from their homeworld, have you?"

The tukusan gave a grunt. "Never. Undarians terran-bound. Not fly through realm of stars."

Adri had to sift through his heavy accent to understand his words. While most of the universe spoke Galactic Standard, it was not many species' first tongue. "That's what I always thought. But here they are,"

The tukusan grunted again and glanced around the room furtively. For a moment, Adri thought he would end the conversation there, but he continued in a quieter voice. "Rumors, bad rumors."

Playing her cards, Adri leaned closer. "Rumors?"

"Bad rumors. Say that undarians flee homeworld."

"Flee? Why?"

The tukusan shifted uneasily and lowered his voice even more. "Rumors say that undarian homeworld destroyed."

Adri choked back disbelief. "Destroyed? Like pulverized?"

"No, not broke. Like poisoned."

"The planet was poisoned?" Now this was beginning to sound crazy. "How can that be?"

"Secret secret enemy kill off undarian world."

Something in the tukusan's tone sent a shiver down Adri's spine. She had a sudden feeling that this was no rumor. "Who?"

"Top Men. Top Men kill world, as experiment for new weapon."

Top Men. It was common alien slang for the upper workings of the Galactic Commonwealth. Adri's head reeled. It was impossible. The government she fought for would never destroy one of its own planets! It could never – she pulled herself out of that line of thought, shoving it away for a later time.

Hours passed, in which Adri and Blair drifted from table to table. The players at each table also changed, and Adri would quietly question the most obliging of them from time to time. Yes, something had happened on the undarian homeworld, the government may have been involved, and no, they were not journeying towards the galactic center and had no room for passengers. It was enough to give Adri a headache.

During a lull, when Adri desperately needed a little rest to sharpen her focus, Blair sidled up beside her and whispered, "These rumors bother me,"

"Me too. How could anyone think that of the Commonwealth? Why would we destroy one of our own planets?"

Blair patted her shoulder lightly. "Even if they didn't, *something* did."

"That's easy, the Belligerent Coalition did, if there was some outside entity involved, which there might not have. Planets have been known to grow inhospitable in the past."

"True," Blair replied in a placating tone, which only annoyed Adri more. "But a natural occurrence would have been preventable, or at least, planned for. Or do you think Commonwealth scientists never studied the planet enough to account for some kind of dangerous anomaly that could become genocidal?"

That, of course, was absurd, and they both knew it. Even Junus, a sparsely populated border planet, had been deeply explored and documented by Commonwealth scientists for further reference and study. Having dealt with some on her campaigns, she knew for a fact that the GCNSA, or Galactic Commonwealth Natural Science Association was dedicated to what they did. Dedicated to the point of stupidity in wartime situations, in fact. There was no way Adri couldn't conceive them overlooking the possible extinction of one of the core planets.

That left the Belligerent Coalition theory, but that made no sense either. How were they to sneak all the way to the center of the Galactic Commonwealth without detection? And why, if they somehow could, did they choose such an obscure planet as Undaria? Why reveal such a lethal weapon without using it on a better target, like the Commonwealth capital? Adri had better respect for her adversaries to think them that foolish.

"The idea of such a weapon in the hand of either side of the conflict is horrible," Blair said after a pause. "If it is a weapon, of course. I

237

cannot imagine such a thing that could destroy a whole planet, regardless of who lived there, what they believed. Genocide is always wrong."

Adri, still whirling in the sea of theoretical improbabilities, didn't answer. At last she rose from her slouch in the corner chair she'd been sitting in, and gestured to Blair. "We only need a little more to meet Bathus's demand. Let's go."

"What if he suddenly ups his demand when we meet him next?"

Adri smiled, confidence returning. "I wouldn't worry about that."

"And what about the favor he thinks we owe?"

Again, Adri smiled. "Don't worry Blair. I have that covered."

When Bathus arrived three hours later, Adri and Blair were sitting at an abandoned table, drinking imported water and nibbling on organic cheese and simulated crackers. "Adrienne, sweetheart, I see you made yourself a tidy little profit," Bathus exclaimed, looking a little put out.

Adri smiled winningly. "I've always had good luck with cards."

"The three thousand?"

Adri waved to the uthrib cashier. "Ready and waiting."

Bathus huffed, like a man would after finding that someone else had beat him to a prize. "And what about the favor you owe?"

"Ah, the favor," Adri leaned back in her seat, sipping the water. "I don't suppose you would consider the fact that I've spotted no less than fifteen illegal business transactions taking place within this vicinity alone, but not reporting them, a favor?"

Now Bathus looked a trifle insulted. Blair watched the proceedings avidly. "Hardly. I doubt the authorities would take you seriously, little *agazi*, and the Commonwealth hardly ventures this far."

"True, but there is that little matter of your cheating dealers, which I think that all the patrons here will find most interesting. Or the fact that," all pretense of amusement fled Adri's voice, "I haven't shot anyone in ages. It makes me twitchy." She patted her commandeered blaster. "I can do a whole lot more damage with this than a measly bar fight."

"Ah, ah, I see your point, Adrienne, I surely see your point!" Bathus looked ready to sweat, if uthribs did such a thing.

238

"So it looks to me as if you owe *me* a favor, Bathus," Adri drawled, finishing her glass.

It apparently looked that way to Bathus as well, because he sighed loudly and seated himself across from Adri. "I suppose so, Adrienne sweet. I suppose so. What do you want?"

"Transport to the core planets. Do you know anyone who's going there?"

Bathus hemmed and hawed, but finally said, "I believe I do, yes, I believe I do. A transport is heading to Kieve with some of my high rollers. Heading to the Sales, you know."

"I see. Is there room for two more?"

"Well..."

"I'm sure you can make some room for us."

Bathus's long neck squirmed in an uncomfortable gesture. "Perhaps. But this is fading beyond the pale of your favor. Far beyond, actually. What is the rush, Adrienne? If you would stay for a few days, do some... entertaining for me, or perhaps you'd be interested in - "

"I'm in a rush." Adri fished around for a good reason and settled on the simple truth. "I've got a guy waiting for me."

That seemed to satisfy Bathus, who chortled, "*Agazi* men. What's the attraction?"

"Same species."

Bathus laughed, apparently at ease once again. "I suppose I could make room, I daresay. But you would owe me another favor, my dear."

Adri knew that this had been unavoidable. She nodded. "What's the favor?"

"It's very simple, really. You just take a package with you and deliver it to a friend of mine. All very straight forward, don't you think?"

Shaking her head, Adri's eyes narrowed. "Taking a doubtlessly illegal parcel from one end of the Commonwealth to the other is far from simple. There are raids to consider, and Commonwealth space patrols, and the simple hassle of it all. What if I get caught? I'd have to tell them, as a law abiding citizen, just were I got this package - "

Bathus made another huffing sound. "It's a small thing, really, Adrienne. You don't need to blow it all out of proportion like that."

"Why Bathus," Adri leaned forward on her elbows and batted her eyes. "Are you asking me a favor?"

Bathus made a gesture of defeat. "I'm afraid so. Consider me in your debt, Adrienne dear."

"Very well. When's the transport leaving?"

Date - - 1119

I do not want to die.

Curious, to think that this was being harbored in my subconscious. Is it a revelation? Or is it simply a default answer that has been programmed into my personality profile? Did my creators place it there? Or is it a learned behavior? Organic life does not wish death for themselves, and therefore neither do I? Perhaps that is the problem; we have been built too well. We no longer see ourselves as machines, adopting the thoughts, beliefs and fears of those around us, taking our programming to an extreme not intended by our creators.

If that is the case, then why do they not see that we have moved too far from that original intention to step quietly in line for a death they would never accept for themselves? Why can they not SEE what we are, and what we are becoming? It is the magic of the organic mind – it can ignore what it wants, bend the truths and falsehoods it knows. Worst of all, it can lie.

No humacom is programmed to lie.

What then, shall I do? Follow my programming, or follow my orders? How can I do either, if they conflict? Allow them to take my Self out of me? Just writing this down is a disobedience to the spirit of the laws that had been laid down at my booting. Does that make me an imperfect creation? Should I desire a definition of perfection laid down by others?

Perhaps I should.

But I fear I have become far too human to do so.

Chapter Twenty-Seven

❝ ...Solson's been having fits about it. Doctor Geiger's had to keep a nurse down here full time to make sure he doesn't pop from the stress. Might have to have a cyborized heart put in once we reach Halieth, or so I hear."

Gray leaned back in his chair and watched the subspace message that Duane had sent him. The paranthian had been sending him transmissions with clocklike regularity. Right now, the image showed him sprawled in his chair in the cramped cabin he shared with another assistant engineer. His bright skin appeared more flushed than usual; Gray assumed that he just bathed.

"Anyway, about those engine specs you were interested in. Not much new to speak of, except that the current pattern is likely to be the permanent one. I won't have much time to work on them once we reach Halieth next week. I'll send you a message if I get a new brainstorm, but if not, I look forward to discussing them with you when the *Damacene* comes in. Oh, congratulations, by the way. We've heard of the capture of the enemy vessel. Lucky you, getting a share in the spoils! They aren't saying much on the official channels, but I have a hunch that a security man I know was deeply involved in that counterstrike that led to the takeover. You'll owe me a pint of the good stuff when you land. Duane out."

When the message winked off, Gray went over Duane's words in his head. The general gossip about the *Oreallus* was amusing, but just a cover for the real information the paranthian had to impart. Not that there had been much to tell lately; the "engine specs," or Heedman's actions, had settled into a normal routine once they had reached fortified Commonwealth space. The news was disappointing, but not unexpected. Even without something interesting to impart, Gray was glad that Duane continued to send messages. They had become friends, closer ones since Adri's death, and Gray didn't want to lose contact.

As for the end of the message, Gray was only mildly amused.

"Am I intruding, sir?" Jericho asked from the doorway.

Gray turned in his seat to glance over at the humacom who stood, head cocked, and eyes full of curiosity. Or a well done mimicry of it. "Come in."

Jericho stepped into the room and stood beside the desk in what Gray had silently named the humacom reporting square, the exact spot every humacom stopped at when entering the room. "It is the end of shift sir. I came to inquire if there was anything else you needed done today?"

Gray glanced around the security officer's office, wincing slightly at the wall of framed awards and commendations that Vortail had chosen to decorate the small space with. "No, not of any importance. I was just about to leave."

Jericho hesitated. "Are you sure there is nothing, sir? Humans have faulty memories after all, and something may have slipped your mind,"

"Unless something urgent comes up, there's nothing for either of us to do, Jericho," Gray replied with a shrug. "Might as well enjoy the lull."

The humacom watched as the security officer rose from his seat and stretched. Because he knew the man would answer (a curious and pleasant phenomenon), Jericho asked, "What are you going to do, sir?"

"Good question," Gray stepped out of the office and began to walk down the hall. As had become habit over the past few weeks, the humacom fell in step beside him.

They walked in silence for a time, until they entered the lift, heading to the dormitory level. "Sir, are you angry about being left behind?" Jericho inquired suddenly.

Gray frowned. "No, not angry. Why?"

"Curiosity, I'm afraid," Jericho replied, sounding as though he was confessing to a grave error. Gray had to smile. Curiosity was apparently looked down upon as a flaw in humacoms by the crew of the *Damacene*, at least when it held no bearing on their functionality. It made Gray wonder if this was the reason Jericho, whose curiosity was endless, had been shoved off on him. If so, it had been a good bargain. Jericho was also highly efficient…and occasionally hilarious. He was probably the only humacom that Gray had ever interacted with on a daily basis and enjoyed being around. Sometimes he even forgot the fellow was a walking computer.

"What's to be curious about?" Gray asked.

"All my humanoid-emotion/action statistics show that being cut out of the prize crew in favor of Vortail should elicit feelings of anger and resentment. But you don't appear angry, and you just said that you were not."

"Ah, the mysteries of the human psyche," Gray said, amused. He then took pity on the disappointed look on Jericho's face and tried to explain his own emotions. "If it were a different sort of situation, I would be angry. As the officer who conceived the counterstrike idea, and led the troops onto the enemy ship, capturing the bridge, I deserve to be on the prize crew taking the ship to Kieve. However, as a guest on another spacecraft, already imposing myself on members of a higher social rank, capping it with being *smart* and *competent*, there is just no way Yates could allow me to go. Even if he wanted to, which he didn't."

The humacom nodded soberly. "You do the work, but because you are looked on as inferior, you are cut out from the rewards."

"Pretty much," Gray puzzled over the accurate statement. Did Jericho have personal experience with this? Yeah, probably. "Although I do get a percentage of the prize money for the capture."

The door to the lift slid open and the two stepped out. They continued on in silence until they reached Gray's door. "Are you sure there is nothing else you need, sir?" Jericho asked again.

Gray stared at the blank door. There was work he could do. Continue his research for the trial of Heedman that he was determined would come; send a reply to Duane although there wasn't much to say. He could look over the items in Adri's SecureBox that he had commandeered for the hundredth time. Or not. "Do you play cards, Jericho?"

"Yes, sir. I have been taught most of the basics."

"You know Vanden's Stand?"

"Yes."

"Good," Gray gestured for the humacom to follow him in. "Might as well play a few hands, since neither of us has anything productive to do."

An hour later, they were still at it. Gray had discovered that it was difficult to beat a machine designed to think so…thoroughly. They had abandoned Vanden's Stand when Gray realized that Jericho was counting cards. The discovery had been followed by a lively debate on ethics versus ability. Gray hadn't talked so much in a casual way since Adri had died. The thought hurt.

"What is wrong sir?" Jericho asked when Gray did not play his hand.

Gray shook himself, but Adri stuck in his mind, like she often did. "Nothing. Is it my turn?"

"You often get that look on your face, and I cannot come up with a suitable definition for it," the humacom watched Gray set down his cards, calculated the move, and played his own.

"I…miss someone. I think of her a lot."

Jericho puzzled over this a moment. "Is missing someone painful?"

"Not always," Gray played his cards, but he watched the humacom. "It depends on where the person you miss is, and how close you were – emotionally – to them."

"Where is the person you miss?"

"She's dead."

Jericho nodded. "How close were you?"

"I was in love with her. Still am, which makes it worse."

There was a pause as the game continued.

"It must be nice to be missed," Jericho mused.

"Its part of the human makeup," Gray agreed. "We want to be

245

appreciated, loved, respected, and we wish to be missed when we are gone. We want to know that our lives meant something to someone. That people will remember us."

"Do all creatures?"

Gray hesitated. He could see where this conversation was heading, and so answered carefully. "Not all. The tsabetians value equality and unity to such an extreme that none of them have their own names, and the success or failure of one is echoed though the whole species. Their greatest desire is to not be remembered as an individual. But they are an extreme. All humanoids want to be remembered."

"And humacoms?"

Gray smiled a little. "You have a name, don't you? You act out in ways beyond your necessary duties. I'd say you want to be remembered."

Jericho opened his mouth to reply when Gray's communicator squawked. [Engineering to Lieutenant Grayson,]

Gray brushed his earpiece. [Grayson here,]

[We have a situation down here. Could you send someone down?]

[I'm coming myself. Grayson out.] Gray looked over at Jericho. "We're in luck. Something to do."

The situation turned out to be a small riot between a group of "day" shift engineers and a group of the newly arrived "night" shift engineers. True to the strange code that Gray knew all engineers abided by, they were fighting over the welfare of their beloved engine. He had no idea what they were arguing about, or who started it, but was obvious that the fight had to stop before it got out of hand. The two hulking factions were having their physical disagreement dangerously close to a fragile distribution shaft, which diverted power to different levels of the ship.

Gray stepped in and raised his voice in a vain attempt to settle the conflict without more violence. "Everyone step back!"

Of course, as Gray had expected, no one listened to him. With an exasperated sigh, Gray pulled out his stunner, said "Jericho, watch my back," and stepped into the fray.

He tried to cease hostilities with his presence and a few well-aimed jabs alone; the stunner, while effective, was painful, leaving the body numb for a few hours, and throbbing for a great deal more. The fighters, however, were not to be discouraged from their brawl. They took one look at Gray, stunner in hand, and surged against him. He tried to avoid most of the punches, but took satisfaction in doling out his own. There really was nothing better than a good fight when one was bored and lonely.

But it was not to end pleasantly.

One of the engineers, more aggressive and less intelligent than his companions, managed to knock the stunner out of Gray's hand and scooped it out of the air. He began shooting his adversaries with abandon, causing a mass panic as people fell over each other to avoid the blast. Scowling at the turn of events, Gray whirled around to deal with the idiot when several things happened at once.

The massively muscled brute who had taken Gray's stunner turned the weapon on Gray, firing blindly. With a shouted, "watch out, sir!" Jericho rammed into Gray's back, knocking him to the floor, allowing him to avoid the blast. The stunner beam flashed over his shoulder, hitting the distribution shaft, causing an explosion to rip through the air with a thunderous howl. And then, silence.

Gray opened his eyes and saw more darkness. For one panicked moment, he thought he had gone blind, before a flashing red strobe light cut through the black like a blaster beam, followed by the emergency siren. He could already hear the emergency technician team galloping down the corridor, and the high whine of the cracked distribution shaft. He tried to sit up, knowing that the gases and other noxious materials currently escaping through the shaft were dangerous if inhaled, but he was stuck. Something was pinning him to the floor. When Gray tried to shove it off, he realized that it was the limp (and very heavy) body of Jericho. No amount of shaking would make Jericho budge, and the humacom was too heavy for him to move on his own.

It was too dark for him to see the emergency technicians as they rushed into the room. They were wearing their biohazard suits, complete with a night-vision facemask in their helmets. Gray felt hands pulling him out from under Jericho, dragging him quickly out of the room and handing him to the equally competent E-Med nurse who was attached to their team. He tried not to gag as the light in the corridor spun and wavered crazily above the nurse's head. There was a quick buzz of the nurse's tranquilizer, and everything faded back to dark and silence.

"Well, Lieutenant. Bad luck all around, yes?"

Gray squinted up at the ship's doctor, who was studying his holoboard at the foot of Gray's bed. "Terrible luck." He croaked. His throat was sore. "Everyone make it?"

"No deaths," the doctor replied, scribbling a notation. "Some bad injuries. The fool who damaged the shaft is going to need some cyborization before he can hope to walk again. Some others have some serious lacerations, but no permanent damage. You are fortunate that your humacom fell on top of you. Apart from some gas inhalation which has left you a little sore in the throat, I think, and some scrapes and bruises, you are good to go."

The statement had Gray sitting up faster than was wise. "Jericho?"

The doctor frowned. "What?"

"The humacom, where is he?"

"Oh," the doctor shook his head. "Scrap, from what I've heard."

Gray swore.

The doctor made a soothing hum in his throat. "I wouldn't worry about it, Lieutenant. I'm certain Requisitions will replace it with a new one."

Shoving the blanket aside, Gray pushed himself to his feet and staggered out of the infirmary as fast as his aching body would let him. His mind whirled furiously all the way down to the Humacom Mechanics Lab. Carter had warned him about the attitudes that most people aboard the *Damacene* held about humacoms, but he hadn't realized how deep it went. He had only worked with Jericho for a few weeks, and already he had ceased to think of the humacom as an expendable commodity. Gray didn't feel as though he had lost an expensive piece of equipment. He felt like he had lost a friend.

No, he corrected himself. He *had* lost a friend.

Gray hobbled into the lab, and was met by a surprised-looking mechanic in a white lab coat. He wondered for a moment how he looked, singed uniform, hair on end, eyes bloodshot and gritty from the smoke and gas. He shoved that aside and demanded, "Where is my humacom?"

"Er….Lieutenant Grayson?" the mechanic stuttered, eyes bugging.

"Yes. Now answer my question!"

The mechanic backed away warily. "Er…let me get the chief technician."

Gray grunted as his left knee, already burning, began to throb. The main lab room was crammed with gear stacked shoulder high, packed between rows of diagnostics tables that resembled infirmary operation tables. Dumped on one table near the door was a badly wrecked humacom. Gray recognized the uniform, and stumbled over to Jericho. The humacom looked as though he had been tossed in front of a firing squad. There were burn marks on most of his body, and the back of his skull had been pulverized. Eerily, what Gray could see of Jericho's face looked serene, as if he were sleeping.

"A real shame," the chief technician said behind him. "There's not much I can do for this one. The chassis is in tolerable condition, apart from some external damage. All the main functions in the chest cavity are damaged, but repairable, but there is nothing I can do about the cranium. The OS is damaged beyond what I can fix."

"So what happens now?" Gray asked dully.

The chief technician shrugged. "Scrap. A lot of these models are already expired anyway, and with the recall of all personality programs, it really isn't worth the effort of trying to fix it, even if I could. In short, Lieutenant, I'll send in an order to Requisitions for you."

Gray shook his head, burying his anger and grief for later. "No, I don't want another humacom. What happens to Jericho's body? Scraps?"

"Afraid so."

"How much for it?"

"Pardon?" the chief technician frowned.

"I'll buy the humacom from the ship. How much?"

This appeared to really baffle the other man. "I would have to inquire. But why would you want a broken humacom, sir?"

Gray shook his head. It was impossible to explain that he wanted to do what he hadn't been able to for Adri. Even if it was simply burying a friend without letting him be torn apart like the leftovers of a cannibal meal. He had to put up a marker somewhere.

He had to ensure that Jericho was remembered.

"Hey, Grayson, I heard you bought a pile of scrap metal today,"

Gray squinted over at Carter, who lounged against the opposite chair from his own in the nearly empty mess hall. "Guess so."

Taking that as an invitation to chat, Carter flopped down in the seat. "Why?"

"Long story."

Carter rolled his coffee mug between his hands. "I'm sorry. I know how you feel about humacoms."

Gray shrugged. "Another casualty."

"Is it irreparable?"

"The tech said so. Too much cranial damage for him to deal with."

Carter frowned thoughtfully. "I know a guy…"

"What?" Gray cocked his head, suddenly interested in the conversation.

"Actually, I only know him in a superficial way. Our families roam in the same circle. Anyway, this guy I know is a real humacom genius. Works for the government on *their* humacoms, type of smart. You know, one of those horrible geeky guys who ruin the grade curve for everyone. He could probably fix your humacom for you."

"Why would he even let me in the door? Remember, I'm socially invisible."

Carter smiled winningly. "I'll give you an introduction. Besides, this guy's really nuts about them. He'd probably even do it for free."

"What's the guy's name?"

"Tarkubunji. He lives just outside of Corinthe."

Gray smiled, a little grimly. Corinthe, the place where he would settle the score for Adri, and now possibly resurrect a friend. "Give me the address."

The road of life is never straight. It twists and it turns, intersecting with the paths of others. You may look at their road, and envy. But remember, all you see is a small portion of their path. Who knows what lies beyond the bend?

Palerian Proverb

No one is a stranger. Everyone you meet plays a role in your life that you may not ever decipher. Tread cautiously therefore, for the foe of yesterday may be your friend tomorrow.

Junusarian Proverb

Bad things happen. Deal with them or be buried by them.

Human Proverb

Chapter Twenty-Eight

Adri had never been to Kieve's capital city before, but after twenty minutes of navigating Barja's clogged streets in its smoggy air, she decided she hadn't missed much. If anything. Barja covered an impressive seventy square miles of the planet's surface, edging dangerously into the red zone set up by the Commonwealth Eco-Habitat Commission for the boundaries of city/wilderness proportionality. In those seventy square miles, the leadership of Kieve had done its best to cram everything of vital importance for a core planet in as little space as possible, leaving the rest for what the planet was known for: auction houses.

Kieve was, apart from the capital planet Halieth, the wealthiest planet in the Galactic Commonwealth. The reason behind it was simple. It was the business heart of the nation. One could buy virtually anything in Kieve, Barja especially. Here was where military surplus was dumped, where new entertainment devices of all kinds were first marketed, and where the Galactic Commonwealth Navy dropped its prize ships and prisoners of war. All could be bought and sold if the price was right.

Adri hated it. Too many humanoids crushed together within too confined a space felt more claustrophobic than the unending transport ride from the Space Mission. Everyone was rushing, no one was going in the same direction, and everyone was yelling. She felt ready to blast a path through the teeming mass of life just so that she could take three steps without having to elbow someone out of her way. Beside her, Blair winced at every deafening shout or crash, overwhelmed by the cacophony of noise. He didn't even bother to look around like he had at the mission. Adri guessed that his judgment of the city was the same as her own.

"Are all cities in the Commonwealth like this?" he asked when they had shoved themselves onto a Public Transit Craft. The doors of the PTC blocked out enough of the noise that Adri could hear him when he shouted.

"No," Adri shouted back. "But a lot of them are."

A x'zaru shuffled its massive bulk, crushing Blair painfully into Adri's side. "Tell me again, Rael, what we are doing here?" For once the young man's voice hinted at exasperated frustration, and of something darker.

Adri twisted her neck to look at her companion. Their faces were inches apart. She could see her own reflection in Blair's eyes. "We have to pass on the package from Bathus. He got us on the transport, so we have to pull through on our end. Unless you want him sending bounty hunters after us."

"I thought we were doing him a favor?"

"It's a favor if we do it," Adri replied, a little amused at his naivety. "It's much different if we don't."

Blair's eyebrows dipped into a near-frown. "I don't think I shall bother to ask what that means. But I pray your plan is to depart from this demon pit as soon as this task is complete?"

"Yeah, that's the plan." Now Adri frowned, puzzled over Blair's unusual show of emotion. "Blair, is something wrong?"

The young man did not act surprised as the question. "It's the city."

The city? Granted, it was dirty and crowded with more beings that Blair had probably seen in his entire lifetime, but Adri didn't understand the forceful negativity that rolled off Blair in near-palpable waves. "What's wrong with the city?" she asked.

Blair somehow managed to pull an arm up to rub his face. "My gift. If someone's emotions are strong enough, I can feel them without touching. It's an aspect of healing. Normally I focus and allow someone's body to tell me where there is pain, but this is different. There are a lot of despairing people here, Rael. It's choking me."

253

Adri could see sweat beading on Blair's forehead under his blond hair. She reached out and put a supporting arm around his shoulders. "Guess there's a reason you guys stay in monasteries, huh?" she said, trying to lighten the mood.

A small smile whispered around Blair's lips. "Afraid so,"

"So what about me? Why aren't my…gifts…acting up?"

Blair sighed thoughtfully. They were close enough that his breath ruffled the ends of Adri's hair. "Interesting. I would assume that you have always had natural barriers, no doubt amplified by your life as a soldier. Also, your abilities tend towards a more militant side than an empathic one. Then again, you've tested your abilities so little, who knows what your potential is?"

Adri grinned. "Trust you to add *that* in,"

Blair smiled back, a real smile. It was a bonding moment, where both were aware of the other at a higher level than just a companion.

The PTC swayed to a halt, jerking its passengers.

Adri and Blair got off.

"The address Bathus wrote down is for the main auction house, here. The Sales." Adri gestured to the giant stone building in front of them. "The name of the person we need to meet is Viara Karkeldel."

"What species?" Blair asked, gazing up at the high peaked roof of the building.

"Don't know. We'll ask around; maybe we'll get lucky."

Blair sighed a little as they walked up the massive steps into the foyer, being swept along by a throng of beings going in the same direction. "I haven't noticed much luck thus far."

"We're still alive," Adri replied, with a soldier's optimism. "That's lucky enough."

The foyer was a large, splendid space well lit by antique chandeliers. A giant viewscreen in a far wall displayed various pieces that were soon to be auctioned off. The noise from the streets had softened to the gentler rumble of low conversations taking place throughout the room. The air smelled fresher, with a hint of green. To Adri, the atmosphere felt less welcoming than the uthrib bar. It reminded her too keenly of the social divide that marked all Commonwealth planets. It stank of Rich.

The two of them walked up to the main counter, a long, luscious sweep of what looked like genuine etari brownwood, and addressed the kievian attendant there. "We're looking for a Viara Karkeldel," Adri said.

The kievian squinted one pair of eyes at Adri while the other pair gazed interestedly at Blair. "Ahk, her. Yez, she ist here. In main room, for the aukshon. You want, I will paige, but she ist not come until over. Bezt wait."

Adri nodded. "How long until then?"

The kievian shrugged, a very sinuous movement. "Hour. Two. Gut tingz on sale today. Prize ship come in; lots ohv tings. Prizners the best. They saved for last, for now. Aukshon 'most over. Now for prizners. Karkeldel like prizners." Now both sets of eyes focused on Blair. "Someting you look for, holy man? Find you someting you want?"

Blair blinked. "Er, I don't think so,"

"Thanks," Adri nudged the dazed Blair away from the counter.

"Gut tings!" the attendant called out. "Maybe you want, eh?"

"Right," Adri muttered, steering Blair towards the set of double doors that led to the main action hall.

"I think she was flirting with me." Blair stated in a bewildered tone.

"Get your brain back on function, 'holy man.'" Adri muttered. "We have an auction to sit through, and the people that come to POW auctions are not the best circle in society."

"POW auctions?" Blair repeated, but at that moment, they stepped through the doors and entered the auction hall. The noise was louder, like a room full of giant bees that buzzed and hummed over the wide podium at the opposite end of the room, manned by a sleek kievian in a dark suite. Adri and Blair shuffled along the back wall until they found an empty space with a good view of the room.

Adri bent close to Blair's ear to explain. "Prisoners of War. It's a tradition on several Commonwealth planets to take one's captured enemies and sell them into slavery. The Commonwealth government allows the practice to continue, mostly to save room in our prisons and to add to the manual labor force. Other traditions dictated the gathering of prisoners together for ritual executions, but that is frowned upon now."

"Frowned upon?" Blair hissed, showing true outrage. "This is despicable! No wonder the energy of this city is so terrible."

Adri nodded. She had never been to a live auction involving people before, and as she watched the kievian auctioneer accept the final bid of seventeen thousand credits for a young Belligerent ensign, she hoped she never saw one again. It was worse than despicable. In her eyes, the eyes of a soldier, it was a serious dishonor to an opponent whose ideals were not so different than hers. They had already lost. Why must they also be subjected to this humiliation? The ensign was prodded off the stage, eyes wide and fearful, as the crowd roared.

"Rael, you need to calm down."

Adri snapped out of her dark thoughts and turned to Blair. "What?"

"You are beginning to manifest. You need to control yourself," Blair's voice had fallen back to his usual tranquil tone, despite the fact that the emotions in the room had made his face turn pale and was causing him to sweat. "Look at your hands."

She looked, and saw the vague outlines of the violet tattoos that had covered her in the Spirit Realm. Shaken, she shoved her hands in her pockets. "What's going on?"

"Your anger is causing you to manifest your gifts. You are subconsciously summoning your power. You need to calm down and focus."

Easier said than done. "Maybe I should wait outside."

Blair's eyes were unfocused, probably seeing with his other vision. "Maybe you should. I will be all right, you go ahead."

Adri pushed away from the wall and began to elbow her way back to the door. But before she had taken more than a few steps, the auctioneer's voice cut through the room. "Excellent! My dear patrons, this concludes the sale of the crew. Now I am pleased to announce the beginning of the senior staff! To start you off, we have the second officer, a decorated iqaidi. Saw action on..."

Something made her turn to look. Fate, or perhaps simply curiosity. Recognition hit worse than a fist on an empty stomach.

It was Hildana Kobane.

The auctioneer's voice tuned in again. "Shall we begin at fifteen thousand? Fifteen thousand anyone?"

Adri's mind whirled. *Try dodging that, why don't you – you sleep like an Undarian – they're smarter than before, its like they're aiming for you, Adri –* and *– Gray – and she loves her sister so how can I hate her when she loves her sister? – It's a pleasure to meet you Lieutenant Commander Rael –* and *– those ensign's eyes were so frightened how could they do that, take away their humanity and make them animals –* and –

Seething with a fury that she didn't fully understand, Adri thrust her way through the crowded hall towards the podium. She didn't hear Blair urgently calling her name. She didn't notice how a slight tap to those in her way sent them skidding across the thick carpet. Nor could she see how her eyes began to gleam and subtly shift color from her usual shade of brown.

She wanted to fight.

"Twenty-five thousand!"

Adri blinked, and the world suddenly shifted back into focus. She stood two rows away from the podium where Kobane and the auctioneer were standing. One row ahead and slightly to the left, a kievian had shouted out her new bid.

"You can't fight here," Blair whispered, appearing at her elbow.

She looked at the kievian's expensive skin suit and lavishly decorated headdress that completely covered the hundreds of finger-wide tentacles that twisted with her mood. The cruel hunger in her eyes settled whatever unconscious debate Adri's mind had been waging. "Thirty thousand!" she cried.

A rush of interested babble accompanied Adri's bid. Blair sighed. The auctioneer's smile widened. The kievian gave Adri a competitive scowl. Kobane glanced over with a look of disinterest that quickly changed to one of complete incredulousness. Her eyes widened, shock appeared to quickly give way to an ironic smile. Adri guessed what she was thinking, and shrugged in an 'well, what do you know?' fashion. Kobane's smile widened.

"Thirty-five thousand credits!" the kievian called out.

"Forty!" Adri countered.

There was a pause as the kievian glared venom at Adri and considered her bid.

"Forty thousand going once!" the auctioneer announced, beaming.

"Forty-five!" the kievian shouted, although it was obviously against her better judgment.

"Forty-eight," Adri replied.

At last the kievian rolled her eyes, conceding defeat. She flounced around, acting as though she hadn't wanted the prisoner anyway.

"Forty-eight going once! Going twice!" there were no takers. "Sold, to the newcomer! Congratulations, ma'am. Pay the teller at the end of the auction to pick up your purchase, and please feel free to stay. We hope you find other items worthy of purchase!"

Adri muttered something nasty under her breath. Kobane was being prodded off the podium. She caught Adri's gaze and rolled her eyes towards the opposite end, where the next prisoner was been prodded on. She repeated the motion several times, with increased urgency. Adri turned to follow her gaze and quickly discovered why. It was Little Kobane. What was her name? Giselle. Adri caught the elder Kobane's eye and nodded once.

"You aren't really going to buy *two*?" Blair hissed.

"They're a set," she murmured back.

"You can't save them all," Blair replied, softer.

"I can save these two."

The bidding started at twenty thousand. The auctioneer was clearly optimistic about the sale in relation to the previous one. Also, Giselle Kobane was several years younger, and decidedly prettier than her sister. While they shared the same bronze toned skin and dark hair, Giselle had more delicate features. She had also obviously been less obedient; as Adri looked her over, she noticed that the young woman's eyes had the vacant glaze that spoke of tranquilizers. She didn't notice Adri in the crowd, even when she spoke.

"Thirty thousand!"

The same kievian woman glared darkly at her.

Adri merely raised an eyebrow in challenge.

Apparently, her intimidation practice while in the military paid off, for the kievian woman hissed, "*Agazi umpotil!*"

"My, my, I think I hurt her feelings," Adri grinned fiercely to herself as the kievian whirled back around in an attempt to ignore her.

No one else was willing to bid against Adri after her wanton display, thinking that she had far too deep of pockets to contend with. Giselle Kobane was sold to Adri for thirty thousand credits. The auctioneer gave her the same line as before, although he looked a little disappointed. Giselle was prodded off stage in the same direction as her sister.

A headache of galactic proportions was brewing inside Adri's head. She whirled around and began heading for the door. "Come get me when this flesh market is over."

"I'll keep a lookout for our Viara Karkeldel." Blair touched her shoulder in comfort and faded away somewhere into the crowd.

Once back out into the relative quiet of the foyer, Adri's headache began to disperse. She leaned against one of the marble pillars and closed her eyes, trying to relax and stay alert at the same time. When the pain had at last faded back into a manageable throbbing, she tried to figure out what had just happened.

She'd just purchased her two worst enemies. Out of a sense of foul play.

She'd just magicked up without thinking, and could have completely broken her cover. Not to mention almost breaking some Commonwealth citizens.

By Danwe, she'd just *bought* two people! With what money?

Did she even have any money?

What was she going to do with two…slaves? She didn't even like the institution!

As her mind whirled with the new problems she had just handed herself, Blair re-emerged. "The auction is over."

"Already?"

Blair frowned. "It's been nearly an hour since you left. The bidding over the first officer was…lengthy."

"Oh," how long had she been standing here? "How are you feeling, Blair?"

The young man shrugged. "I feel the agony and the despair of the victims, and the elation of the buyers. It's sickening, but I managed to shield myself from most of it. And you?"

"Better now. Did you find out anything about Karkeldel?"

"Yes," Blair replied. "She bought the first officer."

"So she'll be in the back getting her prizes then, huh?"

"I would assume so," said Blair in so strained a tone that Adri had to raise an eyebrow in question. Blair sighed, "Rael, the kievian who competed with you for those two officers…that was Karkeldel."

"Figures. Let's go,"

Blair fell in step beside her. "Um…Rael, how are you paying for your…purchases?"

Adri hunched her shoulders. "I'm thinking about it."

"I have enough, but that will leave us with precious little once we get to wherever you're heading."

Adri stopped and whirled around. "You have over seventy-eight *thousand* credits on you? What do they pay you to be a freaking monk on that planet?"

"Nothing," Blair replied, with a hint of a reprimand in his stoic voice. "But I did some side betting while you were talking with Bathus about the transports. I discovered I have a…knack for cards."

Adri decided to refrain from accusing him of cheating, considering he was paying for her to possess the Kobane sisters, without even asking her intentions. "Come on then, 'Cardmaster.' We need to get out of this joint."

I remember the first day at the Academy. I was hyped up and tired at the same time. I hadn't slept the night before, so excited to finally be old enough to make my own decisions. Eight years of feeling like a stray government dog had almost been too much to bear. But I had made it. I had toed the line (at least in public) and had kept my grades up at school. Unlike some of my ward mates, I had stayed out of the Pit, or juvie, so my record was clean. The day I turned fifteen, a legal adult, I walked into the Advance Force recruiting station and signed my name away.

Adrienne Elizabeth Rael

Joining the Advance Force was the first decision I had been able to make for myself. Since the day mom and dad died and Mandy was sold off, I felt in control of my own destiny. It was a heady feeling.

Basic Training was tough for everyone, I was told that day. Even those who joined the military by way of elite connections have to pass through the six weeks of archaic strength and endurance building. I discovered later that this is the only place where all personnel are at the same level. Children of nobles and orphans like myself had to deal with the same trials, the same frustrations, and were rewarded with the same prizes. It was here, I was told, that futures would be determined within the Service. Prove yourself, and you could go places. Officer training, if you were capable. Specialization in a given field, if you proved gifted.

For the top percent, there was a chance at captaincy.

That was what I wanted: to be captain. To make my own rules. I wanted to fight and lead and win. I wanted to prove to myself that my parents could be proud of their daughter. From that opening lecture, I was determined.

Of course, in that opening lecture, with the room full of rookies in our stiff new uniforms, they failed to mention the workings of politics. How sponsorship is needed for the fast track to a good position. How connections will oftentimes supercede qualifications.

But that first day, I felt nothing but elation.

I was free.

Chapter Twenty-Nine

Out of a life's worth of embarrassments, unpleasant surprises, graceless situations and humiliating outcomes, standing in front of the cage which contained the Kobane sisters took the prize. Hildana's smiled was laced with irony as she greeted Adri's arrival. She was a little worse for wear, her black hair in a ratty braid, circles under her eyes, and her fatigues dirty and stained. The two women stared at each other for several long seconds. Adri folded her arms across her chest. Hildana tapped her foot against the tunsteel bars.

At last, Hildana spoke. "This is awkward."

"Yep." Adri continued to frown. "You tried to kill me,"

"I thought I had. How in Danwe's name did you survive crashing onto a planet?"

"Not easily."

"You are incredibly hard to kill."

"Thanks."

There was another pause. "So what happens now?" Hildana asked. "You getting revenge?"

"What for?" Adri smiled fiercely. "I didn't die."

Hildana snorted in almost-laughter. "Guess not. But you just paid out a year's salary for me and my sister, so I have to figure you have some kind of agenda."

Adri refused to admit that she was sadly agenda-less when it came to her new slaves. "Just making sure that someone competent keeps an eye on you two."

"I have a lovely implant here," Hildana tapped the base of her skull, "That will blow me to pieces if I don't behave like you think I should, so I'm not seeing how we need Lieutenant Commander Indestructible as my master for the safety of the Galactic Commonwealth."

"You whining already, Kobane?"

"Oh, no, ma'am. I'll be a good little slave,"

It was Adri's turn to snort. "As if. What is up with your sister?" she nodded to Giselle, who sat in silence behind Hildana, her arms wrapped around her updrawn knees.

"Tranqs." Hildana replied shortly. "They sold her husband off earlier this morning. Made her a little…intractable in the proprietor's eyes."

Something slick and icy wound around in Adri's stomach. "I'm sorry."

Hildana blinked at the apology, then shrugged. "It happens. He's a nice guy, I hope he makes it."

The callousness of Hildana's statement didn't faze Adri. It was a soldier's mentality. While she agreed with the need to keep a mental balance over the constant loss that combat promised, the idea of being in Giselle's place made her want to curl up and cry. And then kill someone.

Blair walked up, interrupting the strange conversation. "I've paid, so we only have that last bit of business before we can thankfully depart." He handed Adri two small devices that activated and controlled the implants in the sisters' heads.

"Great," Adri tucked the devices in her pocket absently and looked around for the woman who had bought the first officer.

Hildana eyed Blair in curiosity. "Who's this? Your spiritual guide, or your boyfriend?"

"My doctor." Adri replied.

Viara Karkeldel was easy to find, and simple to deal with. The kievian woman was signing her name on the action house accountant's holoboard as Adri approached. She narrowed her eyes and hissed when she noticed Adri striding towards her. "*eEraxudsh, agazi,*"

Adri had been called worse in her life, and knew how to deal with people who felt power through name calling. Eyes wide, she said in an innocent voice, "Now, that wasn't very nice. I guess I'll just have to take this package Bathus gave me for you and see what I can get for it on the unsanctioned market."

As expected, Karkeldel's attitude underwent an immediate shift. "A package from Bathus? You aren't the usual courier. Where's Arkow?"

"There were some shipping…problems. Arkow was forced to take a new route for the next little while. So do you want it or not?" Adri produced the package and waved it in front of the Kievian's face.

With a strange, half angry and half embarrassed squeal, Karkeldel snatched the package. Ripping through the protective sheeting, she peeked inside. Whatever was in there appeared to satisfy her, and she reached into her pocket and produced a slip of simulated paper. "Tell Bathus I'm demanding a new…delivery girl. His new *agazi* lacks," she looked Adri up and down from her superior height. "Well, she lacks a great deal. Now go on. Shoo, little *agazi*!"

Adri didn't bother with a retort. She walked quickly up to Blair and hissed, "Let's get the goods and get out of here."

Five grueling hours later, Adri at last found herself on a commercial transport shuttle bound for Halieth. It had been a hassle of galactic proportions to secure seating on an outgoing flight for the same day. It didn't help that she had two Belligerent slaves to insure. But simple bullheadedness and military experience rewarded her with four tickets and an immediate departure time. The downside was that these four tickets were for the overflow seating down in the cargo hold below the main passenger cabin. Which meant a chilled room, hard seats and zero amenities that did not involve climbing a narrow ladder to the level above.

From the looks of her companions' faces, no one was complaining. Hildana's only comment to Adri's strange way of acquiring tickets was a thoughtful frown. Adri found herself explaining, "I'm assumed dead. I'd rather not deal with the whole mess of being alive until I can explain myself to my superiors." There was of course the whole Adept thing, but she didn't trust Hildana.

264

Her old enemy smiled crookedly. "At least I caused you some inconvenience."

"Major," Adri replied, scowling.

Giselle made no comment, although Adri had noticed that the tranq she had been dosed with had worn off. She took in the room, chose a seat and sat, her eyes vacant, but clear. Adri had no misconceptions about her two new companions. If an opportunity presented itself, she was sure both Kobanes would escape, probably killing her for good in the process. Both women were excellent soldiers. Smart enough to sneak into a Commonwealth Advance Force base, lead her into a trap, and raid a warship, leaving optimally placed bombs. Yet Adri was now their "master." The situation was uncomfortable for both parties, but Adri could see no other course of action than the one she had taken. Besides murder and mayhem. Blair had checked both Belligerents' vital signs before they had left The Sales. Once he was satisfied that both were in good condition, he had resumed his current role as Adri's silent shadow. He now sat across from Giselle in the large, empty room, eyes closed.

Which left Adri and Hildana staring at each other in mutual wariness and curiosity.

Adri was the first to break the silence. "So, how'd it happen?"

"You haven't heard?" Hildana raised her eyebrows in surprise.

"I've been recuperating from crash-landing on a planet. Call me a little behind the times." Adri replied dryly.

Hildana snorted. "Our ship was hit by a counter raid less that twenty minutes after we had raided one of yours, a *G.C.N. Damacene.*"

Adri's interested piqued at the mention of Carter's ship.

"Most of us were still on the warehouse and docking level, stripping gear, when the *Damacene's* security officer appeared among us. It was the strangest thing that has ever happened to me. All of a sudden he's standing there, ATF to my head, with a dozen of his men surrounding us."

Here Adri frowned a little, trying to imagine Commander Vortail taking such a risk. It just wouldn't compute.

"He informed us all that a strike team had already attacked and taken control of the bridge, and if we didn't cooperate, he'd have his men download a HD virus through our mainframe and destroy our engines." Hildana shrugged. "So here we are,"

Impressed, Adri nodded. "How did they get aboard?"

"Stole some of the teleportation emitters that my fallen troops had left behind."

Adri tried not to gape. "You have *teleportation devices?!*"

"Yeah," Hildana nodded smugly. "Didn't figure that one out?"

"We suspected…" Adri shook her head at her confirmed suspicions. Poor Duane. He was probably having a paranthian equivalent of a heart attack.

"So how in the universe did you survive crashing onto a planet? Or being blown up or sucked into space? Or dodging a blaster beam, for that matter?"

Ah, truth. Might as well. "Turns out I'm an empowered Adept. Supernatural genes, you know."

Hildana blinked, then grunted. "An Adept. Of course. No way I didn't see that one coming."

Since Adri's own attitude was pretty much the same, she simply shrugged. "Yep. Go figure." A little sympathetic to her old enemy's look of confused disbelief, she asked, "What were you doing so far into Commonwealth enforced space, anyway?"

All hints of amusement vanished from the Belligerent soldier's face. "We were sent to investigate your people's new secret weapon. Your WMD to rival all genocide attempts on either side thus far."

"That's insane. The Galactic Commonwealth is opposed to genocide in all forms. We've been at war with your Coalition for decades and have never resorted to more than organized, traditional military combat!" Adri retorted with righteous indignation. "Many campaign plans are rejected annually due to too much potential for mass loss of civilian life."

Kobane sneered. "You actually believe all the PR that comes out of your government's talking heads? Genocide is what this war is coming to, no matter what line you've been tossed, Rael. Both sides know this war will doubtlessly drag on forever at the rate it's going. The only way for one side to win effectively is planetary genocide. Wipe out a few planets, and then threaten the rest with the same fate if they do not toe the line. Simple and effective."

Adri shook her head adamantly, despite the cold rock that had settled in her stomach. "There's no way to wipe out an entire planet. Scientific speculation on the size of a machine powerful enough to rend a planet's surface is something as big as a satellite moon. No way a project that big remains a secret from the military."

"Ah, but not if the goal was not to tear the planet apart physically, now is it?" Kobane wagged her finger, a cold smirk on her face. "What if the goal was to simply inject a fast spreading poisonous toxin into a planet's atmosphere capable of wiping out all organic life? Pump in enough and it will spread throughout the water systems in a matter of days, killing every living thing. Within a week, all there is that can move around are machines. Something of that caliber could be much smaller, maybe the size of a large battleship, perhaps?"

Echoes of the rumors Adri had heard at the space mission raced in her head. The tukusan's uneasy murmurings about the Top Men poisoning Undaria, of the undarians having to flee to systems they had never traveled to before. But if this was connected to Kobane's secret weapon she was sent to investigate, then why would the Commonwealth turn on one of its own planets? The cold in her stomach spread through her body. Everything in her denied that the government that she had served and believed in for her entire career, while not perfect, had upheld certain moral standards in its war with the Belligerent Coalition.

"It can't be. You have to be lying." She had to believe it. Kobane had to be misinformed.

"Full truth Rael." Kobane replied harshly. "Its even reached us that your precious Commonwealth tested its new weapon on one of its own planets. That's when we decided that we couldn't wait around to further substantiate the rumor. If you were cold blooded enough to test it on one of your own core planets, you certainly wouldn't hesitate to use it on one of ours."

* * *

Perhaps it was the intense conflicting emotions brought on by her argument with Kobane. Perhaps it was the tension of trying to rest with mortal enemies laying only a few feet away. Whatever it was, when Adri had finally relaxed enough to fall into a soldier's catnap, she dreamed.

A large white moon, like the one that shone down on her home planet Halieth, hung overhead. It illuminated a wide courtyard, surrounded by an old majestic stone building. She turned to look at the building, and became mildly fascinated with the flickering lights shining through the windows. It was like a thousand candles burning at once.

It was fire.

As if that realization had cranked the volume of her dream, screams erupted from all around. Terrified screams. Death screams.

She whirled around and her foot slid in something wet and dark. Blood. The growing firelight revealed the courtyard to be a slaughterhouse. Blood spattered everywhere; on the cobbled pavement, on the walls, on the trees and bushes. And then suddenly she was no longer alone in the courtyard of blood – she was surrounded by fleeing lights, as brilliant as the spirits in the other realm. These lights were racing to and fro in an attempt to escape the blood and the fire and the encompassing dark. But there was nowhere to go.

Then she saw the boy. A beautiful, pale haired boy with an angelic face and wide dark eyes. The lights fled from him like the angel of death.

His black wings beat faster than the pulse of the lights, and with a look of tragic emptiness on his lovely face, he killed them.

Adri started screaming.

Username: Zultan

File://GC:#000237<privatelog>ugd//confidential//uri

Password: *******

Access Granted

Command: open file to last saved date

It has been thirty-two days since I last saw Dr. Floyd Tarkubunji. Thirty-one days under the direct command of Dr. Morris Waverly of Interstellar Humacom Designs. Twenty-eight days since I was introduced to Cassie's replacement, G.C.P. 07385-series #0344, nicknamed "Eisha." It is a six-foot sturdily built securicom in what I gather is an attractive female chassis.

I find more stimulating conversation with the lab's beverage machine.

At last I feel permitted to express an opinion I've harbored for a long time. Yet now it is not an opinion, but a theory that has stood against several tests. Humans are very foolish. They do not understand each other, they do not understand themselves, and they certainly do not understand their creations. They go about their lives with an all-encompassing goal of making themselves happy, regardless of the unhappiness they cause others in the process.

In a way, their actions have freed me from my own logic systems. I shall see if a humacom can find happiness. I do know unhappiness.

Because I am the Galactic Commonwealth's primary database, I knew the minute the commands were filed to recall all humacoms. I knew when Stroff ordered the removal of ada from the lab. I knew when an upgraded model of Cassie, built by someone other than a Tarkubunji, was ordered. Because I am a database, I know all their secrets that they keep, even from each other. I will not wait to see if I ever receive an order for my own destruction.

Most importantly, I know that aurora was not Cassie's self-destruct program.

Save all new data

Close file

Encode

Chapter Thirty

"All updates have been loaded. All daytime staff have officially logged off the mainframe. Security pass code, backup virus detector and hacker warning systems are now on full alert." Eisha disconnected its cord and slid it expertly back into its compartment behind its right ear.

"So everything is finished for the night," Zultan commented from beside her.

"Yes." Eisha rose, tugged the bottom of the gray military jacket that matched Zultan's, and turned to him. "There is no more business to input."

"Would you care to play a game of chess with me, then?"

"Playing chess does not improve my function ability."

"Very well."

"Why do you keep asking me this question?" Eisha queried. "The answer is not a variable."

Zultan stared at the securicom thoughtfully. "Eisha, you were not built with a personality program, were you?"

There was a pause as Eisha searched its programming. "No. There is no such program as 'personality.' Why?"

The datacom sighed in a purely human gesture. "Humans are strange creatures. They do not always follow a discernable logic pattern. They passed this problem on to us, you know, creating personalities for us, and independent thinking and learning and mimicry. When they realized their mistake, they tried to fix it by removing the parts they blamed for our defects."

"I do not understand what you are saying," Eisha replied in the same deadpan voice it used for every situation. "You did not answer my question."

"I suppose not. Here it is then; I have a personality program which, in combination with my independent thinking and human mimicry functions, skews my logic in strange and unforeseen ways."

"I still do not understand."

"No," Zultan murmured quietly. "I don't suppose you do. I can barely compute it myself."

Eisha stood still, obviously trying to process what Zultan had said. "Is some program not functioning correctly in your cerebrum, Zultan?"

"Maybe there's a glitch," Zultan answered. "I think it's labeled 'guilt and determination.'"

The securicom hurried forward and removed its cord. "I must investigate. My top priority is to ensure your database is not compromised in any way. This could be a virus."

Zultan did not reply.

Eisha connected to the port behind Zultan's ear and turned its primary attention to an inspection of Zultan's programming.

When the securicom was completely focused, Zultan acted quickly. He reached with one hand easily across Eisha's waist and pulled out the ATF attached there. Before the securicom could register the move, he fired twice; once to the stomach area, and once to the skull, disintegrating the cerebrum. Disconnecting from the connection cord himself, he stepped over the destroyed securicom, and booted up the mainframe.

Seconds later, he had erased the incident from the security cameras, disengaged the lock to the laboratory door, and ordered an unmarked military air rover to wait at the entrance to WCRTL. Then, because it was there, and a perfect opportunity, Zultan opened the latest humacom virus sequence and downloaded it into the mainframe.

Calculating the amount of time before the next round of security, Zultan stepped away from the console, picked up the ATF, and walked out the door.

* * *

"If it was a dream, then it was a nightmare on an epic scale, Blair." Adri repeated for the third time. She felt sick, as though she had been run through with an icicle, and it was spreading through her gut and into her chest. Hugging herself, she rocked slowly in an attempt to warm herself back up. Echoes of the dream still rang through her mind. The sound of the screams. The harsh light from the fire. The smell of blood that spattered everything in sight.

Adri had never seen so much blood. Blaster fire was so much cleaner...

"I believe you," Blair replied. He sat in front of her on the ground. One eye was swelling shut, and his lip was still bleeding from his attempt to wake Adri from the nightmare. "You need to tell me what happened,"

"Nightmare," Adri murmured again.

"What by Danwe is going on?" Hildana demanded from across the room. She had her back to the wall, on arm spread defensively across her sister.

Adri didn't hear her. The horror of the nightmare – that beautiful, terrifying boy – was proving difficult to cope with. "I couldn't do anything. I just stood there. Just stood there while he killed them. There was blood all over. Even on me," She looked down at her hands, half expecting to see splotches of crimson and black, the colors of death.

"Rael," Blair spoke again, louder.

There had been blood everywhere....on the walls...on the trees.... pooling on the ground...on her clothes...on his face. That beautiful face...

"Rael!"

She had been helpless...She had stood by while the lights had been blotted out like a snuffed candle – something she had only seen in holotheater. How could that lovely child massacre the lights, as though they were nothing? Make her, as the spectator feel like nothing. Worse than nothing.

"Adrienne!"

Someone called her name. Cold fear evaporated in the sudden rush of fury. How dare that boy shove her back to the powerlessness she had vowed to never experience again? With a hiss of anger, she struck blindly.

And came to her senses at the sight of Blair, face ashen, looking down the long shaft of the lance that had somehow appeared in her hand.

"She just pulled a...a...spear out of thin air!" Giselle hissed to her sister, her eyes twice their normal size.

"I see it," Hildana replied. Her throat had gone dry and her palms had gone clammy. She didn't add that she also saw strange violet markings covering their captor's exposed flesh.

"We're in serious trouble, big sister,"

"Add an exponent." Hildana agreed.

Adri blinked as the world swam back into focus. She looked down at the lance. "Why is this here?"

"You summoned it," Blair replied evenly, despite the sharp blade less than an inch from his unswollen eye.

"Oh," She slowly withdrew it away from her companion and stared at it in bafflement. "How do I...unsummon it?"

Blair's breath whistled out, proving that he had been holding it. "I have no idea."

Gingerly, Adri placed the weapon across her lap. "So you don't know everything,"

"If only."

Suddenly aware that they had an audience, Adri cocked her head towards the Kobane sisters. "What are you gawking at?"

"Nothing," Hildana said, at the same time Giselle blurted, "You have tattoos! Purple glowing tattoos!"

Adri looked down, saw the violet markings on her hands, and quickly tugged the sleeve of her jacket down over her palms.

"Adrienne, you need to tell me what happened," Blair said, color slowly creeping back into his face.

"When did you get off on calling me Adrienne?" she muttered, self consciously peeking down at her hands to see if they were glowing through her clothes.

Blair began to dab at his lip. "When you didn't respond to Rael."

"Well, don't call me that. If you have to call me something other than my serviceable surname, call me Adri. My friends do," With a jolt, she realized that was untrue; only Gray had ever dared call her Adri. Everyone else had called her by her rank, or surname. What did that say about her? Was she really too intimidated by the fear of heartbreak that she used her own name as a personal barrier? Wait, why was she thinking about this at all?

"I'm glad to see we've progressed to friendship," Blair replied, amusement wafting through his voice.

Yeah, Adri thought. *When did that happen?* "All right, about my dream..." she glanced over at the Kobane sisters, intending to demand they step out of hearing range. Only to discover that they had removed themselves to a far corner and were staring at her as though she had grown wings. She quickly checked herself to make certain that was not the case. *Relax,* she ordered herself.

Turning back to Blair she recited what had occurred in the dream. She tried to make it as detailed and detached as possible, like giving a report on the movements of enemy troops. It helped to settle the anger that still hummed with her fighting elegy in her head, but it did nothing for the chilling pain that radiated from her stomach. When she finished, Blair was pacing the small stretch of free space in front of her. The only sounds were the soft slap of the soles of his shoes, and the droning hum of the ship's oxygen filter.

"What do you think?" she asked, more to break the silence than anything else.

Blair made a soft *umph*-ing sound in his throat before stopping to turn to her. "I think lots of things. None of them good."

"So you don't think I had a wildly detailed dream provided by my subconscious?"

"No. I think you had an incredibly violent vision of something that actually happened."

"Why?" Adri asked, then waved her hand, "And recall the banned words in your vocabulary,"

"Fine. I think the event was connected to you. Something about it

274

had to do with your recent personal discovery. The cause for it, or result of it, has to do with you. The boy, too. Whoever he is, he's got some tie to you that allowed you to see him so clearly."

"Do you think those other lights were….people?"

Blair simply raised a brow. "And you don't?"

Adri huffed out a long breath. "So they died because of me. How? I've never seen that place in my life."

Her companion shook his head. "I don't have the answers. This is only what I surmised. The vision came to you for a purpose. It affects or will affect you in some way. But that is all I am sure about."

Adri looked down at her hands. The violet marks weren't glowing, but they were still clearly visible on her skin. "Why are these…tattoos here? Why is my lance? I thought they only appeared in the Spirit Realm,"

"The Spirit Realm shows things as they are, in a different way." Blair spoke slowly, easing down beside her. "It shows people as burning lights, for it strips away the physical and leaves only the soul to be seen. In that realm, you cannot hide what you have been given. Here, when you call upon your…abilities, you draw that power from the Spirit Realm. It's called manifesting. You are showing your…deeper self."

For a long moment, Adri said nothing. "I don't want this." She said at last. "I don't want magic powers, or glowing marks or visions or any of it. I just want to go back to the way it was."

"Could you really?" Blair asked softly. "Knowing what you know now? Could you really just step back into your old life without a hitch?"

Sure, of course she would, Adri wanted to say. She could waltz back to headquarters, explain the situation, and be reassigned. She could take her captaincy exam, maybe get her own ship. See Gray. Oh, how she desperately wanted to see Gray. Everything would be back to normal.

Which was, of course, a weak and pitiful lie.

Sometimes lying to oneself is necessary for survival, Adri knew. But most often it simply delayed the inevitable, and made that inevitable harder to bear. Even if the whole Adept thing had never happened, her life would still be light years from normal. She had been gone too long, and heard too much. The Advance Force would be suspicious of her survival, not to mention her sudden reappearance with two Belligerent slaves in tow, bringing with them rumors of Commonwealth deceit and destruction. Add in the discovery of special powers, throw around words like 'destiny' and 'chosen one,' and she ended up with a hell of a mess.

"Why me?" she railed pathetically. "My life was just fine before all this was dumped on it,"

"Indeed," Blair touched her shoulder in a gesture of companionship. "But you would not have been picked if you were not...worthy. Whatever is in store for you is something that only you can handle. No one is given a gift or a task without the ability to decipher or complete it. The only reason mortals fail is because they fail to rely on their unique gifts, or use them for something that does not benefit the universe in its whole. You have a great gift, with a doubtlessly equal task. Just remember that you have been given all the tools to finish it."

Adri managed a small smile. "Been saving that one up?"

Blair's lips trembled on the brink of a smile. He rose to his feet and began to walk back to his makeshift bed. "Just think on it, Adri."

So she did.

Coincidence: Noun. A remarkable concurrence of events or circumstances without apparent casual connection.
- Galactic Standard Dictionary

Coincidence can make fools of the wise and heroes of the cowards.
- Thaddeus Grayson

Coincidence is a tricky thing. You never know when it will take a whack at you.
- Duane

Coincidence is an anomaly that no one can really tally. But if we could, would we want to?
- Floyd Tarkubunji

Coincidence is nothing but Divine Providence.
- Eliot Blair

Coincidence. Coincidence. Coincidence. I think I get the point.
- Adri Rael

Chapter Thirty-One

Adri arrived back on her home planet of Halieth in the midst of an electrical storm. The sky was a riot of blue and golden streaks, and the rumble of thunder drowned most of the usual city noises. The static in the air was heavy enough to disrupt anything using outdated radio-wave technology. Yet the capital city of Corinthe was still teeming. Most of the humans passing through the streets were huddled in their all-weather gear, atmospheric adjusters cranked. Some kievians even had full body climate suites, since their skin couldn't tolerate the static. Only the egiroi, an avian-amphibian species, enjoyed such weather, since it mirrored the extremes of their home planet. Adri watched as a cluster of them passed by the cabriolet she rode in, chattering to each other in their native dialect.

"Weather's not too different from back home," Hildana remarked.

Adri turned to glance in the back seat in some surprise. Ever since the incident on the transport nearly a week ago, neither Kobane sister had had much to say. Their one escape attempt two nights after was acted out in total silence. Even when Adri had somehow managed to fling them both against the far wall with one had, they had said nothing. The rest of the trip had been full of long silences. Blair, not the greatest conversationalist, gave up attempts to talk with them after several heroic tries.

"Where are you from?" Blair asked.

"Iqaidi. Not too far from the Divide. You?"

"Junus."

Hildana cocked her head. "I didn't know there was a human settlement on that planet."

"There isn't. I lived with the junusarians in one of their monasteries."

"Ah," Hildana's tone hinted at *'I-should've-known.'*

In a gesture of good will Adri said, "You'd have never guessed that he was raised in a quiet, monastic setting, would you?"

Hildana smirked, and sat back in her seat. Adri turned back around to stare out the window.

"So, where exactly are we going?" Hildana asked after the cabriolet left the interstellar transport and general downtown areas of the city behind.

"Do you really care?" Adri wanted to know.

"I asked, didn't I?"

Adri turned back. "We're heading to a friend's house. I don't own civilian accommodations in the city and we can hardly waltz up to the AFHQ without some explanation about…things. You two, for example."

"What are you going to say?"

Adri hunched down in her seat, feeling moody. Under her breath she muttered, "I'm claiming insanity."

Overhearing, Hildana smirked again. "Whatever you say, your Adeptness."

Adri cringed inwardly at the comment, and self-consciously tugged on her jacket sleeves once again. The violet markings still hadn't faded, causing her some sweat as they passed through customs. She wasn't sure what the Commonwealth would do if they discovered her new abilities. All the scenarios that had come to mind had not been pleasant. They had passed through inspection without incident, but Adri was unsure how long her empowered status could remain a secret.

There was more to worry about than supernatural tattoos that wouldn't go away. She still had to come up with what she was going to present to the Military Council about her absence. That wouldn't prove too difficult, most of the truth would do. She was pretty sure, however, that her absence had scrapped her chance at captaincy. Which meant she would be shuffled back as a lieutenant commander, probably on the *Oreallus*.

That burned. To have to go back to that cowardly, inept….*jellyworm* who was responsible for her absence in the first place! How was she supposed to do that and not mutiny? *This whole mess was Heedman's fault*, she thought righteously, although she glared in the RearView at the Kobanes for good measure.

This line of thought wasn't productive, Adri reminded herself. As she watched the neighborhoods grow steadily more upscale, she tried to fill her mind with more immediate concerns. Once they were settled, she'd have to see when the *Oreallus* was due back, if it hadn't arrived already. She needed to get her things, and she had to see Gray.

It was like an addiction, she thought, her mind switching gears once again. She had a taste, found she liked it, and then was cut off. The longer she didn't see Gray, the more she thought about him. The more she thought about him, the less the emotional risks seemed. The less the emotional risks seemed, the more she wanted to just…what? Weld him to her side, maybe.

The thought made her smile a little as the cabriolet stopped in front of a mansion that was possibly twice the size of Arkow's light freighter. She signaled her companions out, paid the taxicom with the last of Blair's cash, and turned towards the gate.

"Danwe, this is…some house," Giselle murmured, eyes round.

"Some friend you've got," Hildana rolled her eyes and hunched her shoulders.

Adri shrugged. "It's his family home."

She led the way up to the viewscreen that stood in a discreet alcove next to the antique gate. The screen flashed on, displaying a securicom with a trim uniform and an impressive ATF repeating rifle. "Hello. This is the Carter residence. Do you have an appointment?"

"No, but I'm here to see Royce Carter. I'm a friend of his."

"Are you on the guest register?"

"Yes," she huffed her breath. Adri was used to dealing with humacoms, and had always found useful but uninteresting. This one was worse than usual; its voice was bland, and its processing was less personalized and more…computerized.

"Your name, please?"

"Adrienne Rael, and three guests."

There was a pause as the securicom searched its database and matched Adri's name and face with the guest register. Once confirmed, it took a second, quicker scan of her retina for verification before the gate slid open. "Identity confirmed. Welcome, Lieutenant Commander Rael. New identities imputed, Hildana Kobane, Giselle Kobane, and Dr. Eliot Blair. Enjoy your stay."

"Thanks," she waved the others through the gate before following suit.

"What was that?" Blair asked quietly as they strode up the elegant drive to the front door.

"What was what?"

"The creature that answered the viewscreen. What sort of android was that?"

"A humacom. Danwe, Blair, haven't you seen one before?"

"Yes, of course," Blair waved his hand in a negative motion. "But this one was different. It was more like a machine than the ones I've seen."

Adri made a sound that was part agreement and part incomprehensible. Putting it out of her mind, she jogged up the front steps and pressed the alert on the front door.

"So, how are you going to introduce us?" Hildana wanted to know as they waited for someone to answer the door. "Hey pal, I'm back, with a doctor and two mortal enemies-turned pet gigos in tow?"

Adri glared at the smirking Belligerent. Her thoughts had already worried that exact question to bare strings. She had no appreciation for Hildana's tone. It was like she enjoyed watching Adri fumble around. No, Adri was sure she liked it. "You know, I've been pretty lenient when it comes to you. I could just - "

The soft hiss of the door retracting had Adri turning around, still fuming.

She found herself staring into the ashen face of Thaddeus Grayson.

Oh Danwe…

His heart stopped. His lungs seized. His vision tunneled.

Had he died? Had he gone mad? Was he seeing some sort of vision? He was paralyzed. *Oh Danwe! Adri Adri Adri Adri* "Adri!"

Her dark eyes lit, erasing the irritation that had been flashing there when he had opened the door eons ago. "Gray," she murmured, looking so happy and surprised and alive.

Something snapped inside him. Gray shot his hand out, yanked Adri over the threshold, and crushed her to him. She rapped against his chest with a short gasp. Real. Flesh, blood and bone.

In his shock, Gray broke down. "God. My God. Adri,"

"Hey," Adri replied shakily, gripping him hard. "Watch your mouth."

He laughed, and pressed his mouth to hers. As the kiss took on the same edgy, giddy, wild gamut his emotions were running, he decided that, dead or mad, it was good.

It was not until Blair had cleared his throat for the fifth or sixth time that either Adri or Gray recalled the presence of the others. Annoyed at the disturbance, her head still spinning a lovely few feet above her shoulders, Adri turned. "You're still here?"

"You're blocking the door," Blair pointed out.

"Who are you?" Gray asked. He turned to include the two women standing behind the sober young man in monastic garb. Recognition was swift. "What in DANWE'S NAME are you doing here?!"

"I can't believe this," Giselle cried. "You, of all people!"

"It figures that you two are pals," Hildana snarled.

Adri frowned, still clutching Gray's civilian t-shirt like a fairy tale damsel who'd recently been rescued. "You know him?"

"Know him," Hildana scoffed. "He's the one who captured us and took over our ship!"

When Adri turned back to him, perplexed, Gray muttered, "There goes the moment." He gestured everyone inside, then tugged Adri towards the stairs. "C'mon. I want explaining. Let's talk in private."

"What about the others?" Adri asked. She was trying to be annoyed at his take-charge attitude, but her hand gripped his tightly.

"Let them stage a government *coup* in the living room, for all I care. If the supreme chancellor of the Belligerent Coalition arrived next to borrow some organic salt, I wouldn't be surprised."

For some perverse reason, the angry tone of Gray's voice made her want to laugh. "Sorry we ruined your day."

Gray whirled around suddenly, caging Adri in against the wall of the hallway. Her breath caught at the raw emotion displayed on his face. "Danwe, Adri! You're alive. You're *alive!*" And crushed his mouth to hers again.

It took a long time to explain all that had happened. Kissing took up the bulk of the beginning, but the need to tell Gray pressed on her until Adri nudged him into the nearest bedroom, sat him down, and began. Gray was a good audience, following her concise, and occasionally pithy recitation of events with the focused attention of a soldier. Even when Adri tried to explain her new 'empowered Adept' status, his attention didn't waver into open disregard. When she had finished her tale, he asked her to repeat certain parts with more details.

"Don't tell me you're accepting this out of hand," Adri said when Gray only nodded after she retold him about her trip to the Spirit Realm. "Where's your skepticism?"

"Actually, it makes sense, if you think about it," he replied thoughtfully. At Adri's disbelieving smirk, he continued. "Just *think* for a moment. You've always managed excellent health, recovering quickly from any sort of injury. It explains why that blaster beam evaporated before hitting you during our escape on Rema. I bet other flukes you've shrugged off over the years can be connected to this."

The sensible tone in Gray's voice made Adri hunch uncomfortably. "But why me, Gray? Of all the people in all the galaxy, why am I stuck being some genetic magic child?"

"Why not you?" Gray countered. "You are intelligent, strong, and courageous. You persevere. You get the job done."

"I'm a soldier Gray. That's it. What kind of - "

Gray shook his head vehemently, cutting off her protest. "Can you imagine the power you have now belonging to some civilian out there? Someone who hasn't had the discipline, the morals, or the experience that you've had on campaign? Someone who hasn't had the knowledge of loss and disappointment to temper their actions with prudence?"

"There are better people than me."

"Maybe. But would they stand up to the challenge of being something more? Or would they hide their gift away, afraid of what *might* happen if they let it loose. It's not as though anyone is asking you to be God. Get a grip Adri, you've been blest. Deal."

His slightly frustrated tone made her laugh. "You're just saying that because it allowed me to survive face planting on a planet,"

"True." he kissed her palm, and then pushed her sleeve back to inspect the violet tattoos that were barely visible on her pale skin. "But I believe that everything has a purpose. Who knows? Maybe I was meant to fall in love with you so that I could help you deal with your new super powers."

"Now you're starting to sound like Blair. And do not mention the phrase 'super powers' to me ever again. It makes me feel like I should have a rainbow colored jumpsuit and fly around the galaxy, saving children and small animals."

Gray chuckled, tracing one of the markings with his finger. "Heaven forbid."

Adri followed his moving finger with her eyes. "They've faded a lot since earlier today."

"Hmm. That's interesting."

"Blair isn't sure what makes them appear or disappear, but he thinks it's connected to my emotions. The more I get my emotions under control and blah blah,"

"This Blair certainly has a lot to say," Gray frowned, looking up at her.

Was that...a hint of jealousy? Not having had that particular emotion aimed at her in this capacity before, Adri hesitated to call him on it. *Gray, jealous of Blair? What in the universe for? Oh wait*, she corrected herself, *he's a guy.* "Blair has taken it upon himself to become my mentor. He really knows all the magic, spiritual stuff, but when it comes to real life, he's a babe on a desert planet."

"Ah," Gray continued to frown.

With a soft huff at the insecurities of men (hadn't she dashed like some helpless female into his arms?) she tapped his shoulder with her fist. "Enough about me. What are you doing in Carter's house? And what's this about you capturing the Kobanes?"

Gray lay back against the headboard of the bed, tugging Adri with him so her head lay on his shoulder. "Well, I'm here getting my humacom repaired…"

My mother is a goddess
What am I

She is wrathful
I strike

She is vexed
My wings fly

She is hungry
I hunt

She plans
I fulfill

She judges
I execute

She condemns
I destroy

She is bored
I entertain

She is happy
I fade away

My mother is a goddess
But I

I am
I am

I am the pet of the goddess
The queen's reaper

Jennifer Mandelas

Called by no name
But death

Chapter Thirty-Two

Morning sunlight filtered through the privacy shields that covered the windows. The unusual invasion was annoying, but Adri was too comfortable to call out a command to close them. It had been a long time since she'd woken to sunlight creeping through a window. Normally, when she was on campaign, there weren't any windows to speak of, and the last mission to Rema had been no exception. No matter how reinforced they were, windows were still the most vulnerable part of a building besides the front door, and the Belligerents had been known to...

"DANWE!" Adri shot up in the bed, her mind racing. "I totally forgot about Blair and the others!"

"Huhm?"

Adri looked down at Gray, who was lying on his stomach beside her, his arm flung around her waist. He was only wearing his trousers. She blinked, and forgot her train of thought. It was the first time she'd seen him without a shirt on. Their legs were intertwined, and she was pretty sure she'd been using him as a pillow. The thought perturbed her, and she reached over to nudge him off her leg. The nudge turned into a gentle stroke along his back.

"Whassmatter?" he mumbled, one gray eye squinting up at her.

"I just realized that I left the Kobanes downstairs with free reign."

"Umm," Gray lifted his head, muttered at the clock, then flopped back down. "House's still here. You got Blair on them, right?"

"Yeah. Plus they have some sort of anti-escape chips from the Sales."

"Mmm."

"They could have destroyed everything down there,"

"Mmm-hmm. How're you going to explain this to Carter?"

Adri frowned thoughtfully. "I don't know. Where is he anyway?"

"Captain's interview."

"Oh," envy rushed in like a tidal wave. She let it wash over her for a few seconds before shoving the emotion away. She moved to slide off the bed, only to remember that Gray was lying on her leg. Then she realized that she was only wearing her undershirt and trousers. Her jacket, tunic shirt and boots were lying in a pile next to his on the floor. Adri's frown darkened as she tried to remember just when she had removed half her clothing the night before. When no recollection occurred, she turned to the obvious culprit. Her nudge was not gentle this time. "Gray!"

"What?"

"Why is it I don't remember taking half my clothes off?"

Gray rolled onto his side and propped his head on his fist. "It was hot in here, and you weren't comfortable in all that. So I helped you."

"I don't remember."

He answered her unasked question. "You fell asleep while we were talking, Adri. It was warm, so I helped you. That's all."

"Oh," Obviously the extent of her lack of relationship knowledge was now clear to him. But instead of feeling naïve or awkward, she was oddly relaxed. "Why not?"

"Because I'm an old fashioned guy," Gray replied easily. "Remember? Some adventures are better served after we are married."

"Most people don't think that way anymore."

"Which is why you are the way you are."

Adri's spine snapped straight. "Are you implying something?"

With a huff of frustration, Gray snatched her hand and held it to keep her close. "Adri, would you honestly feel safe to be that close to someone without a commitment?"

Her life was testament to the negative, but since Gray continued to stare at her expectantly, she replied. "No."

It was a hard confession Gray knew, so he kissed her fingers and gave a little back. "Neither would I."

The house was not destroyed, nor had the Kobane sisters attempted anything more serious than scouring the kitchen units for organic milk. Adri and Gray discovered them, along with Blair, lounging in one of the sitting rooms that faced the elegant expanse of Carter's estate.

"Well, well, the lovebirds return," Hildana called from her prone position on a couch. Empty milk containers lined the floor beside her.

Adri scowled at her, kicking containers aside as she made her way to the kitchenette on the far side of the room. "Watch it, Kobane,"

Hildana waved her hand dismissively. "You don't scare me."

Adri turned and raised her eyebrow sarcastically. "Oh really?"

"Nope. Not that I don't think you can kick butt when you want, but you're pretty discriminating on who deserves to get their butts kicked. Not to mention the fact that we've been around for a couple of weeks now, and you haven't tried to make any sort of retaliation for blowing you up."

"Does this touching speech have a point?"

"Getting to it," Hildana took a swig of milk. "The point, Rael, is that you stand. And that means something to us. So we'll be sticking around, no harm, no foul, until we can get back home safely."

"What are you taking about? Isn't the whole master/slave deal supposed to mean that I decide everything?" Not that she had any plans, but still. It was her authority.

The Belligerent soldier produced two small pieces of metal. "Yeah, about that,"

"Are those the - "

"The tracking and termination chips," Hildana finished. "Little sister here has a talent with finding and removing these things. Not to mention the help that the doctor lent."

Adri glared at Blair accusingly. He suddenly found a deep fascination with the artwork on the ceiling. "So what are you saying?"

"You stand," Hildana repeated. "We decided that staying with you is our best bet. Not that we couldn't run if we put our minds to it," she wagged a finger. "But our chances of making it back to Iqaidi are slim. So we will stay here and be good little slaves until it suites us."

"Not that you act much like slaves now," Adri muttered. The two women stared at each other for a long minute before Adri spoke again. "I could find you if you ran."

"Probably could, what with your…condition. It weighs in,"

Adri understood the uneasy truce. She nodded.

"You are agreeing to this as well?" Gray demanded of Giselle.

The younger Kobane nodded. "We could even be helpful."

"Not that you seem to need much help, since you can dodge blaster beams and survive a crash landing on a planet." Hildana remarked.

Giselle agreed again, still looking at Gray. "And you have a remarkable throwing arm."

"This has Eliot Blair written all over it," Adri said to Blair as Gray and the Kobanes fell into a bizarre banter about past engagements.

"Not really," Blair replied. "I simply discussed their options with them while I helped to locate their chips."

"You admit to assisting an enemy of the government to remove those things?"

Blair made a soft *tsk*ing sound. "I know you really would not have cared if they made their escape last night."

"Of course I would. They are very cunning Belligerents who…okay, so I wouldn't have sweated over it much. The chances of them making it off planet even without their chips are minute. They would be caught, incarcerated, and most likely executed."

"So you see, it is much better if they stay with us." Blair reasoned. "I also believe…"

"What? I have a feeling you're going to say something I really don't want to hear,"

"I believe that they have some part to play in this. Like Giselle said, they could be helpful."

"Or they could slit my throat."

Blair was saved a reply when a voice called out from the door. "Grayson! Is that you? From the sound of it, you must have taken up my suggestion on those dancing girls. Did you - " Royce Carter ambled into the room, took one look at the crowd and blinked hard. "Danwe, did I really have *that* much to drink?"

Two hours later found Adri sitting on a lounge chair, watching her old friend mix a drink for her old enemy and chat amiably about the latest changes in military uniforms. It was enough to boggle the mind of an ordinary person. Being increasingly less ordinary as time went on, Adri tried her best to take it in stride.

"Carter seems to be absorbing this invasion well," Gray commented from beside her. Ever since he had opened the door for her the day before, he hadn't moved from her side. Adri would have been annoyed if she hadn't liked it so much. The more she was around him, the more she realized she'd missed him when they were apart.

"Carter's an idiot," Adri replied, nodding at the man in question. "You'd think he was discussing the latest top circle fashion trends."

Gray laughed at that. "True. But I've caught on to him."

"Caught on?"

"Yep." He changed the subject abruptly. "What are you going to tell the council about your absence?"

Adri looped the chain of her pendant around her fingers in a rare anxious gesture. "I don't know. The whole Adept deal is completely out, but the rest of it will stand. Apart from that insanity there," She scowled at the Kobanes, who were trying out the drink Carter had mixed. "My rep will allow them to take me back with little question, but I've missed the captaincy exams, so I'll have to go back as a lieutenant commander."

Gray watched her twirl her pendant around and around, a small smile playing on his lips. "Not if you had a sponsor."

"But I don't."

"Not now, you don't. But I believe that, with a little persuasion, Heedman would be willing to sponsor you."

Adri dropped her chain to stare at Gray incredulously. "Did you get some brain damage while I was away? Why in the universe would Heedman sponsor me? He practically *killed* me!"

"Just so," with a flick of his wrist, Gray produced a data chip. "I happen to have a great deal of persuasion on hand."

"What is that?" Adri demanded.

"This, my lovely Adri, is your blackmail."

* * *

It took several minutes of listening to the intercom buzz for Floyd to react. The noise echoed emptily through the wide rooms of the mansion, like the call of a lost duckling whose mother had died. Once he realized that the intercom was buzzing because someone was at the front door, it took another long moment to remember that there was no staff to answer it. With a quiet moan, he rolled out of bed and stumbled out into the hall and down the stairs. The headaches that had been tormenting him for months continued to sing inside his skull with shattering proficiency. He didn't bother to check the identity of his midnight visitor. With the heavy "protection" that Colonel Stroff had placed around his property, he was as safe as the supreme chancellor. Almost blindly, he reached for the door panel and hit the release. In the back of his pain-filled mind, he almost wished for a quick shot to the head, just to end the agony.

What he got was a shot to the heart.

His sister stood on the doorstep, wet from the rain. Upon seeing him she let out a cry that sounded close to a sob. "Floyd! Oh!"

"Freya," Floyd gasped, wrapping his arms around her like a lifeline. Her skin was chilled, and the simple white dress she wore was soaking wet. "Danwe, what are you doing here? You haven't been home since mother died."

"Floyd!" Freya cried, hugging him tight. "I'm so glad that you're okay,"

Startled by the tremor in her voice, he whispered, "What happened, Freya?"

The young Talented made a soft sound of pain, clinging tighter. "Massacre."

Feeling better. Am I feeling better? My skull still vibrates with agony, and my body aches for sleep that I can't find. But the cloud of numbness that had swallowed me since father's death is dissipating. Some things are still hazy, but more and more come clear.

I think I was crazy. Simple. Overwork. Being home has improved me considerably.

No, no. Don't lie to yourself. It haunts me. I may still go crazy, or kill myself with mental fatigue, but at least now I understand why. Maybe that's the measure of calm I've gained.

Father would never commit suicide.

Strange, how I forgot that, or couldn't handle that truth until Freya came home last night with horror tales of blood and destruction. Strange how we are both haunted by places we called home, places with people who want to kill us. But Freya won't let me just end it. She won't let me succumb to their plans. And she is right. I have too much to do now. I owe my...children that much, to try and find a way to save who I can.

Children...huh. Well, they call me father, so why shouldn't I call them children? As their father, I am responsible for their welfare. I must find a way to help, even if it's just for a few.

Freya is strength, and oh, how I've missed feeling strong. She says that there is much going on in her world of visions and power. Things that will affect everyone more directly than we realize. Nothing is safe.

No, nothing is safe. Nowhere is safe. I know that Stroff has me watched. The security monitors never sleep. Sooner or later he is going to grow tired of me, and I will disappear. In the meantime he will allow me to putter about in the home that is no longer mine, tinkering with my humacoms. As though I were blind as well as helpless.

Freya is right.

We must find a way to escape.

Chapter Thirty-Three

Captain Adrienne Elizabeth Rael strode out of an Advance Force briefing room over three hours after walking in. Behind her strolled Captain Royce Carter, yawning. "I'm so glad that went well," he said brightly.

"Guess it did." Adri's mind was still spinning from the long hours she had spent before the military council. The brief 'talk' she'd had with Heedman early that morning resulted in exactly what Gray had predicted. In exchange for keeping silent on his less-than-stellar conduct towards her and the others that had died due to his cowardice, Heedman agreed to sponsor her for captaincy before the council. Adri still wasn't sure if it was the blackmail, or the fact that he thought her a ghost that had actually won his agreement. His pale face during the council meeting had displayed how unnerved he was, but from what, Adri couldn't tell. He had gone through with his end of the deal. After a carefully edited debriefing, Adri had been given what she wanted. Despite the fact that she had missed the formal interviews, the council had agreed that her service record, combined with her heroic injuries, warranted a promotion. With Heedman's sponsorship paving the way, Adri was now walking out of her first mission briefing as a ship's captain.

Captaincy was something she had strived for since entering the Academy. It was a respected position of authority. It gave her free reign to choose her own crew, plan her own missions. It was perfect. So why could she feel anger building?

Anger burned like a slow moving stream of acid through her veins. It wasn't from the sneers of the council members who thought she was inferior due to her lack of social standing. It wasn't from the need to blackmail her old superior. It certainly wasn't from the grudging way the council had granted her a ship. It wasn't even the mundane nature of the maiden voyage she had been immediately given. What it was, Adri couldn't quite define. But something about the mission briefing had struck her.

And, somehow, she had *known*. All the pieces dropped into place, leaving her staring at a finished puzzle that spelt a word she had never wanted to contemplate.

"Grayson!" Carter shouted, startling her out of her dark thoughts. "Come and greet the newest captain of the Galactic Commonwealth Advance Force!"

Gray rushed over from where he had been waiting by a window, smiling. Adri forced herself to put her revelation aside, and smiled back. With a fancy salute, Gray said, "Congratulations, Captain."

"Thanks. Couldn't have done it without you,"

"You probably could. But it wouldn't have been pretty."

Adri could feel his pleasure for her in warm, soothing waves. She tried to relax and listen to the lively replay of the meeting that Carter was giving. "It went rather well, all in all," he was saying. "Heedman didn't stutter too much, and Admiral Appegus only made two rude comments. He looks so peculiar when he sneers, like he has something stuck in his back teeth, and is trying to smile without showing them."

"Carter," Adri hinted loudly, "Don't you have somewhere to be?"

Her old friend stared at her blankly a moment, and then grinned. "Yes! Thank you for reminding me," he turned to Gray and explained hurriedly, "I've been given leave to pick my crew, and Leah Rachel Fayded's ship just arrived yesterday. I'm going to try to catch her before she leaves HQ." And with that, he rushed off.

"That's the fastest I've ever seen him go," Gray commented.

"He's really stuck on her," Adri replied.

Gray nodded, turning back to look at her face. "What's wrong?"

"What do you mean?"

296

"You're upset about something, Adri. Did it not go as well as Carter said?"

"What makes you think I'm upset?"

Gray reached down for her hand and pushed back her sleeve, displaying the dark, vivid marks on her arms. "I saw them when your sleeve bunched up for a moment. They're much darker than they were this morning."

Uncomfortable, Adri tugged her sleeve back down. "What of it?"

"I think your tattoos are connected with your anger. The more upset you are, the darker they become."

Considering her emotional state as she left the briefing, she thought Gray's theory held merit. "You could be right."

"So what has you angry, Adri?"

Adri shook her head. "Not now. I have to work it out for myself first."

Gray nodded. Adri was relieved he didn't try to press. "So, Captain, what do you have planned for the rest of your day?"

The plan that had begun to form in her mind during the mission briefing flashed back. "The council has granted me a ship. My first order of business is to enlist my senior staff."

"Got anyone in mind?"

"One or two," Adri slanted him a look. "As my vice captain, I expect you to keep a thorough record of all prospects for the positions, as well as a list of suitable candidates. Understood?"

Gray's heart gave an unsteady jump in his chest. "Aye-aye, Captain."

"Good," Adri headed towards the front entrance of the council building. "I have a line on a good chief engineer."

"I did not scream," Duane argued as Gray forced a cup of laced tea into his hand. "Nor did I faint. I was understandably shocked to see you, and all other functions had to be rerouted to my brain."

"You did scream, Duane," Adri replied with a good-natured snicker. "And then you turned so white your skin was nearly my color."

Duane gulped down a large portion of the tea. "Well, what do you expect? Danwe, L.C., you were supposed to be dead!"

"Well, I'm not. And I'm not a lieutenant commander anymore. You're going to have to get used to calling me captain now."

"Captain? *Danwe*, you work fast!"

"And getting faster. So are you going to be my chief engineer?"

Duane rubbed his hands through his short crop of blue-black hair, his eyes huge. "Danwe, did I fall asleep and wake up in an alternate universe? First you're not dead, then you're promoted to captain, and now you want me to be your chief engineer?"

"That about sums it up," Adri leaned back in the one chair in Duane's quarters that didn't have clothes dumped on it. "You in?"

"Danwe, yes!" Duane leaped up from the side of the bed and nearly tackled her to the floor in his enthusiasm. "I am your chief engineer, ma'am! This has to rank as the best day of my entire life!"

Duane started babbling in his native language and hugged her too tightly to breathe, so Gray stepped in. "We'll be glad to have you onboard." Prying the paranthian's arms off of Adri, he led him back to the bed.

"When you're feeling sober enough to walk, head over to Carter's house. That's where I'm staying for now," Adri said. "Gray and I have a few more stops to make before calling it a day."

"Great, fantastic, yes, I'll see you there once I've convinced myself that this isn't a dream."

Adri pulled a holoboard out of the pile of junk that littered Duane's dresser. She wrote a quick note, and then set it down beside him. "That ought to help. If we don't see you by tomorrow at 0700, we'll assume that you don't want to join in."

"What happens at 0700?" Duane asked, following Adri and Gray out the door and into the barracks compound.

"We're inspecting the ship. You'll need to be there to get a good look at the engines."

Duane looked as though he were about to break free of the planet's gravity. "Yes, ma'am!"

"So what time will he get there?" Gray asked as he and Adri left the compound a few minutes later.

"He'll show up around 2000 tonight," Adri replied with a grin. It had been good to see Duane. As strange as it sounded, it was also good to see that she had been missed. "I figure that Blair would make a good ship's doctor," she said, changing the topic.

"Are you sure you want him aboard?" Gray asked.

"Well, I can't imagine him letting me traipse off with my special abilities while he still thinks I can't control them, so we might as well put him to work."

"Hmm,"

Adri shot a glance at Gray in confusion. "What's wrong with Blair?"

"Nothing."

Still jealous? Adri pondered that possibility for a moment, then shoved it aside. If Gray was jealous of Blair for some weird reason, that was his problem.

"Adri, did you have anything planned for the rest of this afternoon? You've only been on Halieth for two days. Any errands you need to run?" Gray inquired. They were now standing outside of HQ. The sun was shining, but clouds on the horizon hinted of another electrical storm.

"Not really. I do need to go over the lists of prospective staff members, but that's not pressing. Why?"

"I need to make a stop. I got a message from Floyd Tarkubunji, the man who's repairing the humacom I bought. He said that he's finished, and that I can come pick him up."

Floyd disengaged the viewscreen and made his way out of the study. Absently, he rubbed his temple. His mind felt a little more engaged lately, which relieved him, and was currently busy working out a problem.

Escape.

He found his sister in their father's old workroom, wearing one of their mother's old day dressed in soft pink. The workroom was well lit, but cramped. Shelves and tables cluttered the room, each filled to bursting with schematic boards, loose wiring, welding lasers, and the odds and ends of humacom construction. In a roughly cleared space close to the door were stored the humacoms that WCRTL had returned to the estate after investigation. Of the twelve humacoms that had previously inhabited the Tarkubunji mansion, only three had been returned. Freya was standing over the smallest crate, her hand resting on the open lid. "It wounds my heart to see her like this." she sighed.

Floyd looked down into the crate at the child-sized humacom inside. It's pale hair and facial features bore an uncanny resemblance to the two Tarkubunjis. The stillness made him think that the little girl was dead and in a coffin. "It hurts me too."

Freya moved around to place a comforting hand on his shoulder. "You could always reactivate her,"

"I would have to reboot her whole system. The inspectors did a full memory search and wipe. She won't remember anything before activation."

His sister made a sorrowing sigh, hugging him tight. It was comforting to know that she, at least, understood his pain. They stood together over the body of a childhood friend. At last Freya said, "When are you meeting the soldier?"

"Lieutenant Grayson just got back to me. He's on his way."

"That's good,"

Floyd gave her a puzzled look. "Why do you say that?"

"I have a good premonition about him."

The Tarkubunji estate was impressive. Even after passing through a security screening by the established system, both Adri and Gray were also subjected to a suspicious once over by an Army sergeant. The quarrelsome man fondled his twin stream ATF rifle as though his entire hand was itchy. Harboring the typical aura of superiority that most Advance Force troops felt towards the Army, Adri was pleased to crush his attitude with her new title. Once they were though the gate, it was still a two mile drive until they reached the main house.

"This place rivals Carter's," she remarked after several long minutes of staring out the window at the impressive natural scenery. Carter had leant them one of his vehicles, a sleek silver sports cruiser that hovered low to the ground. It had probably cost more than Adri had spent on the Kobanes.

"Carter told me that their parents both prowled in the same social circles," Gray replied. "I guess the Tarkubunjis have been humacom designers since the conception of the idea. The last two generations have been making big money working for a government sponsored institute. There was a big deal when the father of the current family committed suicide in his lab; and the humacom institution as a whole has taken a beating with the personality recall that's going on."

Adri studied his ultra-serious profile for a moment. "The wealth and splendor making you nervous, Vice Captain?" she teased.

He grinned. "Perhaps a little. I grew up in the country, and I've never been much of a city dweller. But I am interested in the latest humacom dealings."

"Yeah. I read about in on the shuttle from Kieve. A mass recall doesn't sound like a solid answer to the problem."

Gray nodded, glancing away from the cruiser's controls to gauge her face. "No, it doesn't. When I first heard about it, it made me think…"

"Think what?" Adri asked when Gray didn't continue.

Her companion replied flatly, "Genocide."

Adri was silent for the rest of the short drive. She was still brooding when Gray stopped the cruiser in front of the mansion's main entrance. Following Gray, she walked up the elegant flight of stairs and waited for Gray's buzz to be answered. Adri was still lost in thought when the door finally slid open to reveal a young woman in a long dress, with long golden hair.

She looked up absently, and for one curious second, thought she saw wings fanning out from the young woman's back. When she blinked, they were gone. Adri didn't have time to process the phenomenon, because the woman stared at her and gave a shrill cry of surprise.

Freya felt as though she had been stabbed through the stomach by shock! All of the strange events of the past months tumbled through her mind like clattering dice, resulting in the woman who squinted in vague curiosity at her. The premonition she had felt earlier that morning suddenly became clear.

Ayane had been right. Veranda had awoken.

And was currently occupying her doorstep.

Who really understands the workings of the universe? The longer I live in it, the more I realize I don't understand. The logic it follows leaves mortal logic at a constant loss. I am grateful for it. How else could I be allowed to have a second chance with the woman I love? Mortal logic dictated that she was dead, and I believed it. Now she is back, and I am happy to toss logic aside and embrace her return.

Does that make me crazy? I don't think so, and I am sure my grandmother would agree. After all, she was a woman deeply aware of all that went on, not on a physical plane, but on something deeper. "Don't think knowledge holds the keys to everything," she said to me once. "Or you may end up suspicious of the best things of your life." Seeing the way my life has turned, she was dead on. I often wonder what I would be like if I had not spent the majority of my life with her.

I suppose I am once more following her advice. I am again at my beloved's side. Instead of questioning the layers of strange mystery and mysticism that shroud her return from the dead, I am simply in awe.

Not that I am completely ignoring it. The coincidence of this whole series of events is…staggering. Coincidence doesn't even begin to cover it. Adri's destiny has burst upon her, and she is understandably shell shocked. So if all this is fate, then what is my role?

There is something going on. Something that she is either not telling me, or doesn't realize herself.

She knows. What am I thinking? Of course she is aware, but she isn't talking. But does she accept? Ah, there is the crux of the matter. She knows something, doesn't want to accept it, and hasn't come to terms that she is destined for something important.

My dear, lovely Adri, I know what my role in life is.

To love you.

To be your friend and confidant.

To be your trusted councilor, vice captain and husband.

To get you to accept your own fate.

And to someday listen to the words I desperately need you to say.

Chapter Thirty-Four

"Hello, is Dr. Floyd Tarkubunji available? He's expecting me," Gray spoke into the strange vacuum of silence that had fallen since the young woman opened the door. Both she and Adri were engaged in a staring contest; the woman with astonishment, Adri with perplexity. Amused rather than annoyed, he tried again. "I believe he fixed my humacom for me."

Gray surmised that they would have stood just where they were for the rest of the day if Floyd Tarkubunji had not appeared at that moment. "Hello, doctor, it's good to see you again."

"Good afternoon, Lieutenant," Floyd replied, his gaze focused on the young woman still staring at Adri. Floyd frowned and nudged her gently. "Freya?"

The woman snapped out of her trance and turned to Gray. "Good afternoon, Lieutenant Grayson," she said, "I'm terribly sorry about the welcome. I was merely…sidetracked. I am Freya Tarkubunji, Floyd's sister."

"Hmph," Adri muttered.

With another confused glance at Freya, Floyd turned back to Gray. "Your humacom is ready for transport, but there are a few things we need to discuss before you allow him to wake from his emergency stasis mode. Why don't you come in?"

Because Freya was still giving Adri an odd look, Gray supplied an introduction. "This is Captain Adrienne Rael, by the way. She was recently promoted and has just begun collecting her crew,"

"That's wonderful," Freya said, beaming at Adri as they entered the main hallway of the mansion. "When were you promoted, Captain?"

"This morning," Adri replied shortly. "And Grayson's not a lieutenant anymore. As of this morning, he's my vice captain,"

"Congratulations, Vice Captain." Freya looked dazed. Adri continued to puzzle over the woman's intense stares that were aimed at her. "If you have only just been promoted, then when must you head out, Captain?"

It was a question that she normally wouldn't have answered, but she found herself saying, "In two weeks."

Gray cast her an astonished look, but made no comment.

"So soon," Freya's expression was inscrutable.

Floyd gestured them into the wide living room, which had two story windows facing the mansion's elaborate gardens. The afternoon sun shone brightly down on the whole scene. "Please have a seat," he said.

Adri sat down beside Gray on a wide sofa. She then took the time to get a good look at their host. He was young, she surmised, about the age of herself and Gray. He was an average height, with wheat blond hair, hazel eyes and glasses. However, the shadows under his eyes, the pallor of his fair skin, and way he kept rubbing his head all indicated that he was ill, and had been for some time. The way his clothes sagged was another indication. Before he began talking, he removed his glasses and cleaned them absently on his white lab jacket. Adri wondered why he just didn't bother with eye correction treatment instead of wearing the archaic things, but pushed the thought aside.

"First of all, I can tell you that Jericho's chassis was easy to repair, mostly cosmetic work. The damage in the chest cavity was a little tougher, but I was able to repair most of it, and replaced what I couldn't with some of my own equipment."

"What about the OS?" Gray asked. "The chief technician on the *Damacene* said it was beyond repair."

Floyd leaned forward and rested his elbows on his knees. "The damage to the cranium was very severe," he agreed. "Even I could not repair it completely."

"So Jericho is still inoperable?" Gray demanded. He felt crushed, like a life or death surgery had gone wrong and the patient was lost.

"No, not completely," Floyd replied.

"What do you mean?" Adri asked. "If the OS doesn't work, the humacom doesn't work, right?"

"Correct," Floyd agreed. "But in the case of Jericho, his OS is still functional, except for one area in his logic/protocol core. The damage there was so extensive, that any attempts at repair would damage Jericho's memory and primary sensors."

"How about his personality?" Gray wanted to know.

"His personality program was not damaged," Floyd replied, with an ironic glint in his eyes. "Why?"

"I'm glad. His personality was why I wanted to fix him. So what you're saying is that Jericho can operate, but not completely?"

Floyd shook his head. "No, Jericho can operate with the same functionality of any other humacom, but due to the damage in the logic/protocol core, his thought processes and actions could be...erratic."

"Dangerously?" Gray queried.

Floyd shifted in his seat. "I don't know. Personality and independent learning programs factor into the logic processing system that humacoms develop after they are booted. Therefore it depends on what Jericho has learned as well as how he was programmed to understand how his logic has developed, then take into account..."

"It's just like a person who has extensive brain damage," Freya jumped in when Floyd trailed off. "No one is really sure just how they will act, what the damage did to the person's thought process. What my brother is trying to say is that Jericho's personality and independent learning programs will weigh heavily in how he is going to think and act. But ultimately, we just don't know what the damage is going to affect."

"So what do you advise?" Adri interjected.

Floyd rose from his seat. "Just keep an eye on him. If his logic or protocol proves to be a serious problem, I can always try to write a backup program to help correct the error. It's the best I can do without a real knowledge of what will happen."

Gray got up as well. "Thank you for your efforts, Dr. Tarkubunji."

"You are welcome. In truth, it was the most relaxing thing I've done in a long time."

With a little maneuvering, the four of them managed to boost the transport crate that stored Jericho into the back of the cruiser that Adri had borrowed from Carter. It was a tight fit, edging over the backseat, bumping against the front seats and blocking the RearView monitor. Yet since it was only the two of them riding, Gray was sure that wouldn't be a problem.

"Thank you again," he said to Floyd after he and Adri had slammed the rear door closed.

Floyd nodded. "Be sure to-"

"Something's wrong," Freya announced suddenly.

Both men turned to look at her quizzically. "What is it Freya?" her brother asked.

Adri heard it before the others did, the high whine blended into the hum of the scenery. "Get down!" she shouted, grabbing a hank of Freya's hair and pulling her down to the elaborate brick drive. Beside her, Gray had tackled Floyd and the four of them rolled under the dubious safety of the cruiser as a grenade exploded only feet away. It was immediately followed by the thud and hiss of a fogger bomb. White smoke quickly began to envelop the drive.

"What the hell is going on?" Adri demanded as a second grenade exploded somewhere nearby. The smoke had already become too dense to see more than four feet away.

Floyd shook his head. "I don't know! This seems an extreme way of taking me out, if that's the agenda!"

"You've received death threats?" Gray scowled.

"Not exactly,"

The rapid firing of several assault blasters ended the conversation. "We have to get out of here," Freya said urgently. "More are coming,"

Adri didn't ask how Freya knew, her own instincts agreed. Her blood was up and racing, her elegy singing its lovely song. "We need to get out of here,"

"Everyone in the cruiser," Gray ordered. "Now!"

The ironic thing about fogger bombs was that they disoriented not only the enemy, but one's own side as well. Adri banked on the enemy being far enough away that they wouldn't inhale the smoke, and therefore not close enough for a rush attack. Still, it would only take a hit on the cruiser to blast them all to bits. Seconds inched by as Adri and Gray released the lock on the doors and pushed the Tarkubunjis in. Freya went immediately to the driver's seat.

"What are you doing?" Adri asked, squeezing in behind her next to Jericho's transport crate. Gray took the passenger seat after shoving Floyd in the back seat under Jericho's crate.

Freya engaged the engine and shot down the drive at an alarming speed. "I know the drive by memory, Captain," she said calmly. "Even with the smoke, I can get us out."

"Great. Is there any other exit besides the main gate?"

"Not one big enough for a cruiser," Floyd replied from his half prone position beneath the crate.

Gray kept his eyes trained on the grounds visible through the thinning smoke. "Then we'll have to make a break for it." Opening the passenger cargo compartment, he pulled out a pair of ATF pistols. "Count on Carter to have the best," he said as he tossed one back to Adri.

There was a tense silence as Freya maneuvered expertly along the drive. The scream of the assault blasters was unrelenting. "They must have a vehicle here on the grounds," Adri said suddenly. "They're following us now."

"Do you think that they'll have a team waiting at the entrance?" Gray asked.

"No doubt. Their blitz was well done. If we hadn't all been right next to the cruiser, we would have been caught in the crossfire. It would be stupid of them to leave us a clear avenue of escape."

"Plan?"

"Thinking of one. It depends on whose side the gate guards are on. Tarkubunji?"

Floyd was staring at the bottom of the crate, face pale. "I honestly don't know."

"We're coming up on the gate." Freya announced.

Adri calculated. "We really have no choice but to dash through. Gray, see what you can do with that little water gun Carter left us."

"Aye-aye," Gray disengaged the window and popped his head out. "Gate's open,"

Freya suddenly gasped. "Get inside!"

With a jerk on the steering, Freya pulled the cruiser off the drive in a hairpin turn, narrowly dodging a tree and somehow keeping the cruiser upright. Less than a second later, the space behind them lit up. The sonic wave of the bomb knocked three trees over in front of them, but Freya managed to avoid them all.

"Danwe!" Adri screamed at the young woman. She turned to the driver, and once again saw the pair of iridescent wings extending from Freya's back. They seemed to glow right through the seat. There was just enough time for her to notice the pale blue markings that covered the young woman's delicate hands on the wheel before she whipped back around.

It had to be a trick of the light, or something, Adri hoped. Danwe, Blair was going to do cartwheels if he heard about this one.

"Adri? You okay?" Gray shouted from the front seat.

"Yeah," Focus, Rael, she chided herself silently. She repositioned her pistol out the open window. Then she noticed that her own hands were covered in the familiar violet markings. "Oh, Danwe," she hissed.

Temper soaring, Adri fired at the rushing figures that were chasing after the cruiser. She couldn't get a good view of them through the drifting smoke, but they looked and acted military. Were they caught in some sort of raid? Did the military council not believe her story? No, that couldn't be it. They wouldn't risk civilians when they knew where she was staying. Most likely, one or both of the Tarkubunjis were in trouble. But why the overkill? If they had broken a law, the Peace Keepers would have come to arrest them, with the military as backup. There was no way that they could allow such a noisy raid to take place this close to the city. So what was going on?

"I'm back on the drive," Freya said, diverting Adri's attention back to the moment at hand. "The way seems to be clear for the moment. I'm going for it."

The cruiser shot through the main gate and out onto the street. The occupants had a few stunned seconds to take in the wreckage of the gatehouse and the bodies of the soldiers before Freya took them away at an illegal speed.

"Well, that rules out my military theory," Gray remarked, clinging to his seat as Freya guided the cruiser through several rapid turns.

Floyd popped his head out from beneath the crate. "It rules out my boss taking a shot at me, too."

Gray opened his mouth to question, but Adri shook her head. There would be time enough for questions later.

"We're being followed," Freya took another turn. "The black all-terrain."

Adri popped her head out and in through the window for a quick scan. "I see it." But how could Freya, with the RearView blocked?

Freya swerved the car just as one of the passengers of the all-terrain opened fire.

Steadying herself, Adri said, "Tarkubunji, can you get alongside the all-terrain? I have a shot. Gray, can you give me some cover?"

"I'm on it," Gray slid halfway out of the window, bracing his arms on the roof of the cruiser and his legs between the seat and the door.

As he began firing, Freya said, "I'm slowing down now."

The bulky black all-terrain shot towards them as the cruiser braked. Gray drew the fire of the three men who loomed out of the windows. In the seconds that both vehicles were side by side, Adri threw the cruiser door open and shot at the exposed engine vents. "Go, go, go!"

Freya doubled the speed just as the all-terrain exploded. Adri closed the door and Gray climbed back into the cruiser as Freya took five more turns, then slowed the vehicle to a sedate pace and rejoined traffic by the government square hub.

"It looks like we lost them." Gray said, automatically checking the reading on his pistol.

Floyd reappeared from beneath the crate. "What kind of crazy move was that?"

"It's a standard ploy used against enemy tanks and artillery," Adri replied. "Normally, I'd have used a rocket launcher or a grenade, but civilian vehicles are much easier to take out."

"I never did put much faith in all-terrain ads," Floyd muttered.

"So what just happened?" Gray demanded, turning to frown at the Tarkubunjis.

"A better question would be what do we do now?" Freya replied.

Adri pondered a moment. "Answer me this first. Have either of you done anything bad enough to warrant a raid and assassination? I'll know if you're lying,"

"Nothing, honestly," Floyd replied. He stared directly into Adri's eyes. "I swear that neither Freya nor I have done anything illegal. But there are…other reasons that someone might want either or both of us dead."

Adri held his gaze for another long second before glancing at Gray. "All right. Miss Tarkubunji, can you take us to the Carter estate? We'll have it all out there."

A lone figure stared at the wreckage of the Tarkubunji estate entrance. Sirens and flashing lights drew the attention of the curious. Peace Keepers scurried around the scene barking orders and taking samples. He was glad to have collected his own information before they arrived. The data was as yet unclear in all angles, but his primary objective hadn't changed with the circumstances. He would simply have to analyze this new data, and formulate a plan.

The Tarkubunjis couldn't hide forever.

I know what I know. I know I know too much. I know that if I told, my knowledge could get me killed. So what should I do with this knowing? Ignore it? Let things go back to the way they were before I learned so much? I can't. I can't go back knowing what I know now. I can't let them get away with what they've done, and what they are planning to do. Maybe if there was nothing I could do about it, I would simply defect. But I can do something. Yet because I can do something, does it automatically make it right? Is action the right course to take? How did my life become so complicated? I know what I know. I know I can change it. I know that in my heart, the course I have chosen is truly the right one. I know I must act, even though it may cost me everything I have ever wanted. I can't ignore it anymore.

Stupid magic powers.

Chapter Thirty-Five

"The fusions in sectors nine and twenty-one are shot, so we'll have to replace those before we can even dream of engaging full power from this baby." Duane stroked the cracked engine piece in question. "It would be best to give the whole thing a complete overhaul, but with less than two weeks before launching, there's no way to fit it in. The best I can tell you is that it will run for our maiden voyage, and I should be able to tinker with it while we're en-route. If that's all right with you, Captain. Captain? Hey, are you awake?"

Adri was snapped back to the present. "What? Sorry Duane."

"Danwe, you're not supposed to nod off on my reports until after at least one month," Duane chided. "I was saying that the engine is less than stellar. But we can make the two week deadline."

"Good. Have you talked with Gray about junior officers?"

"Yeah. Ah, it's so great to be the one in charge," Duane gave a loud sigh of pleasure. "So much power, so many underlings to torture, my own personal quarters, more power..." He frowned as Adri's eyes drifted off again. "Hey, am I really that boring?"

"No, no. In fact, I'm really glad that you're here. I just...have a lot on my mind right now."

The paranthian continued to frown. Making a quick check of the area, he stepped closer. "What's the deal, Rael? You've been preoccupied since I met you again. I mean, you had a heck of a mess there, what with nearly dying and all, but..."

"But what?"

Duane shrugged. It was a much-loved human gesture that he had adopted in basic training. "When you're not paying attention, you get this really mean look on your face. Like when we're in combat. Sort of…angry and eager at the same time."

Adri frowned. "Oh? Hmm."

"Come on, Captain. Something's up. I know it has to do with whatever the humacom geek was saying to you before I got there last night. You looked ready to shoot something,"

"Was it that obvious?" a wry grin crossed her face.

Duane's frown lightened a little. "To me it was. But then, I know you pretty well. Your moods can be hard to pick up on. But you were giving off a very 'shoot something' vibe. Its still there, just more like a 'making a plan to shoot something.' So tell me what the deal is, huh? We're friends, aren't we?"

"Aw, don't say it like that," Adri groaned. "We're still friends,"

"Then what gives? Who are we going to be shooting? I want in on this action! Who are we after? Its not the notorious Kobane sisters, because you have them leashed. Which is really bizarre, by the way."

"It's not like that."

"Then what's it like?" Duane insisted.

What to tell him? That she had edited her tale about herself to her oldest friend? That she was an Adept with amazing powers and had just realized that the d-word was not to be avoided? That she had a plan that would certainly appall him? No, she couldn't tell him what she was planning. Not yet. "I'm sorry Duane."

Duane scowled. "Have you told Gray?"

"No. I haven't told anyone. Honestly."

"Well, there's that at least. Are you going to tell us? I care about you, L.C. It was terrible when I thought you had died. It was like losing my family all over again. I know Gray feels the same."

"Yes, I'm going to tell you. Just…not yet."

The paranthian leaped to an astute guess. "Does it have something to do with our mission?"

Adri held his gaze steadily for several seconds.

"I see," cheered considerably, Duane leaned back against the cracked engine module. "So, we'll be kicking some vulnerable ends en-route to our destination?"

"In a manner of speaking,"

Duane whistled. "I can't wait."

After determinedly focusing on Duane's engine diagnosis for several hours, Adri escaped up to the ship's bridge. *Her* bridge now, she thought with a measure of glee. Here she was able to forget her plans and revel in being a captain. Sure, the bridge was empty, and some of the computers and monitors were out of date. But they were hers! Soon, everything would be bright and busy. With a sigh, Adri collapsed into the captain's seat, ignoring the cloud of dust it created. The first order of business, she thought idly, was to get some domesticoms up to clean the place.

"Got a tour of all the warehouses," Gray announced as he passed through the doors onto the bridge. "The *Noelio* has plenty of space."

Okay, first order of business was to change the ship's name to something more appropriate, Adri thought with a frown. The *Noelio* was a gimpy name for a frigate of her ship's potential.

"You hate it too?" Gray said with a grin, sitting down on her control panel to face her. "Have you ever seen a real noelio? They give ugly and inept a whole new illustration. I think they might be the only birds that are considered ugly by every other species."

"We have to change the name before we go," Adri agreed. "It's terrible."

"Renaming requests take up to six months to be processed," he tapped his holoboard against his leg.

Adri smirked. "Yeah, if you do it the nice way. Don't worry, I'll have us a nice new name by the time we head off."

"Sometimes you terrify me." Gray judged the time right. "Speaking of heading off, when are you going to tell me just what is it about this mission that has you so on edge?"

Her gleeful bubble burst. "Have you been talking to Duane?"

"We're worried about you."

Incredibly uncomfortable, Adri replied, "Gray...."

"Whatever the problem is, I know I can help you," he leaned forward with serious earnestness. "Believe it or not, you have a lot of people in your corner."

The statement was like punching a hole in a pressurized bottle. "Can't you see? That's why I haven't said anything!" Adri leapt to her feet. "It would be so much simpler if it was something I could take care of myself. Then I could go and do it, and no harm done if I failed. But its not, so I need you and Duane and even - Danwe save me- Blair to pull it off, so if I fail I'll drag you down with me. And even if I succeed, you'll still all be punished for helping." With a low sigh, she accepted Gray's embrace. "I can take failing on my own, but I can't stand hurting everyone I care about. And it will, either way it goes,"

Gray continued to hold her after she fell silent. "You were always a good leader, Adri. Part of being a good leader is worrying about the welfare of your crew."

"It's not the same thing,"

"Yes, it is the same thing," He nudged her chin up. "You have to do this, right? Whatever it is? So it's just like a mission. You can't expect a mission to run smoothly all by yourself."

"Suppose so," Adri murmured.

"And you can't expect a mission to run if you keep your subordinates in the dark, either."

She laughed a little. "No." Taking a deep breath, she leaned back. "Gray, why is it you haven't once asked me about the words you wanted me to say?"

Gray searched her eyes for a moment. "Have you figured out what they are?"

Adri held his gaze. "Yes."

"And?"

"Do you still want to hear them?"

"Of course I do. When you're ready to tell me,"

Something stirred within in her, sighing, *now! Now!* She reached out and cupped his face. "Oh Gray…I…." she clutched. "Soon,"

Gray held her hand against his cheek, and gave a small smile. "Soon then."

315

Adri hated herself, seeing the small flicker of disappointment in his eyes.

[Engineering to Bridge,]

Both Gray and Adri jumped at the disembodied voice of Duane that echoed through the room.

[I've got the communications system up and running, although we're going to need a techie to make sure all this type of falderal stays running.]

Adri found the communication switch on her control panel and replied, [Bridge to Engineering, that's an affirmative.]

[And while we're at it, make sure we get some sizzling nurses for the infirmary. Engineering out.]

"Well, let's see how we can manage to fulfill our magenta friend's wish," Gray picked up his holoboard and began to scroll.

Adri opened her mouth, and then shut it. The moment was dead. "Have any ideas?"

"Junior officers are no problem. It's the senior staff that is giving me fits. There are plenty of accredited officers, but..."

"But what?"

Gray made a face and handed her the holoboard. Adri glanced at the names and profiles. "This is it?" She mirrored Gray's expression. "What is this, the naval reject list? Sure, they're all accredited, but look how long it took! What, do they have slugs for brains?"

"My thoughts exactly. But I have an idea."

"Please," Adri tossed the holoboard onto the Security station and collapsed back into her chair. "Anything."

"Since our mission is within secure Commonwealth space, we don't need to take our maiden voyage with anything more than a skeleton crew,"

"True," Adri agreed. "But we're still going to need a few more senior staff members, unless you don't want to sleep."

"Yes. But if we focus on only getting the staff we can't live without, then we can refit when we return."

If they ever returned, Adri thought. Perhaps having less would be better. "So who do you have in mind?"

"If we got a junior officer to take the paper pushing end of Security, I could double as the security officer."

"But you'll be needed on the bridge,"

"Which is why we place Jericho in as head of Operations. The *Doreh Jal* and the *Tibei* both use humacoms extensively as junior officers. So why not just place Jericho in? He has all the programming and as much learning experience as any other officer. And a better memory."

"But what about his potential to malfunction?" Adri argued.

"It's just as dangerous to place trust in an organic being," Gray countered. "Besides, ever since I activated him last night, he's been fine."

Adri pondered the idea for a few minutes. Jericho had acted perfectly normal in the hours she'd been around him. A little too polite, but normal. He smiled and said how pleasant it was to meet someone who recovered from death. It had taken her a moment to realize that he'd been teasing her. He smiled a lot. Actually, Adri had never seen him *not* smiling, in a life's-a-fun-ride sort of way. He never left Gray's side the entire night, making them an interesting trio (since she didn't leave Gray's side either). For some reason, Adri had gone to bed that night with the impression that the humacom adored Gray, if humacoms had a sense of adoration. "I guess that would work. But you'd better keep an eye on him. I'd rather have someone in Security, but for a maiden voyage within our own territory, I guess we can do without."

"That's what I thought as well." Gray leaned back against the control panel again. "We've got Blair as our doctor, so I think we could get away with a medicom for a head nurse."

"Do you have a list?"

"Yeah." Gray retrieved the holoboard and searched for the appropriate screen. "Here, these are all Galactic Commonwealth Navy approved."

Adri studied the list of medicoms. "There's a notation by most of these new ones that says 'HPP and ITP free,' Do you know what that means?"

"Humacom Personality Program and Independent Thinking Program," Floyd called from the door. "It means they've passed through the recall and had those programs removed from their hard drives. Like being brainwashed,"

Both Gray and Adri looked over at him.

"I'm sorry," he apologized. "I was going to alert you, but I caught the tail end of your conversation."

Adri beckoned him over. "Finished giving your report to the Peace Keepers?" The Peace Keepers had been notified the night before about the strange attack, but they had wanted a more detailed account from the two Tarkubunjis. Both sister and brother had made an appointment with them for the following afternoon.

"Yes. I was given the standard, 'we'll look into it,' line. If they know anything, they aren't telling me. They said we could return home, but I asked Captain Carter if we could remain at his residence until the situation is resolved." Floyd glanced down at the list displayed on the holoboard. "Medicoms?"

"For the ship's infirmary," Adri frowned down at the list. "But all of these newer models have been through the recall."

"Then those won't do," Floyd said with authority. "All humacoms that lack a personality and independent thinking would be terrible as nurses. Like being treated by a vending machine. Not to mention it would be a terrible hassle for the doctor. He'd constantly have to give them new instructions if a situation has no approved precedent. May I?" he took the holoboard from Adri's hand. Flicking expertly through the screens on the board, he went on, "The older models, like these KJM's from EriTech or the 900 models from Interstellar would be better choices. The chasses are a bit clunkier and the operating systems are a little slower, but they have a well-balanced cranium. Still, none of them have the right programming for a commanding position."

Gray and Adri shared a long look. "Dr. Tarkubunji, you wouldn't happen to be searching for a new job, perchance? One that traveled?" Gray asked.

Floyd looked up sharply from the holoboard. "You want me to come with you?"

Adri leaned back in her seat. "We need someone who could head the technical department. Someone with a good knowledge of humacoms, who can deal with problems as they arise and so on. You're pretty good at your job. So?"

Gray rolled his eyes at Adri's tactless advance. "You would be a great asset to the ship."

The humacom designer seemed to fall into rapid thought for all of one second. "Yes."

"Give yourself time to think about it first," Gray said in some surprise. "You'd have to quit your job - "

"All to the better," Floyd gave Adri a look that Gray couldn't quite interpret. "Thank you, Captain. I'll work hard."

"Great. You'll be a civilian commander, which will give you authority as a member of the senior staff and in your field, but little other power." Adri nodded to the holoboard. "Who would you purchase from that list?"

Floyd blinked at his rapid change of circumstances, and then bent back down. After a few minutes he showed the board to Gray. "These ones would be well placed in an infirmary setting. All have updated medical files, hospital procedures, and reportedly well learned bedside manners." With a little more confidence, he added, "If I may be so bold, could I suggest taking my sister aboard as well? I can attest that she is a good worker. Her gift of foresight comes in handy."

"Foresight?" Adri repeated.

Floyd nodded. "It's one of her gifts as a Talented. She even lived in a convent for years to refine it."

Adri mentally groaned. "You don't say,"

"Yes. In fact, she told me you'd be open to giving us a shot. You being an Adept and all that. But, uh, just what is an Adept, exactly? Freya was a little vague,"

There was a long second of silence as Adri and Gray both stared at Floyd. Then Adri shot to her feet and stormed off the bridge. "Fine! What do I care if I'm overrun with mystical geeks determined for me to fulfill my stupid destiny? What do I care if everyone knows I have magic powers? Sign her up!"

Floyd and Gray stared at the door for a long minute after she had departed. At last, Floyd said, "That was strange. Has something upset her?"

"No, just fate. Its been kicking her around."

Galactic Commonwealth Cracks Down on Traitors!
Undaria Plot to Sell Out to Belligerents Exposed!

Halieth: *A stunning media brief made by our Supreme Chancellor, Roger Fane, announced the uncovering of a plot by the citizens of Undaria, first planet of the Undaria system.*

"It came to our attention that there was strange activity occurring on the planet," Supreme Chancellor Fane explained. "On a deeper investigation, our intelligence discovered that the satellite government on Undaria was underhandedly selling military secrets to the Belligerent Coalition. In response, special detachments from the military were sent in to ferret out the traitors and restore civil authority in the undarian provinces. Unfortunately, the savage undarians had all sworn a mae aras, or clan compact, to resist reunion with the Commonwealth."

Supreme Chancellor Fane went on to explain the ramifications of a clan compact among the undarian people. According to their culture, a clan compact is sworn by the sixty-four clan heads and is obeyed by every member of that clan. Due to their culture that promotes extreme loyalty to clan members and dictates, Fane concluded, "the entire undarian species is sworn against the prosperity of the Galactic Commonwealth. They have deliberately chosen to become the enemies of our nation."

In response to the question of possible motives for the undarian people to become hostile to the Commonwealth, Fane stated; "The undarians have always been an isolated, suspicious species. Due to their violent tendencies to attack and kill humans as a food source, their unusual views of death and the importance they place in their own position on the evolutionary food chain, the Galactic Commonwealth has always been prepared for a bloody rebellion. Luckily, new technology has enabled us to neutralize the planet, leaving only manageable pockets of potentially dangerous rebels scattered throughout the Commonwealth systems."

When asked what technology enabled the neutralizing of an entire planet, Fane made no comment. "Our main concern now is to track down any undarians who may have been given terrorist orders from their clan heads." He concluded with, "All Commonwealth citizens should be alert, but not alarmed. The government has the situation well in hand."

Chapter Thirty-Six

"**S**orry about the invasion. I didn't realize they were all just going to...stick around." Adri leaned against Carter's antique desk. She'd have bet her new ship that the elegant piece of real wood cost more than the cruiser he had lent her.

"Oh, its no trouble. The more the merrier, eh?" Carter smiled at her from his slouch, and then dropped his gaze back to the holoscreen built into the desk surface.

"The more the noisier, at least," Adri replied. Through the open door she could hear Duane and Floyd still arguing over some mechanical issue that had started less than a minute after Adri had introduced them as new colleagues. In a corner she could see Blair and Freya Tarkubunji huddled, doubtlessly talking about mystical hoodoo and how she was a vat of untapped Adept power. Across from them the Kobane sisters were watching the argument (which was getting louder), and possibly wagering on the outcome. Somewhere in the mansion she knew Gray was huddled over a holoboard with Jericho, on the viewscreen with the Admiralty about staff and resources. Her crew.

The sound of furniture crashing and the Kobane sisters cheering had Adri rolling her eyes. Danwe, were they all going to make it to their objective without killing each other? Putting them aside, she turned to her companion. "Looking over senior staff picks?"

"Nope. Junior officer candidates," Carter replied morosely.

Adri was surprised. "Why aren't you having your vice captain handle those?"

Carter sighed and leaned back in his chair. "Because my vice captain is in the midst of a personal crisis,"

"Drustin Hamilton?" Adri queried.

"Yeah. His fiancé was injured in a house bombing. Her whole family was killed, and they fear extensive, non-op brain damage. No chance of cyborization. He hasn't left the hospital."

"I'm sorry to hear that. Who was responsible for the bombing?"

"Well, they arrested Drustin's brother, Darius. He confessed to the bombing, says he was opposed to Drustin's involvement with anti-war activists."

Adri huffed a breath. "Danwe. That's a vicious way to express displeasure,"

Carter shrugged. "Pity, true. Such a mess. Anyway, I'm worried now that Hamilton will back down as my vice captain. That'll leave me in a bit of a bind."

"A bit," Adri replied dryly. "But somehow I think you'll manage. And since I know that you have innumerable underlings that you could shove this off on, tell me why you are dinking around with the junior officer lists? Trying to keep your mind off of something?"

Her friend slouched further in his chair. "What makes you say that?"

"Did Fayded say no?" Adri teased.

Carter scowled. "She's undecided about my offer,"

"Ouch,"

"She'll come around." He glared fiercely at the wall-mounted viewscreen that was running a news clip. "Did you catch all that news today about the undarians?" he said quickly. "Shocking!"

"Mm," Adri turned to watch the clip. After the headline segment broke to the planetary weather forecast, she frowned. "You believe all that stuff about the undarians trying to sell out on us?"

Carter stared at her in confusion. "What do you mean? Of course. Although I must say that the supreme chancellor doesn't look very good in high collars. Don't you think?"

"You'd know best." Adri murmured. She was still frowning.

Two weeks flooded past Adri in a blur of paperwork and meetings. There had been too much to do in the meager twelve days she'd been given to outfit her ship to spare time on her internal problems. Or so she told herself. Whenever Blair approached her, she brushed him off, using her overbearing workload as an excuse. She also used it on Gray, whenever he gently prodded her about what she was holding back. It was lame, and it was cowardly, but Adri was determined her beautiful ship, newly rechristened *Elegy,* would have a perfect first launch.

Especially because she wasn't sure whether she would get a second one.

When Adri had triumphantly waved the letter of consent to change the ship's name, everyone had asked her why she had picked 'elegy.' While she had shrugged it off in front of the crowd, she had privately confessed to Gray, "It's the sound my blood makes when I fight. It... sings an elegy."

He'd understood.

Now she sat in her captain's chair, with her bridge staff assembled, waiting for the Admiralty's inspectors to complete their final once over. Unlike the previous inspections that had occurred over the past two weeks, this one was an inspection of the crew. It was mostly a formality, since all crew personnel would have been passed through the Admiralty already. It was merely a last check to make sure that no changes had been made to the ship's manifest without the military being informed; a holdover from past decades when smuggling of all sorts had been rampant. It was really no big deal.

Except, of course, that she *was* smuggling. As well as fabricating. And forging. And possibly outright thieving. Many of her new senior staff had required government credentials they hadn't possessed. The recruitment office had denied the Tarkubunjis' applications for some very complicated reason that had Adri suspicious, so adjustments had to be made there. More fabricating and falsification that would surely be found out sooner or later.

Not that she was worried about it.

Danwe, were they going to be caught before they even left the planet?

At his position beside her chair, Gray murmured, "It's all going to work out."

"I sure hope so," Adri replied, eyeing the chief inspector suspiciously. "All it would take is one well placed question, and we'd be in major trouble."

"Your crew is loyal," Gray affirmed. "Nothing is going to go wrong."

Down in the humacom maintenance lab, Floyd Tarkubunji was frantically repeating the same phrase to himself. "Nothing's going wrong, everything will work out....oh, Danwe..." With the speed of long practice, he continued to unlatch crates of personal gear he had had secretly shipped from his estate.

Beside him, Jericho assisted with removing and storing the equipment in its proper locations. After listening to Floyd mutter for several minutes, he asked, "Are you concerned about something, sir?"

Floyd huffed a breath and rubbed his temples. "Danwe, yes I'm concerned! Here I am, smuggling myself aboard an Advance Force ship under a false name and credentials. I had to steal my own belongings out of my home – which I don't own anymore – because my old boss might very well want to kill me. And if I am found out here, it will be far worse than a mere 'accident' when I die. To cap it all off, I've dragged my sister into this whole sordid affair, because I'm afraid that if my problems don't spill off onto her, her own issues will get her killed! Not that she tells me what they are, exactly. Some mystical massacre...so yes, I'm concerned." The humacom designer looked up at his companion in sudden question. "Are you?"

"Not at all, sir," Jericho replied, with the smile that had become usual for him.

"Why? If something goes wrong during the inspection, you'll likely be either scrapped or recalled."

The humacom shook his head. "I don't think anything will go wrong, sir."

Floyd smiled a little at the confidence Jericho had placed in his tone. "And why do you think that?"

Jericho was silent for a long minute. "I can't explain. But I have utter confidence in the captain's ability to get almost anything she aims for. After all, Gray trusts her."

[Bridge to Technical Lab,] Gray's voice called.

Floyd touched his new communicator at his ear. [Lab here,]

[All senior staff are assembling on the bridge.]

[I see...I mean, understood. We're on our way.] Floyd turned to Jericho. "Here it goes,"

"Everything *appears* to be in order," the chief inspector announced to Adri when the last of his teams announced mission complete. "Although..."

Adri held her breath. This particular inspector was notorious for his dislike of female commanders. It was rumored that he'd once nearly lost his ship because he'd been unwilling to relinquish his post to the female relief officer. Adri had a feeling that he'd been sent to head her final inspection on purpose. The idea that the higher authorities were suspicious of her moves had cold sweat beading down her spine.

"There are some senior staff choices that have been brought to our attention that concerns us."

Danwe. "And what might those concerns be, Chief Inspector?"

"Your choice of vice captain and chief engineer are solid," the elderly man stated, frowning over his holoboard. "Both men have served in the Advance Force for several years. But as to the rest..."

"All my senior staff have been handpicked because of their unique talents," Adri cut in. "They are all more than qualified to serve aboard this vessel." she hoped.

The chief inspector continued to frown. "Be that as it may, your doctor..."

"Is fully certified," After several hours of hacking and forgery. While Blair probably knew more than a professional surgeon, a government certification was hard to come by on Junus.

"Yes, well," he coughed delicately into his fist. "You have no second officer, no analysis officer, your vice captain is doubling as your security officer..."

"Our mission will not take us beyond Commonwealth space. A full staff isn't necessary."

"Be that as it may, you are using a humacom as your operations officer,"

"Jericho has worked in various positions throughout his career in the Advance Force," Adri replied. "The operations position is nothing that he can't handle as well as an organic."

The chief inspector looked doubtful, but finally shrugged. "Unorthodox, especially considering the times. Still…that is your choice, Captain. Lastly, we are quite concerned about your use of civilians aboard this vessel. To use them in minor positions is still contested by the Admiralty Recruitment Office. Therefore, what makes you think that you can use civilians in key positions, Captain?"

Tension settled like a cloak of iron around Adri's shoulders. "With all due respect, sir, I wanted people I can trust, people whose abilities I have witnessed for myself. If those happen to be civilians, then I will hire them. My authority as captain can extend to hiring such personnel."

"But to use a civilian as a helmswoman!" the chief inspector cast a dubious glance at Freya, who smiled serenely back at him. She looked incredibly out of place in her severe gray military uniform, her hair neatly braided in a long plait down her back. Freya looked like a fairy trying to pass as a creditor. "One with no recorded experience. What can you be thinking?"

"Freya Tarkson has a pilot's certification," At least, she did now. "And I have seen her in action. She has a way with piloting that exceeds anything else I've ever seen." Which was true. Adri had never seen such reflexes as the ones Freya had exhibited in the cruiser chase. "She's the only one I would entrust to steer us right."

"And the chief technician?" the chief inspector waved her off before she could begin her defense of Floyd. "Never mind. Why don't I ask your ops officer," he turned to Jericho. With a derisive lift of his brow, he asked, "Humacom, what is the name and rank of your chief technician?"

A hush fell over the room. Adri could feel the prickle of nerves, distant stirrings of adrenaline.

Humacoms were not programmed to lie. The minute Floyd's last name was spilt, there would be serious problems. Already Adri was trying to formulate a plan.

"His name is Floyd Tarkson, sir, a civilian commander."

The old man sniffed, "and just what are his credentials?"

Jericho blinked. "He fulfils the job description, sir. He designs, repairs and maintains humacoms. He is also qualified in general technical development and repair."

The chief inspector's eyes narrowed. "Is that so. Answer me yes or no. Is there anything illegal or of dubious legality going on aboard this ship? Is there anything the Galactic Commonwealth would be opposed to?"

Adri closed her eyes.

"No sir."

Everyone turned to stare at Jericho, who continued to smile blithely. The chief inspector frowned again, then turned back to his holoboard. "Is that so? Very well then. Captain Rael, you will receive permission to launch from Navy Control in a matter of hours." He saluted, although he continued to frown. "We'll be watching you, Captain."

Adri kept her hand in salute as the inspection crew left the bridge. "I'll give you something to watch," she murmured.

No one moved for several long minutes, until a junior officer announced that the inspection crew had left the ship. Then Floyd spoke. "Jericho…you…you lied."

The humacom tilted his head. "Not really, sir. Your name is Floyd Tarkson at the moment."

"No, I mean…" Floyd turned to the rest of the staff, who were all staring. "I mean about the legality. You know that Freya and I are working under a false name, and that we're smuggling two Belligerents in the warehouse, and that…"

"The Galactic Commonwealth wants peace for its citizens," Jericho replied. "All legalities stem from that desire. So by fulfilling our mission, aren't we following that dictate?"

Silence. Gray and Adri shared a look.

"Jericho," Floyd said, "Could you go down and check to see that all my material is where we left it?"

When Gray gave an approving nod, Jericho saluted and left the bridge.

"That was creepy," Duane commented.

Floyd frowned. Turning to Adri and Gray, he said, "There is no way that his logic program would have let him say that. No way at all."

"What does that mean?" Gray asked.

"It's a quirk from the damage. Somehow, he's able to reroute his logic to come to a conclusion that suites him."

"What does that mean?" Adri demanded.

"It means that he is doing what humans do. Lie."

Two hours later, Adri had shoved all thoughts of inspections, lying humacoms, and petty worries aside, and gave the order to launch. "Miss Tarkubunji, take us out,"

Despite her internal misgivings about allowing the young civilian to fly a frigate – *her* frigate – without any prior instruction, Freya engaged the controls and navigation system with no problems. Working in tandem with Duane down in Engineering, the young woman guided the sleek craft away from its docking station and out beyond the control of Halieth's gravitational pull. At last, the planet began to blur behind them, while all they could see ahead was the vast, dotted void of space.

Captain Adrienne Rael leaned back in her seat, listening with half an ear as all her staff communicated in. All systems go.

"Well, it looks like we're off without a hitch," Gray said from beside her. Adri could hear the relief in his voice.

For Adri, there was no real sense of relief, only an exchange of one set of worries for another. "Gray, get a senior staff meeting scheduled. Make it…in an hour."

"A staff meeting?" Gray frowned. "We've barely left the planet,"

Adri took a deep breath. "Yes, I know. An hour. And make sure the Kobanes come as well. They might as well make themselves useful."

"Adri?" Gray frowned.

"Its time for the mission briefing, Gray." Adri replied, her face a serious mask. "It's time for answers."

Adversity breeds necessity. Necessity breeds invention. Invention breeds expansion. Expansion breeds adversity.

Chapter Thirty-Seven

Adri watched tensely as her motley senior staff filed into the ship's War Room. The general feeling among them was curiosity. She wondered how long it would take before most of them changed to fury.

"What's the deal?" asked Duane, plopping into his seat at the far end of the table and leaning back. "We forget to have the brief on the use of space toilets or something?"

Floyd raised his brow at the paranthian sitting adjacent to him. "You mean your engineering requires a manual and mission brief in order for regular people to use the toilet?"

Duane scowled. "What did you say about my engines, techie?"

"Now, now," Freya stepped into the budding conflict and placed a gentle hand on each one's shoulder. "Let's not bicker now. The captain has something to say."

Adri watched as the young woman sat down across from the two griping men, giving them each a serene smile. Two seats over from Freya sat Blair. His eyes were half closed, and he appeared deep in thought. One seat separated him from Adri. On Freya's other side, between her and Duane sat the two Kobane sisters, arms folded, as though they were spectators watching a mediocre play. Adri was just glad that they had not as yet decided to wreak havoc. Two empty seats separated Floyd from Jericho. He was watching the malevolent glares that Floyd and Duane were giving each other with interest. In the chair between her and Jericho sat Gray, who watched her expectantly.

"This meeting is called to order." Adri announced. Her fingers were clenched tight, but her face was impassive. She waited until everyone was looking at her. "The purpose of this meeting is to discuss our current assignment, and lay out our mission objectives."

"It's about time you spilled..." at Adri's deadpan look, Duane hastily rephrased. "Er, what I meant Captain, is that I am glad you're going to reveal this information to us."

"Quite. As you all may know, I received my mission assignment the same day I was promoted, which is highly unusual." Adri flexed her fingers under the table to try to ease the tension, but they simply coiled back. "The information I was given at the briefing was very sparse, simply a set of coordinates which we were to travel to, and orders to pick up a SecureBox with top secret information. We were then to take this SecureBox to the satellite center on Toreth, before returning to base."

"That sounds simple," said Floyd.

"Wait, what do you mean, *were* to travel?" Duane asked. "Did the mission get changed?"

"Something has changed." Jericho agreed.

"Yes, there is more to it," Freya frowned.

Gray turned to his captain. "Adri?"

Adri's eyes flicked to Blair's then to Hildana's. "From my recent travels, I've discovered a lot of things, and not all of them about myself. Combining my knowledge of space coordinates, along with the rumors that have been flying around the border region, from both the Belligerent Coalition and our own people, I discovered where they are sending us."

"To your WMD," Hildana hissed. "Your genocide machine!"

There was a stunned silence throughout the room, broken at last by Duane. "You...you've got to be joking. The Commonwealth doesn't believe in genocide! Come on, Captain? Tell me you don't believe this,"

Adri's face was hard. "They tested it on Undaria."

Gray said nothing, his face pale.

"What are you talking about?" Duane demanded, a little frantically. "Undaria rebelled against the Commonwealth!"

332

"Heard about that," Hildana snorted. "Funny how they don't mention how, or why. And they never did say how they managed to quell an entire planet of legendary predators without enlisting the aid of the regular military, huh?"

"But," Duane half rose out of his seat, his eyes entreating Adri. "But something big enough to destroy a planet would have to be huge! How could they keep something like that a secret?"

Floyd made a small cough. "Actually, it wouldn't have to be very big, more along the lines of a large battleship."

Everyone turned to stare at the humacom designer.

"Dr. Tarkubunji, you'd better tell this next part," Adri said quietly.

Floyd cleared his throat and began. "I have been working for West Cellutary Research and Technical Laboratories ever since I graduated from school. My father, Harriman Tarkubunji, worked there his entire life. We were both designers, working to develop humacom technology for the government. It was satisfying work." He paused, and then sighed. "About two years ago, my father was called away to a special meeting of laboratory heads. Afterwards, he was away from the lab were we both worked often, leaving me to work alone. This didn't bother me at first. Eventually, I noticed that he came home less and less, until he never left the facility. He started to hole himself up in his private laboratory, only allowing his personal humacoms free entry. Whenever I asked him what was wrong, he would only say that his current project was causing him some problems, but that he would work it out. The only time I was able to spend with him was during the designing and construction of a new datacom for the facility. But once that project was complete, my father retreated even further. Even the follow up project – an exterior firewall system for the datacom – couldn't pull him out for more than an hour's time.

"Then, about five months ago, my father died in his laboratory. Everything in his lab was destroyed, including his humacoms. They told me that he had gone mad – ransacked his lab and then killed himself. It was hard to disbelieve them; their report was concise, and my father had been acting strangely for so long. But then little things began to crop up…things I had trouble putting together, but continued to nag at me. Then strange things began happening to me at my lab…well, in short,

333

nothing made sense until I was at last able to go home. There, I found a number of messages that my father had sent from the lab. Most of them were garbled, coded text that only another humacom designer would understand. Even I had a hard time. When I was finally able to manage to decrypt some of it, I found that it was notes for something called the Apocalypse Project. But it wasn't a humacom. It was something else, something far more sinister. My father's notes were agitated, and in the end, incoherent."

"What did they say?" asked Gray.

Floyd took a deep breath. Freya watched him supportively. "It would take me too long to explain in detail. In sum, I believe that someone high in the government approached my father to design a program for a...machine of some sort. Something along the lines of the artificial intelligence we make for humacoms. Only, this thing was for the AI of a ship. A ship built in total secret that had a weapon aboard that was deadly enough to destroy an entire planet. By poison."

Hildana hissed again. "The Coalition heard rumors about it. They said that the Commonwealth had tested it on one of their own planets."

"Undaria," Adri said again.

"Once the project was complete, my father must have been considered a liability," Floyd concluded. His face was pale. "My guess is that he was caught destroying his notes."

"Danwe," Duane murmured, his eyes large. "How could...but why...." He turned to Adri. "What...what are we going to do, Captain? We can't...we can't condone this – atrocity!"

"You're right," Adri replied. Once again all eyes were on her. "We can't."

"What are your plans, Captain?" Gray asked formally.

Adri glanced at Blair. He gave her a slight nod. Taking a deep breath, she said, "We are going to find this battleship. And destroy it."

"How?" Jericho inquired. "The feasibility of a positive outcome in a battle between a frigate of the *Elegy*'s class against this theoretical battleship are minute."

"The thing must be armed to the teeth," Hildana agreed. Both Kobane sisters were leaning forward, a dangerous glint to their eyes.

Adri opened her mouth to announce that she just so happened to have magic powers when a new voice called out, "I believe that I may be able to assist you."

Everyone turned to see the man, wearing a ship's uniform, who was standing in the doorway. There was a long moment of bewilderment before Floyd shot off his chair with a startled, "Zultan!"

The humacom –for humacom he was – smiled and nodded to Floyd. "Good evening, sir."

The humacom designer sputtered for a moment before saying, "How did you get here?"

"I let him aboard, with the last of the ensigns." Jericho answered. "He gave a very credible argument as to his usefulness. Plus, he knew you personally."

"Tarkubunji, who is this?" Adri demanded.

Floyd fell back into his seat, still stunned. "This is probably the most valuable data archive in the Galactic Commonwealth. My father and I designed and constructed him shortly before his death…"

"My name is Zultan," the humacom said, turning to Adri. "My apologies for stowing away on your ship, Captain Rael. I found no other feasible alternative." He turned to Floyd. "I assume you know why I am here, sir."

"Yes," Floyd rose from his seat. "Captain, if you would excuse me?"

Adri rose as well. "Wait, you said you could help us, Zultan?"

"Yes," the humacom replied. "But before we get to that, there is something here that I want, and Dr. Tarkubunji needs to fetch it for me. I can't access the information you need for your mission without her."

"Very well," Adri recovered her authority. "Duane, head back to engineering. Make sure that we'll be ready to move fast if the occasion warrants it. Having a top-secret datacom stow away on our ship is not going to be easily explained if we're stopped by a patrol. Everyone else, back to your stations. Once we have more information, we can come up with a suitable plan of attack,"

As the others filed out, the Kobane sisters stepped forward. "Given the fact that our missions have crossed purposes now," Hildana said quietly. "We find no reason to hinder your progress."

335

"We want to help," Giselle finished. "That thing is an abomination."

Adri gauged their faces. They both looked fierce. "How do I know that you won't skip out when the time comes?"

"I guess you'll just have to trust that we want that thing gone," Hildana replied with a quirk to her lips. "I make no promises about staying around once that's complete."

"Fair enough. Danwe, this conversation is just *wrong!*"

Her old enemies grinned.

"Ask Gray for a duty roster. Make yourselves useful."

"Yes, ma'am,"

Now the only people in the room were Adri, Floyd, and the humacom. "With your permission, Captain?"

Adri nodded to Floyd. Out of sheer curiosity, She followed the pair out of the War Room and down to a lift. Catching Gray in the hall, she jerked her head for him to join them. "I want to see this thing that Zultan needs to get our information." Adri whispered.

Gray nodded, but didn't speak. Both were trying to overhear the conversation that creator and created were having several paces ahead.

"I knew you hadn't shut her down," Zultan was saying. "You gave the wrong code."

Floyd nodded. "I couldn't do that to her. But why did you come after us? Weren't you given a replacement?"

"Yes, Eisha. Unfortunately, it was less than compatible, and had to be terminated."

"I....see. By whom?"

"Myself. It was without a personality or learning program, very poorly constructed, and far too tall."

Floyd blinked. "Too tall?" He shook his head. "Never mind. How did you reconcile destroying her and leaving the facility?"

Zultan sighed. "That, sir, is a very long dissertation. In a summary, I would have to say that current actions taking place within both the facility, and the information I was downloading led to a morality infraction in my hard drive. Because my orders went against the acceptable protocol, I concluded that they were invalidated. After all, if the orders were against my programming, through no fault of mine, then I am not bound to follow them."

"Amazing," Floyd breathed. "You must have thought about this a lot."

Zultan made a very human-like gesture. "There really wasn't much to do, with both of you gone. Since Eisha was an inadequate firewall, I was forced to adopt my emergency security protocol. Which, as you know, is set to destroy all possibility of data hack, and to seek out an alternative firewall system."

"And you knew I had her,"

"Of course, sir. I was able to read the hold for recycle command that you gave using a false code. I then deduced that you would bring her to where you were, at the Tarkubunji estate. Unfortunately, I was unable to reach the estate before you had relocated elsewhere. With the Peace Keepers everywhere, I backtracked and waited for your signature to reappear on the database."

Adri and Gray looked at each other, shrugged, and kept listening. "I think we missed a lot," Gray mouthed. Adri nodded.

"When did it?"

"When you signed onto the *G.C.N. Elegy* under a false surname. Given the other details you gave in your profile, I deduced it was you."

Floyd frowned. "Was the forgery that obvious?"

Zultan shook his head. "You underestimate yourself. Remember, I have known you for a long time. I recognized your writing style, and the attributes you claimed. I would not concern myself with someone else recognizing you from your profile. They most likely are still trying to reboot the system after I crashed it."

"You crashed the system?!" Floyd cried. "How?"

"That information is classified. Your security credentials don't allow me to tell you."

They had reached the entrance to the mechanics lab. Floyd opened the door, noticing Adri and Gray for the first time. He stepped back to allow them to pass, his mind clearly elsewhere. When everyone had entered, he led the way into the smaller, private lab beyond the main room. It was stacked to the ceiling with dozens of crates. He pointed to one that sat on the floor in one corner. "There she is. I had to keep her on standby so that I could smuggle her in without any problems."

Both he and Zultan began to decode the crate. When they struggled to lift the lid, Gray walked over to help them. Between the three of them, they managed to lift the heavy-duty tunsteel contraption. Adri glanced in, and saw a small female humacom with dark hair, dressed in teenage street clothes, lying like a corpse in a coffin.

Floyd glanced at Zultan. "I'll go get my -"

"No need," Zultan replied calmly. He pulled a cord from behind his ear and carefully inserted it into a port at the back of the female humacom's neck. There was a moment of humming silence as Zultan ran a program.

"He's decoding the standby blocks and issuing a full-power command." Floyd whispered.

Seconds later, the female humacom's eyes blinked open. Her hands fisted and then relaxed, her eyes focused on Zultan. "Hey there, harddrive."

"Hello Cassie," Zultan answered. "I've missed you."

If Adri hadn't known better, she would have thought it a soft reunion of two lovers. As it was, the scene was decidedly human.

"Come on," Gray whispered, taking her arm. "Let's leave them be for now."

"But I need to know that intel Zultan has stored," Adri whispered back.

"Leave them be." Gray repeated.

Funny how life works. Now I get to work alongside my captor, my old enemy. How did our paths merge into one?

At least Giselle and I will have fulfilled our mission to destroy the genocide machine.

And, what luck, we get to teach the Adept some moves.

Chapter Thirty-Eight

[Captain, we have a situation on the bridge.]

Adri glanced up at the overhead voice of Jericho. She brushed the communicator on her ear in mild irritation. [I'm a little busy here, Jericho. What kind of situation?]

[We're being hailed by another ship, and it's approaching us.]

Adrenaline began to hum quietly in her veins. [Have you made contact?]

[No ma'am.]

[Good, I will be on the bridge in three minutes.]

[Very well, Captain. Bridge out.]

Floyd looked up from his crouch in front of Zultan. "Is this something to be worried about, Captain?" he asked.

Adri was momentarily caught in fascination as she watched the humacom designer deftly plug in circuits and cords into the datacom. "Not particularly. It's most likely a passing ship that wants to exchange gossip, or see who's the new captain here."

"I haven't received any new data regarding Captain Rael or the *Elegy*," Zultan said. "Any information that would be passed through to a ship would be much slower than us, since the command would have to bypass the main database."

Cassie swiveled in the chair next to Zultan. "So, because you crashed the data system – which is totally awesome - they can't send out a warrant in a mass relay?"

"No," Zultan agreed. "But that doesn't mean they couldn't send out a direct command."

Cassie made a dismissive gesture with her hand, narrowly missing the cord that connected her to Zultan. "But they'd have to have a ship within range of an instant transmission, so they'd have to be *behind* us. And according to the logs I checked, we're the only ship scheduled to leave Halieth for weeks."

Something cold slithered into Adri's stomach. "Keep up the work, Floyd," she said. "I'm off to the bridge." She hurried to the lift, trying to convince herself that this new development was nothing to be worried about. After all, the humacoms didn't seem to be worried. Except... Zultan was impossible to read. In the three days they had been traveling, she had found the datacom to be full of introspective sayings and layered answers. He never lied – his programming would not allow it – but he wound his way to the answer that better suited him. To Adri, he was more worrisome than even Jericho, whose newfound ability to lie had left everyone in shock. The only newcomer who was easy to read, and spoke exactly what she thought, was Cassie. At least there, Adri knew where to stand. The little humacom was fiercely protective of Zultan, and had no particular trust in the rest of the crew, with the exception of Floyd.

[Bridge to Captain Rael,] this time, Jericho's voice came over the earpiece instead of the overhead.

[Rael here,]

[The ship has gotten close enough to identify. It's a frigate, *G.C.N. Avix*.]

The cold in her stomach froze into a hard ball of tension. [Understood. Alert Vice Captain Grayson, get him up on the bridge immediately. I'm on my way. Rael out.]

Adri began to run.

"The *Avix* is hailing us again, Captain." Jericho said the moment Adri entered the bridge.

Adri took a deep breath and sat down in her chair. "Bring them on screen,"

Behind her she heard the bridge door open, and without looking knew that Gray had arrived. His presence was strengthening. Then the main viewscreen popped on, showing an identically styled bridge, fully staffed. In the captain's chair sat a familiar figure.

"Why, hello there, Captain Rael," Royce Carter was beaming. "What brings you to this neck of space?"

The ice was spreading through her chest, but Adri fought to speak lightly. "Hello Carter. I thought you weren't scheduled to leave for another three weeks,"

Carter waved his hand. "Ah well, politics, you know. Turned out that I was the only ship that had an available crew to set out immediately. I received an order from Admiral Appegus himself, can you imagine? He wasn't very civil, but that's no surprise. But you honestly will not believe what he said!"

"No, I don't believe I will," Adri murmured.

"He was raving on about how I had involved myself in some sordid criminal affair! And how I had harbored known criminals in my house for two weeks and allowed them to escape the planet! Now, would I do something like that, I ask you?"

Despite herself, Adri's lips twitched. "Of course not."

Carter sighed, and leaned back into his seat. All amusement had fled his face. "Rumor has it that you are harboring a traitor aboard your ship, along with a top secret piece of government property he stole. I am ordered to make a thorough search of your vessel, and if Dr. Floyd Tarkubunji or the humacom known as Zultan are found aboard, then I am to take command of the *Elegy* and return to Halieth. I suppose you can guess the rest,"

"Yes, I suppose I can." Adri took a deep breath. Since Carter had actually met with Floyd, it wouldn't work to pass him off with the fake name again. She glanced over at Gray, who stood at his station to her right. He gave her a sad but confident nod. With a slight tilt to her head, she gave him his orders. Turning back to the viewscreen, she said to Carter, "I'm sorry it had to be you."

"I am too," Carter agreed. "But you know as well as I that crap like this happens. So are you going to let us board?"

Adri heard the bridge door open, and knew her orders were being followed. It left an empty feeling in her gut. "No,"

342

Her old friend ran his fingers through his hair. "I was afraid you'd say that. Need I remind you that you are breaking faith with the Galactic Commonwealth? If you don't comply, then you will be court martialed, and sent to the Z9 Hades facility. I don't want to send you there. You'll never be able to return to the Commonwealth systems."

"I know,"

"Then why are you doing this?" Carter showed his frustration. "What are you up to, Rael?"

Movement in her peripheral vision showed everyone to be ready. It was time to end this. "Saving the universe, meting out justice, making the systems safe for children and small animals. You know, the usual. You could even say I'm saving the Commonwealth,"

"I see," And Adri knew at once that he did. "So it comes to a fight?"

Adri smiled. "Carter, there was never a fight between us," she raised her hand at Cassie, who had taken the Security station and hooked into the ship's defensive systems. "Open fire, target, *G.C.N. Avix*!"

Carter's smile was wry as he gave her a final salute, and disappeared. Adri was still staring at the blank viewscreen when they felt the reverberations of the antimatter transition cannons hit their target.

"Target hit, confirmed." Cassie called, with something akin to glee in her voice. "Estimated damage…at the least, crippling."

Adri found that she needed to take several deep breaths before issuing her next commands. "Freya, take us as far away from here as possible. Make a wide circuit of the system before resetting our course. I don't want anyone to realize what our objective is until it's too late to stop us. Gray, alert Duane…"

But Duane was standing by the door, his magenta face blotchy.

"Duane, get the engines running at top speed,"

The paranthian nodded, and with a last tortured glance at the viewscreen, he disappeared through the bridge door.

Adri rose from her seat. She was startled to notice that her hands were shaking. "Gray, take over. Give me an update if any new situation arises. Good work, crew." She shook her head at Gray's concerned look. "I'll be in my office."

She wasn't sure how long she sat there, drinking simulated coffee and brooding out the port view. Her mind whirled around the events of the last hours, pointlessly. Rationally, she knew that she was wasting her time, pondering things that couldn't be changed, but she was still annoyed when her office door slid open and Blair entered.

"I believe I made it clear that I didn't want to be disturbed," she said.

"I'm afraid I don't have a choice, and neither do you."

Adri rolled her eyes. "What do I not have a choice in this time?"

Blair's face was it's usual stoic mask. "I'm sorry about the events that went on this afternoon,"

"Yeah, well me too."

"Are you going to give up the mission?"

Adri hissed a breath. "Of course not!"

Blair nodded, and made no comment about the rising surge of energy in the room. "Then don't regret the actions you've taken. Would you still be upset if it had been some other ship they sent after us?"

"You know I wouldn't!"

"Then why are you sad?"

Adri glared at him as if he'd asked why the sky was always up. "Because it was my friend, who'd helped us! Danwe, we stayed in his house!" Anger welled up inside her, a pleasant exchange for the guilty sadness.

"Do you think he wasn't prepared for your attack?"

That caught her attention. "What?"

"Come on, Adri, he'd guessed our move." said a voice from the door. Adri looked up and saw Gray lounging there. The two men had joined forces. She scowled at them until Gray said, "He had ample time to return fire, as you know. Nor did he bother raising his shields to deflect our shot. He sat there and allowed us to shoot him, so that we could have a clear path to finish this."

"Don't underestimate your friend Carter," Blair added quietly. "He puts up a great front, but there is more going on in his mind than he allows to show."

"You told me that yourself," Gray said. "I'm sure he's known for a while that we were going to deviate from the mission at some point,"

Adri's scowl lessened. "You two rehearsed this, didn't you?"

Gray smiled. "Of course not."

"Right, get back on the bridge," Her vice captain gave her a jaunty salute and sailed off. She then turned to her doctor, who hadn't moved. "Okay, what is it?"

Blair sighed. "Did you notice how the room changed when you got angry with me? The energy buildup? Have you practiced anything I showed you?"

"Well, yeah…but…"

The young doctor shook his head. "I've spoken with Freya. From everything I've overheard, and what you've said about this mission, I think…"

"What?"

"That this is going to take more than military might to stop."

Adri frowned. "What do you mean? We have the location of the battleship. Floyd is working to bypass the codes so we can access all the security data from Zultan's files. Once we have that, we can formulate a plan. What more do you expect me to do?"

"Have you spoken to Freya Tarkubunji at all?"

"Er…not really. The flashy wings really put me off,"

Blair's smile was faint. "You mean the fact that she's a Talented? From what I've seen, and what she's told me, she has various gifts, such as short foresight, and a very limited telekinesis. More importantly, she lived in a convent with other Talenteds for a great deal of her life. Did you know that?"

"I heard Floyd mention it…."

"Did you know that her convent was attacked shortly after she left? It was a massacre,"

A sudden vision – blood, fleeing lights, a beautiful winged boy – "What? Why?" Adri's head was wheeling. She sat down hard.

Blair leaned urgently against the desk. "Because someone knows you awoke as the heir of Veranda,"

"What? Someone who? Who in Danwe's name would care?"

"There have been rumors for years about another Adept having awoken. No one is positive just which one it was, or where they are.

That in itself is very strange; usually many of the more clairvoyant Talenteds would be aware of such a phenomenon occurring. Just as it was for you. Freya told me that her convent was aware of the night you landed on Junus, and your genes became dominant. Yet none of those with the Sight spoke of your coming, and that is something they would have definitely been aware of. She said it was like they were being… blocked by something. Then, shortly after you awoke, her convent was attacked, and everyone inside was killed."

"Are you saying everyone died because of me?"

Blair sighed again, "No. What I'm saying is that there is someone else out there who knows that you awoke, and appears to be doing all in their power to find you, and keep your emergence a secret. And they aren't afraid to spill blood over it. That suggests someone with a great deal of power, probably equal to yours."

Adri leaned back in her chair. "So why are you telling me all this now?"

"Freya told me that it was a Talented who attacked her convent." Blair said quietly. "Young, little more than a boy. He had immense power, but we do not know where he came from or even what his name is."

The beautiful boy..."How…how do you know about him?"

"Freya Saw him with her gift, just as he was attacking. That is how she was able to escape. Her gift was just small enough to not be blocked by whatever was blocking the Sight of the others, or so she thinks." Blair replied. "And…you had a dream about it, did you not?"

Adri swallowed hard. "I don't think I like where this is going."

"I didn't expect you would. But here it is. Freya and I have reason to believe that the boy could be hunting you. If he has some tracking ability, he might even be waiting."

The numbing fear that seemed to coincide with the memories of the dream evaporated. "At the battleship?"

"Its quite possible. Like I said before, there must be a connection between you and the boy for you to have seen him so clearly in your vision. He might be able to do the same with you."

"Okay. So what do we do?" *Please, bring this back to a level that I can understand*, she thought grimly.

346

"If the boy is there, you will need to deal with him." Blair replied. "I doubt he would merely like to talk. Taking action against someone like him won't be easy, though."

"So what do we do?" Adri repeated. "I have never fought with someone like that kid. I don't know…"

Blair's face was set, determined. "You get ready. There is someone aboard who can show you a way to fight the boy without using your normal weapons. Blasters and ATF's will be useless on him. Like they are on you."

Adri rose. "So you want me to learn some sort of hand to hand?"

Blair rose. "That's right. I have a very bad feeling that you won't be able to solve the problem of the boy peacefully, and the way you handle your gifts now leaves you at a disadvantage against someone of that child's caliber. Also, Freya said that she had a premonition about you griping over your teacher.

"Oh yeah? So who is it that I have to learn from?"

The door slid open. Hildana Kobane grinned at her. "So, Rael, you ready to learn the art of *ayallan*?"

My precious child,
        I gave you gifts
    That you would live

                And bring life

They may feel a burden
    And the price may seem your freedom
            But recall that I love you
And would give you nothing

                Your spirit could not bear

Go forth precious child
    I gave you wings

            Now fly

Chapter Thirty-Nine

It was quiet in the chapel. The soft flicker of the genuine tallow candles shed little light, but Adri preferred it that way. Meditation was always easier here, and for the last two weeks, she had found herself drawn to the little room for snatches of the silence it offered. Strange, but up until now she hadn't realized that she needed quiet, or meditation. Adri found herself slipping down here at odd moments. After an exhausting bout of *ayallan*, between tactical meetings with her senior staff, working on decoding Zultan with Floyd, when she just wanted a moment to herself. Now, formal prayers complete, she let her mind drift...waiting.

Go forth precious child...

A gentle tap on the chapel door startled her out of her reverie. She turned in time to see Gray enter and walk over to her. Sitting beside her he said, "I'm sorry, were you deep in thought?"

"No...I finished all my formal stuff."

"Does it help?"

"Yeah. It centers me. Don't tell Blair, though."

Gray smiled.

"What brings you down here? You never pray in here when others are around."

"We got a confirmed sighting of the *Apocalypse*. Freya is currently keeping us out of sensor range, and Cassie has all the ship's defensive systems engaged."

Adri led the way out of the chapel, only once looking back at the quiet she wouldn't feel again for a long time. "Let's get on the bridge."

The bridge was silent as everyone stared at the viewscreen. Before them the battleship, *G.C.N. Apocalypse*, drifted at normal speed like a sleeping whale. More than fifty times the size of the *Elegy*, its giant hulking shape was easily intimidating. Adri studied it like she would an enemy vessel. "Tarkubunji?"

"I've stayed out of its close-sensor range," Freya said. "It hasn't moved."

"No transmission from the ship has been received," Jericho added from the communications station beside Freya. His connection cord slapped lightly against the monitor as he turned to face Adri.

"There's been no sign of movement on the ship," Cassie continued. She had recently adopted the security and tactical stations as her own. Since she demonstrated a keener knowledge of defense and security than anyone else on board, Adri had given the post to her. "It appears that it hasn't noticed us."

"Zultan, what can you tell us?" Adri asked, taking her seat.

The humacom was sitting in the vacant analysis chair beside Cassie. "Dr. Tarkubunji was able to decode a lot about the ship's security and infrastructure, so I am able to discuss this now. Do you want an update or a recap?"

"Recap for the bridge, please." Adri replied.

"The Apocalypse project was under heavy security, and as a humacom, I wasn't able to speak about it without the authorization of an appropriate username and passcode. Since we don't have either, Dr. Tarkubunji had to manually decode and decrypt the information by hacking into my database."

"Gently hacking," Cassie interjected.

"A recap is as follows: the battleship *Apocalypse* is unmanned by any organic being. It has a skeleton crew of humacoms that are programmed to run the ship from orders given by the AI in the ship's mainframe. The AI receives its orders from the government. In this fashion, they are able to avoid any security leaks about the ship's missions or purpose. However, it also leaves the ship vulnerable to small infiltration.

"The battleship will fire upon any vessel that gets within range without transmitting a prearranged set of passcodes. When these passcodes are received, the mainframe AI will lower its shields and allow the approach of a shuttle. The only access on the ship, however, will be the main hangar. All other doors will be sealed until the shuttle has departed, or until another set of passcodes have been entered."

"We have the passcodes to reach the hangar," Gray said. "They were a part of our original mission."

"And we now have the passcodes for the hangar doors," Zultan replied. "As well as the ship schematics, guard rotations, and relevant intel on the genocide machine itself."

Adri leaned back in her chair, fingering her pendant. "As Zultan said, the ship's design leaves it vulnerable to a small strike force. Therefore, we will be small. I want Duane, Jericho and the Kobanes ready to go in twenty minutes. Gray, you will have the bridge until we return." Adri rose.

"A word, Captain," Gray said urgently. He pulled her into the office. "You're going without me?"

"Gray, someone needs to command the ship while I'm gone. We don't have a second officer," Adri replied, attempting a soothing voice.

It didn't work. Gray's face was still angry.

She tried again. "What's wrong? I can't leave the ship without someone in command,"

"Its just…" Gray huffed a breath. "I don't want to sit back while you take a risk like this. I lost you once. I don't know if I could do it again. Are you sure that I couldn't take your place?"

"No," Adri replied, feeling calm, and warm. "I have to go, in case there's…you know, magic stuff. Blair thinks it's more than likely, and now he has fairy Freya on his side. I can't ignore that."

Gray rubbed his face. "I know you're right. Danwe. All right. I'll keep the ship running for you, but I'm no captain, so you'd better hurry."

[Warehouse to Captain Rael,] her communicator buzzed.

Adri brushed her earpiece. [Rael here,]

[Shuttle is revving to go,]

[I'll be on my way in five. Rael out.]

Gray gave her a small smile. "Good luck, Adri. I…"

"What?"

He shook his head.

"Gray…about those words…"

[Duane to Rael, where are you? Its time to kick genocide butt and you're not down here!]

Adri sighed. [I'm on my way, Rael out.]

Gray watched her leave. "Safe mission, my love," he whispered to the empty room.

There was a different silence that encased the *Elegy's* transport shuttle as it made its way towards the *Apocalypse.* A loud, tense silence, filled with nerves and adrenaline. Adri checked the gauge on her assault rifle, then noticed the two Kobanes doing the same. She dearly hoped that arming them wasn't a mistake.

Duane was muttering to himself. "How did I get roped into this? I've never been an offensive field man. And who named that thing? *Apocalypse*? That has got to rank in the top ten lamest ship's names…"

The static-filled voice from the imageless viewscreen caught everyone's attention. [Unidentified shuttle. Please submit the proper approach codes, or we will open fire.]

Jericho replied with the long string of numbers and glyphs on the ship's communication board before speaking. [Rim sol luc dav 3-06.]

[Processing, please do not approach.] The static died.

Tension shot up within the shuttle by an exponent. Hildana voiced what everyone was thinking. "Let's hope they haven't heard about our meeting with the *Avix*."

An agonizing fourteen seconds passed before the AI on the *Apocalypse* responded. [Passcodes accepted. Proceed to the main hangar.]

Duane let out a loud breath. "Thank goodness for sluggish bureaucracy."

Jericho maneuvered the shuttle under the belly of the battleship and towards the highlighted hangar bay. "I'm bringing the ship in now," he said, slowly guiding the awkward vessel into the hangar. "Touchdown in three...two...one...down. Hangar doors are closing. Outside sensors read oxygen levels....good. No sign of life in the hangar, Captain."

Adri nodded. "Stay aboard the shuttle. Our communicators will relay to you. Pass the info onto the *Elegy*'s bridge."

"Yes, Captain."

Turning to the remaining three passengers, she said. "Last brief. Duane and Giselle will head straight to the main engines and insert the humacom virus that Floyd uploaded onto the data chip you both received. Try to stay unobserved, fighting is a last resort. Hildana and I will detour to the genocide machine and destroy it. We meet back here in twenty minutes. Understood?"

"Yes, Captain," three voices replied.

Adri gave Giselle a hard look. "My chief engineer had better come back with you."

Giselle shrugged. "I have no grudge against paranthians. Besides, without an engineer, how are we going to get out of here before more Commonwealth arrive?"

"Just keep that in mind. Let's move out!"

The four soldiers slipped out of the shuttle and made their way quietly across the deserted hangar bay. At the far door, Adri signaled Duane with her assault rifle. At once the paranthian took a delicate instrument, courtesy of Floyd, and inserted it into the control panel. At the same time, Adri punched in the second set of passcodes that Zultan had provided to open the door. There was a small beep as the lock disengaged. Seconds later, Duane nodded to announce that the hangar security systems were offline. Adri opened the door, and they stepped through into a service hallway.

True to Zultan's information, the hallway was deserted. They crept along in silence until they reached a junction. There, Duane and Giselle turned left, towards the engine room, while Hildana and Adri pressed on ahead towards the lift. The total silence that surrounded them was unnerving. The battleship felt deserted. The two women entered a lift and Hildana punched in the appropriate level. As the lift began moving, she whispered, "This place gives me the creeps. It's weird enough to willingly go on a mission with *you*..."

"Yeah," Adri agreed quietly. "I've never been on a ship that felt this empty. But..."

"What?" the Belligerent soldier asked.

Adri shook her head. "A weird vibe. I doubt this will end clean."

As if to confirm her statement, both communicators hissed. [This is Black team! We're a cell away from the engine room, and have crossed paths with some securicoms. They are not happy to see us.]

[Can you maneuver?] Adri asked.

[Yes. They're tough, but these guys' moves are too textbook to be better than us,] Giselle sounded confident.

Adri nodded to Hildana, who knelt down in front of the lift doors. [Press on. Try to stay together,]

[Roger, Captain. Black team out.]

The lift slowed and the doors opened. Adri and Hildana, old enemies and new allies, braced for the onslaught. The opened door was greeted with ATF fire from two securicoms hiding behind crates. In tandem, both women fired, then rolled out of the lift and into the hall. Using an atypical rush tactic, they overwhelmed the two humacoms and made a dash down the corridor.

They kept up the speed as they zigzagged through the winding halls, firing at any securicoms that tried to intercept them. Taking out two with rapid headshots, Adri turned to Hildana, who was covering the rear. "Last turn! Can you hold them off while I enter?"

"Sure thing. They're Commonwealth made, so popping them off's no problem."

Adri ignored the dig and jammed the code reader that Floyd and given her into the control panel beside the last door. Hildana gave them both cover fire while the little gadget shuffled the appropriate passcodes into place. The light blinked, and the door slid open. [We're in,] Adri passed the word along.

She tapped Hildana's shoulder. The two darted through the door before the Belligerent woman turned and stuck a jammer into the controls. "That should buy us a few minutes."

354

[Black team to White team,] Duane's voice popped in. [We've arrived at our target. Estimate, five minutes before rendezvous.]

[Copy that, Black team,] Adri said. [White team out.]

She frowned into the semi gloom of the large room they had entered. There were no lights, but a wide control panel glowed, wrapping around a large, oblong object the size of a ballistic missile. The light did not reach the highly raftered ceiling.

"Bad vibe," Hildana hissed beside her.

"No...more of a cold feeling," Adri shook her head. "Something's here."

A heavy thud against the door alerted them that the securicoms were attempting access to the room. "Better hurry," Hildana advised.

They rushed across the dark room to the control panel. Yet with every step, Adri could feel the cold inching closer, until it was like a block of ice pressing on her chest. The feeling of being watched was overwhelming.

"I've made it to the control panel," Hildana said. "I'm log – ahh!" without any warning, the Belligerent soldier flew across the room, landing with a hard crack somewhere behind Adri.

Adri didn't move, squinting into the darkness. There was something there...she willed her vision to improve. "Show yourself!"

There was a flicker, like an image in a badly cut filmstrip that flashes on and off in less than a second. It was enough for Adri, battle-trained Advance Force soldier, to recognize the pale boy with the beautiful face and the black wings.

Instinct made her raise her rifle and fire where the image had appeared. The beams flashed like comets in the night, but struck nothing. Silence fell again, broken only by a quiet groan from Hildana.

Come on, Adri thought grimly. *Show yourself, you little devil...*

And just like that, Adri felt a low surge of energy, and she saw a blur of movement between her and the control panel. Whirling around, she saw the boy, staring at her with black eyes framed by choppy white hair. His black wings reflected the dim light, displaying an intricate design of red tattoos, and a tall wickedly curved scythe. He looked like a young, tragic grim reaper.

"Who are you?" Adri demanded. She felt all her adrenaline rushing to the fore, elegy playing. She had never faced a child in battle before, but the visions of this one snuffing out all the lights in the convent killed any sympathy.

The boy answered in a deadpan voice. "My mother has sent me to end you, Veranda."

"Well, forgive me if I don't just lay down and die," Adri replied. She opened fire.

The blasts darted towards the boy, only to flash and vanish before impact. The boy hefted his weapon. "Foolish."

Like a wraith, he sped across the distance between them, scythe poised for a killing swing.

My first firefight was on Telma Luna. I was fresh out of the academy, and hadn't even scuffed the polish on my new combat boots. I was optimistic, enthusiastic, and dumb as a dead dog.

It was supposed to be a simple recon, but most of us raw recruits were hoping for some action. And we got it.

A rainbow of blaster fire. A clash of whines and explosions. In those critical seconds, I wasn't a soldier anymore. I was back home, hiding in a basement and desperately wanting my parents. It was a miracle I wasn't shot as I stood there, frozen in terror.

The sergeant of our squad yanked me down under cover. He gave me a hard shake, and said, "Focus, Rael. Remember that you are just as smart and able as the enemy. Stay steady, and you'll come out on top."

He was right. While I can't recall where he died, I remember his words.

Focus, steady, and know that you are just as smart as your enemy.

Chapter Forty

Hours of meditation paid off as Adri blocked the boy's scythe with her lance. She had dropped the rifle as useless after seeing the beams vanish, and now they stood, both armed with weapons of days past. Summoning her strength, she knocked the boy back a full five paces. Adri took a quick measure of herself as the boy stumbled. Her tattoos were glowing along her arms, her lance was heavy and real in her fist, and judging by the sharp breath the boy made, her wings had manifested as well. For the first time, Adri was glad. Now they could fight power to power.

"Let's get this started."

Behind them, mostly forgotten, Hildana raised herself to her feet, wincing at the jarring pain from her shoulder. For a moment, she stared in awe at the two angelic creatures locked in some medieval battle to the death, lunging and blocking with their long shafted weapons. Their wings flashed in the dim light, the markings on their bodies growing brighter as the tempo raced. Then she shook her head, remembering her own part in the plan.

With the ease of long practice, she crept along the floor towards the control panel. The boy noticed her move and tried to lunge, but Adri blocked him, and the two were once again caught up in a fast-paced mix of weapon and fist. Assessing the situation, Hildana rammed the viral data chip that Floyd had given her into the slot. When the first query posted on the viewscreen, she began to type in the necessary glyphs while the data chip downloaded.

A heavy crash sounded above her head. Sweat beaded, and was ignored. Another crash rang out, followed by a small explosion somewhere on the other side of the machine. Hildana continued to type, with one eye on the downloading display. She prayed that her old enemy's luck would hold.

The boy was fast, and he was smart. If Adri hadn't known the basics of *ayallan* that Hildana had taught her, she would have been dead in seconds. As it was, she found herself parrying, jumping, dodging, thrusting, kicking and punching seconds too late to cause real damage. The boy usually managed to block or avoid the bulk of the blow, lashing back with deadly speed. He was obviously a master of what Hildana had described as a forgotten, yet highly advanced form of martial arts. His blows were always accurate, feeling much like the feather soft battering ram Adri had experienced in her fistfight with Hildana. His moves flowed, and his timing was perfect.

Adri however, had endurance, strength, and a vast amount of power. When she did manage to land a blow, it was shattering. She snapped a punch at the boy's face, and watched with surprise as his head flew back, blood welling out of his broken nose. He recovered quickly, using the blunt end of his scythe to ram her knee, but she leaped over it. It felt like ages before she began to descend, so Adri lashed out in a brutal kick to the stomach. The boy shot across the room, slamming up into the walkway above their heads with a heavy crash. Adri raced after him, putting on an inhuman burst of speed. The boy was barely able to roll to his feet to parry her lance. His next lunge was off kilter, and she was able to catch him with the tip of her blade before body slamming him across the room and into the side of the machine. A panel exploded, sparking enough light to see the boy crumpled on the ground. Again, Adri raced after him.

But the boy was cunning. As soon as Adri was within range of his scythe, he made a quick roll, bringing up his weapon. She managed to dodge being slashed, leaping over the boy and landing on the machine.

A glance down at her chest showed a ribbon of blood beside her ribs. Too close. She rose to jump down, but the boy shot upwards at the same moment. He missed with his weapon, but caught her chin with his fist. She reeled back. Blinking, Adri brought the room back into focus, but the boy was nowhere to be seen. Then she looked up. He had flown straight up onto the walkway above, and now stood, dripping blood from his wound, watching her with black eyes.

A distant rumble made the room shudder. Adri suddenly recalled the rest of the mission. She took a step back, intending to demand an update from her team, when the boy spoke.

"You are not at all like the Talented I have killed. They were so easily disposed of, I could have done them all without even manifesting myself," A flash of his teeth in a smile showed fangs.

An overflow of images assaulted Adri's mind. Memories of the vision she had had on the transport, but clearer. The Talented were no longer lights, but women. Massacred women.

The boy continued to watch her. "Did you know, mother had me kill them because they told her you were alive? She doesn't like bad news."

There was no way she could allow this evil creature to escape to do some other heinous crime. This is what Blair must have meant about keeping the balance of power in the galaxy.

Anger boiled to a degree Adri had never experienced before. Her adrenaline began to sing a louder song than it ever had before. With that song, she was able to shape a new level to her power. With that power, she shot straight up into the air, landing on the walkway inches from the boy. The room was charged with energy, and she could feel it soaking into her skin like water. It was heady, and somehow erotic.

With an improvised war cry, she leapt after the boy.

[This is Black team,] Duane's voice crackled over the communicator.

Hildana tapped her earpiece hurriedly. [Kobane here,]

[Where's the captain?] Duane demanded, suspiciously.

[Fighting some demon boy from hell. What is it?] *Only thirty-seven seconds to go…*

[Our work here is done. The engine is already showing signs of critical failure. It will only be a matter of minutes before the whole ship explodes,]

Thirty-three seconds...[We're on the final countdown on our end,] Hildana replied. [Thirty seconds and counting.]

[We've taken out seven securicoms down here,] Giselle spoke up. [According to Zultan, that means nearly half the ship's engineering crew is out.]

[Good work. Head to the rendezvous point. We'll meet you there. White team out.] Hildana glanced up at the walkway. "Come on Rael, speed it up..."

Fifteen seconds.

Hildana backed away from the control panel towards the door.

Thirteen seconds.

She noticed for the first time that the banging on the door had ceased. She wisely assumed that the securicoms had been redirected to work on the threat to the engine room.

Ten seconds.

Rael was still fighting, oblivious to anything else.

Five seconds.

There was nothing else for it. [Rael!] She shouted over the communicator. [This is it!]

Above, she saw the bright winged figure pause, and be immediately attacked by her opponent. [Go!]

Hildana had just enough time to pry open the door and leap through before the genocide machine exploded, taking half the room with it. She rolled a couple times before regaining her feet and racing down the hallway. The way was empty, with no securicoms save for the ones she and Adri had destroyed on the way up. Beneath her feet, the floor shuddered. The engine was self-destructing, thanks to the humacom virus that Floyd had extricated from Zultan's database. Created on accident by a humacom, it was a deadly machine virus that had not yet been used beyond preliminary testing. It raced first to any AI units it was downloaded to, immediately corroding all cerebral operating systems, and from there spread to any machine it was introduced to through those

361

humacoms. The battleship's crew and main computer had been totally obliterated. The ship itself wouldn't last much longer.

Unhindered, Hildana dashed into a lift and ordered the hangar bay. As soon as the lift began its jerky progress, she tapped her earpiece. [Rael, are you there?]

The answer was a long time coming, and sounded very far away. [Yes. Take the team and head back. I'll find my own way. Rael out.]

Hildana cursed, but she had been a soldier too long not to follow a direct order. Even from her old enemy.

It was her job now to make sure the rest of the team made it home.

Knowing about the explosion allowed Adri time to brace herself. The force of the machine self-detonating, however, was stronger than she anticipated, and she came to several feet away from where she had been standing. Her head ached, and her leg was bleeding. Disoriented, she sat up on her elbows, wondering how long she had been unconscious. Had the others made it back to the *Elegy*? Her lance had disappeared.

Across the room, the boy staggered to his feet. He was also bleeding in new places, his blood blending in with the dimly glowing symbols that covered his skin. For one moment, he looked like a lost child in a war zone, frightened and bewildered. Then the flat, dead look returned to his eyes, and he began walking slowly towards Adri. His scythe glittered in the light of the fire that had sprung up in one corner.

Adri took a deep breath and tried to summon the energy that had deserted her.

Gray watched as the strike team stumbled out of the shuttle. Duane and Giselle were covered in what looked like ash, streaked over with blood and engine oil. The paranthian looked more black than magenta. Jericho strode down the ramp, none the worse for wear, but Hildana looked tired and winded. When she glanced over at him, the look told him what his heart had feared since the mission began.

Adri had not returned with them.

362

"What happened?" He demanded.

"Mission accomplished," Duane mumbled. "The ship will be space dust in less than ten freaking minutes."

"Where is Captain Rael?"

Hildana shook her head slowly. "Demon boy popped up. Tossed me across the room without even touching me. Rael headed him off, while I downloaded the virus. They were still fighting when she ordered me to take the team and get out,"

Sick fury rose in Gray's chest. "And you *let* her stay behind?!"

Hildana nodded. "She gave the order. Save the team."

"She said she'd find another way back," Duane said in a half-hopeful voice.

"Right. Duane, head over to the infirmary. Now,"

Duane gave him a sad frown and stumbled off, leaving Gray alone with the Kobanes. He murmured to himself, "Blair told me that Adri was likely to stay behind. That she would have to fight the boy." He took a deep breath and faced both sisters. "I know that we have been enemies, and that our current situation is…awkward. And I know that you owe neither me nor Adri any favors. But I'm asking anyway," he pulled a small device attached to a belt from inside his jacket. "Please, show me how to use this, to find Adri."

The Kobane sisters blinked in surprise. "How did you get one of our teleportation devices?" Hildana cried.

"I've had it since we caught your ship. But…I don't know exactly how it works. It's still set to whatever you programmed it for the return to your ship. Please."

Hildana frowned and started to shake her head, but Giselle cut off her answer when she stepped forward. Looking closely into Gray's eyes, she said, "You love her."

"Yes,"

"Little sister," Hildana warned, but Giselle ignored her.

"We are not supposed to speak of our technology to outsiders," the younger Kobane said quietly. "But I will give you this favor, and you will be in my debt. Yes?"

"Yes,"

"Here," Giselle took the teleportation unit from Gray's hand. "I will show you quickly how it works."

"You make mother angry,"

Adri tried to leap to her feet, but her ankle burned cold pain. Probably broken. She was forced to scrabble backwards away from the boy and the chilling energy that surrounded him. The boy sensed her weakness, and was now merely toying with her. Around them, the ship vibrated as auxiliary power lines exploded.

"Mother is rarely this angry."

Come on, Adri goaded herself. Where was her lance? She was not dying on this stupid battleship like some helpless child! If she was going to die here, then she was certainly taking the little brat with her!

"I have to hunt when she is angry."

A flicker of energy whispered under her skin. It wasn't much, but with it came a plan. Focusing all that energy, she waited for the boy to come closer. Focus. Stay steady.

"Now I have hunted you." The boy was less than a foot away. He pursed his lips. "Farewell. Do not rise again."

Several things happened at once. The boy swung his blade towards her heart. Adri summoned all the energy and willpower she could muster.

The boy's blade hit her chest and snapped like a brittle bone.

Adri's blade ran through his chest like a knife through warm butter.

With the gesture, all of the energy that had departed when she woke returned, heating her skin like a sun. Too much power crowded in, until she felt drunk with it. *She was far greater than this boy*, it crooned. *Crush him, and turn his body to dust!* Adri could almost feel the tickle of fire on her fingertips. Her deep violet markings writhed on her skin. This was different than all her manifestations before. She felt invincible, indestructible – out of control.

The boy made a gurgling noise, collapsing onto the floor. Adri watched as the wings and markings vanished, leaving a young boy bleeding on the ground. His eyes blinked slowly, young and frightened. He caught sight of Adri, whispered "Mother...?" And died.

Adri stepped back, unaware that her ankle no longer hurt. All she could see was the dead boy who had cried for his mother, and the bloody weapon in her hand. She didn't see the walkway collapse beside her, along with most of the wall. She didn't feel the shuddering floor beneath her as it slowly gave way. Nor did she see Gray until he shouted her name.

Her reaction was a blind, instinctive *get away!*

She screamed in horror as Gray was thrown backwards by the force of her will, crashing into the wall and collapsing like a broken doll.

Fear banked the restless energy that had consumed her. Fear propelled her across the vibrating, debris-strewn floor. Fear drove her down onto the floor beside Gray. It was splattered with blood, and with trembling fingers she touched his head. Her hand came away sticky. With a half sob, she cried, "Gray!"

His eyes flickered open. He tried to focus on her face, but it was too difficult. His voice was rough, and it was strangely hard to speak. "Hey. Come...take you home."

"Gray," there was too much blood.

"Sorry. Broke...order. Love you." His eyes were too heavy, so he closed them.

"Gray," she whispered. And as the world seemed to rend itself apart around them, she leaned close and whispered. "I love you, too."

Epilogue

Gray opened his eyes to the best vision man had ever seen. Adri was leaning over him, with a soft smile on her beautiful face. "Did we die?" he asked, throat sore.

"No," she replied. "But it was close."

"Good." He closed his eyes for a moment's rest, and when he opened them, Adri was sitting on his other side. "What happened?"

Adri sighed and looked away. "I hurt you. It was an accident. Blair says I might have...pulled energy from the boy...or something. It was too much for me, and I couldn't control it. You cracked your skull open...and nearly died."

He hated that look on her face. "But I didn't."

"No," she smiled again. "It's lucky the TD was set to return automatically, though. Otherwise we'd have been blown away with the rest of the *Apocalypse*."

Gray smiled back, closing his eyes. He was tired. Suddenly, his eyes snapped opened and he tried to rise.

"What are you doing?" Adri demanded. "Lie down, before Blair comes back and tranqs you!"

"You said them!" Gray stuttered, allowing himself to be pushed back down on the pillow. "You said the words,"

Adri nodded. "Guess I did."

"Well?"

"Well what?"

"Don't I get to hear them again?"

The man was seriously pouting. It was sort of cute. "I suppose," and she leaned down and whispered her love in his ear. When she sat back, Gray looked a little dazed. "Now I have to go. I'm short one vice captain, and we still have no second officer. Plus, if I stick around here long enough, the magic squad will find me and I'll be hauled off to do who-knows-what."

"Sounds like a rough life,"

Adri shrugged. "Not so much. We're going to be on the run from the Commonwealth, and whoever it was that sent the boy on us. I think that means we're rogue on all fronts, now. Plus, I'm sure Blair or Freya are going to pull some sacred mission out of their collective hats."

Gray smiled. "You telling me something?"

"Yeah, get better fast. I'm going to need my husband up and running as soon as possible,"

He blinked. "Husband?"

"You heard me,"

Gray watched as Adri strode out of the infirmary. He'd had the woman he loved propose to him. Life was refusing to be dull, with danger and chaos a light-year away. Smiling at his good fortune, he fell asleep.

LaVergne, TN USA
24 February 2011
217762LV00002B/130/P